"GET OUT NOW . . ."

"Alana Marks?"

She looked up at the waitress. "There's a call for you."

"Me? Are you sure?"

"Blue top, dark hair, knapsack. Alana Marks."

It didn't make sense. David, sitting across from her, showed he thought the same.

"My friend probably wants me to bring back pirogies," she told the assistant district attorney. "Back in a sec." She followed the waitress to a wall phone and picked up the receiver. "Hello?"

"I'm at a pay phone down the block," Nick said. "Two cop cruisers just pulled up in front of the joint you're in. Get out now."

"What? How—"

"David set you up."

"No, he wouldn't do—"

"Alana, I gotta take off. And you'd better too, fast. Because if the cops bring you in, Knelman's gonna get you. I gotta go. I wish you . . . *baxt*." He hung up.

Baxt. Gypsy luck.

PRAISE FOR THE NOVELS OF STEPHEN KYLE

After Shock

"A wonderfully intelligent, highly readable, and thoroughly enjoyable thriller. I enjoyed it tremendously."

—Heather Graham, *New York Times* bestselling author of *Night of the Blackbird*

"A wild, thrilling ride through cutting-edge technology, love, and betrayal and the ultimate triumph of the human spirit."

—T. J. MacGregor, author of *The Other Extreme*

"Science and politics clash in Kyle's feverish techno-thriller."

—Publishers Weekly

Beyond Recall

"*Beyond Recall* has everything—a compelling hero, a complex and fascinating villain, heart-stopping action, and a dynamite opening that explodes into a ripping good read."

—Steven Spruill, author of *Daughters of Darkness*

"Entertaining . . . dramatic showdowns, soul-wrenching . . . a tale to be read and enjoyed . . . a pleasure."

—Toronto Star

THE EXPERIMENT

ALSO BY STEPHEN KYLE

Beyond Recall

After Shock

THE EXPERIMENT

STEPHEN KYLE

An AOL Time Warner Company

WARNER BOOKS EDITION

Cover design by Diane Luger
Cover art by Stanislaw Fernandez

Warner Books, Inc.
1271 Avenue of the Americas
New York, NY 10020

Visit our Web site at
www.twbookmark.com.

 An AOL Time Warner Company

Printed in the United States of America

First Printing: January 2003

10 9 8 7 6 5 4 3 2 1

Acknowledgments

Special thanks to the following:

Simon Girard, actor and stunt performer, for an intriguing and constructive explanation of various details of film stunt work.

Hilde Leavitt for advice on German words and phrases, and George Miczak for details about World War II Germany.

Al Zuckerman, my agent at Writers House, whose counsel and guidance in shaping this story was, as always, simply invaluable.

Dan Ambrosio, my editor at Warner Books, for perceptive suggestions and deft fine-tuning that yielded a better book.

Fay Greenfield of Writers House, for being my very helpful guide to New York City.

Sandy Weissman and Elaine Bulger, for a fine autumn sail off City Island that gave me the perspective I needed on Long Island Sound.

And my gratitude once again to Stephen Best.

"He that increaseth knowledge increaseth sorrow."
—ECCLESIASTES

"Many children, much luck."
—GYPSY PROVERB

GLOSSARY OF ROMANY (GYPSY) WORDS

Pronunciation note: *x* is pronounced like the "ch" in the Scottish *loch.*

baxt	good luck
boojo	literally, a dishcloth; a swindle in which a cloth bag is switched
bori	bride; daughter-in-law; woman who marries into one's family
diwano	a group convened to discuss a matter publicly, often to settle a dispute
gudjo (sing.)	an adult nongypsy
gadje (pl.)	nongypsies
kirvo	godfather
kris	a trial attended and judged by Rom; gypsy court
kumpania	a group of extended families living, working, and traveling in a territory
marimé	impure, polluted, defiled; rejected or outcast by trial

ofisa	fortune-telling parlor
papio	grandfather
pomana	death feast, memorial celebration
Rom	the gypsy people; also the term used for a gypsy man
Romany	the language of the Rom
rom baro	a leader, literally "big man"; the chief in a kumpania
shori	daughter
taté	father, daddy
vitsa	a loose federation of extended families; a category of kin; a tribe

THE EXPERIMENT

CHAPTER 1

April 30, 1945

DR. VIKTOR SCHILLER'S laboratory in Berlin had had no running water for days. The lights were flickering again, and it was so cold that his breath fogged the slide under his microscope. After five years of war's hardships he had grimly learned to carry on without enough to eat or enough sleep, but he cursed the cold for making his fingers stiff and clumsy on the microscope, hindering his research. No scientist could work in these impossible conditions. He turned his head to divert his breath, and to force down his alarm. He knew it wasn't the cold. No scientist had ever faced the appalling evidence that lay beneath his lens.

Fritz's radio down the hall crackled with static over "The Blue Danube." The cheery music was supposed to calm the terrified citizenry, but it only reminded Schiller of the Allies' morning broadcast declaring that the Americans had reached the Elbe River seventy kilometers away and were sweeping south to the Danube. Yesterday, Dr. Verschuer had ordered all staff to destroy correspondence with colleagues in Auschwitz and other camps. How like a Nazi, Schiller thought in disgust. Did Verschuer really think that by whitewashing the Kaiser Wilhelm Institute of Human Heredity and Eugenics he could make the Nazis' sins disappear?

He felt a shiver, for he was officially a Nazi himself—a reserve captain, a Hauptstürmführer, in the Schutzstaffel. Without membership in the Nazi party, of course, he would have had no laboratory privileges, no research funding, no professional advancement, but he loathed Hitler's band of thugs and everything they stood for, and had always worn his SS uniform with contempt. And now with a piercing shame as well. For he was just beginning to realize the extent of his own sin—his breakthrough trial in genetic manipulation that enabled knowledge to be passed from mother to child. He had envisioned his experiment as pure research, and it had been wholly benign for the three subjects. His dream had been to advance mankind's wisdom. But now he saw, with a growing horror, how it had gone awry. In the wrong hands it might even be used to breed a race of killers.

Could the evidence before him be wrong? He looked again through the lens at the brain tissue from the stillborn child. He had dissected the hippocampus, vital for laying down new memory traces, and the amygdala, gateway to the limbic system, whose neural pathways mediated emotional arousal. As he peered again at the tissue on the slide, the darkened, damaged cells answered his question. Not a definitive answer; for that he would need more equipment, more assistance, more *time*. But his lab supplies had been pilfered, his assistants had been sent to the front months ago, and time had run out. If the Americans had reached the Danube, they were on the threshold of the camp at Otzenhausen. That would mean liberation for the inmates. He felt a swell of happiness for his friend Heinrich Knelmann, who finally would be free. But so would the three women who were Schiller's experimental subjects. Like infected research animals escaping the lab. Given this new evidence, the potential for evil embodied in the women terrified him.

The radio music stopped. The lights flickered, then went out. Lifting his head in the darkness, Schiller felt the death of the light as a sign. Further investigation was impossible. It forced on him an appalling task, but one he could not shirk. Elimination of the carriers.

It sickened him. He'd never killed anyone in his life—he was a *scientist*. His fingers felt for the gold crucifix on the chain under his shirt. "Dear God," he whispered into the confessional darkness, "forgive me."

On Charlottenburger Chaussee dirty snow lay piled against smoking ruins, and people in threadbare clothes scurried in the wake of Schiller's Audi Horch, one of the few civilian vehicles on the road. Driving out of the bombed capital, he was dismayed, as always, by the devastation. He thought of ancient Rome, sacked by barbarians. In the once lovely Grunewald section, his own family lay dead in the rubble, his wife Clara and their two young daughters, killed instantly last March when huge American air fleets had dumped their deadly tonnage. Thirteen long months later his grief still smoldered, but the flame was exhausted. As he drove across the Glienicker Bridge over the Havel River and through the miraculously undamaged suburb of Potsdam, he thought of the eastern barbarians approaching—the Soviet army. Marching westward, they would soon fall upon the city. Everyone was predicting fierce street battles with Hitler's fanatic troops. But Schiller's thoughts were on the Americans to the south. Could he reach Otzenhausen before them?

* * *

Cresting a hill on the edge of the Thuringian Forest, Schiller saw American tanks on the horizon. So near the camp! He drove on, passing snow-patchy fields where a farmer was out with his team of horses. Schiller had seen the man cultivating his land throughout the war, while ash from the camp crematoriums drifted over the countryside.

"Heil Hitler!" The nervous, acne-faced guard at the main gate looked hardly more than a teenager, Schiller thought as he returned the idiotic salute and drove in. He rarely came to this awful place. Even its peripheral sights made him slightly nauseous: the railroad tracks that brought transports of frightened prisoners to the gates, the rows of electrified barbed wire, the watchtowers. Last summer, driving past a half-dead work gang shuffling to labor in the village munitions factory while their guards barked orders, Schiller had noticed a corpse entangled in the barbed-wire fence. The prisoner had been shot days before, trying to escape, and they'd left his body to rot on the wire, the stench overpowering in the August sun. But on this cold spring afternoon as Schiller drove in, the din of cruelty and the smell of fear had vanished. It was as though the camp itself were holding its breath, waiting for the Americans. The broad Appellplatz, used for roll call, was vacant. Commandant Reinhardt had probably confined all prisoners to barracks, terrified of a last-minute uprising. No officers in sight. Schiller had heard that in the past days most of the SS men had left. But the rank-and-file guards were still stationed on the watch towers. Their life was following orders; they had nowhere to go.

He parked and went into the hospital block, passing the central office where soldiers were destroying documents. No wonder; he knew of the vile experiments that went on in F Block under the direction of the sadistic Dr. Helmut Kleist. Kleist had infected prisoners with typhus and polio to test experimental drugs for pharmaceutical firms. He'd injected women with caustic sterilizing chemicals directly into the uterus without anesthetic, just to observe toxicity levels. He'd conducted tests for the navy, observing how long men lasted when given nothing but salt water, and how long before they perished in freezing water. To Schiller, Kleist was a butcher. Yet what am I? he thought, suddenly rocked with guilt. He'd held to the moral justification that the three subjects of his own experiment had enjoyed improved rations and had suffered no discomfort, not even the mental distress of being told what the operation was for. *But now, because of me, these women have to die.*

In his office he found Heinrich Knelmann writing at the desk. Looking up in surprise, Heinrich got to his feet. It always jarred Schiller to see his friend in that faded striped uniform with its yellow double-triangle badge, "J" for *Jude*, Jew, his eyes haggard from long imprisonment, and his face, once handsome, now bony and pale. They were both thirty-four and both taller than average, but Heinrich had become stooped and looked a decade older. Yet in Schiller's eyes Heinrich would always remain the athletic, gregarious undergraduate of their medical school days.

"They're coming," Schiller said. "Maybe by nightfall, maybe just hours."

"We've heard."

"You'll be free."

They stood still, aware of the extraordinary moment. Then they both strode forward and embraced.

"Viktor, how can I ever thank you?"

Schiller waved away the thanks, though pulling the strings had been far from easy. He'd told Verschuer and Commandant Reinhardt that this exceptional Jewish researcher was essential to his ongoing genetic experiment and must not go to the gas chamber yet; he needed him as an assistant here. But only by going to the top and exploiting Reichsführer Himmler's interest in the project had Schiller been able to stretch that "yet" to over two years. "Where will you go?" he asked.

"America, on the first boat I can get. I've prayed that my son got to my sister's. I'll find her, and raise my boy." Tears glinted in his sunken eyes. "You won't accept thanks for my life, but I swear I'll somehow find a way to repay you for the life of my child. Hannah would have thanked you too."

Schiller had to look away. He hadn't been able to save Heinrich's wife in this hellish place, but he had succeeded in smuggling their baby son to Switzerland in the care of a Red Cross nurse, with instructions to send the child to Heinrich's sister in America. Still, Heinrich hadn't seen his sister since they were children. Given all the unknowns, who could say if his boy was even alive?

A rumble made them both turn. Mortar fire in the distance. American guns.

"Viktor, why have you come?" Heinrich's bewildered look said it all: Why would an SS medical officer walk straight into the Americans' hands?

Schiller felt a clammy dread sweep over him. He took a key from his pocket and unlocked the desk's left drawer, from which he pulled out his Luger pistol. It was standard issue to all SS officers, but he had never used it. He hoped he could remember how to load it.

He turned to Heinrich. "Where are the subjects?"

"Sophie Grossmann's in the infirmary, recovering after the stillbirth. Hilde Wentzler's back in G Block barracks after her miscarriage."

Schiller realized that he'd never known the women's first

names. How like Heinrich to distinguish such a human detail.

"The gypsy woman's in the infirmary, too," Heinrich added, "with her newborn, a girl."

A baby, Schiller thought. Dear God.

"You've come to tell them, is that it? Explain the gene to them, before they're set free?"

Stricken, Schiller looked down at the gun in his hand. "No." When he looked up, Heinrich too was regarding the gun, and his eyes filled with alarm.

"You're not thinking of—"

"Heinrich, don't you see? They were never expected to leave this place!"

The grim reality of it silenced them both.

There was a shout down the corridor. Then a commotion of voices. A corporal ran past the open door, yelling, "The commandant has hanged himself!"

It rocked Schiller. There was so little time. He opened the right drawer, burrowed beneath papers and files, and found the box of bullets.

Heinrich gripped his arm. "Viktor, there's no certainty that the gene implantation was even successful."

"I fear it was," he said, loading bullets. "And worse. I dissected the Grossmann infant's brain."

"Worse? What do you mean?"

With the gun loaded, Schiller turned to him. "My only intention was to advance knowledge. You understand that, don't you? I thought it might one day lead to an elevated human consciousness. Something magnificent—the inheritance of wisdom. Instead, it appears to produce a chromosomal mutation in the offspring that deadens the limbic pathways. Deadens conscience itself. Think what that means, Heinrich. If the subjects live to reproduce, their progeny will constitute a new subspecies with enhanced abilities but with no sense of right and wrong. They could one day wield a tyranny more brutal even than the Nazis."

"Viktor, calm down. What analysis did you do? What tests? Who's corroborated your findings?"

"None. No one. There's been no time!"

"Then you could be mistaken." He took the gun and laid it on the desk, beyond Schiller's reach. "You can't take that chance."

"Can I take the chance that I'm not? Heinrich, don't you see how appalling this is? I have a theory. The infant was a male, and that's the crux of this thing. It's because the chromosomal change—"

A gunshot exploded down the hall. Schiller heard frantic shouting.

"Jew, out!" a voice barked at the doorway. It was Helmut Kleist. The fat little doctor was sweating in fear, and his Luger was pointed at Heinrich. Glancing at the hall Schiller saw that Kleist had rounded up a half-dozen other inmates, physicians like Heinrich, and armed guards were marching them toward the door to the courtyard. In horror, he realized what Kleist was doing. These prisoner physicians had been forced to assist in Kleist's depraved experiments. He was going to eliminate them.

Two corporals grabbed Heinrich and began to drag him to the door.

Schiller lurched to block their way. "No!"

"Hauptstürmführer, step aside," Kleist said. "He knows too much. If these Jew doctors testify, we'll hang."

Schiller stood firm. Kleist aimed his revolver at Heinrich's forehead. He fired. Heinrich was thrown back by the blast, and fell. Kleist and his men ran out.

Stunned, Schiller dropped to his knees at his friend's

side. The obscene red-black hole in Heinrich's forehead wept bright blood. His eyes were glazed. "Viktor . . . I beg you . . . see about my son . . ."

Schiller watched in anguish as blood trickled down Heinrich's temple to the floor. It felt like his own life's blood draining. A moment later, his friend was dead.

Rage roared into Schiller, possessing him. He got up, grabbed the Luger, and burst into the hall. Kleist's men, marching the prisoners, had almost reached the far door, with Kleist bringing up the rear.

Schiller aimed at the fat man's back. "Butcher!" He fired. Kleist fell.

The two corporals stared at him, aghast. The prisoners blinked at one another, then silently and swiftly ran.

A gleeful shout outside: "The Americans! They're coming!"

Schiller yelled at the corporals, "Get out!"

They fled. Schiller was alone.

He went to a hall window. Prisoners were leaving barracks, hundreds swarming onto the Appellplatz, some running, many more shuffling and limping. Skinny men, women, children, all in rags. Their voices set up a low hum of hope. The guard on the main gate watchtower was staring down the road in dumb shock. Schiller felt in shock himself, his heart still raging at Heinrich's death, his hand still trembling from the murder he'd just done. But his ears picked up the faint growl of tanks, the whir of motorcycles. He couldn't see past the gate, but he could tell from the guard's gaze that the enemy was near. They'd come on so fast!

His mind lurched. *They'll arrest me . . . just another SS officer.*

There might still be time to escape. Drive out the rear gate and through the village, and make a run for the Swiss border. But that would mean leaving the subjects. His heart was hammering. If he took the time to finish what he'd come to do, he would surely be arrested. He closed his eyes, silently begging God for an answer.

It came. When he opened his eyes, he knew. *The mutation must not leave the camp.*

He dashed down the hall to the infirmary and crossed the corridor to the women's ward. All but the sickest had gone out to greet their liberators, and even some of the feeble ones who remained were shuffling toward the door, making a bottleneck Schiller had to squeeze through. He heard a tank rumble through the main gates, and faint cheers. At the far end of the ward he saw a woman hurrying out the back. A flash of wiry red hair: Grossmann. His mind jumped to Wentzler in G Block. He'd go after Grossman, then take a shortcut to G Block.

A baby cried. He wheeled around. The gypsy woman, his third subject, lay in the corner on a cot with her newborn. The young mother looked pale and anemic, but fiercely self-possessed. As Schiller approached, her dark eyes, wary and calculating, met his. It shook him to his core. Kleist had deserved to die . . . but this innocent young woman? He knew that if he hesitated, he could not go through with it. He quickly made the sign of the cross, aimed down at her heart, and fired. Trembling, he moved to shoot the baby next. The tiny girl looked at him—*into* him—freezing his heart. Would God ever forgive him?

A crash at the door jolted his aim, and his wild shot hit the floor. Several prisoners ran into the ward, swarthy men, shouting. Schiller saw their shirt badges, black triangles with a *Z* for *Zigeuner*—gypsy. One big-boned young man rushed to the cot where the dead woman lay with her squirming baby. "Lina!" he cried. His furious eyes turned to

Schiller, and he lunged at him and slammed him against the wall. The blow to his backbone made Schiller drop the Luger, and it skidded along the floorboards. His eyes locked with the gypsy's as a voice burst over a loudspeaker outside: "Greetings from the American people!"

The gypsy stepped back, his face dark with rage. He snatched up the baby and ran out the back.

Schiller grabbed the gun and ran out after him. In the warren of barracks alleys the man and baby had vanished.

Schiller hurried down the alley toward G Block. The camp was in chaos. A gray tank with an American flag waving from the turret was rumbling over the Appellplatz. Prisoners had roped the huge Nazi eagle over the gate and were pulling it down. Others swarmed the incoming troop trucks and motorcycles, grabbing at the soldiers' boots and sleeves. Many were rushing for the now-open main gates.

The voice on the loudspeaker called, "Stay where you are! Food and medical care will be available to you all! Stay where you are!"

But the prisoners kept running. Schiller had to back up against the G Block barracks as a gang of them rushed headlong past him for the gate. Among them he glimpsed a tall, stout woman, dirty and bedraggled but still strong looking. Wentzler. He thought: She's going to make it out. So will Grossmann.

Panic gripped him. He had failed to destroy the mutation. And now his arrest was inevitable—as a war criminal. Incarcerated, he could never track the escapees. Never contain what he had unleashed.

A desperate idea took hold. *Heinrich.*

He ran back to his office. The bullet that had ended his friend's life had gone through his brain: on the inmate uniform, no blood. Schiller stripped. He pulled off Heinrich's grimy clothes and wooden shoes and put them on. He emptied his own wallet of Reichsmarks and then, using a roll of bandage gauze, strapped the Luger to his calf, stuffed the money in beside the gun, and rolled the pant leg down. Finally, he turned Heinrich's left wrist, still warm, to check the prisoner number tattooed on the inner forearm. 17233. Shaking, he gathered the experiment files from his desk and dumped them in his metal wastebasket, along with his wallet, then got matches from the drawer and set the papers alight. At the last moment he remembered the crucifix around his neck. A gift from Clara. When he'd lost her and their daughters in the bombing, only his faith had saved him from despair. Lifting the chain over his head, he dropped the crucifix in the wastebasket, where it disappeared among the flames. The desecration chilled him.

On an impulse too strong to ignore, and too raw to question, he kneeled by Heinrich's body as he would to a priest in the confessional. "Forgive me," he whispered. The sins on his conscience were terrible—two murders, and something far worse: for joining his research to the Nazis' vision, the world would pay a horrific price, unless he could stop what he had set in motion. He had to destroy the evil he had spawned.

He pulled Heinrich's body into the closet and closed the door.

Across the courtyard he found the prisoner induction office empty, but the tattooing equipment was all there. He closed the door and picked up the tattoo needle.

A half hour later he walked out the open gates of Otzenhausen with a mass of those prisoners most determined to leave. He felt dazed and battered, almost disoriented. Heinrich's foul clothes were tight, the wooden shoes painful. His spine ached from the gypsy's assault, and the fresh tattoo on his inner forearm stung. But in the maelstrom of his mind lay a still center of certainty: he would track down those two remaining subjects. And the gypsy baby. And, somehow, honor his friend's dying plea for his son.

It all seemed staggeringly impossible. The only thing he could deal with now was escape. The future was a fog.

CHAPTER 2

September 1973

THE WAR WAS over. "Peace with honor" was how President Nixon had described the treaty he'd made in January, and with it the last U.S. combat troops had left Vietnam and the first POWs had come home. The Watergate scandal, though, raged on: the president had been implicated in the criminal cover-up, and insiders had begun to whisper about impeachment. But for ordinary Americans, life went on. *The Joy of Sex* was a best-seller. *The Exorcist* was the year's top-grossing movie, giving the devil a revival. *Kojak* premiered on TV, Mary Tyler Moore was everyone's favorite working girl, and *Gunsmoke* was still going strong. The average household's yearly income was about ten thousand dollars, and a first-class stamp cost eight cents. Elvis gave Priscilla three quarters of a million in their divorce settlement. So much for ordinary Americans.

Alana Marks had always known she was different. From her gypsy childhood to the way she now made her living in the movies, she'd always lived on the edge. She'd been paid to leap from a sixteenth-story window, roll a car to a cliff edge, get thrown off a speeding train, and be dragged into a river by a runaway horse. At the moment, she was about to set herself on fire and jump out of a burning barn.

She stood on the lip of the loft, checking everything one last time. She and the crew had already been through an intensive cue-to-cue rehearsal, but a high fall plus full-body burn was not something she undertook lightly. Beneath her Civil War period nightgown she wore a fire retardant suit, and under that a protective film of Nomex gel. Her skin tingled with the cold, because she kept her Nomex on ice; it helped against the heat of the burn. There was fire retardant on her wig, too; it was her bare feet she was concerned about. Still, they were freezing from the gel, so that reassured her.

She looked down at the box rig she would fall onto forty feet below, satisfied at how she and her crew had stacked the layers of folded cardboard boxes. She mentally ran through the midair rotation she would do. When she'd planned this fire gag with Ian Turnbull, the stunt coordinator, he'd suggested air bags, but that would have meant she'd have to do a flawless three-quarter rotation to land on her back so the bag would clam up around her. If this were a straight high fall, she could spot the landing and ace it, but with a full-body burn the fire would drastically limit her vision, so everything depended on her spatial awareness being perfect. If she over-rotated, she'd hit with her feet; if she under-rotated, she'd hit with her head. Either way she could spear the bag and go through it—and if she was lucky only break an ankle or blow out her knee. Eleven years ago, at the start of her stunt career, when she was seventeen, she'd broken her nose by landing in a tuck that had cracked her knee into her face. They called it eating your knee, but eating the damn thing would've hurt less. So she preferred the box rig; it took longer to set up and was a bit harder on the bones than an air bag, but it would forgive a less than perfect rotation.

Below, the crew was setting up the dolly shot. Gaffers hauled electrical cables, and grips pushed the camera along the track, rehearsing the shot, while the director and the AD discussed it. As directors went, Alana thought, this one was okay—didn't pretend to be David Lean and didn't bark at the extras. Ian stood flirting with the script assistant, but Alana knew he and his crew were on top of things; she could see that they had the fire extinguishers ready near the box rig. She trusted these guys to reach her fast. They'd better—on fire, she wouldn't have any air to breathe until they put out the flames. She felt a small shiver, knowing the liquid nitrogen would feel cold as hell, but so very welcome. The local fire marshal sat on a picnic table, looking bored; his fire truck was waiting on the service road, out of sight. Nobody was looking up at Alana. She liked that—that no one was nervous about her. She'd earned it. In her work, two things made her happy: the rush from doing a dangerous gag well, and being one of the best. It meant she was in control. At least, of everything she *could* control.

Still, she sensed the tension below. Only one take would be possible, and about that the production people *were* nervous. They'd already shot sections of the barn with the illusion of it burning, using movable propane bars. This wide shot would be the grand finale: the whole building truly in flames, and Alana's jump. There would be no second chance once the barn was razed. It gave her goose bumps, knowing how much rested on her getting it right, and not just for the shot—for her future. Ian had hired her scores of times, but his friendship had cooled after she'd told him of her ambition to become a stunt coordinator herself. She was more than qualified, but the job was a male preserve; the boys didn't want girls in their fort. Alana needed tonight's spectacular to go perfectly, to clinch her status. Then she'd feel easier about approaching producers directly. Ian might grumble at her advancement, but she doubted he would stand in her way.

She noticed that the production manager had brought his two little kids to watch. That bothered her; they were too young. He stood between them, bending to speak to them, and the wide-eyed girl, maybe six or seven, was staring up at Alana, looking afraid. Her dad was probably saying how the stuntwoman was going to be on fire. What a jerk, she thought; the kid would have nightmares for weeks. She waved down at the little girl and mugged, grinning, to show that she was enjoying herself. *See? It's just fun.* The girl looked amazed, but shyly waved back. Great, Alana thought, if I kick the bucket now the kid'll never sleep again.

She made herself concentrate, get centered. She looked past the bright lights at the shadowy Connecticut countryside. Night-dark woods, black stubbled fields. The night was calm, windless, hot for the last week of September: summer's last kick. Faintly, above the crew's voices, she could hear cicadas. And there was a scent of hay. That smell gave her a creepy sensation. Reminded her of the smell of a newly scythed flax field one summer night in Austria's Burgenland on the border of Hungary. *I slept in that field, on the run. The village people were turning in gypsies to the Nazi governor's police.* It jolted her. *No, not me. Lina.* Then she reminded herself with a shudder: *And I made it up.*

Alana knew she was seriously weird. All her life she'd had these intense visions of her mother's life. Why she fabricated such things, she didn't know. But the flax scent felt as real as the chemical whiff of Nomex on her skin.

"All set up there, sweetheart?" the AD called.

She shook off the disturbing sensation, glad of the job at hand. She relied on her work: it kept her rooted in reality. "You bet," she called down. She gave him a clear thumbs-up.

"Okay, people," he announced to the crew, "let's get this in the can."

Alana felt the familiar adrenaline rush: a hot spike of fear bathed by cold confidence. It was a sweet thrill, and she knew it would get sweeter. She held the igniter in the folds of her nightgown, ready to set herself ablaze. She was prepared.

The crew set the rear of the barn alight, and the cameras rolled. Alana could hear the flames' faint crackle far behind her. Now all eyes were on her. All the lights too. She turned her head to "play away," not let the cameras see that her face wasn't the starlet's she was doubling for.

Something was wrong. Her peripheral vision caught a movement inside on the barn floor. Beyond the lit-up shelf of the loft, it was dark down there. As she focused on a spot among the shadowy straw bales, her breath caught. A man lay in the straw. Gus? He'd been her safety inside the barn for the cue-to-cue, and he must have stayed there and passed out. Drunk again.

She could have killed him. She'd met Gus Yuill back when he was a top stuntman, and she probably owed him her life, but he'd let booze ruin him, and lately he'd become such a burden on her she'd had it up to here. More than once he'd crashed at her place after a landlord had locked him out, then he'd stayed for weeks on end. More than once she'd paid his sky-high bar bills, a bite on her bank account. And what the hell was she supposed to do now? She'd have to alert the AD that Gus was here so they could pull him out before the flames roared through, but as soon as they saw he was drunk, they'd fire him on the spot. He was fifty-two and already reduced to doing NDs, nondescripts: man-on-the-street falling in an earthquake or bomb blast, or knocked down by a running hero or villain. NDs barely paid his rent. Once word got out how he'd been fired tonight, he'd be washed up in this business.

Then he'd be on her hands for good. Damn him. He was a millstone around her neck.

What if she said nothing? He'd burn to death. No more millstone. It seemed so simple as a vision flashed: Lina, in the camp. So simple . . .

January morning. Fucking cold. Snowing again, and me foraging for scraps at the SS kennel fence. I found out the Standartenführer always sends his Sunday-night roast leftovers to his favorite dogs. I'm gnawing pork gristle off a bone when I see a prisoner across the path by the compound fence. A Jew. Scarecrow like the rest of us. Maybe he's hoping the falling snow will mask him, because he's poking something through the fence to a prisoner in the next compound. Passing a paper? A crust of bread? Very dangerous. Not just the electrified wires. Talking to inmates in another compound is forbidden, and like all offenses there's only one punishment. Death. I turn to go, wanting to get far away from this loser, but then I see that fat little doctor, Kleist, leaving the stable on his mare at a walk. He rides across the countryside every morning, no matter the weather—the asshole must imagine he's some hero in a folktale. But what luck for me.

I shove the bone up my sleeve and shuffle forward as he comes, my head down like a slave, the way the Nazis like. "Herr Doktor, beg pardon, forgive me, but look." I point out the prisoner at the wire—you can just see him through the falling snow. Kleist trots toward him, pulling out his pistol. The Jew turns in terror. Kleist shoots him in the face. He doesn't look back at me as he reholsters his gun. That's it? He's just going to ride off? Shit, it wasn't even worth my trouble. But then he trots over to me. He looks at the black "Z" badge on my sleeve. "Gypsy, why are you here at the kennel? For scraps? Did your block kapo authorize you?"

What answer will satisfy the asshole? If I say I have permission, I'll be clear. But he could check the lie. I hang my head, say nothing.

He glances back at the Jew's body already dusted with snow. "I wish the kapos were as conscientious as you. Go to my kitchen door. My maid's just put a pan of scraps on the back step to go to the dogs. They're yours. Then report to me in Medical Block F. Dr. Kleist. I could use a clear-headed helper." He trots off.

And I run, mouth watering, for his kitchen door . . .

Alana's heart was thumping. She could smell the gunpowder in the frigid air, see the German's jackboot in his stirrup, taste the sweet pork fat congealed on the bones. The vision was as vivid as a memory. And this wasn't the first time. It terrified her. She'd never even *known* her mother. Lina had died in that camp, killed on the day of liberation when Alana was just days old. Her father had told her that. *So I've made it all up. Created this vicious person as my mother. What does that make me, but insane?* The sickening image of turning in the Jew was only one vision; there were so many others. It seemed as though she knew everything about Lina. Terrible things. She'd *always* known, and it had poisoned her life. Because worst of all was the dark appeal of becoming just like Lina. The Lina who said: Do anything you have to. Steal, betray, kill. *Survive.*

She felt it now, that dark thrill. *Screw Gus. He's not my responsibility. Let the drunk burn.*

Flames crackled nearer. She smelled smoke, heard voices, Ian's and the AD's, yelling up at her: "Jump! Now!"

She saw Gus struggling to sit up among the bales, coughing at the smoke. It rocked her to her senses. That she'd considered, even for a second, letting him die! Gus had taken her in off the street when she was fifteen, trained her, given her her first job. Of *course* she had to save him. But now the problem hit her: if she alerted the AD to haul him out, they'd see how wasted he was, and he'd never work again. She couldn't let that happen either.

She had an idea.

"Abort!" she called down. "I've made a mistake."

"You *what*?" the AD yelled.

"Let my gel get too dry. Can't do it. Abort!"

"Oh, fuck—" He sounded freaked. He yelled for the crew to put out the fire and barked an order over his radio to the fire truck.

The director burst out, "What the hell? No, we're not cutting! Do the jump, Alana! Just *do* it!" But she was already on the ladder going down from the loft to the interior. She heard the pandemonium outside. The AD: "If she says she can't, we gotta stop!" And the furious director: "Jesus fucking Christ—yeah, yeah, cut—put out the fire. *Fuck* this!" And Ian's irate voice punching through: "Alana, get your ass out here!"

She reached Gus among the straw bales. Coughing, bleary-eyed, he looked up at her in bewilderment. The smoke was so strong it stung her eyes. She slung his limp arm around her neck. "Dumb old fart. Let's go. Hold on to me."

She dragged him out the back door, and they made it into the adjacent woods just as the crew swarmed around the barn with fire extinguishers and the fire truck roared up. As the crew sprang into action putting out the flames, Alana prayed that no one could see her and Gus crouching in the trees, catching their breath.

He flopped onto his back in the dry leaves. His voice came out wobbly, but with his roguish laugh. "Holy shit."

Her anger surged back. "What the hell was going through your pea brain?"

"Thought it was a run-through."

"No, Gus, the real thing."

He blinked up at her and swallowed. "Thanks."

She stood up, violently brushing leaves from the hem of her nightgown. "Thanks, nothing. I saved your sorry ass because you once saved mine. But that was a long time ago, Gus. We're square now. Next time, I'll let you burn. You got that?"

He was barely following her. The poor dumb lush. "Stay here awhile," she said, not so harshly. "Then go the long way back to the trailer, okay? With any luck, they'll never know you were gone."

When she reached the set again, they were all waiting to tear a strip off her.

"What the hell was that about?" the AD demanded.

"Sorry," she muttered. "Made a mistake in my prep."

The director yelled in her face, "You are a total fuckup!"

"Jesus, and I thought I could trust you," Ian growled. He was so mad he swore he'd never hire her again, and threatened to put out the word how unreliable she was. That scared her. Without work, all she had was her craziness.

"See that?" the production manager shouted at her as he pointed to the barn. "That's *money* burning! Do you realize what you've cost us?"

She did. For a reshoot the burned section would have to be restored. A very expensive screwup. She stood there taking the abuse but inwardly cursing Gus, and herself.

"Henry? Are you with us?"

Henry Knelman pulled himself from the turmoil of his thoughts. "Indeed, Dimitri. Mrs. Aylward, a wrenching case. And yet, does she qualify?"

He had arrived late at the Mount Sinai Hospital neurology department on East 100th Street for this evening meeting of the cingulotomy assessment committee. Late, and in torment about the phone call he'd got as he was leaving his clinic. Sheldon Bender, calling from his practice in the Bronx: "Henry, remember that MPD case of mine? Unfortunately the patient didn't show for her Monday appointment, and my secretary can't locate her. Sorry, seems we've lost her."

Again, Knelman thought. He could still feel the shock of that moment twenty-eight years ago when he'd been about to shoot the baby, but her gypsy father had snatched her from the cot. *Lost her.*

He glanced at his colleagues in the stuffy meeting room decorated with photographs of flowers and gardens and made himself focus on the agenda. The committee was himself, three psychiatrists, and a neurophysiologist. They assessed all prospects, though of the fifty or so patients who applied for the cingulotomy procedure each year, only about a third could be accepted. The present discussion concerned a woman with a profound obsessive-compulsive disorder. Mrs. Aylward believed that any object that might have come in contact with a dog was dangerously contaminated, even objects that might have been touched by a person who owned a dog. Any such object that she herself touched made her so agitated, her only relief was to wash everything the article might have tainted, including all her clothes, the walls of her apartment, outdoor stairs, even money. The OC disorder had taken over her life. She could not handle cash or the mail, ride public transit, or sit in a chair outside her home.

"She's in purgatory, Henry," the psychiatrist went on. A weedy man with bushy gray eyebrows, he hunched over his file folder on the table. "Last week she found a hair in a book she was reading and was convinced it was a dog hair. She had a cleaning fit, threw out all her clothes, had to dress herself in garbage bags to go to the store and buy something to wear. She's ready to try anything. She's begging me."

In purgatory. It was how Knelman felt about his long search for the gypsy girl. Over the years he had made frequent trips back to Germany, where he'd hired a private investigator in Frankfurt, the center closest to Otzenhausen, and hired others in Hanover and Munich, even all the way to Vienna, but there wasn't a trace. Gypsies were elusive, drifting around Europe like smoke, disappearing like smoke. And then, two months ago, he'd dared to hope he might have found her. At a conference in Chicago, Sheldon Bender, a psychiatrist from the Bronx, had presented a paper on multiple personality disorder that included an MPD clinical study from his own files about a young woman of ethnic extraction, as he'd put it, whose obsession lay in mentally creating every detail of her mother's life in Austria as minutely as if she'd lived it herself. Hearing this, Knelman's pulse had quickened. It had never occurred to him to look for the girl in his own backyard! He took Bender to lunch and asked about the patient.

"Never seen anything quite like her disorder," Bender had said over his second gin and tonic. "She has a fixation about her mother's life first as an itinerant gypsy, then in a concentration camp. Uncanny knack for pinpointing details. She must have heard them somewhere, or read them."

Knelman had thought in excitement, It *has* to be her. "Interesting," he'd said. "Care to refer her to me for a consult? She might be a candidate for psychosurgical therapy."

"Hmmm. Worth a try."

Now Bender's office had lost track of her, and Knelman despaired that after coming so close, the gypsy had again slipped through his fingers. Smoke. Still, he had learned one thing from Bender. The girl's name was Alana Marks.

"Henry, cingulotomy may be Mrs. Aylward's last hope," said Tom Barrick, the neurophysiologist. Handsome, still blond in middle age, he sat idly scratching his tanned cheek, waiting for a response. They were all looking at Knelman. Knelman had perfected the bilateral stereotactic cingulotomy.

"Tom, there are always patients desperate for the procedure who do not qualify to receive it," he replied. "We must maintain our policy of accepting only those who have tried the appropriate drug and behavioral therapy, yet remain chronically sick. Since Mrs. Aylward has not yet completed her cycle of Thorazine, surgery may be premature. We must not forget, the procedure is not without risk. Yes, by burning small incisions in the frontal lobes we disrupt the limbic pathways' mediation of emotional responses. It usually works. But we still don't know how it works, or why."

"Well, you learn the art of detachment in this business, but in twenty years I've never seen a more pitiful case." Barrick gave Knelman a deferential smile. "I say she needs your magic touch."

"Hardly magic, Tom."

"Oh? Sixty percent, moderate improvement. Thirty-five percent, *significant* improvement. Those are fabulous numbers. If you're not a wizard, Henry, I don't know who is."

Knelman acknowledged this with a modest nod. God had given him a gift, and it filled him with humility. But he knew what God's plan for him was. Evading arrest at the end of the war by assuming his dead friend's identity, he had reached America and prospered, but he'd been allowed this good fortune for one reason only: to put right the terrible wrong of his genetic experiment. For almost thirty years he'd done all he could to atone. Charity cases, and breakthrough work on psychosurgical therapies like the cingulotomy to help the most pitiful: the intractable obsessive-compulsives and the lost souls frozen in profound depression. "Life unworthy of life," the Nazis had labeled the mentally ill, killing thousands through a program of so-called euthanasia even before turning their murderous sights on the Jews. The Nazis' sins were beyond redemption, of course; Knelman could only pray that his own were not. He might yet hope for absolution if he could successfully eradicate the mutation.

He was halfway there. Years ago he had tracked down the two surviving subjects. And terminated them. It had been dreadful, but necessary. He didn't like to dwell on that.

The subjects' two offspring who'd slipped through his fingers were his focus now. Young Jacob Wentzler was one. Alana Marks had to be the other.

"Well, Henry, you're the expert," the psychiatrist said, closing his file folder, "and if you say this patient isn't a candidate for surgery, at least not yet, I'll continue monitoring her on the drug therapy. I only ask that you keep an open mind if I bring up her case again soon."

There was a knock on the door, and a nurse poked her head in. "Excuse me. Doctor Knelman, there's a call for you."

He took the phone at the nurse's station.

"Doc, it's Jacob. I think I just killed a girl."

The woman was alive, barely. Knelman kneeled by her bloodied body on the linoleum floor, checking her vital signs. The moment he'd entered the apartment, he had closed the door behind him and locked it, using a handkerchief to cover his fingerprints, then went to the victim. Multiple contusions. Thready pulse. Low blood pressure. Blood smeared her face and matted patches of her straw-textured hair and the gauze of her skimpy lime nightie. On the floor beside her lay a flea-market desk lamp, and the sharp edge of its heavy iron base was bright with blood. Knelman turned away, trying to regain his professional composure. The fourth floor walk-up held a whiff of garbage that turned his stomach. Outside, a siren screamed by on East Thirteenth Street, then faded. "How long has she been unconscious?"

"Since I called you. Took you long enough." Jacob Wentzler, sixteen years old, sat on a kitchen chair, legs apart, elbows on his knees, and flipped playing cards into a plastic bowl on the floor. Knelman saw that some of the card faces had finger smudges of blood. He also noted the tension in Jacob's movements despite his mask of indifference: if Jacob wasn't concerned about the woman, he was about the prospect of prison. "What now?"

"We must get help for her. Who is she?"

"Angela or something. Picked her up on Second Avenue. I don't think her johns are gonna miss her much."

Knelman stood up, fighting back his dread. He had known this moment would come sooner or later. Jacob Wentzler, at his birth, had been biologically destined to be a killer. "Did you call anyone else?"

"You said not to." Jacob sat back, unfazed at the speckles of blood on his white T-shirt and tan slacks. He was well built, with muscled arms, back, and thighs. Knelman knew he'd worked out at the gym in the South Boston Correctional Facility for Young Offenders. He also knew that Jacob's immigrant father had washed his hands of his son when the boy had been sent to the reform school. Most important, he knew that Jacob, having completed his sentence three weeks ago, had been released.

"Jacob, get up. You cannot be found here. I know you're not responsible for this—it's your condition. But the police won't understand. We cannot let them arrest you. Come." Knelman grabbed a grimy kitchen towel and used it to pick up the bloodied desk lamp. He found a paper shopping bag and dropped the lamp in, and then, using the towel to lift the plastic bowl, he dumped the blood-smudged cards into the bag too. He looked around for further incriminating evidence. "Did you bring anything in with you?"

"Just a hard-on."

"Come away, now. Here, put on my jacket to cover the blood. We shall go back to your hotel."

From a pay phone on Second Avenue Knelman made an anonymous emergency call requesting an ambulance for the woman, then hailed a taxi and got in with Jacob. Midtown, he asked the driver to make a stop at a newsstand, where he got out, dropped the paper bag with the evidence into a trash bin, bought a *Wall Street Journal*, and got back in the cab. At the St. Moritz Hotel on Central Park he and Jacob took the elevator in silence to Jacob's room. Closing the door, weak-kneed with tension, Knelman asked, "Did you copulate with the woman? Did you ejaculate?"

"What's this, dirty-old-man question hour?"

"Answer me. Did you penetrate her and ejaculate?"

Jacob was pulling off his blood flecked clothes. "Didn't get that far. The bitch was bugging me."

Knelman felt immense relief. He would not have to deal with a pregnancy, at least.

Jacob flopped down on the bed in his shorts, lying on his back, one hand under his head. "The other bitch was bugging me, too. Good ol' Mom. I could hear her saying, 'The whore's trouble, hit her.' Drives me nuts, Doc."

Knelman's mouth was dry. Hilde Wentzler—one of the three experimental subjects, dead for fifteen years. Jacob knew that she was his mother, but nothing about the gene. The subjects hadn't known the purpose of the experiment. And, sedated, they hadn't seen who'd operated on them. Knelman had let Jacob believe that his visions of his mother sprang from a mental illness. "Jacob, all of that unpleasantness will soon be finished. The neurosurgical therapy will end your visions."

Jacob regarded him with cold eyes. "Makes me feel funny, though, the idea of you drilling in here." He tapped his forehead with one finger.

"Nonsense." They'd been through all this. Last spring Knelman had contacted the psychologist at the correction center and offered a consultation with the problematic teen. In a private session he'd persuaded Jacob to become his patient, and after several intense counseling sessions had got him to agree to a cingulotomy upon his release. Jacob had now traveled here for the operation and Knelman had put him up at the hotel. The procedure was scheduled at his private clinic in four days. "You know there is no drilling. We merely introduce a thin heated needle into the cingulate gyrus for a matter of seconds. It creates small lesions that disrupt specific neural pathways whose crossed wires, as it were, brought on the undesirable behavior. You will feel nothing, and will leave my clinic an hour later, cured."

"Tell you the truth, Doc, I'm not sure I wanna go through with it. Gives me the willies. I'll pass. You just give me a drug refill, and I'll take the next train back to Beantown."

"That is not an option. We will go ahead with the procedure."

"Or else what?" Jacob smirked. "No more sessions? Scary."

"Or else I shall inform the police about Angela."

The young man's face hardened. He didn't break eye contact as he slowly got up from the bed. He had about two inches on Knelman, plus youth, far superior strength, and a vicious glint in his eye.

Knelman didn't move. "Don't even consider it, Jacob. Perhaps few people would miss Angela, but many would miss me. You'd spend the rest of your life in prison."

Jacob seemed to assess the threat. "Why the hell does operating on me mean so much to you?"

"You are my responsibility." *You're the monster I created.* By the time he'd traced the Wentzler woman, he'd learned that she had previously been reunited with the man she'd been married to before the war, and had given birth to Jacob. The marriage hadn't lasted, and the father had emigrated to the States with the child. Through the 1960s Knelman had often gone to observe the run-down bungalow in South Boston and watch the child from a distance. He'd waited, hoping desperately that some accident or illness would remove the boy without any intervention on his part. When Jacob, at thirteen, had assaulted a teacher and been sent to the reform school, it had given Knelman a temporary reprieve: locked away, the boy could do little harm. But now, having been released, he'd almost killed this prostitute, and Knelman couldn't wait any longer. In their sessions in Boston Jacob had told him about the arsenal of guns he planned to acquire, and his urge to mow down all the people who "bugged" him. Knelman was sure that unless he acted now, he would be hearing one day soon about the crazed young gunman who'd walked into some busy restaurant and murdered fifty people in a killing spree. As for the thought of Jacob ever impregnating a woman, passing along the gene, the progeny forever beyond Knelman's control . . . that was too horrible to contemplate. Jacob had refused sterilization outright. Which had brought them to this crisis point.

"In fact, Jacob, it is now evident to me that we must advance the schedule." He could not risk the police tracking the youth before he could operate. "Come to my clinic in the morning, first thing. I will perform the therapy then."

"So that's my choice? The operation tomorrow, or jail?"

"Yes."

"Christ, I called you tonight for *help*."

"Believe me, this therapy is the only help. It will cure you."

He was lying, of course. A cingulotomy could do nothing to cure Jacob. That had never been Knelman's intention. His goal was to render the mutation harmless by incapacitating the carrier. After the surgery, Jacob would be lucky if he could say his own name.

The young man slumped down on the edge of the bed, sullenly accepting the ultimatum, and Knelman gave him a comforting pat on the shoulder. He pitied Jacob, but God had given him a mission, and he must not fail. He had taken care of all three original subjects. He would take care of

Jacob tomorrow. Then there would be only one carrier left. The gypsy girl. He prayed he would not have to harm her.

First, he had to find her.

It was after ten when he reached his apartment building on Seventy-third at Park, took the elevator, and opened the door to his penthouse. Esther had left the light on in the foyer, but the living room lay in gloom. He was used to it. Before she went to her bedroom each night she turned off lights, perhaps a habit from her hard-up childhood, so different from his own. Or had she gone out? The thought disturbed him. She used to go to a movie or a play with her women friends, but these days it was more likely to be with Howard Jaffe. He snapped on a lamp, curbing the jealous pang, telling himself: She's your *sister*. Except it wasn't true; not by blood, and not in his heart.

In the kitchen he found that she'd left cherry kugel out for him on the kitchen counter, a large slice on a Delft china plate neatly covered in plastic wrap. He was famished, and ate the whole slice standing.

"Henry, I didn't hear you come in."

He turned. Esther stood in the doorway, regarding him with her gentle smile. She was still trim at fifty-nine, her hair coiffed, its rich auburn color maintained by her hairdresser. He knew that she took such care over her appearance not from vanity but from sensitivity about her one turned eye. Strabismus, a hereditary condition. She still lowered her face a little whenever she met strangers. He found her faintly unfocused gaze endearing. To him, she'd always seemed lovely.

"Well?" she asked.

Well, what? he wondered. Had he forgotten to pick up something she'd wanted? Something at the cleaners perhaps?

"The dress, Henry. What do you think?"

He realized she was wearing a formal gown. Floor-length green brocade. "Very nice," he said, then added, unsure, "Is it new?"

She laughed. "You remind me of that story about the woman who'd bought a horribly expensive new dress and was afraid her husband would be angry. When he came home she waited upstairs until he'd had a scotch and was comfortable, then she came down wearing it, and said casually, 'Do you like this dress?' As he stared at it, she was afraid the storm was coming. Then he said, 'It's always been my favorite.' "

Knelman smiled, feeling the tension flow out of him. It wasn't the little story, it was Esther's way. She always relaxed him.

"I got it at Bergdorf's for the gala next week," she said, coming in and taking his bare plate to the sink. "Just trying it on with the right shoes." She rinsed the plate and wiped crumbs from the counter with a dishcloth, chattering all the while about the preparations for the upcoming party at the Isaac Rosenthal Center where she worked as a special functions coordinator. She'd lost all but a trace of her German accent. Knelman had found it difficult to shed his own.

He watched her. Years ago, living together as brother and sister like this, he had suffered such lust. Eventually he'd taken a mistress. Jeanne had had her own apartment and her own life as an art buyer, and never asked for more than the monthly check he discreetly left, nor for more of a commitment. After sixteen years, he'd found out why: she'd been seeing another man for a decade. Knelman had been almost relieved when he and Jeanne had parted. He had his work. Esther made his home charming. And he had David, the son he loved as his own flesh and blood. David had filled his empty heart from the moment he'd first seen the child twenty-seven years ago, an open-faced three-year-old standing at that Brooklyn Heights apartment door holding Esther's skirt hem. His small hand had reached out to touch the flimsy suitcase Knelman held. Knelman still felt the wonder of that meeting. On the ocean crossing he had studied books on Jewish customs, and racked his memory to recall every detail Heinrich had told him about his family, how he and his sister had been separated as young children when their parents divorced, each going with one parent, never seeing each other again. But now that he had arrived at Heinrich's sister's door, his courage faltered. It seemed impossible that she would not see through him.

"Esther?" he'd said as the shy young woman opened the door. "Do you know me? It's Heinrich."

Her hand had flown to her mouth in amazement. "Bruder!" *Brother.*

Her innocent acceptance had so moved him, he had loved her then and there. And understood in the same moment that he could never have her.

Wiping up cake crumbs, she was careful to keep her new gown from touching the counter. "David called. He said he'll try to make it to the gala, but he's awfully busy. Said he's got an interesting case in court tomorrow. Something about a gypsy." She shook crumbs into the sink then put down the cloth. "I didn't even know there *were* gypsies in New York. You learn something every day." She turned and walked out. "Switch off the lights when you're done, won't you, dear?"

He stared after her. David. Was that the way to find the gypsy girl?

CHAPTER 3

DAVID KNELMAN STRODE down the busy hall outside the second-floor courtroom at One Hundred Center Street, passing a cluster of black women, one of them crying, likely over some guy in the holding cells. He was heading for a portly, balding, pink-faced man sitting on a bench beside the elevator. Sunday-best suit, not new. Battered suitcase on his lap. Looked like a hard-up salesman, David thought. He hoped this man knew his stuff. A magician, apparently well known on the B nightclub circuit for his sleight-of-hand theatrics, he was to be David's make-or-break witness.

"Mr. Eaves? I'm David Knelman. Thanks for coming. Sorry I couldn't get to the meeting yesterday to see your work, but my cocounsel said you knocked his socks off."

The magician's lips pursed in a smile as he got up and they shook hands. "Mr. Fielding was a good audience."

Smug smile, David thought. Maybe the guy *is* good. "We have a few minutes. Did Rudy fill you in about the case? Any questions?"

"Well, he said it was about a fortune-teller. I must say I

was wondering, why such a fuss? I mean, isn't that sort of thing just petty crime?"

"Grand larceny. To the tune of forty-seven thousand dollars." He looked down the hall to the bird-thin spinster in her sixties outside the courtroom door. The plaintiff, Ada McCall. Blue-rinse hair, dowdy brown dress. Waiting to go in, she looked anxious and bewildered, twisting a handkerchief in her hands. At thirty, David had been a Manhattan assistant district attorney for four years, long enough to become infected with cynicism, but it hadn't taken. This lady had been bilked of her entire life's savings by a parasitical con artist, and that made him mad. "It's called a boojo scam, and it's one of the oldest of gypsy swindles," he explained. "Starts in a fortune-telling parlor with a two-dollar palm reading. In this case, on Lexington at a Hundred-and-Sixteenth Street, but you've passed them everywhere, those little shop windows with painted tarot cards and zodiac signs. They advertise as 'Reader and Advisor,' because fortune-telling's illegal in New York. The two-buck trade covers the rent, but what the boojo woman is looking for is that one person in a hundred, in five hundred, that she can exploit in a major haul."

"Really? How?"

"Victim's usually a single female, lonely, a little gullible. For months, maybe years, she's been anxious about some personal problem. So she wanders into the little parlor, and it's cozy there, and the fortune-teller seems so understanding and wise. Once the victim opens her heart, she's hooked. Comes back again and again, soaks up the astrological advice, starts to think of the fortune-teller as her friend. But in their chats the boojo woman's coaxing out financial information. How much money does the mark have in the bank? What savings? Any stocks or bonds? Eventually, if she decides the victim's ripe, she tells her what the root of all her bad luck is: her cash in the bank is cursed. If the poor lady believes it, the boojo woman makes a promise to do her best to lift the curse." David noticed Rudy Fielding, his cocounsel, open the courtroom door for Miss McCall and go in with her. "All set?" he asked the magician, nodding at the suitcase. "Let's go."

As they walked, Eaves seemed hooked himself. "But how does the gypsy get the victim's money?"

"Gives instructions." David's eyes were on the defendant coming down the hall with her attorney. She had to be doing well if she could afford Ned Dewart and had posted bail. Middle-aged and thick-waisted, she wore a conservative navy dress and had her hair in an old-fashioned bun; she was smart enough—or Dewart had coached her—to make herself look innocuous. But her hard eyes raked David with contempt before she went into the courtroom with the lawyer. "The victim's told to bring in her cash, sometimes tens of thousands of dollars," he went on to Eaves. "She's told to wrap it up in a kerchief—a special one the fortune-teller loans her. *Boojo* means 'dishcloth' in Romany, the gypsy language. When the victim comes back with the money, the boojo woman, who's a sleight-of-hand expert, switches the cash-filled kerchief for an identical one stuffed with paper. She makes incantations over what the victim still believes is the money, then sends her home with a warning not to open the bundle for at least a week, or the curse could come back."

"But once the woman finds she's been swindled, she'd tell the police and they'd arrest the gypsy, wouldn't they? So where's the profit?"

"Usually the victim keeps quiet. She's too ashamed. Knows she's been had. And often by the time the hoax is discovered, the con artist has skipped town. That's what happened in this case. I had the defendant extradited from Virginia."

They reached the courtroom doors, where David stopped. "Mr. Eaves, my challenge is the jury. Though people may feel sorry for a gullible little old lady, deep down they're thinking, What a fool, how could anyone fall for a switcheroo like that? That's why you're here. I want you to show the jury exactly how. I want you to make them see how even *they* could fall for it."

Eaves flashed his smug smile. "That I can do."

Turned out the man did know his stuff. In front of the judge and jury David played patsy for the demonstration, dumping his wallet and watch and keys into an empty cloth bag Eaves supplied. Eaves did some swift and clever misdirection, and when David opened the bag that he was sure still held his things, even he was surprised when he poured out the contents onto the table: just pebbles. He heard a jurywoman suck in a breath of astonishment, while the foreman, a flinty Chase Manhattan accountant David had feared would be a tough nut to crack, looked alarmed and unconsciously felt for his own wallet. The case wrapped up fast. David won a conviction.

"Congratulations, Knelman," Fielding said as they gathered up their notes.

"Thanks." No feeling like it, he thought. As good as a clean downhill run plus a slam dunk, rolled into one. Yet, as he caught the eye of the bewildered plaintiff, he felt a needle of frustration. Justice had been done, but the poor lady would likely never recover her savings.

The defendant, led past the prosecution table by the bailiff, sneered at David. "I put a gypsy curse on you. You will never marry, and will never have children."

As she was led out, David said dryly to Fielding, "And I put a Jewish curse on her. It's called lock-up."

"She's expecting you, Mr. Knelman," the doorman said breezily, holding open the apartment lobby door. He eyed the gifts David carried, a bottle of Dom Perignon and a silver-wrapped gift box. "Looks like you'll be mighty welcome, too."

"How's your boy, Bill?

"Home from the hospital, proud as heck of his cast. Thanks for asking."

"And a Little League hero, I'll bet, for his battle wounds." David walked briskly to the elevator. In court all day, then in a drawn-out meeting in the judge's chambers about another case, he was running late.

As he opened the door the apartment held the familiar smells of gardenia eau de cologne and cinnamon. Even today, his aunt had been baking.

"David? Is that you?" She came into the marble-floored foyer, beaming. Pink linen shirtwaist dress, pearl necklace, every hair in place.

"Happy birthday, Aunt Es." He kissed her powdered cheek. "You old enough now to vote?"

She playfully swatted his arm, and as he handed her the silver-wrapped package, she said, "Oh, David, you shouldn't have."

"That? I just picked it up at the five-and-dime. *This,* however, is the real thing," he said, lifting the champagne. "Time for a glass? Sorry I'm so late."

"Just a glass, I'm afraid, our dinner reservation's at seven. Come and say hello to Howard. We were just having a drink before we go."

"Dad's not home yet?"

"Still at the hospital." The click of David's shoes on the foyer marble was silenced by the thick Persian carpet as they walked into the living room. The apricot silk drapes filtered the evening sun.

"How are you, Howard?" David strode forward to shake hands.

"Can't complain, David, except the old ticker's showing its age. I blame Esther. Too much excitement. Just what my doctor warned against."

Esther blushed and returned Howard's fond gaze. David liked his aunt's beau. Howard Jaffe was more than a decade older than Esther, slight of build and bald as an egg, but he was lively and quick, and the penetrating blue eyes in his liver-spotted face hinted at the sharp mind that had made him a millionaire in a clothing business before his twenty-fifth birthday. A widower, he was a benefactor of the Isaac Rosenthal Center where Esther worked, and a few months ago they'd started keeping company—Esther's phrase. David wasn't sure if the old gentleman's casual comment about a heart problem was serious or not. Whatever, it did his own heart good to see his aunt so cheerful. She'd been his surrogate mother, taking him in as a baby after his father had smuggled him out of Germany before being caught in the Nazis' net. Before the war there'd been some episode of an American fiancé she'd come to marry but who'd left her at the altar; David didn't know the details. Then her family were murdered in the holocaust, all except Dad, who'd turned up on her doorstep. The upshot was that she'd devoted herself to raising a nephew and keeping house for a brother, so in David's opinion her belated happiness with Howard was long overdue.

"I hear you and Aunt Es were just leaving. Sorry I got held up."

"Don't be," Howard said. "Someone's got to put the bad guys behind bars. You going to open that, Esther?" He nodded at the little gift box she held.

She pulled off the paper and lifted out the antique snuffbox. She collected them, and David was pleased to see her obvious delight at this one—silver inlaid with tiny emeralds and rubies. "It's exquisite, David."

"Czarist, the dealer told me."

"Yes, early Romanoff, I'd say." She looked up at him, her face clouding with concern. "But, dear, you shouldn't have. You work so hard for your paycheck. You can't afford it."

"Don't worry, I used my Mafia kickback. Usually I just fritter it on dope and fast women."

Her smile was playful. "So that's your problem, you're *buying* them. That's not how to find a nice girl, you know."

He laughed. "Don't start, Aunt Es."

They had only enough time for a glass of champagne and the crab hors d'oeuvres Esther had made, and then it was time for her and Howard to go.

"I'll stay and see Dad," David said. When they'd spoken on the phone this morning, his father had said there was something he wanted to talk to him about.

"Yes, do, dear, he'll be so glad. Now, there are leftover chicken crêpes in the fridge, and some spinach soufflé. And fresh strudel I made today. Just heat the crêpes in a slow oven for—"

"Howard," he laughed, "get her out of here."

When he was alone, he took off his jacket and loosened his tie. Long day. He'd been at his desk at seven, preparing for an eight A.M. charging conference with his boss to appraise the merits of all the weeks indictments. Then in and out of court all day. He sank into an easy chair, glad to relax in the familiar surroundings. The cream brocade sofas, the grand piano where his father's dog-eared music books were spread, the solid wall of books. The raised dining room with its soft lighting over the case that held Esther's snuffbox collection. The glassed-in terrace with his father's tiers of rare orchids. David's apartment on Riverside Drive was spartan, and the decor, now that he thought of it, kind of a blend of waiting room and frat house. This place still felt like home.

"David, how good to see you."

He got to his feet. Hadn't even heard the door. "How are you, Dad?"

Knelman looked around. "I missed them?"

"Just. Only got here myself in time to say hello and goodbye."

His father shook his head in mock disapproval. "All work and no play, son?"

David had always liked his father's German accent: his W's were soft V's. The syntax, though, was as flawless as an English professor's. "You should talk. When's the last time you took a holiday from the hospital?"

"Sickness, mental or corporeal, respects no man's rest."

"Neither do my perps." David lifted the champagne from the wine bucket and grinned. "But being late has an upside. Champagne doesn't keep. Join me?"

Smiling, his father gave his peculiar slight bow of the head, and they started for the glassed-in terrace. David had always found that small bow so elegant, emblematic of a lost world of cultured European Jewry. Dad was the essence of elegance, David thought. Not just his erect carriage, his close-cropped white hair and trim white beard, his fine taste in English wool suits and Italian silk shirts. It was his style of mind that David admired. His quiet courtesy. His erudition, both as a neurosurgeon and in private life; for pleasure he read nineteenth-century German poetry and played

Stravinsky and Schoenberg. And his generosity: he was known for his philanthropy at the Rosenthal Center, and he often took cases for no fee in his specialized field of psychosurgery. David sometimes felt humbled in his father's presence. Not that he had an inferiority complex: he knew he was a good prosecutor, his friendships were solid, and the women he'd been with made it clear that whatever it was women found attractive, he seemed to have it. But no man inspired him more than his father, who showed all of this nobility of mind and spirit despite having suffered in a concentration camp. Or maybe because of it, David sometimes thought. There was a permanent hint of tragedy in Dad's gray-green eyes. David's mother had died in that camp. He'd had no such brutal test by which to measure himself. Did his national service after Columbia Law by clerking in the navy's JAG office in Washington—Vietnam as far away as the moon. He hoped that if he ever did face such a test, he'd be able to muster his father's stoic dignity.

Knelman sat, folding one long leg over the other, as David poured champagne and handed him a glass. The lights of Park Avenue lit up the night. David nodded at the glow as he sat. "Look at that. And I thought this OPEC oil embargo was supposed to get us all conserving."

Knelman smiled absently. "How about a tennis game next week? Could you make Thursday evening?"

"You're on."

They drank champagne. Dad seemed preoccupied, David thought. Maybe tired.

"How are things at work?" Knelman asked.

"Busy. The DA's on a roll with all these mob indictments. Oh, Greg Owens—the guy who shares my office?—he's leaving for McCarthy, Roth, Vineberg uptown. Can't wait to move on." Settling back in the chair, David stretched out his legs, wondering what his father had wanted to talk to him about.

"And you?"

"What, move on?" David shrugged. "Call me crazy, I like working for the people."

"The people should be grateful."

The understated approval pleased David. The district attorney's office was widely regarded by the four hundred assistant DAs as a stopover on the way to lucrative private law firms, or as an arena for making the political connections that led to judgeships. David had ambition, but he meant what he'd said. He was shooting for his boss's job, executive ADA. Maybe one day the top spot, DA. Defense work didn't interest him. The money would be nice, but he'd seen too much evidence of how that money corrupted the system—drug barons and corporate crooks walking. Something deep down in him liked helping the ordinary joe who got steamrolled. Maybe it's in the blood, he thought. The Nazis had perfected the steamroller.

"How did the gypsy case go today?"

David looked a question at him.

"Esther told me," Knelman explained.

"Ah. Well, I won a conviction. Actually, it's become cases, plural. Seems I'm carving out a gypsy crime niche. My boss likes my conviction record on these perps, so he's loaded me up. Interesting work, though. My friend Lip—Detective Lipranski, the gypsy specialist on the force—he recently brought me something new, or at least an original twist on an old scam. We're investigating, and I have a feeling it's tip-of-the-iceberg stuff. And not pretty."

His father seemed to be only half listening. His expression became sober. "To be truthful, David, I have an ulterior motive in asking. It's what I wanted to speak to you about. I have a favor to ask."

"Shoot."

"I'm not certain I have any right to bother you with this, but . . . you see, it concerns a young gypsy woman. And it seems you have made contacts in that community."

David was surprised. What possible business could Dad have with gypsies?

"Don't worry," his father said, looking vaguely amused. "I haven't compromised myself with a hussy." At the old-fashioned, slightly priggish word, David had to smile.

His father explained that she was the patient of a psychiatrist colleague in the Bronx who'd contacted him about the girl's mental disorder, but then the colleague lost contact with her. "She didn't show up for her appointment, and she left an indecipherable address and no phone number."

"They do that," David said dryly.

"I would like to find her, to offer her my services. From what Bender tells me, I believe her condition might be treatable through a minor neurosurgical procedure. It is—" He stopped, spreading his hands in a gesture of apology. "As you know, patient confidentiality prohibits my discussing her case."

David waved that away; the details didn't concern him. He felt torn. Much as he wanted to help with his father's good deed, he found it hard to get into the spirit of it when he thought of his desk stacked with booking sheets and prosecution reports and indictments awaiting completion. Checking out this gypsy would be a big drain on him.

He could see that his hesitation wasn't lost on his father. "Forgive me, David, I know you have a punishing caseload. Please, forget I even asked." He stood, moved to the glass shelves where his orchids were ranged, and picked up pruning scissors. "I'll speak to someone else about this." Snipping at dead leaves, he whistled softly.

David wondered, What's eating him? He only whistles when he's worried. "Hold on, Dad. I didn't say no."

His father turned. "Her name is Alana Marks."

"Might as well be Smith or Jones."

"Pardon?"

"Marks, Stanley, Mitchell—they're the most common gypsy names. But the bigger challenge is, these people use a lot of aliases. Can be hard to trace."

"But surely not all of them do. And there must be so few in New York City."

David leaned forward, elbows on his knees. "Okay, crash course on gypsies. There are over a million in the United States. They live in tightly knit clans, they maintain age-old customs, and they generally keep apart from the *gadje*—that's their name for nongypsies. They're often taken for Hispanics or Greeks, a mistake they don't discourage. Among themselves they speak Romany. It's an unwritten language with a base of Sanskrit—shows their ancient origins in India. Most are barely literate—they keep their kids out of the school system like it's poison. But a lot of them are far from poor. They don't travel in caravans these days; it's Cadillacs and RVs. And they have their own version of organized crime, though it's almost always nonviolent. Fly-by-night body-and-fender fixers, fairground used-car hucksters, insurance-fraud artists, slip-and-fall experts, pickpockets, welfare cheats, and of course the fortune-telling trade is their bread and butter. If they feel the law getting too near, they disappear in one city and resurface in another under a new name. Using aliases is almost universal among them. One insurance scammer I busted had eleven driver's licenses. Police right across the country find it tough to track down and convict a gypsy perp." He shook his head. "The gypsies' philosophy seems to be that the U.S.A. is one big plum tree, and they're just picking plums. They usually get away with it."

"But does it necessarily follow that you could not find this girl?"

David found his father's persistence odd, like a dog who'd got hold of a bone and wouldn't let go. But then, he hadn't survived a death camp and climbed to the top of his profession without being tenacious. David sighed, half smiling. "Let me see what I can find out."

Next day on his lunch break David left his seventh-floor office at Eighty Center Street next to the courthouse and walked the six blocks to Oliver Street among the Lower East Side tenements to meet his gypsy informant. It was hot, and on the way he slung his jacket over his shoulder. Laundry drooped from a maze of clotheslines between fire escapes, and drifting trash papers littered the sidewalk. He and Augie Denver met in front of the Mariners Temple Baptist Church, forlorn and seedy. Spray-painted graffiti covered the church's noticeboard. Nearby, a Chinese fishmonger was tossing a bin of crushed ice into the gutter, and the air reeked of fish.

Augie was about David's age, but shaggy-haired and mustached. As he took the ten dollars David handed over, he scratched the beer belly that grinned between his tight purple tie-dyed T-shirt and low-slung yellow bell-bottoms. David never could figure the gypsy mind-set about clothes. From the seventeen-year-old who ran his mother's fortune-telling parlor on the Bowery and owned a red Corvette to the Jersey City *rom baro,* clan leader, who regularly flew to California and Texas for clan weddings and funerals and to judge at the *kris,* the gypsy court—no matter how well-off they were, they dressed in things that looked like donations to the Salvation Army. Size didn't seem to matter much, or style, or vintage. Color was the only constant—the brighter the better.

"I been checkin' around, like you asked," Augie said. "Seems she might be the daughter of Rajko Marks."

It wasn't a name David knew.

"He goes by other handles, too. Maybe you heard of one. Roman Mitchell?"

David felt a jolt of excitement. Mitchell was the *rom baro* of his Kalderash clan in Queens, owner of various fortune-telling parlors there and in Manhattan, and probably of a hoard of stolen goods as well, according to Lipranski, though there was no hard evidence, just Lip's gut instinct. Slippery and secretive, this *rom baro* was also, by all accounts, autocratic as a tyrant. "Does she live with him?"

"No way. They say when she started acting up as a teen, the *kris* made her *marimé*. Rajko threw her out."

The way he pronounced the Romany word, like "Mary may," it sounded like something from a nursery rhyme, but David knew how grave a punishment this gypsy verdict was. Anyone declared *marimé* was forbidden to keep company with other gypsies for months, even years. Gypsies lived communally, and family meant everything—there was no such thing as a lone gypsy—so the excommunication was a hard sentence.

"What do you mean, acting up?"

"Guy I talked to said Rajko called her *dili*. You know, touched in the head?"

It fit. A Marks/Mitchell girl who was considered unstable was almost certainly the girl Dad was looking for. But it would be tricky getting access to the family to ask about her. Few gypsy households would open up to a *gadje,* and none would to a DA. Or if they did, it would only be a ruse; David would never get straight answers. "Could you get to Marks, ask about his daughter?"

The gypsy made a face at such ignorance. "He's Kalderash, I'm Machwaya. Our people don't mix a whole lot."

David understood. The four gypsy *vitsas,* or nations, kept a cool distance from one another. "Any idea where I might find the girl?"

"Nope." Augie was tucking the ten into his hip pocket. "Last anybody heard, though, she was working in the movies. Stunts."

A second assistant director, he called himself, this kid in the Jefferson Airplane T-shirt with hair to his shoulders; couldn't be more than eighteen. In the twilight he was leading David through the crowd of film people across a trampled farm meadow. On the phone, when they'd called it a set, David had imagined a space the size of a basketball court, but it seemed as though whole acres had been taken over by trailers and trucks and equipment, to say nothing of a small army of crewmen. Everyone's focus was on an old wooden barn, which David and the kid were approaching in the gathering dusk. When he'd traced the Marks girl through the Screen Actors' Guild, they'd told him she was working on a Civil War adventure picture: "On location. Tilverton, Connecticut. Little farming town." He'd taken a department car. If he could help his father, and even better, if the girl had anything to tell him about Rajko Marks, the trip would be worth it.

"Had trouble with this stunt the other day, so we're a bit antsy," the second assistant director said as he stopped behind a forest of light stands. He held up his clipboard to halt David too. They were about as far from the barn as home plate from second base. "Also, we've got a stiff wind this time, not good. The fire marshal's making noises about shutting us down another day until it's calmer. Production manager's sweating bullets. Time is serious money around here. So," he added in a conspiratorial whisper, although people were moving around them in a din of activity, "before the ax falls we're going ahead fast with the shot, toot sweet." David nodded with a small smile. *Toot sweet* was fast, all right. "Stand here and don't move," the kid said. "I'll be back in a bit." As he hurried away he said over his shoulder, pointing up at the barn, "That's her."

David looked up. The barn's loft door was open, making a kind of small stage, and on the lip of it a girl stood in an ankle-length white nightgown, barefoot. The wind was lifting her long blond hair and tugging the nightgown tight against her body. He'd pictured a stunt woman as rugged, somewhat butch. She wasn't. Nice shape. He'd recently seen a movie featuring the starlet she was doubling for, and for his money this girl was better looking, not so Barbie doll. She seemed to be checking some handheld gear and looked very focused, her actions methodical. She looked anything but mentally disturbed.

Darkness had fallen by the time they set the rear of the barn on fire. It was spectacular, exciting in a visceral way David hadn't anticipated. The flames swept the weathered wood, the orange blaze lit up the night with a low roar, and even at this distance he felt the heat. The crowd of film workers watched in silence, apparently as entranced as he was. But when the flames reached the front where the girl stood at the loft edge, trapped, David tensed. Her nightgown caught on fire. As she jerked and twisted in terror, he felt an urge to race forward and help her. It was all he could do to keep still with the others as she leaped and tumbled down in flames.

CHAPTER 4

"THE DISTRICT ATTORNEY? For *me*?" Alana laughed. "Yeah, right, Tina. Pull the other one." She was still shivering from the cold white residue of liquid nitrogen that left her looking like a powdered doughnut, as Tina, the lone girl in the FX crew, cut her out of her charred nightgown. Around them in the wardrobe trailer the wardrobe assistants were busy cataloging rows of costumes on racks, eager to call it a night. The cramped space smelled of perfumy film makeup, coffee, and the chemical tang of the Nomex on Alana's skin.

"No, really, honey. He's waiting outside. Kinda cute, too." Tina gingerly pulled away what was left of the nightgown. "And he's come for you, all right. He watched you work."

These FX guys had a reputation for cooking up some whoppers, Alana thought, but she quickly showered and got dressed. If she was being set up for some practical joke, she didn't mind. She felt energized, felt terrific. Nobody could have done the high fall better, and the fire gag had worked like a dream. Even Gus, sober and contrite, had been a big help rigging the box rig, and this time, instead of curses from the director, Alana had gotten compliments. After giving her a brief burst of applause, the crew had gone right back to work, plenty to do to put out the fire and strike the set; as far as they were concerned, she'd only done her job. Which was just the way she liked it. It meant this location shoot was wrapped, and everybody could go home and get some sleep. She was satisfied it had gone so well.

She stepped out of the trailer, and there he was. Tall, fit looking. Well-cut dark suit, maroon silk tie, brown hair short like a cop, polished city shoes in the grass. Jesus, maybe this was no joke. *Nobody* on set dressed like that.

"Miss Marks?" He was looking at her with a puzzled expression, as though not sure it was her.

Alana realized why. He'd watched her fall—as a blond. "It was a wig," she said, running her hand through her dark hair, almost as short as his. Catching his quick once-over, she added, "The rest is real." She thought she saw him blush a bit, but it was dark out here, she couldn't be sure. She made a gesture that took in her red tank top, faded jeans, flat sandals. "My civvies." Not exactly the Victorian damsel in distress he'd seen minutes ago.

"Of course, I forgot, you're an actress."

"Not me, I just do the grunt work. And you are—?"

"David Knelman. Manhattan assistant district attorney."

A flag of caution went up in her mind. It was reflexive, a habit ingrained since childhood. Gypsies would do almost anything to avoid the law.

"Don't worry," he said. "There's no problem."

Then why drag your ass out to Connecticut? she thought. They stood in the shadows around the corner from a stark battery lamp clamped to the end of the trailer. The wind carried the acrid odor of smoke and wet wood from the drenched barn.

He looked around. "Is there some place we could talk, inside?"

She jerked her chin at the trailers scattered around the chewed-up meadow. "What you see is what you get. Which means being underfoot with tired, cranky people busting their humps to get the set struck before overtime kicks in."

He nodded toward a picnic table under a tree. "How about over there? We could sit at least."

He'd barely got the words out when two big grips reached the table, hoisted it, and carted it off to a props van. Alana caught the DA's eye. "Gotta be quick."

"So I see."

"There's always a Johnny-on-the-spot."

He smiled as though her lame crack had actually been funny. Tina was right. He was cute, in a square kind of way.

"So," she asked, "what's this about?"

"I've actually come for two reasons. My father is Dr. Henry Knelman, chief of neurology at Mount Sinai Hospital in Manhattan. As I understand it, your doctor referred you to him but then lost contact with you. My father feels his specialized expertise might be of use, and he'd like to offer you a consultation."

Alana was taken aback. She'd given up on that shrink, Bender. Like the two others she'd gone to before him, he didn't have a clue about why she was plagued by her visions. He'd tried to cover with patronizing jargon about a multiple personality disorder. Load of crap. Worse, he'd put her on Thorazine, which had made her so dozy she couldn't do her job. To hell with that. She didn't remember him mentioning anything about a referral. But if this neurology man really could cure her, she was ready to listen. Only, why send his son? "What's the other reason?"

"I'm investigating a situation in which there may be a gypsy connection. I understand you were raised in that community. I came mainly to convey my father's offer, but I was also hoping you might supply some background for my case."

She said flatly, "You want the word on my father."

"Yes."

This was new—somebody who wanted something coming right out with it. No soft soap, no faked disinterest. "You'd make a lousy gypsy, Mr. Knelman. We'd rather tell any story but the truth."

He smiled, but there was something stern in his eyes. "I don't intend to apply for admission."

No kidding. "Wish I could help, but I've been an exile from the *kumpania* too long. Haven't seen my father in years. Haven't a clue what he's up to."

"Kumpania?"

"Extended family. Maybe thirty families altogether. You know anything about gypsies?"

"Always ready to learn more."

He looked as though he meant it. She sensed no hidden agenda, just straightforward interest. "About *your* father. You mentioned his special expertise. What exactly would that be?"

"Psychosurgery. He's the best." He handed her a business card with two phone numbers penciled on the back. "The top one is his private clinic on Park Avenue. The bottom's his office at the hospital. He said to call either one, anytime."

Alana suddenly wasn't so sure. "Psychosurgery? Doesn't that mean cutting into your skull?"

"Sorry, that's beyond my scope. I'm just the messenger."

She turned the card over. It was this assistant DA's own card. She couldn't help a wry smile. Guys had given her their numbers before, but never like this.

"Alana, we're going into Stamford for beers. You coming?" It was Lorri, the script assistant, stopping on her way to the parking area. Alana's Fiat was in for servicing, so Lorri had driven her here this morning. She noticed a couple of gaffers waiting by Lorri's aqua Fairlane, chatting, happy to be wrapped. Seeing Gus joshing with them, she felt a jab of annoyance. They'd do beers, but he'd do bourbon. Well, hell, she wasn't Gus's mother.

"No, thanks," she told Lorri. She was teetotal, because any alcohol kick-started mean head-movies of her mother, which she could live without. "I'll get a ride with Manny." The prop man was a pal.

"You sure? The strike's a bitch. He'll be forever."

"No problem. Have fun." Lorri walked on. Alana toed the grass.

"Do you need a ride?" the DA asked. "I'm heading back to the city. Let me give you a lift."

She looked up at him.

"Where do you live?" he asked.

"The Bronx."

"Fine. We can talk in the car."

Why not? It beat hanging out here for hours. "Just let me get my gear and sign out."

They pulled out of the parking area in his spick-and-span office car, a boring brown new Plymouth. Alana thought affectionately of her '64 Fiat Cabriolet. It had belonged to a seat-of-the-pants independent director-producer just out of film school who'd had drive and guts, but no budget for the flick he'd hired her for, so he'd given her his dinged old convertible in lieu of her fee. She'd fixed it up, painted it yellow, and loved it. As the DA drove down the gravel road in the darkness, Alana opened her army-surplus knapsack. It was sturdy khaki canvas; she had no time for purses. Rummaging inside under the library books, she pulled out the sweater panel she'd half finished and the last of its ball of blue yarn, then a fresh ball and knitting needles. As she set to work knitting in the faint light from the dashboard, she caught the DA's look of mild surprise. "I like to keep busy," she said. She'd learned long ago that if she didn't have a concrete task to focus her thoughts, her mother would invade her mind.

He glanced at the book poking out of her pack, a manual on the Atomic Four marine engine. "A little light reading?"

"I like to learn things, too." She read a lot when she wasn't working, and she'd learned a lot. She'd taught herself passable Spanish, could rebuild an Atomic Four marine engine, and was practically an expert on the Revolutionary War. "Ask me anything about the 1775 attack by the Green Mountain Boys on the British at Fort Ticonderoga."

"Was history your major?"

"No, nuclear physics." She shot him a sardonic glance. "Mr. Knelman, my father pulled me out of school when I was eleven."

"I'd rather ask about that. Your people."

"Aha. The price of the lift. Sure, ask away. Just remember, I've been out of that world a long time."

He hit the brake at a four-way stop. Not a car in sight at the dark farmland crossroads. He accelerated jerkily, his foot a little heavy on the gas for Alana's taste. He said, "Alana isn't a gypsy name I've heard before."

"It was the name of a woman my father saw on the boat

coming to America, some rich *gadja*. He needed a quick name for me."

"Were you born on the boat?"

She shook her head. "Germany. My mother died right after I was born, killed by the Nazis. My father grabbed me and beat it to the States." And never had a day's peace with me, she thought grimly. "He was looking for a new name for me because gypsies believe that if a baby's struck by trauma or sickness, it has to be renamed to trick the evil ghosts, so they won't take it. They pick the name of some sleazy person, because they believe the ghosts aren't interested in taking somebody like that. A drunkard, say, or a *gadjo*. All *gadje* are dirt to gypsies." She glanced at him. "No offense."

"All? Why is that?"

"*Gadje* are immoral."

He laughed. "But gypsies aren't? That's one I haven't heard."

"No, really, that's what they're taught to think. And moral behavior is very important to gypsies." She tried to keep the bitterness out of her voice but knew a trace was there, always would be, like ink on cloth. "The way they see it, the *gadje* act so remote with each other that bad people among them can get away with bad stuff—adultery, wife-beating, child abuse. With gypsies all of that gets exposed and judged at the *kris,* so it—" She lowered her needles. "You know about the *kris*?"

"Gypsy court."

"Right. Well, because complaints are hashed out in front of everybody at the *kris,* a family's moral behavior is public knowledge. Gossip and scorn make pretty good deterrents. There're no secrets in the gypsy community." She went back to knitting and purling. "Also, no police and no jails. Carrying out the judgment of the *kris* is up to the whole community. Whereas look at the *gadje* way. Closed sessions, plea bargaining, out-of court settlements." She stole a glance. "Which, I guess, is your line of work, isn't it? Sorry—to gypsies that's sneaky and unjust. Another thing, they don't feed off their own like the *gadje* do. Crimes like protection rackets and contract murder just don't exist among gypsies."

"Okay, but moral superiority? I mean, swindling seems to be almost a way of life."

Needles clicking, she glanced at him under her eyebrows. "A tad prejudiced, are we?"

He looked taken aback. "Me? Not at all. I just look at facts. And the fact is, in the main, gypsies avoid honest labor. They don't hold down jobs, don't pay taxes. They don't *work*."

"Wrong, they work like crazy, just not at occupations you'd call steady jobs. They won't work nine-to-five as wage slaves, and they won't work for a *gadje* boss. But they'll often have several deals going at a time. Blacktopping driveways, roofing, scrap metal collection. And whole families travel out every summer to pick crops—damn hard work. And they're always into selling used cars, just like they once sold horses. You have to understand, a gypsy sees his job as making money, plain and simple. How he gets the money is a detail. But put a gypsy down anywhere in the world, he can earn a living."

"Fleecing the *gadje*?"

She shrugged. "They're fair game."

They were on a paved road now, not far from the highway intersection. A guy zoomed past on a Honda 400, and the DA swerved like an old lady.

Alana said dryly, "Drive much?"

"I hate driving. Didn't even pass my driver's test the first time. Only exam I ever failed."

She caught his rueful smile. No macho hang-ups with this guy. He was a good listener, too. Made it easy to rattle on about this stuff from her past. "As for sex," she went on as she knitted, "gypsies are actually quite prudish. Virginity's important, and girls are chaperoned, and adultery's a serious wrongdoing for both sexes. And you'll never see a gypsy prostitute. The *gadje* get that all wrong. I've seen *gadje* men with their tongues hanging out when they watch gypsy women, because the gypsies sometimes expose their breasts kind of casually. But to gypsies breasts are just for nursing. It's the lower part of the body that's taboo. And it's a big taboo. Everything below the waist is *marimé*. Unclean. Which is why there are such elaborate precautions in washing. You know about that?"

"No."

"Oh, yeah, different bars of soap to wash the top of the body and the bottom. And when the women do laundry, they separate upper-body clothes from lower-body clothes, and also separate men's clothes from women's. Cleanliness is a big deal. Gypsy homes are kept very clean and tidy."

"Come on. They throw trash out the windows into the yard."

"Because inside is all that matters. Outside is nothing, it's kind of invisible to them. Gypsy culture's fanatical about inside purity—the body, the house, the *kumpania*. They even hate cats because cats lick themselves and take outside dirt into their mouths. It's also why they don't like indoor toilets. They'd rather use an outhouse or a hedge."

He said skeptically, "That's cleaner?"

"To them, definitely. They're revolted by the way the *gadje* defecate inside a home."

His eyebrows went up. "I guess it does have a certain logic."

She snorted a laugh. "Logic has nothing to do with it. It's the code of *marimé*."

"Which, I admit, I find it hard to get a handle on."

"It's the central thing about gypsy life. It keeps everybody in line, and also keeps the barrier clear between gypsy and *gadje*. *Marimé* means impure, polluted, and it covers a whole mixed bag. Cleanliness, food, sex, business dealings, and of course, the biggest pollution of all, mixing with the *gadje*. I think it's some centuries-old throwback to India, the idea of untouchability. But it's also very much about disciplining an individual in the group. *Marimé* also means outcast. It's how they weed out someone who won't conform."

"I notice you keep saying 'they.' Don't you consider yourself a gypsy?"

"Oh, I'll always be gypsy. But I've been on my own half my life."

"Weeded out?"

He doesn't miss much, she thought. "How about you? Is it 'they' or 'we'?"

He gave her a keen look. "My family's not much into religion—my aunt says her parents actually used to have a Christmas tree. And I wasn't even bar mitzvahed. But I take your point. I'll always be Jewish."

She couldn't resist. "That's okay, I'm not prejudiced."

His laugh was quick and good-natured. "Touché."

She smiled. She liked this guy.

Traffic was backed up on Route 95, and he slowed to a crawl behind a big white Allied moving van. Ahead, and in her side minor, Alana could see irritated drivers butting in and out between lanes. The DA, too, flipped on his signal, checking in his rearview. What for? she thought. Stay put. One lane's as good as another.

A wind-tossed half page of newspaper jerked between

them and the van. It hung for a moment in the air like a puppet, then flattened against their windshield, stuck. Alana stiffened. Felt a lurch of nausea. Saw a 1944 newspaper, *Die Berliner Morgenpost* . . . and something wrapped inside, with the sickening odor of phenol . . .

They got me spritzing kids again in F Block. Shitty work, but it gets me in Kleist's good books, and he lets me keep booty once they're dead. Yesterday I bagged a cigarette tucked in one kid's cuff and a hunk of apple another was hoarding in her shoe. Not bad. Anyway, it's easier than spritzing the women, because some of them figure it out and then I have to tie them down. Most don't, of course, too dazed, maybe from stripping in front of the male kapos outside. The kids never have a clue. Kleist leaves them to me, and I do it right in the heart, like he does, with a long needle. At first he did it into their vein, but sometimes it took them a few minutes to die. One boy shuddered for nearly an hour. The heart's much faster, about fifteen seconds.

Kleist and me, we've got a system with the women. First, the kapo tells them they're just going to be examined, so that keeps them calm. Then I bring them in, one at a time, naked, through a side door of F Block into the little room. The woman thinks it's just a part of the clinic when she sees it's all painted white, even the windows—sees the doctor's rubber apron hanging on the wall, and the little table with syringes and a bottle of yellowish pinkish stuff. She doesn't know it's phenol. I sit her on a footstool, get her to bend her right arm behind her neck and the left one behind her back. The idea is to get her chest stuck out so the heart area's clear. Then Kleist fills up the syringe and fin-

gers her rib cage—I've learned how he finds the fifth rib space—and he drives the needle in. Spritzes her. Me and a Jew prisoner pick her up as she falls, and we throw her into a pile of corpses in the next room. Weird sight—the phenol turns the bodies bright pink. I go bring in the next woman, sit her on the stool. We get through about fifty in two hours. None on Sunday, though. The doctors go to church in the village. Makes a nice day off for me.

But today it's the kids' ward. One of the doctors here, Grabner, is doing a study of their eyes, so I'm measuring the kids. Nazis are crazy for measuring everything. Grabner says his eye work's being published, whatever that means. I draw a pencil line on the wall at my shoulder height. Grabner gave me a measuring stick, said something about centimeters, but I don't know anything about numbers, and my shoulder works fine. If a kid's head doesn't reach the line on the wall, they get sent to the gas chamber, or else we spritz them. These kids watching me now, they stand quiet, no energy, legs and arms like sticks—poor dumb creatures. We can all smell the smoke from the crematoriums that burn day and night. I'm glad me and Rajko don't have kids.

Grabner in his white coat strides through the ward. "Gypsy, follow me." He's carrying something wrapped in newspaper, and he motions for me to come with him into the lab. "I've brought a specimen back for postmortem study," he says, and unwraps the newspaper bundle on the counter. Inside is a child's head, smelling of phenol. "Get out the eyes," he tells me, "and get my measuring tape." Shit. I swear they measure everything . . .

"Miss Marks? Are you all right?"

Alana's stomach was rocky; her palms damp.

"You don't look well. Is something wrong?"

She stared at her knitting needle tip. *Yeah. I know how to ram this into the fifth rib space.*

The van ahead pulled forward. The traffic was moving. As the DA shifted jerkily into gear, the newspaper on the windshield drifted up and disappeared.

Alana took a deep breath. "Guess I got a little carsick, knitting. Do me a favor? Let me drive?"

"What? I offered *you* the lift."

"You said you hate it. And I'm good. I get paid for driving. Crashes, rollovers."

He deadpanned, "That's reassuring."

"Mr. Knelman, I'm good because I'm careful. I promise I won't even break the speed limit. How about you pull into that filling station up there? Please. It'd really help me out."

They stopped and switched places. Alana merged smoothly back into the traffic, glad to be behind the wheel, relieved to be on the move. But she wiped one damp palm on her jeans. Once again, she couldn't shake the terrible fear that came with these repulsive fantasies of her mother. Why would she imagine such things unless she was like that herself, deep down? Cold-blooded and brutal. A murderer in her heart. She had a horror that one day she'd act on it. One day she'd hurt people.

"Can I ask you something?" she said, eyes ahead. "You know criminals. Do they ever change? I mean, the brutal ones. Do they ever reform, or do they just . . . get worse?"

No answer.

She turned and found him looking at her with the same slightly puzzled expression as when he'd first seen her out of costume. "Anyone can change," he said. "Can I ask you something? Why did you leave your father's *kumpania*?"

"Long story." And not one of her favorites.

"I'm not going anywhere."

There was something in his look, probing but gentle, that she found strangely settling. Reminded her of that day years before the war, a stormy day on an Austrian roadside, when her grandfather had gentled her mother's nervous pony. *No, stop making things up,* she told herself, exasperated, scared, her hands tightening on the steering wheel. She thought of the card in her jeans pocket with the neurosurgeon's phone numbers. Could he really help her? Maybe she'd check him out. If he was anything like his son, maybe it wouldn't be so bad. Her grip relaxed. "I wasn't exactly my father's dream daughter," she said. "I've always had a bit of a problem with reality."

"You seem pretty together to me."

"Yeah, well, when I was about fifteen I got a little out of hand. Heavy fights with him." She'd never forget the day she told him about her gruesome visions of Lina helping the Nazi doctors. He blew up, said she was crazy, said it had been just the opposite, that Lina had been murdered by a Nazi doctor, and he accused Alana of stirring up trouble with such malicious stories. Scared and confused, afraid she *was* crazy, she'd lashed out at him in turn. "Fact is, I got *way* out of hand. Stormed out. Slept with a *gadje* boy. Very bad. When my father heard, he was so furious he dragged me to the *kris*. In a way, he had to. As *rom baro* he's responsible for the actions of everybody in the *kumpania,* and if he hadn't made an example of me he could have faced trial himself, lost his leadership. It was actually hard to find a judge at first, because of my father's status—lots of people owed him. They finally brought in a powerful Machwaya *rom baro* from Monterey, figuring he'd be impartial. I remember he showed up driving a silver LTD and wearing a big cowboy hat, and his wife wore all the jewelry she owned. There must have been three hundred people in the rented hall. That judge sentenced me *marimé*. After, my father wouldn't speak to me, arranged to marry me into a broke Kuneshti family in San Francisco, the only ones who'd have me. He couldn't even get a hundred bucks for the bride price. Anyway, it didn't come off, because I ran away."

"He'd have sold you into marriage? At fifteen?"

"That's common. Sometimes even younger."

"It's barbaric."

"If you want to understand about gypsies, you'll have to keep an open mind. Early marriage is how they hold the culture together. My father was doing his job."

"I'm amazed you can defend him."

"I'm just saying I understand him. Look, I'm sure your father's proud of you, but say you hadn't aced law school, say you flunked and he came down hard on you. He's still your father, right? Family's family. I didn't fit in—big-time. Doesn't mean I don't miss them."

The memories were getting her down. She switched on the radio. Stevie Wonder singing "You Are the Sunshine of My Life." So sweet it hurt her teeth. She punched another button. "Midnight Train to Georgia," Gladys Knight and the Pips. Better.

She drove into the Bronx to Orchard Beach and crossed the bridge to City Island. He asked, "You have a house out here?"

"I wish. Ever been on the island?"

"No. It's nice. Looks like Nantucket." He was taking in the tree-lined street of boat chandleries and modest art galleries and antique shops that hugged the harbor around the boatyards. Sailboat masts rose from the scattered marinas like thickets of night-dark woods.

"Yeah, it's a real old seaport. Late 1600s." She turned into the Beacon Marina parking lot and pulled up at the deserted dock. "That's where I'm headed." She pointed across the water to *Seawitch* at its mooring.

"The sailboat? How do you get out to it?"

"Same way I came from it. Dinghy."

They got out of the car. From the way the pier flags were rippling, Alana figured it was blowing maybe twelve knots. Bits of paper were skittering along the dock toward the restaurant and bar. She pulled on her jean jacket. It'd be cold on the water.

"Looks like a nice boat," he said as they both went to the trunk to get her gear.

"A Pearson 35. Not mine, at least not yet. Belongs to a stockbroker friend. I live aboard."

Before she could reach her two gym bags in the trunk, he pulled them out for her. "With the broker?" he asked, holding onto the bags.

No. Crazy women don't get boyfriends. "We're just partners in the boat. We race together, and I keep her in shape. I've been buying her in installments. She'll be mine next month." She took the bags. "Thanks for the message from your father. Maybe I'll call him."

"Do. You'll like him."

"Sorry I couldn't be more help, Mr. Knelman. For your case."

"No, it was instructive. It was great. And my name's David."

Warm blood rushed to her face. It was the way he was looking at her. His interest was so direct he didn't give her anywhere to hide. Only, she wasn't sure she wanted to hide. The feeling was nice. He was nice.

The Crow's Nest bar down the pier had a new neon sign that caught her eye, a giant martini glass beside a miniature naked girl, pink-fleshed. *Pink corpses . . . from phenol.* Horror washed over her, a mental nausea, both at the image and at her own sick head. She looked back at the DA. *Go away, nice man. You don't want to get mixed up with me.*

"No phone on the boat, I guess," he said.

"Nope."

"Is there some way I could get in touch, in case?"

"In case?"

"If I have a question about gypsies." He smiled. "So you can set me straight."

Climbing aboard alone, she tied the dink's bowline to the stern cleat. *Seawitch* rocked gently from her boarding, but otherwise lay calm in the moonlight, just dancing a little in the breeze. Alana was the only live-aboard at the marina, and although the sounds of belowdecks partying came from one dockside powerboat, out here at the mooring it was quiet. The other moored boats around her lay in darkness, looking lonely, their shrouds faintly whistling in the wind. She stood on deck for a moment with the breeze in her face, looking westward at the lights on the mainland—the Bronx, and the glow of Manhattan beyond. This channel of Long Island Sound was narrow, but barrier enough between her and the world. She'd given David Knelman her message service number, knowing that if he did call, she wouldn't call back.

She'd long ago accepted being alone. That wasn't what bothered her. It was the fear. Like a cancer, it grew minutely every day. She had honed a regimented life so she could keep this thing that poisoned her mind under control, and it had worked so far. But what if her mental sickness got worse? What if it was degenerative? She was afraid it would one day control *her,* and if that happened, if she could no longer work and support herself, how would she live?

She went below, switched on the light over the galley, and closed the hatch against the wind. She loved any boat's cabin for its coziness, and *Seawitch* wrapped you in that. Her shrink had warned her that she'd made it a hiding hole, a place to shut out the world. *Well, we do what we have to, Doc.* Despite the lush teak paneling, the boat was set up for racing; Blake, the owner, wouldn't condone a rug or even a framed picture. Alana didn't mind; nest building had never been her style. This year alone she'd spent two months working in L.A., a month and a half on locations in Mexico and Canada, and had just got back from three weeks in Spain on the latest James Bond flick's second-unit shoot. She did have plans, though. Next month, once *Seawitch* was hers, she was going to sail her to Florida. She was looking forward to taking some time between jobs there throughout the winter and fitting out the boat for more comfortable living and cruising.

She put on an Otis Redding tape and ate a quick snack of cheese and a pear that wouldn't last another day. As Otis slid into "Try a Little Tenderness" she opened the engine cover and got out her toolbox. She had a few days off and had planned to use them to rebuild the carburetor and replace the fuel pump, starting tomorrow morning, but she couldn't go to bed yet, didn't even dare lie down, not with Lina and her needles lying in wait. At two A.M. she was still kneeling on the cabin sole, and her tools clinked at the engine block, an out-of-sync percussion backing up Otis, while the wind in the rigging keened a tuneless alto dirge.

CHAPTER 5

"THE FIRST STEP is boringly conventional, Miss Marks. The taking of a history. It will allow me to ascertain whether your situation qualifies you for therapeutic psychosurgery. It will also allow *you* to judge whether this pompous old man bores you too much to continue. You see? We'll both observe, learn, and reach a decision."

Alana managed a smile across Dr. Knelman's gleaming mahogany desk. "I'm all for conventional first steps, doctor. When I'm rehearsing a stunt, that's what saves my neck."

"Excellent." He unscrewed the top of a gold fountain pen, preparing to take notes.

She tugged the hem of her floral dress closer to her bare knees. She rarely wore dresses, but an appointment on Park Avenue had seemed to call for it. She'd even put on heels at first, the only pair she owned, but when she went topside on *Seawitch,* wobbling on deck, she rejected the shoes as idiotic and changed to her all-purpose sandals. She felt foolish being so nervous. This office in Dr. Knelman's private clinic could hardly be more restful: comfortable forest green armchairs, Persian carpet, ivory fabric with a linen texture on the walls. There were pretty orchids on glass shelves at a bay window alcove, and Impressionist prints, and honorary degrees in silver frames, and a pitcher of water with crystal tumblers. But she'd felt a shiver as she'd followed his receptionist here and caught a glimpse down a hallway into the clinic. Though all she'd seen was sunny lighting and creamy walls, her unease had been honed by her upbringing. Gypsies hated any kind of hospital. Hospitals meant death.

"We'll start with the basics," he said, smoothing the blank page before him, poised to write. "Your background."

She found his manner calming. Reassuring. Or maybe she was just searching for his son in him. Not that they looked much alike, except for both being tall and immaculately dressed. The father was so lean he was almost bony, and his trimmed silver hair and beard intensified the gray-green light in his eyes in a way that made her think of sun on granite. She remembered his son's dark good looks as altogether more gentle. But both men had a disarming quality—courteousness. She'd found it hard to ignore David Knelman's messages on her service, two friendly requests to get back to him, which she hadn't. The weekend had gone by. By now, he'd have given up. Better that way, she told herself. Though it didn't feel better.

"Tell me about your family," Dr. Knelman said. "Where did they come from originally? Go back as far as you know."

Alana hesitated, not sure if she wanted to go through this again, putting her trust in a doctor, getting her hopes up. But she knew she'd reached a crossroads. She wouldn't go again to a shrink, and she couldn't take therapeutic drugs and still function at her work, yet neither could she go on living as she was, a prisoner of her own sick mind. Though uneasy at the very thought of psychosurgery, she was ready to hear this doctor out. He might hold her chance for a cure.

"Austria," she answered. "The Burgenland." As she started telling him how the Nazis had persecuted the gypsies, she watched him write. Briefly, she told him that her parents had been sent to a concentration camp, that her mother had died there, and that her father had emigrated to America when she was still a baby. He asked who of her immediate family were still alive. She told him her father was, here in New York, and her stepmother, though she hadn't seen them in thirteen years. Also her seven half-brothers and half-sisters, who'd probably all got married and had a pack of kids each. "I took off when I was fifteen. Met a top film stuntman, Gus Yuill, and he trained me. No funny stuff—he didn't hit on me, just gave me my start in the business. We're still friends."

He seemed to be writing all this down, then asked about her general health, including nutrition. Did she smoke? No. Drink or take recreational drugs? No. Exercise? Yes, at a gym in the Bronx. "Admirable habits," he murmured, jotting notes. It made her impatient. She hadn't come for a pat on the back. She had the rebellious thought that a doctor taking a history wasn't so very different from a fortune-teller teasing out information to feed back to the client, build their trust, get them hooked. Her stepmother, Yanka, had been a master at it.

Finally he said, "Now, let us discuss the manifestation of this multiple personality disorder."

Alana's hope sank. "Look, Dr. Knelman, we're not going to get anywhere if Dr. Bender convinced you that's my problem. I don't think I'm somebody else. I'm crazy in a different way. It's like I *know* about her. My mother. I mean, know everything."

"Yes. That is what we must confirm."

He was looking at her with an intensity that made her uncomfortable, yet it was bracing: he hadn't dismissed what she'd said. She asked cautiously, "Confirm?"

He put down his pen and touched a button on his intercom as if to make sure that they couldn't be overheard. He glanced at the closed door as if to check that too. "Miss Marks, the reason for so many questions was to satisfy myself about your identity. And now, please forgive me, but I must be absolutely sure." He stood and removed his tweed jacket, draped it on his chair, then came around the desk to her, rolling up his left shirtsleeve. He held out his arm, showing her a tattooed number on his inner forearm: .17233. Pointing to the number while watching her face, he asked, "What camp?"

Alana swallowed. "Otzenhausen."

"How do you know?"

"Because of the dot."

"Why?"

"It was for inmates admitted after the first year, when there'd been a mass escape. The new commandant ordered a dot before the number to mark his new management. His name was Reinhardt. When my mother was brought in, she heard this from a Polish woman, a longtime survivor—a low number, no dot. The low numbers had the respect of all the other prisoners, because to survive so long meant they were either tough or lucky, and in the camp you prayed to be both."

He nodded with a thin smile, looking almost relieved. Alana's heart was pounding. He'd been in Otzenhausen! But even more wonderful, he *believed* her! He rolled down his sleeve but didn't go back to his chair, and as he went on questioning her, she sensed that he expected her to know the answers. It was bewildering. Yet it felt dangerously exciting to answer him—the first person who'd ever believed her. She wanted to tell him everything.

"When was your mother brought to Otzenhausen? What day?"

"Night." She remembered Lina's fear at the shrill locomotive whistle as the train stopped, then the boxcar doors rumbling open, the blinding lights on the ramp, the leashed dogs barking, the uniformed guards in the snow, the doctors making selections as people stepped onto the ramp: *"Rechts! Links!"* Right! Left! Sending to the right the strong ones who would be admitted into the work camp, and to the left the ones who would go straight to the gas chamber. "It was the fifth of February, 1943. She didn't know calendars, but she'd heard an old Jewish man mutter it as he wrote in his diary on the train. He went right to the gas."

"What went on in F Block?"

"Medical experiments on prisoners. Horrible things, using people like lab rats. They'd give them nothing to eat or drink except sea water and take notes on how long they survived. They injected people with typhus and smallpox and tested experimental drugs on them. Outside doctors came too, and rented research space to try things out, like new amputation techniques. The suffering was terrible."

"What part did your mother play?"

"She helped control the prisoners. When they were in agony from the experiments, screaming or raving, she tied them down. Sometimes she helped in the killing, too, using phenol injections." It made her queasy saying these things, but she had a sense that there was no going back. She felt as though Dr. Knelman had her on trial, and her life depended on convincing him with her answers.

"Did your mother herself become a subject in a research project? A benign one?"

She stared at him in wonder. How did he know to ask such questions? And why did he seem to know the answers? She found her voice. "Yes. She heard from a medical-block kapo that a subject of this new experiment would get triple rations, and if she got pregnant she'd stay out of the gas chamber, at least until she produced the baby. Nine months in the camp was an eternity. The slave laborers lasted three on average. My mother bribed the kapo to choose her."

Knelman seemed startled. "I didn't know that. Bribed him with what?"

She hesitated, then plowed on. "Oral sex, whenever he wanted."

He let it pass. "Nevertheless, she wasn't aware of the project's objectives, was she?"

"No. No one ever told her that. But whatever it was, it didn't hurt her."

"One last question. Did you know me before you came in here?"

"You?" It threw her completely. "Why—have we met before?"

"You don't remember me? From Otzenhausen?"

A shudder went through her. What did he mean, *remember*?

"Evidently not." He let out a tense, pent-up breath. "Miss Marks, I am now going to explain the objective of that experimental project. Though, in fact, you already know it."

It was the most amazing few minutes of her life. What he told her next, she drank in like someone so parched with thirst it hurt to swallow, but she craved to go on drinking. Craved to understand.

"One of the doctors in Otzenhausen was a visiting researcher from Berlin," Knelman said. "His name was Schiller, a neurologist with a background in the emerging field of genetics. His goal was to enable a woman to genetically pass on learned information to her offspring—literacy, scientific acumen if any, musical accomplishment, accumulated insight. In short, culture and wisdom. Himmler himself, the head of Hitler's Schutzstaffel, the SS, encouraged Schiller's research in the hope that it would one day enable the Aryan people to produce, literally, a master race." A shadow crept into his eyes. "Such evil arrogance."

He seemed to shake it off, and went on briskly, more like a professor, "The science of genetics was embryonic then, but rich with potential. In 1928 a biologist had proved that when a chemical substance from a heat-killed bacterium of one species, Strain 5, was injected into animals simultaneously with another strain, Strain R, the latter strain was transformed into the former, and in the 1940s a team showed that this reaction was caused by deoxyribonucleic acid, DNA. The implication that DNA contains the genetic code should have sent shock waves throughout the field of biology, but in fact it caused only a mild stir. Scientists often do not grasp revolutionary ideas. It wasn't until 1953 that Watson and Crick amazed the world with their theory of the role of DNA in heredity. Nevertheless, during the war, a new operational matrix had begun to take shape in a few select German labs when cytologists, studying the workings of cells, found ways of locating chromosomes and genes, and organizing them for analysis under a microscope, a process called karyotyping. Schiller understood this breakthrough, and saw it with the eyes of a neurologist trained in biology.

"You see, Miss Marks, besides the DNA in the nucleus of every cell, humans also carry a small amount of DNA in the mitochondria outside the nucleus. Mitochondrial DNA is inherited from our mothers alone. This is because the father's mitochondria are in the sperm tail, which is lost when the egg is fertilized. Schiller knew that the rate of synthesis of a protein was partially under genetic control and partially determined by the external chemical environment. Working with matrilinear mitochondrial DNA, he engineered a gene that would link the nervous systems of mother and fetus, allowing the fetus to draw in the woman's knowledge, and he devised a chemical graft to implant it in the brain. In effect, the offspring would evolve a specialized neural circuitry."

He took a steadying breath. "You have such a circuitry, Miss Marks. The gene was implanted in your mother. That is why you know everything she knew—although, without context, the information has naturally alarmed and confused you. You could not know that the alien images you saw were, in effect, memories."

Memories. A sob tore through her. Tears blurred her vision. It was like a floodgate opening. She wept—couldn't stop. It humiliated her, the streaming tears, the spasms of sobs. She stood, wanting to get away, not let him see her like this. She reached the window alcove, but her legs felt like straw and she grabbed at a wing-back chair. She barely made it around before her knees buckled and she thudded down in the seat. Her vision dimmed. She felt she was going to pass out.

"Lower your head," Knelman said. "Lower still, that's right, between your knees. Take deep breaths. You have had a terrible shock, Miss Marks. Please, you must go slowly."

She heard him pouring her a glass of water. "I deal every day with the human brain," he went on gently. "It is a resilient and versatile organ, but it can bear only so much stress. I am so sorry for inflicting this news on you."

She raised her head. She'd got control. No more tears.

"I'm okay. Thanks." He handed her the water. She drank it down, but her hand was shaking.

"That's better," he said, taking back the empty glass. He pulled the other wing-back easy chair close and sat opposite her, a look of compassion on his face, and gave her a handkerchief. They were sitting almost knee to knee. Alana was aware of the alcove's coziness, the delicate mauve orchids, the warm sunshine. But her heart was thudding, and her mind was tripping over itself to catch up. "The visions," she said, using the handkerchief to wipe her wet cheeks. "These things I've always thought I'd made up—thought were psychotic fantasies. They're true?"

"They are real, authentic memories."

"So I'm not . . . mentally ill."

"Quite the contrary. You are enhanced."

She remembered a line she'd once heard on TV: "The burden of truth." That's what this felt like, a heavy weight of reality holding her down in the chair. She felt cold; she was trembling. But not from fear. Inside her, beneath the weight, was a bubble of relief so intense it felt like joy. It rose in her, lifting the weight, and as she looked at the doctor she saw him in a whole new light, as a liberator. He had set her free.

But something snagged in her mind. Like a bent green twig, it sprang back—that original bewilderment she'd felt. "Doctor Knelman, how do you know all of this?"

"I was a prisoner physician in Otzenhausen. I was forced to assist with Schiller's operation. Assist, or go to the gas."

"My God, how terrible for you."

He looked away. "Yes."

"*That's* why you asked if I remembered you." She was piecing together memories of the morning her mother had reported to the hospital block to become a subject. Lina hadn't been told what the operation was about, and was startled when the kapo instructed her that they would want her to get pregnant after it. Since coming to Otzenhausen she'd been keeping Rajko off her, because all women who got pregnant were immediately sent to the gas chamber. But this experiment turned that rule on its head: pregnancy would keep her alive, and also keep her out of the slave labor gang. No matter what the operation entailed, a nine-month guarantee of life with triple rations was worth the risk.

For Alana, it felt strange to *want* to coax these images back, as memories. But she did—wanted to recall everything. Except, the morning of the operation wasn't clear. "I remember the disinfectant smell of the anteroom where the orderly took her clothes and gave her a white cotton smock and a yellow pill, and I remember the drowsiness after she lay down. But after that it's hazy." She vaguely recalled a small operating room. "I think there were two men in surgical gowns and masks. It must have been you, Dr. Knelman, and this Schiller. But the voices sounded garbled. She was so dozy by then."

"Yes, sedated. It's not surprising that you do not remember." He went on quickly, "And I must caution you, Miss Marks, that should you have flickering recollections of such details in the future, do not belabor them. Your memory, like everyone's, will be unreliable at times. None of us has perfect recall. We embellish memories, revise them. Records show that even a simple traffic accident is recounted in as many differing ways as there are witnesses. Your memory, of course, is very special, yet I suggest that it may be just as fallible as anyone's. Do not trust it totally."

It sounded like good advice. But she was barely taking it in, still reeling from the whole incredible revelation.

"Naturally," he went on, "what happened to your mother *after* your birth is unknown to you."

"Not quite. My father told me."

"Oh?" He gave her a keen look. "What, exactly?"

"That the day the camp was liberated, a Nazi doctor murdered her. I don't recall the details—my father and I were screaming at each other at the time he told me." It was painful to recall that fight. She'd claimed to know how brutal Lina had been, and her father had called her a crazy troublemaker, and Alana had feared she must be. It gave her a cold shock now to realize she'd been right all along about Lina.

Still struggling to take it in, she asked, "What happened to Schiller?"

"Many SS went into hiding. Brazil, South Africa, Australia." He shrugged. "Who knows?"

Alana felt a surge of hatred for the callous scientist who'd gotten away. But she let it go. After almost thirty years he was probably dead. And she had a life to get on with—somehow. She had the light-headed sensation that her world had changed forever.

"Miss Marks," Knelman said, again fixing her with that intense look, "it is time for you to put all of this behind you. I can see that you are an impressively levelheaded young woman, and I admire your obvious strength of character in coping with this condition imposed upon you. It must have been most trying, being ignorant of its root cause. But now you must forget the past, and face the grave obligation of the future."

"I can hardly think straight about the next few minutes. But I do know I'll always be grateful to you, Dr. Knelman. It's like you've opened a prison door."

"Thank you. However, I don't think you quite understand. I am not referring to just *your* future, but future generations." He leaned forward and gripped her hand. She flinched, his hand felt so icy. "You carry the gene. You alone can propagate it. Unwittingly, you are the prototype of the Nazi's grand plan—you embody the curse of the master race. If ever you have children, they would be the beginning of that race, small in number, but carrying the latent potential of a virus to wreak devastating change. Because those children, too, would pass along the gene—and on and on. Consider the exponential result over time. Proliferating through the population, the gene could not help but create a destabilizing imbalance. We would very quickly become a society of two classes, enhanced and unenhanced. Think of it—individuals with inbred knowledge, born with superior skills and understanding, for endless generations to come. Their advanced abilities would almost certainly make them powerful. Constantly growing in numbers, these people would split society, and eventually change our world. A master race indeed. Do you see, Miss Marks? You constitute, in effect, a new branch in evolution. You are the first of a new subpecies. It is as though you are a potential new Eve, but a dangerous one, however unintentionally, because of this mutation you carry. Yes, a mutation. So, please, listen carefully. There is only one way to prevent such a destabilizing threat to the future. The knowledge gene must never be propagated. I urge you most strongly to consider sterilization."

She was finding it hard to breathe.

He went on grimly, "And there is a factor even more serious. It concerns male offspring. You see, when the genetic—"

"Stop." She held up one rigid palm. "Please . . . stop."

"Forgive me, but this is too grave a situation to leave to—"

"No. You don't understand. It's too late. Sterilization."

"Too late?"

She forced out the words. "I have a son."

They stared at each other. For Alana, the world seemed to have shrunk to this alcove, and everything in it was as stark as under a spotlight. A fly buzzed over an orchid. Sunlight glanced off Dr. Knelman's gold cuff link. She saw a vein at his temple pulse thickly. When she spoke again, her own voice sounded unfamiliar, low and shaky, like a confession.

"When my father threw me out, I was pregnant. I had the baby, but I was fifteen. Penniless. And I thought I might be insane. I wasn't sure I was going to make it myself, let alone with a baby. I gave him up for adoption."

A knock at the door made her jump. The receptionist poked her head in. "Sorry to disturb you, doctor, but your intercom is off, and there's an urgent call from Parkview. It's Jacob Wentzler's doctor."

Knelman shot to his feet. "Not now." The receptionist quickly closed the door.

Wentzler . . . the name plucked a faint string of memory in Alana's mind. She had no idea why.

Knelman's gaze slid away to the window. His face had gone pale. "So . . . another boy."

"What?"

His attention snapped back to her. "How old would he be?"

"Thirteen."

"Do you know where he is?"

She shook her head. Knelman walked away as though lost in thought. Alana felt swamped by guilt. She had put the baby out of her mind almost the day she'd given him up. Unable to cope, she'd been sure of one thing only: that no matter where he grew up, he'd be better off than with her. Now she began to see what she'd done: she had abandoned her son to the mental torture of these visions. A shocking thought struck her. "He knows everything I know too, doesn't he?"

"Pardon?" Knelman turned to her, looking distracted.

"Because of the gene. He knows everything about *my* life."

"Yes. That is, everything you knew up till the moment you gave birth to him."

"Plus my mother's knowledge, right? Hers *and* mine."

He nodded.

She thought, How could the kid possibly manage? "I've got to find him," she said. She was the only one who understood what he was going through. The only one who could help him. "I've got to explain everything to him, like you've done for me. It changes everything." She got up and came to him. "Don't you see, Doctor Knelman? He's got to be told so that his mind makes *sense* to him. So that he can live with himself."

"Indeed. You must find the boy, Miss Marks. To prepare him to live with this burden of knowledge."

"You said there was something more serious. What was that?"

"Pardon?"

"You said, a factor even more serious. Something about males?"

"Nothing. The priority now is for you to find your son. Is there anything I can do to help?"

She thanked him, but said the only thing she could think to do was to apply to the adoption agency for information, which she'd have to do herself. "And I'll see where that takes me. I'll go right now."

"It's almost five o'clock."

She looked at her watch. "Hell."

"Perhaps it is for the best. You need an evening to recover. You're going to need all your strength, Miss Marks. Nevertheless, your impulse to find your son without delay is the right one. And, please, the moment you locate him, contact me. He'll need professional counseling, and I think you will agree that that role must fall to me alone. You will bring the boy to me?"

"Yes. If I can find him."

"He must be made to understand the danger, and urged, as I again urge you, to consider sterilization. You do understand that, don't you? Sterilization is the only responsible option."

She felt out of her depth. He was the expert. "I guess so."

"There is one more thing."

A frazzled laugh escaped her. "Don't know if I can take another hit."

"Forgive me, but I must make one request. What I have divulged must remain confidential, for both our sakes. Should word of the knowledge gene get out, you could become the target of unscrupulous individuals. Sadly, people will try to make money from anything. As for me, my family and my patients know nothing about my . . . enforced collaboration in this Nazi experiment. I daresay it is craven of me to have hidden such a thing from them, but it would mean a great deal to me to preserve their good opinion. It is a matter of . . . reputation."

"Of course, I won't breathe a word."

"Thank you."

"No, thank *you,* Dr. Knelman. Crazy though this is, I feel as though you've just saved my life."

Knelman got out of the taxi in front of the cathedral of St. John the Divine, and as the cab drove on up Amsterdam

Avenue, he stood motionless before the magnificent Gothic building, trying to resist its sacred pull. He felt such a desperate need to unburden himself. *Forgive me. Father, for I have sinned.* Twenty-eight years without confession. Living as a Jew, he had no business going into a church. Once or twice a year, and only when he was out of town, he had weakened and slipped in for mass, always choosing a church large enough that he might be taken for a tourist. The liturgy transported him back to childhood Sundays with his parents in Berlin's Grunewald district by the lake; in a Catholic church he was home. But he'd always stopped short of entering the confessional; too great a risk. What if some acquaintance should see him?

Today, he craved the balm of confession. He was in torment. Alana Marks's news had changed everything. Another male! When he'd been so sure that Jacob was the last! And so desperately hopeful that he would have to do no more harm.

He turned away from the cathedral and crossed the street to the Parkview Psychiatric Institute.

The nurse, leading him through the men's ward noisy with distressed patients and overworked staff, gave him an admiring glance. "So good of you to stop by, Doctor, what with your schedule." She opened the door of Jacob's room, a private room that Knelman himself was paying for, anonymously. *So many sins to atone for.*

Jacob, in pajamas, sat in a wheelchair in front of a television tuned to a soap opera. His mouth hung open, slack, a froth of saliva in one corner. He didn't look up as they entered; nothing registered in his vacant eyes. Knelman regarded the young man he had destroyed, and remorse overwhelmed him. Going to his side, he took a handkerchief from his jacket pocket and gently wiped away Jacob's spittle.

"You're one in a million Dr. Knelman," the nurse said.

He pulled himself together. "No need for you to stay for this examination, Mrs. Enwright. I know your own schedule has demands enough."

On her way out she added, "Oh, try not to move his chair. If he can't see the TV, he cries."

When the door closed behind her, Knelman could no longer hold himself back. His guilt was fed by such a terrible new fear. He went down on his knees beside the wheelchair. Jacob continued to stare blankly at the screen, and Knelman had no trouble imagining that the expressionless face belonged to a young priest in the confessional, staring off in detachment as he prepared to hear his parishioner's transgressions.

"Forgive me, Father, for I have sinned," he whispered. "It's been twenty-eight years since my last confession."

He unfastened the shirt button just above his waist. Reaching in to a hidden money belt, he withdrew the rosary he kept there. Whenever he could steal a few private moments to pray at home or work, the smooth beads of onyx slipping through his fingers brought a touch of comfort. "My sin was horrible," he whispered. "I experimented on human beings. I've tried so hard to atone. I prayed it would soon be over. But this gypsy girl . . ."

He glanced at the closed door, knowing he had only moments to unburden himself. It all came out in a hoarse rush. "Since the last carrier was female, I hoped I'd only have to explain the gene to her, drive home the seriousness of her situation, and instruct her to agree to sterilization. But she's *not* the last. She has a son. Males are the terrible danger. I saw the evidence under my microscope that morning the camp was freed. An unexpected result. The male Y chromosome mutates the genetic material. It damages the brain's limbic pathways that regulate the sense of right and wrong. The gene passes on knowledge, but in boys it *switches off conscience.* Father, I've never confessed this to anyone. I planted a monstrous seed—generations of men who will feel superior and have no compunction against doing harm. In the wrong hands they could be molded into a race of killers. Hands like the Nazis."

He took a steadying breath. "I alone can stop it. I must find this woman's son. I didn't tell her about the chromosomal mutation, because it might have scared her away, and she alone can lead me to the boy. He's just thirteen, but undoubtedly precocious, so he could soon become sexually active, capable of disseminating the gene. An evolutionary time-bomb is ticking. I've got to get to him."

A blade of dread entered him. "But, Father . . . I'm afraid. I was a fool to risk meeting her face to face. She says she has a vague recollection of two men operating on her mother. What if, one day, she remembers me—as Viktor Schiller? She could expose me. Ruin me."

The onyx beads were slippery in his hand, slick with perspiration. "Another danger. She said her father is living right here. I shot his wife in Otzenhausen, and he saw me do it. After all these years, can he identify me?" In a flash of memory he saw the young gypsy woman in the cot, bleeding from the bullet he'd put into her heart. Saw her baby look at him, freezing his hand from firing next at her small body.

"Father, Father," he moaned, "so many sins. What am I to do?"

A noise beyond the door startled him—and snapped him to his senses. He quickly got to his feet and stuffed away his rosary. Buttoning his shirt, regaining control of himself, he looked again into the vacant face, achingly aware that it was young Jacob Wentzler, a pitiful shell. Not a priest. It didn't matter. He had the haunting belief that no priest on earth had the power to release him from his living purgatory.

Only God can do that. And not until my task is done.

CHAPTER 6

ALANA SKIPPERED *SEAWITCH*'S six-man crew for the regular club race that evening, but her mind was on everything but sailing. Bearing down with the fleet on an inflated orange course marker, her bow touched the marker and so she had to sail a three-sixty penalty turn, as the rules stipulated, while the rest of the fleet raced on. Her crew groaned at the killer delay, and Blake Luscombe, the boat's ultracompetitive owner, shot her glowering looks as he trimmed the main. They limped over the finish behind boats they usually left in their wake.

Alana flexed her stiff hand on the tiller, thinking how weird it was that she used to race to keep her problems at bay; now she couldn't focus on anything *but* her problems. Her thoughts kept dragging back to her son. Could she find him? How had he been raised? How was he coping? He'd have to be a thirteen-year-old unlike any other, but had his special gift made him a prodigy, or had the visions cowed him? She felt terrible at having been so ignorant when she'd had him; so little knowledge to pass along, nothing but the gypsy dodges she'd been brought up with. That snuffed out the happy prodigy fantasy. More likely he was suffering, a victim of the inexplicable, bizarre "visions." It made her feel so keen to find him. She planned to be on the adoption agency's doorstep the moment they opened tomorrow.

"Sorry about tonight, guys," she said to the crew as she turned on the engine and they headed in. "Got a lot on my mind."

Blake nodded glumly as he went to the mast to drop the main.

"Hey, it's just a sport," said Andy, preparing the stern dock line beside her. An avuncular advertising executive from Westchester, he had a simple love of campaigning the boat, win or lose.

"We'll whup 'em next week," Pam offered from the foredeck, raising her voice above the engine noise. The only other woman on the crew, she was almost as competitive as Blake. "Hey," she added, eyeing the headsail, "there's a rip starting in the jib. Between the lower hanks."

Blake turned and told Alana, "Better get it in to the loft tonight for repairs. I want to bring a client sailing tomorrow."

"Will do." As she steered into the harbor, she spotted a man standing on the dock, looking out their way. Dark business suit, while everyone around him was in shorts and T-shirts. Alana felt a dart of pleasure. No one could be as consistently overdressed for his surroundings as David Knelman. But the pleasure was tinged with unease. Her world had shifted this afternoon with Dr. Knelman. Night had become day, and she hadn't got her bearings yet in this new terrain.

At the dock her crew traipsed off to the clubhouse for pizza and beer and the regular postmortem with the other racers, but Alana stayed on board, coiling lines in the cockpit, planning to take the headsail in right away. David Knelman walked over, coming as close as he could without stepping aboard.

"Hello," he said.

She glanced up, thinking how grungy she must look in her ratty blue shorts and gray sweat shirt, with salt spray on her sunglasses and a scraped knee. "What brings you out here?"

"Ever think of switching to a better answering service? They obviously didn't relay my messages to you." His tone was tongue-in-cheek. Diplomatic. He had a knack for this; Alana didn't. His tact only made her feel how rude she'd been in not returning his calls.

"Been pretty busy." She hung the mainsheet on the boom and secured it.

"You left something in the car the other night." Reaching into his jacket he brought out a flattened ball of blue yarn the size of his fist.

Alana was taken aback. The yarn cost about fifty cents. "If you're always this conscientious, I feel sorry for the bad guys you go after."

He deadpanned, "Guess you could say I don't like loose ends."

She smiled. Good one.

He tossed her the yarn, then crouched so that his eye level was nearer hers down in the cockpit. "Have dinner with me?"

It surprised her. Excited her. But it confused her too. She didn't know how to act. For years, she'd never let a man get close. "I've got chores."

"Anything I can help with?"

"Not here. Have to take the jib in for repairs."

"I'll come along."

The sail loft was at the back of the Nugents' musty old chandlery overlooking the harbor. Alana waved hi to the two middle-aged brothers she never could tell apart, fifth-generation proprietors, then led David, who'd insisted on carrying the sail bag, through the cramped aisles that smelled of hemp rope, oil, paint, and the sea. Opening the door to the loft where a huge Dacron mainsail was spread out on the floor, she told him, "Careful, don't step on it." As they skirted the expanse of white sailcloth, she called to the angular woman at the sewing machine, an Olive Oyl lookalike, the sister of the men out front, "Hey, Phyllis, how's it going?"

"Good. You beat the pants off 'em?"

"Not tonight."

"Too bad, dear." Phyllis had barely glanced up as she sat working, gnomelike, at the whirring machine. Only her head and shoulders were visible; she and the machine cabinet were sunk in a well in the floor, allowing the fabric to pass smoothly along under the needle.

Alana saw that David was intrigued by the arrangement. "Makes it easier to work with the miles of material," she explained.

"I can see that. Smart." He set down the sail bag, looking around, taking in the loft's mammoth bolts of snowy fabric on huge spools. Seeing the place through his eyes, Alana thought it must look like the haberdashery of some giant angel. He'd asked questions about sailing on the way, too, and she remembered how she'd liked that right away about him, the way he listened, was interested.

She left the torn jib, asking Phyllis if she could possibly get to repairing it first thing in the morning because Blake wanted it for the afternoon.

"Yeah, him and every other fair-weather sailor. Damn

season's too short." She winked at Alana. "For you, dear, no sweat."

"Thanks, Phyl."

"Now what?" David asked as they stepped out into the golden evening sunlight. "Swab some decks?"

She hesitated, then took the plunge. "Thought you said something about dinner."

He looked startled, then grinned. "Absolutely."

She showered at the marina facilities and put on a swirly mauve peasant skirt and a sleeveless white top. Good choice, judging by David's smile when he saw her.

They ate lobster at the Crab Shack on City Island Avenue, sitting at a plastic-covered picnic table on the patio, and watched the sun go down behind Manhattan. Sailboats bobbed at moorings in the wake of a returning fishing skiff. Seagulls swooped with lazy squawks above an old man fishing from the pier beside Buddy's Marine Supplies, and a young couple eating ice cream cones strolled the little promenade toward the bridge. David had taken off his jacket and rolled up his sleeves to eat the messy lobster, and once again, as on the drive they'd shared the other night, Alana found it easy to chat with him. But this time it was even better, because she felt a glow of liberation, felt blessed by this new understanding that she wasn't destined to be like her mother, that she hadn't made up Lina's savagery out of a dark impulse in her own soul. She hadn't made up anything; she truly had Lina's knowledge. She wasn't insane. Watching David eat, it was easy to imagine that she was just any girl enjoying the company of a nice guy on a quiet summer evening. The last thing she wanted to do was burst this happy bubble, this sense of being normal. But that was wrong. She wasn't just any girl—she was very, very different. And she didn't want to pretend otherwise. Not to David.

"I saw your father today. For that consultation."

"Oh? Great." Swallowing a chunk of lobster claw, he wiped melted butter off his chin with the back of his hand, then looked at her, obviously waiting for her to go on.

"He gave me a kind of surprising diagnosis."

"Surprising good, I hope."

She didn't know where to begin. She looked out at the water. In the growing dusk, lights winked off buoys and beacons, and she could just make out Stepping Stone Lighthouse to the south. There was a glow from the traffic on the Throgs Neck Bridge far off on Long Island. A steady breeze funneled up the Sound. "I have a friend named Curt, a cameraman, real happy-go-lucky guy—until last year. He started getting moody, morose. Couldn't concentrate. Said he thought he was going nuts. I was worried about him." She stirred her last inch of soda water with her straw. "He finally went to see a doctor, and a few days later I got a call from him. 'Remember that shoot I did in Peru?' he said. 'Turns out I'm laced with intestinal parasites. That's been the problem. Doctor's put me on a drug that'll knock 'em out in no time. Isn't it great? I'm not crazy, I'm sick!' "

David chuckled. "The bad news is the good news."

She nodded. "Seems my mental problem is kind of like that. I've found out that it's . . . controllable. So I guess I feel the same relief my friend did. Thank God I'm sick."

He leaned his elbows on the table as if to get nearer, and watched her, waiting. She was grateful he had the good sense, or good manners, not to ask: What exactly *is* your problem? They were both feeling their way here. She had the impression he was ready for whatever she felt like giving him—she just wasn't sure how much that should be. The whole truth was so bizarre, she couldn't even imagine how he'd take it. Anyway, she didn't have the *right* to tell: she'd promised Dr. Knelman that she wouldn't breathe a word. He'd seemed so anxious about anyone learning of his collaboration with the Nazis. She had a sense of how close this father and son were, and she would hate to undermine David's regard for his father in any way. No, she wouldn't betray Dr. Knelman's secret.

He said, "You free tomorrow night? I've got tickets to the ball game. Yankees playing the Red Sox."

She hesitated. "You mean, a date?"

"Well . . . yes. Isn't that what this is?"

"Is it?" She hadn't let a man get close for so long because she'd always dreaded that moment of confession: *Oh, by the way, honey. I'm psychotic.* But what she'd learned about herself today swept away her fear. The freedom was thrilling—better than a perfect high fall, better than screaming along at twelve knots, better than the sky-dive gag she'd done for a Disney film, coming down in a field of pink clover. And now, like a gift, this terrific man wanted her. The way he looked at her sent a sweet shiver through her.

But she couldn't ignore the problem. "David, there's something you should know about me. All my life I've thought I was a little insane. I've coped thanks to my work. *Real* stuff. Fires, crashing cars, explosions, falls. I've gotten through those things the same way I've gotten through life—careful prep, one step at a time. Then I met your father, and he explained that I'm *not* crazy. That my . . . condition can be managed. It feels terrific to know that, and I'm ready as hell to lighten up, let life take me where it leads. But, well, all of this is new to me. I mean . . . dating. I honestly don't know how to play the game. I don't even know what the game is."

He hadn't taken his eyes off her. "How about we start by letting the Yankees play the game? We'll just watch."

She laughed. Oh, she liked this man.

Then a shudder brought her up cold, remembering the boy she'd abandoned. Dr. Knelman's words had liberated her, but her son was still in the dungeon. And no one could free him but her.

She hugged herself, suddenly chilly. "This condition of mine. The thing is, it's hereditary. My mother to me, and me to . . . well, and so on."

"Ah. Is that a worry?"

She met his gaze. "David, I have a son."

He didn't move.

"I was fifteen. No legal abortion back in 1960. I gave him up for adoption. No idea where he is."

If it threw him, she didn't see it. "And now you need to contact him," he said. "About this condition. Is that it?"

"Yes. But first I've got to find him."

He sat back. "Did the adoption take place here in New York City?"

She nodded. "St. Luke's Hospital."

"What agency?"

"New Life Advocates."

"Adoption records are sealed by the court. You can make an application to have the file opened if good cause can be shown, and I'd think the need to share medical information would be deemed good cause." He reached across the table and took her hand. "Don't worry, Alana. We'll find him."

It surprised her. And pleased her more than she could say.

Beating the shit out of three guys he didn't even know wasn't his idea of fun. Risky, if they turned out to be fighters. Stupid, too, because it could bring the cops. Nick Morgan, at thirteen, didn't take any risk he couldn't see a percentage in.

He and the nine other guys in the gang turned the trash-strewn corner, following the three, who were about a half block ahead. They looked about sixteen, very uncool, carrying book bags, minding their own business. And they were black. Which was the whole point. Anybody's guess what they were doing in Bensonhurst at ten-thirty on a Tuesday night—maybe just dumb-ass lost—but Nardi and his gang were out to make sure they didn't make the same mistake again. Yup, Nick thought, Nardi and the guys had a big job to do, keeping their world safe for Italians. What horseshit. It wasn't *his* world, this crummy stretch of Bensonhurst beneath the elevated subway. He'd just been slumming here for the last few weeks because he needed cover, and their hangout made a good hiding hole. He was on the run from the Nassau County cops.

The street was quiet. Tacky little stores, closed and barred. A few parked cars, mostly heaps. One, a fin-tailed green Buick, was picked clean of all four tires. They passed a wino hunkered on a basement stoop and a couple of shuffling old bags in black, nattering in Italian. Nick was sticking to the back of the pack, keeping his eyes peeled, ready to take off if he saw a cop.

"Come on, man, let's move up," Tank whispered to him, eager to get to the front and bust heads. Tank had four years, two feet, and about a hundred pounds on Nick. He had fat lips and little ears, and blue eyes as blank as a baby's. His legs were like tree trunks, his fists like rocks. One of the first things Nick had done when he'd joined the gang was to get Tank on his side; good protection. Now, the two of them smoked up most nights. Tank was dumb as a toad, but he scored good weed.

"Nah, back here's good," Nick said.

"You all set?"

Nick nodded, indicating the thick borrowed hockey sock he carried, lumpy with rocks in the foot. The hit on these blacks was his initiation. Nardi's idea. More horseshit. Nick's plan was to just get through it with as little damage to himself as possible.

Tank grinned, hugging the steel pipe under his camouflage jacket. "Let's split watermelons."

"Shut up, lardass," Nardi said from the front of the pack, glaring back at Tank as they all kept walking. Nick didn't know what Nardi's first name was; he didn't seem to have one. Early twenties, he looked like no Italian Nick had ever seen. Rust-colored crew cut, pissed-off green eyes in a long bony face, and beneath a mass of freckles his skin was as milky as a girl's. Nardi was a mongrel, all right. Probably why he was so hot about staking territory, Nick figured. Also probably why he got such a hard-on over the Nazi stuff he collected—SS pistols and posters and swastika flags, shit like that. Nick knew Nardi made good bucks trading the stuff with underground buyers. It's what turned him on. That, plus he'd pulled together this bunch of mongrels like himself and called the gang White Pride. Tonight as always, Nardi had on his brown leather bomber jacket, German Luftwaffe issue. Loved it so much he probably fucked it at night. On the back of his neck, just above the fleece collar, was a swastika tattoo the size of a thumbnail.

Swastikas gave Nick the creeps. Just like they had to Lina in the camp, he thought. Lina . . . the tough gypsy broad had been in his mind for as long as he could remember. Her and another gypsy, a teenager named Alana. Nick knew he was wacko. He'd known it all his life.

Still, it came in handy. Lina always reminded him of the golden rule: Do what you have to do to survive.

"Why the fuck would I want a runt like you around?"

Nardi had sneered the day Nick had showed up at the Tre Stelle bar. Nick had been watching the back of the place from the parking lot next door. Drinking a Dr Pepper, he'd seen guys coming and going through the back door. Dropout types. He figured they had to live there. "I'm good at stuff big guys get caught at," he'd answered. "I'm kind of invisible to people. You could use a runt like me."

He'd got his chance to get in good with Nardi the very next night, with the Twinkies theft. Guys had been flaked out on the bar couches and on the floor, pissed on beer. Nardi was out. Nick knew by then that Nardi's uncle Sal owned the Tre Stelle, but Uncle Sal was in the joint for armed robbery, so Nardi was running the place. Running it into the ground, it seemed to Nick. It was a crummy little hangout wedged between Petroccelli's Grocery and the Uneeda Check Cashing shop. It had crappy fake-wood paneling, fluorescent strip lights, sticky linoleum a puke-green color, and nobody swept up the butts and mouse turds in the corners behind the bar. The bar itself was so small, Nick figured his dad's desk was bigger. But enough die-hard locals came in for the beer and pinball, so Nardi scraped by. Lying on a sleeping bag on the floor around two a.m., Nick heard him come in the back, in the dark. Heard him go down the hall to the Office, his private room. Then a bellow: "Who the fuck took my Twinkies?"

The light over the bar snapped on, and groggy guys staggered to their feet, blinking like idiots, but there wasn't a peep from anybody. Tank looked scared, and Nick knew why. He'd seen Tank wolfing the cupcakes that afternoon. When Nardi came out and demanded to know who'd eaten his Twinkies, everybody looked at the floor. Nardi said he wasn't going to punish the culprit, he just wanted to know who did it, because White Pride brothers had to respect each other, including their private property. Property was a sacred thing in America, he said, and the niggers and slant-eyes flooding in didn't respect that, they didn't respect shit and they were wrecking the country, and he only wanted to get this important point across to whoever had filched his property.

Silence.

Nick cleared his throat. "Uh . . . Nardi? I have a confession."

He saw the jaws drop on a couple of the real losers. Boner was one. They called him that because he was always beating off.

Nardi's green eyes bored into Nick's. "You took my Twinkies?"

"No way. But I saw who did. Should've told you before." His eyes flicked to Tank, whose face had gone pale. "It was Boner."

That's when Nick discovered how dangerous this mongrel leader could be. Nardi didn't listen as Boner squealed his innocence. Didn't lay a finger on him either. He ordered the others to do it. They punched Boner till he dropped, whacked him with pipes, kicked him in the head. Nardi watched from a bar stool, obviously enjoying it, and Nick hung back, watching Nardi. Tank threw himself into it, a dull gleam in his eyes, and between kicks to the bleeding kid he glanced at Nick like a dog at its master. Nick helped haul what was left of Boner down the alley behind Tony's Pizza, where they tipped him into a Dumpster, then came back to the Tre Stelle to sleep. Nick was shaking a bit, but he didn't let anyone see that.

It had been a good call. He'd got Nardi's trust and Tank's loyalty—two birds with one stone. Just like Lina had done by turning in the Jew at the fence. Got Kleist's trust, which had got her the job at the hospital block—no more slow death on the work gang.

The next day Nick had followed up.

"That's a cool collection," he said as he came into Nardi's office carrying the dog's water bowl. He indicated the Nazi memorabilia, shelves of the stuff in a corner book-case festooned with a big red-and-black swastika flag. Looked like a shrine. The rest of the room was a shithole—a mattress on the floor, a desk covered with pizza boxes and gun magazines, and a pool table where Nardi was racking balls. Nick put down the water bowl for the Alsatian. Her name was Heidi. She growled as he moved over to the book-case.

"Nice pistol," he said, nodding at the gun with the long, skinny barrel and swept-back grip. "1940 Krieghoff Luger."

Nardi glanced at him. "You know guns?"

"I know Nazi stuff. That cap there is Waffen SS. And that," he said pointing to a belt buckle stamped with a skull and crossbones, "is Totenkopfverbände—Death's Head Units. They got the name from their insignia. They were the guards at the camps." He picked up the Luger. "Magazine holds eight rounds. When a round's chambered, this little in-dicator here sticks up. See, it says 'Geladen'? Means loaded. That's only on German military pistols. And when the safety's on, it says 'Gesichert.' Means safe."

"No shit?" Nardi looked impressed. "You read up on this or something?"

Something, Nick thought. Maybe he'd sucked in details from movies; maybe he'd made it up. He didn't have a clue why it was in his head. Whatever, he went on to tell Nardi about the Totenkopfverbände soldiers—their barracks, their drills, their parties, their whores. He felt he knew it all. Be-cause of Lina.

He was wacko, all right; he knew that. He'd made up whole lives for his fantasy characters—childhoods and adventures and tragedy and all. Lina, traveling through Austria with her clan in horse-drawn wagons until they were rounded up and shipped to the camp. Alana, growing up here in New York, in Sunnyside, until her old man threw her out. Nick had even made them mother and daughter, Lina married to a crafty guy named Rajko; Alana as Rajko's daughter. It was totally nuts; he'd never even *met* a gypsy. He'd grown up on a Glen Cove estate, and his adoptive parents were pure Long Island white bread. Yet his visions of these two gypsies' lives were as vivid as memories.

And two *women*—how sick was that? He knew how Lina had felt having sex with Rajko. Knew how nervous Alana had been getting laid at fifteen, and how scared shitless when she'd found she was pregnant. It used to freak him out, figuring he was a pervert. He'd never fit in with the blazer-and-tie boys at St. Andrews Academy. Never felt close to his parents, either. He knew he scared them. God, all those shrinks' offices, with Mom and Dad sitting tight-lipped and wet-eyed, listening to the quack drone on. More horseshit. Nick knew before he was ten that he was on his own. By then he'd figured out how to turn around his confusion and fear and make it work for him. Like Lina did with the Nazis. At eight he was stealing cash at school from kids' clothes in the locker room. At nine he was picking pockets at Jones Beach. At ten he'd robbed a house in Brooklyn Heights, picked up just cash and jewelry and beat it fast, then hocked the jewelry. He did it because he was good at it. As good as a gypsy. It was the one thing that made him feel all right about himself. And his parents never had a clue.

Until three weeks ago. Mom found the stack of stolen record albums in his room, then the watches and some jewelry. What a scene. Mom crying, Dad saying they had no choice, they were at their wits' end, so they were sending him to a military school in New Hampshire. Nick knew he couldn't stand that—rules and curfews, like a prison. So he ran away. Bensonhurst seemed like a good place to go to ground. For weeks he'd been getting by picking pockets in New Utrecht, living in the basement of an abandoned apartment building where he'd kicked in the boarded-up window. The concrete boiler room stank of mildew, and at night, with no lights, it got very dark. He ate Kentucky Fried Chicken and pissed in the bushes out back. He figured his folks had to have called the cops, but nobody came around. It was lonely, though. He hadn't expected that—feeling lonely. Besides, whenever he went out it seemed liked there were police cruisers at every corner. Then he'd spotted the Tre Stelle, and the guys coming and going at the rear. He went over, and when he saw the black swastika spray-painted on the back door, he'd felt a shudder of fear—but also knew in his gut that he could make it work for him.

"Stick close to me, man," Tank told him now as they stalked the black kids down the street. "You let me take care of business."

"Tank, shut your mouth, you dumb fuck," Nardi ordered. "Nick, get up here. Come on, runt, these jungle bunnies are yours."

"Right," Nick said. But his hands were sweating as he shouldered through the pack to reach Nardi's side. He looked at the three black kids innocently walking on ahead, unaware. Book bags, clean white shirts, half-assed Afros. Strangers who'd done nothing to Nardi. What was the point?

But it's them or me, he knew. If he didn't show Nardi he could pull his weight, he'd be dead meat, like Boner. He could try to take off. But even if Nardi let him go, he'd just be on his own again, hiding, taking his chances alone against the cops. Bad odds. If they found him, he'd do time in juvenile detention for theft. Fuck that. This was about survival now. Just like what Lina had faced: help the Nazis or go to the gas. Wacko or not, he was in too deep. This was the only way.

They were past the barred stores. The black kids were cutting through a vacant lot, where weeds grew high under an electric tower. Nardi and the guys picked up their pace. Nick could practically smell the bloodlust coming off Nardi's skin.

His hand tightened around the rock-packed sock. He could hear Lina. *Do what you have to do.*

CHAPTER 7

ESTHER KNELMAN PRESSED her hand to her bosom, looking dismayed. “But aren’t such stunts terribly dangerous? However do you find the courage? My dear, I’d be frightened out of my wits.”

“It’s really not that different from any other job involving a bit of risk, Miss Knelman,” Alana said. “You learn the ropes and keep your eyes open.”

“And I’m the queen of the Nile,” David said wryly.

It had actually taken more courage to come *here,* Alana thought: this was like meeting his mother. Their talk had turned to Alana’s work as Esther had given her a brief tour of the Isaac Rosenthal Center’s administrative offices, ending in the third floor atrium used for the special functions Esther arranged. The center was a modern new building on Eighty-second Street between Fifth and Madison, and they stood in this glamorous, sunlit room surrounded by posters and paintings extolling the determination of the Jewish people throughout history. Yet, anxious though Alana had felt before coming here, after five minutes with David’s soft-spoken aunt she'd felt at ease. Esther's one crossed eye, disconcerting at first, was already forgotten, though Alana did notice her tendency to slightly lower her face when speaking. She found it touching. Esther seemed intent on making a friend of her, and Alana couldn't help wondering if that was at David's prompting. It made her happy to think so. She felt herself ready to meet as many Knelmans as he cared to produce, if they were anything like him and his father and aunt.

She'd been so grateful for David's help in her effort to contact her son's adoptive parents. After their lobster dinner on the Island three days ago, Alana had visited the adoption agency, New Life Advocates on Bleeker Street, and spoken to a Mrs. Burard, who'd seemed genuinely sympathetic but explained the hurdles. "There is a state adoption registry, where adoptees can apply to get background information about their birth parents, and birth parents can apply if they're seeking contact with the child. But that process is open only to adoptees over the age of eighteen. Unfortunately, that won't help us here." It was David who'd got the ball rolling by entering an application with the court on Alana's behalf: a request to open the 1960 adoption file on medical grounds, citing a congenital condition, unspecified, but naming Dr. Knelman as a medical reference. Still, when they met at Yankee Stadium that evening, David had warned her that even if the court did contact the adoptive parents, the couple would be under no legal obligation to respond to Alana's request for an actual meeting. So she'd spent the last days edgy with impatience.

The ball game had been a welcome break. Fun, too. Also, she'd kept working. Yesterday, she'd spent the afternoon in discussions with a director in preproduction on a low-budget horror picture, her first crack as a stunt coordinator, which had felt pretty damn good. Lining up her talent, she'd called Gus. He fell over himself apologizing for the disaster in the barn, and she granted that her temper had sharpened her tongue that night, and they patched things up. She and Gus went way back; besides, he'd never change. She offered him a job. "Fuckin' A," he'd crowed, and she knew he was pleased and proud to see her moving up. That felt good too. In the evening she'd met David downtown and they took in a new hit movie, *Serpico,* and over pizza afterward she'd explained the stunts in it to him and he'd explained the police work to her. But throughout all of this, her son was always on her mind.

"I hate the waiting," she'd told David on their way to see his aunt on his lunch break. "Hate doing nothing."

"I've been thinking about that woman at the agency. You said she sounded supportive."

"Mrs. Burard?"

"Yeah. Sometimes goodwill can go a long way." He'd squeezed her hand. "Let me see if I can speed things up."

Their budding romance still surprised her: the worlds they lived in could hardly have been more different. Yet she was happy when she was with him. He hadn't made a move beyond a brief kiss after the movie last night, though she felt he'd wanted to, and the kiss had stirred her. But the tension about her son lay between them: they were both waiting for it to be resolved. Alana wondered, alone late at night on the boat, if it ever could be. Could she go on seeing David without explaining her "condition" to him? She was trying not to think about that. First things first.

"David tells me you lost your mother in the war," Esther said, her voice gentle with sympathy. "Was it in a camp?"

Alana hesitated. She saw where this was heading and didn't want to go there. David had told her how seriously his aunt took the center's work; she should have anticipated this compassionate scrutiny. "Yes," she said, steeling herself. "In Otzenhausen."

Esther's eyes widened. But it was David who looked more astonished. "Incredible," he said. "That's where my father was."

Alana nodded. "He told me."

"Not so surprising, David," Esther said, her expression turning grim. "The Nazis sent over five hundred thousand people to that camp over four years, and murdered three quarters of them. And few are aware that they persecuted the gypsies along with the Jews. We lost six million, the gypsies lost a half million. I believe they have a word for the Holocaust that's equally apt."

"They call it *poraimos*—the devouring," Alana said. "But they don't talk about it. It's the gypsy way to put bad things behind them."

"Ah. Our way is different. To never forget." Esther's sad smile was kindly. "It is a bond, nevertheless, my dear, don't you agree?"

Alana did. "David told me you lost all your family except your brother. It's you who have courage, Miss Knelman."

Esther colored slightly, then glanced between Alana and David as if struck by a thought. "Both of you lost your mothers there. Truly a bond." She asked Alana solemnly, "May I show you our center's files on Otzenhausen?"

It startled Alana. Yet she felt a surge of curiosity. "What sort of files?"

Esther nodded, her look inscrutable. "Yes, everyone craves knowledge of their past. Come with me."

In the second-floor archive room David went to ask the librarian for the files while Alana and Esther sat down at a research table. Two adolescent boys sat hunched at the other end, brows furrowed as they scribbled in notebooks. Alana wondered about her son. Was he a bookworm like these two, or slow at school? She felt terrible that she'd been so uneducated when she'd had him—had so little to pass on. It struck her that if she had him *now*, he'd be born knowing everything she'd taught herself since then. Spanish, the history of the Revolutionary War, sailing skills, boat mechanics. And he'd be terrific at stunts: literally, a natural. It was jarring to look at the knowledge gene in this positive new light—as an asset.

Esther lowered her voice. "David was a gift to me, Alana. Did he tell you? How he came to me?"

"No. What happened?"

"Well," she said, folding her hands in her lap, "I'd come here before the war to marry a boy from Brooklyn I'd met on holiday in London, but the wedding didn't come off." She shrugged. "Nothing dramatic, he just got cold feet. It was November 1938, and I was planning to go home to Dusseldorf when the frightening news came out about Kristallnacht—Nazi thugs attacking Jews, killing them, smashing their shops. President Roosevelt issued an executive order allowing any German or Austrian then in the United States on a visa to stay in the country if they wanted to. My parents sent a telegram telling me to stay." She looked down at her hands. "I never saw them again."

"I'm so sorry."

Esther looked up with the faintest twinkle in her eye. "I was in good company—Albert Einstein stayed too. Eventually, I got a job at a printer's shop and was grateful for it. I needed the money. The war ground on, and the news got worse—by '42 my parents and sisters, cousins, aunts and uncles, had all disappeared into the camps. Then one morning in '43 I got a telegram from the Red Cross in Switzerland. David's father had managed to get him smuggled out with a Red Cross nurse. Congress had passed a resolution allowing five thousand Jewish children into the States, and the World Jewish Congress, working with the Quakers and the Red Cross, were transporting them. Naturally they contacted any relatives here. Seven weeks later a Quaker lady brought David to my door—this sober-faced toddler clutching a grimy Steiff teddy bear. It was days before I could get that bear away from him while he slept, so I could wash it. For the next two years it was just David and me. He's the son I never had, Alana. Then, in the summer of 1945, his father arrived. It felt strange at first—we'd come from a broken home, and I hadn't seen Henry since we were children. He looked like a man who'd been to hell and back. My heart broke for him, and I felt so glad to be able to reunite him and his son. It made us whole again, all three of us. We scraped by on my job while Henry went to Columbia to qualify to practice medicine here; then he established himself, and he's taken care of us ever since. Wonderful, isn't it, how even when we feel we can't go on with life, life goes on with us? Now, of course, after twenty-eight years with Henry, I can't imagine living without him."

"Don't tell Howard that," David said as he joined them, carrying a large box of files. "He might feel three's a crowd."

Esther playfully swatted his arm. "Hush, you." Alana had to smile. David had told her about his aunt's beau and their talk of marriage.

As David set down the box on the table, Esther said, "There's a lot of material, Alana, as you can see. Official memorandums, affidavits, survivor accounts, prisoner lists, plus reams of photos. You'll find various summaries in English, but naturally the original documents are in German. I'd be happy to translate, if you'd like."

"Actually, I know some German. Picked it up from my father."

"Ah, *zehr gut*. Come, David, buy me a cup of coffee. Alana really should do this alone." She got up. "We'll be in the cafeteria downstairs, my dear. Take your time."

As she watched them go, Alana felt unnerved at what she'd just claimed. She'd always *believed* she'd picked up German from her father; it hadn't meant much to her because she'd never had any call to use it. But now that she thought about it, she remembered him once bragging that from the moment he'd set foot in America he hadn't spoken a word of the "Nazi language," only Romany, then English. Which meant the real reason she knew German was because Lina had known it. She felt a shiver. This thing was so incredible.

She opened a binder of photos, and right away they hit her hard. The horror of the place. Yet she felt a buoyant sense of lightness, of distance. Just days ago these pictures would have sent her into a tailspin of fear at her madness, every sight so *familiar*. Now, she could look at them feeling safe—though full of wonder that the familiarity was genuine. How had Dr. Knelman put it? *"Real, authentic memories."*

An aerial U.S. Army photo showed the camp as a wound on the wooded countryside, the railroad tracks leading past it like a scar. There were the rows of prisoner blockhouses, the hospital block, gas chambers, crematorium, SS barracks, watch towers. There was Commandant Reinhardt's house, set apart behind high hedges, with his rose garden and his children's swing set. Near the gas chambers were the burial pits for use when the crematorium was overtaxed. *I remem-*

ber passing the pits and hearing a tire-puncture sound—a bloated corpse left out too long, bursting.

Another photo showed three-tiered wooden bunks crammed with male prisoners in rags. All the blockhouses were identical, built on a German army blueprint of the field shelter for horses: drafty barns with leaking roofs, dirt floors, no windows. The straw mattresses crawled with lice. You lived every day with hunger, fear, and constant thirst. *I remember checking a ditch behind that men's blockhouse after it rained, a spot beneath the roof overhang. The water tasted like mud, but it was fresh.*

Another showed a crowd of women in summery print dresses sitting on the ground with their children among leafy trees, as though on a picnic. A woman with barrettes in her hair; a child in a sailor suit. The caption read: "These women and children, unaware that they have been selected for death in the gas chamber, wait in the nearby wooded area next to the killing facility." *I remember how a fine ash from the crematorium smokestacks fell on everything. First you tried not to breathe it. Then you got used to it.*

Another showed thousands of prisoners standing at roll call on the Appellplatz. Roll call was the horror of every day: if you weren't dead you had to appear, to be counted. People with fevers of 104, people with frozen hands and feet, people like sticks. Twice a day, in the dark predawn before marching to work in the munitions factory, and again in the dark after work. Each roll call lasted at least two hours and often much longer, because if even one person was missing, everybody had to stand until all numbers were accounted for, sometimes all night. If you fell, you were beaten; if you didn't get up, you were shot. You stood in broiling sun, in rain, in subzero weather. You stood in clammy tatters with nothing in your stomach. *I remember a woman silently sobbing, sure she wasn't going to make it.*

There were photos of the German officers, too, some taken at the war crimes trials. One was a mug shot of the dentist who took care of the SS officers' teeth. A friendly young man, he liked having pretty gypsy prisoners around, and Lina was summoned to a Christmas party he held for the officers. His dental clinic was festooned with fir boughs and brightly lit with colored candles, and Lina and other gypsy women danced as Jewish musician prisoners accompanied them on violins, then played Christmas carols. You did anything you could to stay healthy enough to get picked to perform so you wouldn't get sent to the gas. *I remember being handed Berlin pancakes and Viennese apple strudel beside the Christmas tree, wolfing them down, after months without enough bread and water.*

There were Nazi photos of SS officers getting out of chauffeured cars in their black uniforms with the silver double-lightning insignia. And a shot of *Totenkopfverbände* camp guards lounging outside their barracks, the so-called Death's Head Units with their skull-and-crossbones insignia. Some were pals with the prisoner kapos, the block leaders. *I remember that kapo swine Mueller taking his payment behind the hospital block latrines, his stinking cock choking my throat, his fingers like claws at the back of my head.*

It made Alana nauseous. She quickly turned to the next photograph. It showed three ranks of nearly bald women in prisoner garb, gray dresses of rough cotton. Some huddled arm-in-arm, looking dazed and frightened. The caption read, "New Jewish women prisoners selected for work march toward the camp after having their heads shaved, being deloused, given camp clothing, and being tattooed with their prisoner numbers." A woman in the middle rank, tall and stout like a peasant, scowled at the camera, her beefy arms folded as she marched. Something in her hard eyes made Alana tense. *I know her.* Because the women were walking, the picture was slightly blurred, but a name surfaced from her memory. Hilde Wentzler.

An image rose in her mind. A hot night on the way back from roll call. Hilde had come to Lina and gruffly introduced herself, said she'd heard a rumor from a woman in her blockhouse before she died, a rumor about an experiment that would bring the subjects extra rations. Since Lina worked at the hospital block, Hilde wanted her to ask Mueller, the kapo there, about it. Said that for any information she'd pay Lina with the dead woman's shoes.

Alana stared at the coarse face. Wentzler. She'd heard that name recently, but where? Then she remembered—at Dr. Knelman's office. His receptionist had interrupted them with a message about a man named Wentzler. James? Or Jake? Jacob. Every moment of that incredible meeting with Dr. Knelman was still so vivid.

There was a dark recollection about Hilde that she couldn't quite bring into focus. An image of a gold nugget? The connection hovered at the edge of her memory. Then she recalled Dr. Knelman's warning that her memories could be as patchy and unstable as anyone's—and just as suspect. She quickly closed the binder of photos. Enough. She didn't want this to become an obsession, digging for details of lives that were over and done with. She had her own life to live.

She took the elevator down to the first floor to join David and his aunt, and in the lobby with its wall of windows onto the street, she looked around for a sign to the cafeteria. Starting down a corridor, she realized she'd taken a wrong turn.

She was among displays of artifacts of Jewish heritage, where a sign read, "Tradition and Community." Torah scrolls, prayer shawls, nineteenth-century wedding photos taken outside Old World synagogues. A few museum visitors were strolling, peering at captions beside the items. Alana kept going, thinking the path would soon bring her back to the lobby. But one display room led to another, on and on, the "Tradition and Community" sections leading into a series called "Persecution and Holocaust." Nazi Germany election posters. Hitler Youth uniforms and flags. Photos of Kristallnacht, of the Warsaw ghetto, of the camps. She turned the corner, and before her was a high-ceilinged room, much larger than the others, with a lifelike camp tableau. Her breath caught.

She could have been in Otzenhausen. To her right, a boxcar on tracks. Ahead, a guard's wooden watchtower. To her left, a cross-section of a prisoner barracks: tiers of wooden bunks with matted straw. Fronting the barracks, barbed wire ten feet high ran in zigzag lines, fencing the invisible inmates.

She felt dread as she stared at the boxcar. It was the real thing, of wood and iron, its maroon paint flaking, its lockbolts rusted, its steel wheels on the track drifted with some white material to look like snow. The door was open, a black emptiness inside. She felt a sharp pain in her chest, remembering the stench and thirst and terror, over a hundred people jammed inside, many dead by the time that door rolled open . . . here at the railroad ramp. *Freezing night, blowing snow. Searchlight beams from the watchtower blinding us as they herded us off. Guards with machine guns. Leashed dogs barking. Doctors making selections. Rechts! Links! Right! Left!*

"This is boring," a little girl whined at the barbed wire. "I have to go to the bathroom."

"Can't you wait five minutes?" a woman beside her snapped. "This is history. It's important."

It brought Alana back with a rush of relief. Fantasy and reality, she reminded herself. Dr. Knelman had given her the key to separate them, and she meant to hold onto that liberation. Never again would she fall back into the darkness.

She quickly retraced her steps to the lobby and found the cafeteria, so relieved to see David notice her and get up from the table, smiling.

"Henry, I think David's in love."

"Really? That professor? I forget her name." Knelman was squinting at the bathroom mirror as he worked on the tricky bow tie. He wore a formal shirt and cummerbund, tuxedo trousers, and patent leather shoes. He'd raised his voice to be heard through the open door of his en suite bathroom to his bedroom, where Esther was brushing his tuxedo jacket on its hanger. He added, "Is she the reason he begged off tonight?"

"Do you mean that sociologist at NYU?"

"Yes. Hasn't he been seeing her? He spoke very highly of her."

"No, no, that's all over. She's not his type."

"Oh. What is his type?"

"Well, you know, someone with a heart."

He had to smile as he glanced at her. Brushing his jacket, she looked very nice, he thought. She had on the gown she'd showed him last week, green brocade with a high collar and long sleeves, and she seemed in high spirits. He knew why, and it brought a twinge. Howard Jaffe was coming soon to go with them to the twenty-fifth anniversary gala at the

Rosenthal Center. The possibility of her leaving to get married unsettled Knelman. It was so selfish of Jaffe, a man of seventy-eight with a heart condition. Ester had given no indication of any firm marriage plans, but from the way she talked, Knelman sensed the two had discussed it. He could only hope that she would come to her senses if Jaffe pressed the matter. He felt it very strongly: Her home is here with me. "Do I take it you feel David has found such a person?"

"I hope so. She's very different, heaven knows. But in a good way. Independent. Not like some of these hoity-toity princesses."

"Oh? What does this worthy young lady do?"

"Film stunts, of all things. Imagine! But Henry, you know her. She came to you for a consultation, David said. Her name's Alana Marks."

His fingers stilled on the tie. Leaving it dangling, he stepped into the bedroom. "Are you saying . . . he's involved with her?"

"That's not a problem, is it? That she's a patient—or was?" Sitting on his bed, she was poking through cuff links that she'd spread on the coverlet and didn't even look up as she went on, "Though I don't see that should matter. I've seen too much suffering in this world from people being labeled. Whatever she came to you for, clearly you've helped her. Mentally, I'd say she's as right as rain."

His mouth had gone dry. "How did this happen?"

Esther looked at him, eyes twinkling. "Well, Henry, how does it ever happen? My, you should have seen the way David looked at her. Perfectly understandable, she's very pretty. Very . . . modern, but I'll get used to that. I liked her right away. She's no fool, and no sweet-talker either. I'm not surprised David's fallen."

Knelman felt a tightening in his chest. "He said nothing to me."

"Nor to me, dear, but does any young man tell his parents such things? Besides, he's just met the girl. Give it time. But remember, you heard it from me first. It's love." She frowned, looking at his shirt cuffs. "Just as I thought—those dreary old black cuff links. Try these gold ones instead. Much more distinguished."

He stood stiffly, reeling inside from the shock, as Esther busied herself with changing his cuff links, then finished tying his tie. "Isn't it sad and strange, Henry, that both you and this girl's mother were in Otzenhausen?" she said as she fussed. "Dear God, what a world. I showed Alana the files. It's important for these young people to know their history. She was very quiet afterward. A thoughtful girl, you see—sensitive, for all her independence." She helped him on with his jacket, then stood back, inspecting him. "There, you're done."

At the gala, Knelman stood silent and alone amid the chattering crowd. The third-floor atrium sparkled with candlelight and jeweled women and flutes of champagne, but he was in a dark place of his own, shaken by a horror that events were moving beyond his control. Why had he ever asked David to find this girl? The thought of a liaison between them, if it were true, terrified him. And that Esther had shown her the Otzenhausen files filled him with dread. What might the girl have seen there? What might she remember? *What might she tell David?* It made him feel almost unsteady on his feet. In his office she had given him her promise of silence, but if she became seriously involved with his son, it was inconceivable that she would keep her word. Even if she wanted to, the risk was still huge. Given what she innately knows, he thought, the closer she gets to

David, the greater the chance that she'll recall my identity. And then, how could she not expose me? The consequences would be shattering. The ruin of his life. David's hatred. And Esther's. He'd rather die than face that. He realized, with a sharp pang, that this development might force him into an action he abhorred. He might have to eliminate Alana Marks.

"Canapé, sir?"

"No . . . thank you."

The white-coated waiter glided away. Knelman forced himself to nod and smile at a woman waggling her fingers at him across the room. He was well known here. Soon after he'd settled in New York he'd joined the center, then just a one-room office midtown on Lexington, and for many years he had donated to their building fund for this modern headquarters with its museum, and contributed to their programs as well. Who would look for a former SS doctor among Jewish Nazi hunters? For beyond the center's public focus on education, their core work was tracking war criminals and bringing them to justice. Knelman had always approved. He'd despised the Nazis.

"The president's a crook, and he's got to go," said a jowly man in a nearby cluster. Their talk was all about Watergate.

"Don't get your hopes up," a leather-faced woman replied. "Nixon'll never resign. Not with Haldeman managing the cover-up."

"But now Haldeman's gone and the senate committee's got the tapes. They're out for Nixon's blood."

"Well, you know what they say about blood from a stone."

Laughter.

Knelman blocked the chatter out. The danger from Alana Marks had to be faced. Yet how? The thought of doing more violence with his own hands sickened him. In any case, it would only pose new risks. The girl's death would surely lead to a coroner's investigation, and too many people knew of his link to her: her former psychiatrist, his own secretary, and now David. No, he had to maintain distance. If the thing became necessary, it would have to be done by a third party

But who? How did one arrange such a thing?

His eyes were drawn to a small group across the room: Esther, Howard Jaffe, a rabbi named Ziegler, and Julius Bick, the center's suave director. They were listening to a portly Israeli diplomat exuberantly holding forth. Knelman's attention fixed on Bick, and an idea crept into his mind. *Nazi hunters.*

Bick drifted away, taking the diplomat in tow, and Knelman made his way toward the remaining trio.

"Hello, Henry." Ziegler extended his hand. "Glad you could make it."

"Good evening, Rabbi. A fine turnout." Knelman shook hands, aware that his generous support of the center made up, in Zielger's mind, for his noninvolvement with any synagogue. "Esther, could I speak to you a moment?" His tone was light. "I will return her momentarily, Howard." He guided her past guests and out to the hall and stopped beside the elevator, where they were alone. "I have a small gift for Julius, but I don't want to make a fuss. Could you lend me your keys?" He knew that she had access to Bick's office files when he was away, and that she kept her center keys on a ring with her apartment keys. "I'll leave the envelope on his desk while he's busy here."

"How nice. A surprise for him in the morning." She snapped open her evening bag and handed him her key ring. "It's this little silver one."

He stepped into the elevator, and the doors closed on the party voices and the strains of Mozart. When the doors opened on the second floor, he stepped out into a corridor that was empty and quiet. He unlocked the door of Bick's spacious office and switched on the light. There was a huge cherrywood desk, a wall tapestry depicting a golden menorah, and a glass coffee table with fawn-colored leather easy chairs around it. In February Knelman and a select handful of other donors had passed a pleasant snowy evening here over cigars and twenty-year-old Courvoisier. At that cozy gathering Julius Bick, relaxed and expansive, had made reference to a confidential file he kept here on "special operatives." Everyone in the room understood. Sometimes, when a former Nazi was traced but there was not enough evidence to prosecute him in a court of law, the center hired operatives to ensure that definitive justice was achieved outside the court. Bick's tone that snowy evening had revealed pride in managing a hazardous operation, but also clear-eyed caution: he was dealing with mercenaries. The very type Knelman needed now.

It took only minutes to locate the file. In the filing cabinet the nondescript buff letter-size folder was literally labeled: "Special." Knelman opened it. It held a single sheet, without letterhead, on which were typed a list of five phone numbers. No names, but beside each number was an animal designation. Lynx. Falcon. Wolf. Python. Narwhal. Obviously code names.

Knelman copied the numbers and names onto a slip of paper, folded it, and put it in his wallet. He replaced the file, then quickly wrote out a check, a donation to the center, slipped it into an envelope that he found in Bick's desk drawer, and wrote on the front, "Twenty-five years: Congratulations." He propped it against the desk lamp, turned out the light, and relocked the door behind him.

It's only a precaution, he told himself as he made his way back upstairs. It might not be necessary; perhaps Esther was only being fanciful about a romance between David and the gypsy girl. Yet Esther, he knew, had an unerring empathy with David. It would be foolish not to prepare. He'd been foolish enough already by simply meeting the girl, opening himself up to this. He had to protect himself.

Besides, there was her son. There was no question about *that* threat. The gene's extinction was Knelman's sworn mission. The boy had to go. And now, with this paper in his wallet, he had a way to do it.

Forcing a smile as he rejoined Esther and Howard, he reassured himself that no harm need come to Alana Marks yet. After all, she alone could lead him to the boy.

"Oh, lord," Alana laughed, "I'm so full I can hardly reach the taps."

David aped a big belly. "Pigs. The two of us, pigs."

They were doing the dishes in his kitchen after polishing off huge mounds of spaghetti. She was washing; he was drying. Elton John sang from a tinny radio on the counter "Goodbye Yellow Brick Road"—and when the chorus came, they both sang along in exaggerated falsettos: "Ro-o-o-oad." She cracked up. He grinned like a kid. They'd both had quite a lot of red wine.

Up to her elbows in soapy water, Alana stood barefoot in jeans and a blue knit halter top. Feeling mellow in the humid evening, she'd left her sandals in the living room, and had tied her paisley shawl around her waist, sarong-style, to do the dishes. She'd taken a chance on the wine: alcohol had always been a risk, firing up nightmare images. But the sweet relaxation she felt with David had led her to try a glass tonight, and she'd found, with a growing delight at her new mental freedom, that the memories she'd once thought of as demons she could now accept without a qualm. Or, if she wanted to, just sweep the damn things aside. She'd let herself get happily tipsy.

At the song's final chord they bumped hips, Alana's hands deep in suds, David's plate up like a tambourine. It tickled her to see him loosen up. She was even getting used to seeing him in jeans and a sweatshirt, first at the ball game, now at his place. Getting used to liking it, too. His slim hips, his broad shoulders. She liked looking at him, a lot. Wine or no wine, she realized, she was crazy about David.

A sappy Jackson Five tune came on. Alana made a face. "No offence, Counselor, but what you need is a good stereo system."

"I had one, just sold it to a buddy from law school. He said I needed to upgrade."

"Get a good deal?"

"Tell you the truth, I lost my shirt."

Alana pulled the plug, the dishes done, and as David put on coffee, she drifted into the living room. They'd eaten in the small kitchen bright with spotlights, but here there was just the half-light of dusk, filtered through the drizzly rain falling on Riverside Park, and it silvered the room. It was the first time she'd been to his place. Because of the rain, they'd shelved their original after-work plan to check out a Greenwich Village outdoor arts festival. They'd bought food to cook at home instead and come back here to his corner apartment on West Ninety-seventh overlooking Riverside Drive. They'd cooked together, chatting nonstop, giving heated opinions: vociferous dissension about the Yankees' pitcher, whole-hearted agreement that Esther and Howard should tie the knot, and a shared suspicion that TV's Six Million Dollar Man had received only a six-dollar brain. Important issues.

She moseyed over to the big bookcase. Funny, she thought, how an apartment so nondescript—white walls, commonplace parquet flooring—could feel so homey, just because of David's personality. Hardback novels and coffee-table art books crammed the shelves. Several days worth of the *New York Times* were scattered on the worn black corduroy sofa, where his briefcase sat open. Magazines littered the coffee table: the *New Yorker, Esquire,* back issues of a law journal. A top-quality silver ten-speed bike was propped against the wall by the front door. A tennis racquet lay on the floor beside a rack of albums for the now-departed stereo system. She flipped through the front albums. Chet Atkins, Miles Davis, Dave Brubeck. A jazz fan. The removal of the speakers, though, left obvious blank places on the bookshelf. There were no plants anywhere. No rugs. Nothing on the white walls except a big, dramatic black-and-white photograph of Einstein.

"You know what?" she said, raising her voice with wine-husky emphasis so he could hear her in the kitchen. "You live in black and white." She looked into Einstein's soulful eyes and absently slid one barefoot arch up and down her other ankle.

"You add a little color," he said quietly.

She turned. He was leaning against the kitchen doorjamb, arms folded, watching her, smiling. A sweet warmth washed through her.

She slowly untied the shawl at her waist. "Maybe I'll leave you some of it." She turned on a lamp on a side table and draped the shawl over the shade, creating a warm rosy light that suffused the room.

"Pretty," he said.

"Mmmm." Smoothing the shawl, she'd unconsciously begun moving her hips to the soul tune now drifting from the kitchen. Marvin Gaye, "What's Going On?" Good stuff. She let the feeling take her. Hands sliding up behind her head, eyes half closed, she began to dance. For long, lush minutes she moved almost on the spot, turning as the music turned her, spreading her arms as an air current tingled her bare back. Dancing in a mellow fog of wine and contentment, she felt David's gaze on her, first as a glow all over her body, then as a tangible force, like arms drawing her closer. It excited her. Slowly, she danced toward him until she was swaying just an arm's length away, wrists crossed over her head. She could hear his breathing get heavier, almost harsh. When their eyes met, arousal overtook her, a shaft of heat. She felt her nipples harden, brushing inside her knit halter as she moved, inflaming her more. Him too, she knew.

His voice came thick. "Where'd you learn to dance like that?"

"Learn?" She smiled. "I'm a gypsy, I was born knowing how."

He seized her. Pressed her against the doorjamb. Her body melted to his. Her thighs somehow opened, and she went up on her toes to get closer to his hardness, to get it to the spot. His hand on her bare back sent a shiver that made her arch toward him. His other hand found her breast, and she gasped in pleasure. When his mouth reached her mouth, his kiss lit such a fire, she ached.

It wasn't until he'd almost undone the halter knot, his breath hot on her neck, that her mind kicked in. *What am I doing?*

She froze. She had no business leading him on. No business even being here. The words she'd just spoken frightened her: *"Born knowing . . ."*

"Stop." She tried to pull away. "David, *stop.* I . . . I can't do this."

He snapped out of the trance of sex. His hands lifted off her, but his voice sounded half strangled. "What's wrong? Did I—"

"You didn't do anything. It's me." She was still catching her breath. "I'm not . . . on the pill."

"I have safes."

"No, it's me." A mutation, Dr. Knelman had called her. His horrible words were rushing back. *"You embody the curse of the master race . . . You are the first of a new subspecies . . . a potential new Eve, but a dangerous one, because of this mutation you carry."*

It wasn't condoms she should be thinking of—it was sterilization.

Panic swept her. "Don't touch me." She pushed him away. Hurrying to the sofa, she snatched up her sandals from the floor, grabbed her knapsack, and started for the door.

"Alana, for God's sake, what's wrong?"

"Everything." She opened the door.

"Don't go." He'd caught up to her. "Not like this." He pushed the door shut. "I'm a jerk. Forgive me. Give me another chance."

"You don't understand. This will never work. You don't know me . . . know what's wrong with me."

"Then *tell* me. Let me help, be part of it, whatever it is. Alana, I love you."

A thrill shot through her, a split-second fantasy of a future with him. Marriage, a family. Then, like a slap, reality stung her to her senses. *I can't have that.* She'd been swept away by the freedom, pretending she could live like a normal woman. But she wasn't normal . . . and she couldn't even tell him *what* she was. *A freak.*

"Please, talk to me," he said. "You're worried about your son—that's it, isn't it?"

Him, too. "Oh, Christ, yes." She opened the door. "Forget me, David. For your own sake. Don't call again."

CHAPTER 8

ALANA STOOD ON a flower-boxed doorstep off Pheasant Lane in Glen Cove, Long Island, and rang the doorbell. The house was of ivy-trellised brick, two stories, with a three-car garage. Birds twittered in broad maple trees that filtered the afternoon sunshine, and somewhere a gardener's hedge clippers were snipping with serene monotony. Despite the peacefulness, she was more nervous than she'd ever been performing the most dangerous stunt. When a middle-aged maid opened the door, she thought in astonishment: *My son lives in a house with a servant.* But beneath her agitation was a flicker of pride. She may have been a teenage basket case, but the boy had grown up amid comfort and opportunity. She'd done right by him.

"Miss Marks?" The maid spoke with a thick accent. "Please come in. Mr. and Mrs. Morgan, they expecting you."

"Is their son here?" The message hadn't said anything about that.

"Not today. Gone. Please come."

Sure that the accent was Spanish, Alana said, "Muchos gracias."

The maid beamed.

Alana followed her down the hallway's polished hardwood floor, still astonished at how quickly the summons had come about. Yesterday morning she'd got a call from Mrs. Burard at New Life Advocates. "Miss Marks, I've been sent a copy of the court application you made to open the adoption file on medical grounds. I'm glad you're taking that route, but these things can take a very long time, dragging through the system. I'd really hate to see this medical information kept from the adoptive parents—it could be bad for the child. So I propose we nudge things along. Slightly unorthodox, but I didn't build this agency without cutting a corner now and then for the sake of the children. On my own initiative, I'd like to inform the adoptive parents of your wish to contact them. They can, of course, refuse the request, but if they're agreeable, well, we'll take it from there. How does that sound?"

Alana said it sounded great, and thanked her. Coming home to the marina that evening, she'd checked for messages, and the service operator told her that a Leland Morgan had called, suggesting they meet to discuss what he called their "mutual interest in my son," and asking if she could visit him and his wife the next day. He'd left his number, adding, "As it's Saturday, we'll be home." Alana was amazed. Fast work on Mrs. Burard's part. She'd immediately called Mr. Morgan, and in a terse exchange they'd arranged this meeting. Today, keyed up as she got ready aboard *Seawitch,* she'd put on the conservative floral dress she'd worn to meet Dr. Knelman, and this time heels as well. At hearing the Morgans' upscale address, she'd decided the encounter would be tough enough without her turning up like a braless hippie. In her Fiat she'd driven faster than she should, eyes peeled for traffic cops as she crossed the Throgs Neck Bridge.

The couple met her in their immaculate living room, standing side by side as if for a formal function, while a small terrier wearing a plaid bow sat at their feet. Their age surprised her: they looked a generation older than she was. Then she realized it made sense: she'd given up her baby at fifteen; they would have adopted after many infertile years. Mrs. Morgan's hands were clasped tightly at her waist, and her husband, straight as a soldier, held her elbow as if to reassure her. Their clothes looked fit for church; their faces for a funeral. God, Alana thought, this is going to be hard.

"Thank you for seeing me," she said after the awkward moment of shared stares.

"We wanted to." Mrs. Morgan managed a rigid smile.

"Do sit down," her husband said, gesturing to a chair decorated with a seat of needlepoint roses.

They all sat, the Morgans side by side on a pale green sofa, the dog curling up at their feet, a gleaming coffee table between them and Alana. The sad bewilderment in both their faces threw her. Her goal in coming was to get their permission to see the boy alone, because only in private could she explain his incredible situation to him, so she'd been thinking of them largely as an obstacle to get past. Now, confronted with the very human faces before her, she felt how ignorant that write-off of hers had been. These anxious people loved their son.

Mrs. Morgan offered to have the maid bring coffee, or would she prefer iced tea on such a warm day? Alana declined both. The woman's eyes seemed to search hers as though hoping for clues to their mutual son. Alana found herself doing the same. Had the boy been molded to be like this nice, nervous woman, so tensely correct?

Mrs. Morgan lifted a photo album from the coffee table, set it in her lap, and opened it. "We thought you might like to see a picture of Nick."

Something snagged in Alana's chest. "That's his name?"

"Yes, Nicholas," Morgan said as his wife took out a photo and handed it across to Alana. "My father's name. Quite common in the English north country where my people came from."

Nothing had prepared her for the visceral shock of seeing him. A slightly built boy with clear, pale skin and unruly, lank hair. He was lounging back against a brick wall, hands jammed in his pockets, feet crossed at the ankles, head tilted as though in a challenge to the camera. A pose of disdain, if not contempt. He wore a prep-school uniform—gray trousers, navy jacket with a crest, white shirt, striped red-and-gray tie—but the clothes looked slept-in. Alana studied his face, fascinated that the features were so much like her own—high cheekbones, large dark eyes—but as though someone had taken a pencil and sharpened all the angles. Arched eyebrows, where hers were smooth. Pointed cupid's bow on the upper lip, and a narrow lower lip, where hers were full. A small, chiseled nose—well, that was just like hers. The hair was lighter. Like his father's? She had no recollection of the father. Hadn't even known his name. It hadn't been even a one-night stand, just a half-hour grope at a dark and drunken teenage party. She'd thrown up after. But the boy in the photo, despite these hints of his parents, had a gleam in his eyes that was all his own. A glitter of cleverness, of hidden knowing. Before this moment her son had been an abstraction to Alana; now he was startlingly real. Nick Morgan, just thirteen, but watch out world.

"Thank you." She handed back the picture, and tried to gather her wits to broach the subject she'd come about.

"Difficult, isn't it?" Morgan said. "The timing. We've been so worried. And then, when Mr. Knelman arrived to tell—"

"Mr. Knelman?"

"Yes, from the district attorney's office. He came yesterday afternoon."

Alana was amazed. "He did?"

Mrs. Morgan said with fretful precision, "We assumed he was a new police investigator. After all, they've been searching for weeks. But he said he'd come about something quite different. About you. A congenital condition that might affect Nick."

"Not life-threatening, Mr. Knelman assured us," Morgan quickly added. "Still, we thought it responsible of the authorities to take such an interest, and, of course, Janet and I want to cooperate, do the right thing. We are . . . extremely concerned."

So David had engineered this! He must have gotten the Morgans' name from Mrs. Burard and come here on his own. Then Morgan had called Alana's service. Clearly, it hadn't been Mrs. Burard's persuasion alone that had prompted Morgan, but David's influence, using his position, to nail down this meeting. She felt a glow of gratitude, tinged with shame. David should hate her for the other night; instead, he'd pushed things to this point—for her.

"You mentioned the police," she said warily. "Is there a problem? With Nick?"

Mrs. Morgan's eyes widened. "Didn't they tell you?"

"Ah," her husband said, looking flustered. "Miss Marks, it seems that we must bring you up to date. Nick's gone."

"Gone?"

"Disappeared three weeks ago. We had a row over plans for his education. He ran off that very night. Not a word since."

"Have you tried his friends?"

"He has no friends. None that I'm aware of." A pained look, faintly like distaste, came over Morgan's face. "He's a strange child. Always has been."

Alana felt a prick of anger. *You don't understand him.* She'd bolted from home herself when she wasn't much older than Nick. She'd never really been a child, not like others. Nick wasn't either. No one knew how truly strange he was, except her.

Mrs. Morgan said, her voice almost breaking, "I can't imagine how he must be living, all alone, at thirteen . . ." Her voice trailed off, the concept seemingly beyond her.

He's on the street, just like I was, Alana thought. Picking pockets, doing petty scams. He's got inborn knowledge of those gypsy skills—*my* skills. It shocked her, and yet, strangely, it also settled her a little: Nick would be doing all right. What disturbed her more was a deep unease about how he might be coping with his visions. At that age, they'd tormented her almost to suicide. She'd been lucky; Gus Yuill had found her, taken her in, trained her in his trade. But Nick was all alone.

She thought: These nice people are useless to him. There's only me.

"If you hear anything from him, would you call me?" She was thinking that if they'd really had just a spat, Nick might come home. She dug into her knapsack for her wallet and a pen, pulled out the Beacon Marina business card, and wrote her answering-service number on the back. "Here's where you can leave a message for me. If he gets in touch, or if he comes home, please call me." She handed the card to Morgan. "Please, the moment you hear." She got up. "It was very kind of you to see me. I won't take any more of your time."

"But I don't understand," he said, rising with her, flustered again. "Won't you tell us about this . . . condition? Isn't that why you came?"

"Mr. Morgan, there'll be time for that later. Let's find Nick first." Holding back information as a sort of bargaining chip felt awful, but it was the only way she could be sure they'd keep her in the loop.

She hoped to get to Nick before the police did. Given his gypsy smarts, if he suspected the cops were coming for him, he might bolt for good. Truly disappear. Then she'd never be able to help him. She had to reach him first. No one else understood.

Except Dr. Knelman. As she left the quiet house and pulled away in her Fiat, she decided to call him right away. She'd promised to keep him up to date. Besides, he was the only person she could open her heart to about Nick. In Dr. Knelman, at least, she had one ally.

Nick left the Beacon Marina office and walked down the dock. He hadn't trusted himself to ask any more questions of the guy behind the desk. He was too rattled. And there were too *many* questions; he could hardly keep them straight. He was hungry and hot, too. The hike out to City Island had taken a lot longer than he'd expected; subway forever, two buses, and finally on foot down to the water. Almost six by the time he'd got here. Soon he'd have to haul ass all the way back to Bensonhurt and get in before Nardi blew his top that he'd left the dog so long: it was Nick's job to feed and water Heidi. But he couldn't go yet. He had to see if he could find this woman.

He reached the end of the dock and looked out at the moored sailboats, a couple dozen maybe, about as far away as half a city block. He'd gone straight to the office because he'd figured she must work there, but the guy at the desk said, No, she was a club member, she had a boat; lived on it. Picking out the red-and-white hull the guy had described, Nick squinted and could just make out the lettering on the bow. "Seawitch." He stared at it, his heart thumping. Who was she? Why had she gone to see his parents? And—the question that freaked him most—why did she have the same name as the teenage gypsy in his visions?

"A lady," Mariella had said. Nick had been relieved when the maid had answered his call from the phone booth in the Tre Stelle. His first call home. He'd timed it so that Mom would be getting her hair done; she had an appointment every Saturday at four. Dad almost never answered the phone, but if he did, Nick planned to hang up. He'd only wanted to call in, let them know he wasn't dead under some bridge; it seemed kind of sadistic to keep them hanging. Besides, the sooner they accepted that he was on his own, gone for good, the sooner they'd call off any police search. But there was no way he'd talk to them, and he'd planned it so that Mariella would take his message.

But she'd done more than that. "Oh, Nick, somebody come ask about you today." She sounded startled by his call, her accent thicker than ever in trying to keep him on the line. "Mr. Morgan, he out in the garden. I go get him, yes?"

"No, don't. Who came asking about me?"

"She drive up in pretty yellow car. A lady."

A cop? Nick wondered. Maybe they sent women cops when they were looking for a kid. "What kind of lady?"

"Nice lady. She talk to Mr. and Mrs. Morgan. They say she name Alana Marks."

At the name, his mind spun into overdrive, then stalled.

"Nick? You there?"

"Yeah. What . . . what did she want?"

"Don't know. But she leave a card. Mr. Morgan, he put it here in the kitchen."

"What's it say?"

She read with careful precision, "Beacon Marina, City Island. Nick, you come home now, like good boy, yes? Mr. and Mrs. Morgan, they worried sick."

"Tell them I'm fine, Mariella. Tell them I'll send them a coconut from the South Seas. And I'll send you a pot of gold."

Now he gazed out at the sailboat, feeling kind of dizzy, wondering what to do next. Was she there, on the boat? Or maybe, he thought with a shiver, she was right nearby, on the dock. He looked around. The place was busy. Behind him, in the parking lot, people were carrying groceries and duffel bags from their cars to boats at the finger docks. The whole marina was bustling. The nice Saturday weather, he figured. Sailboats and power boats chugged past him, coming and going, some of them jockeying for position to gas up at the fuel dock. Little dinghies with whining outboard motors zipped around the harbor. The yacht club workers looked especially busy, setting up for some shindig tomorrow—a big banner tacked across the clubhouse read, "Founder's Day Regatta. Sunday 8:00 till 8:00. Races All Day! Fun for the Whole Family!" On the grass beside the parking lot some sweaty guys in shorts were setting up a white tent, and more at the far end of the dock were stringing colored plastic flags between high pylons. Others were manhandling inflated orange triangle buoys onto a powerboat, the buoys as big as Nick but lighter, the way they were tossing them. Yeah, everybody looked mighty busy, he thought. Loaded, too, some of these yachty types. A Mercedes and a new Jaguar at the edge of the lot. Rolex watches on wrists. Wallet bulges in the old guys' baggy shorts. Great territory for a pickpocket. Nick figured he could clean up if he had a mind to. But he turned his thoughts away from that and concentrated on the women. In any crowd he mostly looked at girls anyway, so this was just a variation. Except he wasn't looking at tits and ass now. He thought: This is ridiculous, I didn't even get a description of her from Mariella. What do I look for?

Then he saw a face that froze him. She sat alone in an inflatable dinghy, speeding away across the water, one hand controlling the motor, but she'd turned to look over her shoulder at something on the dock. Then she looked ahead again, her back to him. It had been just a glance, and not even at him, but in that moment Nick's heart seemed to have stopped. It was her . . . a little older, but her. Alana Marks.

Pins and needles shot along his arms. His legs went weak as water. This can't be happening. *I invented her . . . didn't I?*

But, holy hell, there she is!

She reached the *Seawitch,* away from the harbor bustle. He watched her stand up in the dinghy and tie up to the boat. She was in a flowery dress, but seemed to be barefoot as she braced one foot up on the dinghy gunnel. Sure enough, she tossed what looked like two shoes onto the boat. It electrified Nick—the way she'd done that, it felt familiar right down to his bones. She climbed aboard and checked some ropes, moving around like an athlete. He strained to get a good look at her face, but at this distance he couldn't make out her features. Then she slid open a kind of door to go below, went down the steps, and disappeared.

He shivered, cold from the shock, but on fire with curiosity. *Who is she?*

His first thought was to grab a dinghy and get out there. He hurried over to where people had left a couple of inflatables bobbing at the dock. But nabbing somebody's dinghy would bring trouble. He twisted around, looking for the launch that he'd noticed ferrying some people to a moored boat. He spotted it waiting at the end of the dock and started for it on the run. Then he stopped, got hold of himself, made himself think. He couldn't just climb aboard her boat like some pirate. What if she wasn't alone? Maybe some muscled guy would come up from below and yell at him. That kind of thing could draw the cops. He'd seen a police boat casually cruising the harbor with two life-jacketed officers. He couldn't risk that.

Ask the desk guy to ferry her a message? But the thought of her coming straight over to meet him made him feel trapped. He just wanted to get close enough to watch her, check her out.

Think. She wasn't going to sail away; the desk guy had said she was fixing up her boat. So she had to come ashore again. Maybe to buy food. Maybe for a shower: he'd seen people going in and out of the shower wing carrying towels and stuff. He went to a bench and made himself sit down, sit still, though it felt like every muscle was twitching. He could see her boat from here. He would watch and wait. He felt shivery, shaky. One of his fantasy people had come to life . . . and had been to his house to find him. It scared the hell out of him. He had to be insane. *But she's not a fantasy—Mariella saw her.* Finding out who she was seemed his only lifeline. If he had to sit here all night, he would.

Earlier that day, Sergeant DiNovi of the Brooklyn police frowned as he studied the boy's photograph David had handed him. Watching the cop wipe his damp upper lip,

David thought how little the sluggish overhead fans were accomplishing on this hot Saturday. The uniforms of the few officers at their desks showed armpits black with sweat, and DiNovi, a paunchy guy, looked irritable, as though he took the heat as a personal affront.

"His name's Nick Morgan," David said, his suit jacket hooked on his thumb over his shoulder. "A runaway." The Morgans had given him the photo when they'd explained Nick's disappearance to him yesterday, confiding to him about the stolen albums and watches they'd found in the boy's bedroom. On a hunch, David had gone first to the Glen Cove police station to check detention sheets, then to Long Beach, and now he was at the Jay Street station in Brooklyn Heights. If he came up empty here as well, he planned to check downtown. The Glen Cove police were looking for the boy, but what they had in mind was a runaway child in hiding. David was looking for a juvenile delinquent on the move.

DiNovi's frown deepened, as though at a nagging suspicion. "This could fit a description. Hang on a minute." Taking the photo, he disappeared into an office.

David walked to the water cooler for a drink. It troubled him that his hunch might be right. Still, he longed to bring about the meeting Alana wanted with her son. He'd got the Morgans' name from Mrs. Burard at New Life Advocates and gone to see the couple, and despite learning from them of the boy's disappearance, his objective hadn't changed. He wanted to connect Alana with her son, because once she'd given the boy the personal information she felt was so important, and he was returned to his parents, then maybe she could get on with her life. And David could reconnect with her. He couldn't believe she didn't want that too. Not after how she'd kissed him the other night. Not after that flash of passion. It thrilled him just remembering. And shook him all over again, the way she'd taken off. She was so extreme; all or nothing. Probably why she was so great at her job. He thought of her with a kind of wonder: she seemed fearless. Which was why he couldn't fathom what had spooked her so badly. Obviously, she was anxious about her son, but whatever this inherited problem was, it seemed to him that she'd blown it way out of proportion. Again, all or nothing. Whatever, he hoped he could get her over it by bringing her and the boy together. The sooner the better: it was taking him away from a deskload of work. He was carefully avoiding his boss in the halls. Worse, he'd taken dubious license in using his position to force the meeting with the Morgans. He had to ask himself, was finding the boy worth risking his job? He didn't believe the risk was all that great—still, he had to shake his head at what he was doing. Fool in love. As he filled a paper cone with water and drank it down, a line from an old song ran through his mind:

I never had the least notion
That I could fall with so much emotion.

"It's the eyebrows," DiNovi said as he reached him at the cooler. He had a report sheet in one hand and the photo of Nick in the other. "A witness described one of the perps as about twelve, dark hair, a runty kid." He read from the notes, "'Eyebrows like upside-down V's.'"

"Witness to what?"

"A nasty piece of business in Bensonhurt Tuesday night, assault on three black youths. Assailants unknown. Apparently not gang-related—the victims were on a Baptist Church exchange. Two of them are still in the hospital. One lost an eye."

David stood speechless. DiNovi seemed to be gauging him. "Up for a little gumshoe work, Mr. Knelman?"

By the time he got into the cruiser beside DiNovi, heading to Bensonhurst to interview the witness, David had absorbed the shock, but he couldn't shake his worry about Alana. If the boy was guilty of such a brutal act, she'd take it hard. Probably blame herself—blame this hereditary thing. He felt so frustrated not knowing what her problem was, but she wouldn't say, and neither would his father. Dad had made that painfully clear on Thursday night. After she'd run out, David had gone over to speak to him. Dad and Aunt Es had just got back from the gala at the Rosenthal Center, and David found him in his bedroom, hanging up his tux jacket. He'd put the question right to him, and got a scowl of disapproval in return.

"I am amazed you ask, David. You know I cannot discuss a patient."

"Alana's more than a patient, Dad. To me, a lot more."

The scowl turned stony. "Then it's true what Esther tells me—that you have been seeing this young woman? That you and she have . . . a relationship?"

"I'm not sure what we have at this point. But, yes, I've been seeing her every chance I get. If I could, I'd be with her right now. But something's scared her. That's why I wish you'd just explain what she—"

"I am deeply disappointed, David. I cannot pretend otherwise. I sent you on an errand of trust in finding her. I must ask that you end this relationship immediately."

David was taken aback. And annoyed. This wasn't exactly his father's business. He let the anger slide—it was petty. But he did want to make his position clear. "She may have beat you to it. Seems I'm not her favorite person right now. But I've got to tell you, if I get another chance, I'm grabbing it. I'm in love with her."

"You don't know what you're talking about. And, frankly, I find your behavior highly improper. Exploitative. Miss Marks is sadly vulnerable. Since you cannot marry her, to trifle with her is to abuse her."

David flared at the insult. "Who says I can't marry her?"

His father went ashen. "Marriage is out of the question."

"Why? Because she's got gypsy blood? Think it'll taint our Jewish purity?"

"Don't be vulgar. You know I harbor no such intolerance. To suggest such a thing is beneath you."

"Then why, for God's sake?"

"Because she is a very troubled young woman! Believe me, you have no idea what you are dealing with."

David reined in his exasperation. "Nothing I've seen convinces me she's any more troubled than any of us. Who *isn't* a little screwed up? And she's a lot more courageous and honest about herself than most. No dice, you can't scare me with the bugaboo of mental instability. I'm the son of a man who's cured hundreds of patients and sent them home happy, remember?" At his father's grim silence, David took a breath. "Look, Dad, I'm thirty years old, I've lived a little, and I've been with some very nice women. But Alana's special. I know it's happened fast, and I'm sorry if it bothers you right now. But I won't give her up just because you feel it goes against some impersonal professional code. That's that."

The walk-up apartment above Corradini's Shoe Repair was hot as an oven and smelled of rancid cooking oil. The shrunken woman was all in black, hunched in a moldering plaid easy chair before the nattering TV. She took a look at the photograph and said with a heavy Italian accent, and surprising bitterness, "That's the young one. I see him a-running away after they do it. That whole bunch, they all a-running when they finish what they do, and the young one, eyes sharp like a fox, he run right under my nose. There." She pointed to the window, shaking her head at the wickedness of the world. "That boy, he gonna bring people nothing but bad."

David went to the window she'd indicated. There was a clear view of the street, and of the vacant lot with an electrical tower, kitty-corner, where the three kids said they'd been jumped.

As they left, DiNovi asked if he could take Nick's photograph to the victims, see if they could make a positive ID. David left it with him; he couldn't spend any more time on Nick Morgan. Before this had come up, he'd planned to use his Saturday catching up on paperwork at the office. He'd already lost the morning.

"I'll keep you posted, Mr. Kuelman. Thanks for this tip."

Arriving at his seventh-floor office at Eighty Center Street, David called Alana's service and left a message with the operator: "Please ask her to call me. Tell her it's about Nick." He left both his numbers, office and home.

He was about a third of the way through his pile of booking sheets when Detective Rick Lipranski walked in.

"The chain on that desk's detachable, you know, Counselor. Had lunch yet?"

David realized he was famished. They went to a street vendor beside the park across from the courthouse, and as they wolfed hot dogs Lipranski updated him on the latest multicase con they'd been investigating. In his fifties, Lip had the manner of the classic hard-boiled cop. Skinny as a junkie, though. Thinning black strands of Vitalis-shiny hair combed straight back. Bloodshot eyes narrowed from the Marlboros he chain-smoked. Or maybe it was a permanent sneer from seeing too much of the citizenry's viciousness in his three decades on the force. David found him invaluable. Attached to the NYPD's confidence squad, Lip was their longtime gypsy expert.

The con they were investigating was something new: personable young gypsy, male or female, befriends wealthy ailing elderly recluse, moves in as companion, and charms the mark into signing a joint tenancy agreement. Only after the sick old person dies and the con artist takes possession of his or her property does the stunned family discover that joint tenancy in law means joint ownership. David and Lipranski were calling it the "elder scam." Prosecution was dicey: there was no law against gold digging. But after their investigation of two previous cases, what concerned the two men was that maybe these elderly folks were being hastened to their graves.

"Magic salt, sprinkled in the old girl's soup," Lipranski said through a mouthful of hot dog with sauerkraut. "That's what the neighbor overheard the gypsy tell his girlfriend. Maybe they're just giving her something innocent like a ground-up sleeping pill, but 'magic salt' sure makes me wonder."

Made David wonder too. Lip's report was a follow-up on a complaint made by the neighbor of an elderly widow named Iris Larson who lived in a fine brownstone on Irving Place at Gramercy Park. The friend claimed that a swarthy young couple had recently befriended Mrs. Larson, made themselves invaluable by doing her grocery shopping and odd jobs around her spacious apartment, then moved in as companions, and were now controlling her life: they'd canceled her phone and allowed her no visitors. David had checked the municipal records and found that a joint tenancy agreement had recently been filed. "This makes three," he said as he polished off his hot dog, jutting his chin to keep mustard from dripping on his tie. "Three that we know of."

Swallowing his last bite, Lipranski jammed a Marlboro in his mouth and rummaged in his pockets for a light. "Fucking cottage industry."

David balled his paper napkin between his palms and tossed it in the trash bin. Was Iris Larson being slowly poisoned? Gypsy swindles rarely involved violence, a strategy that usually kept them clear of the overworked cops. But you never knew what people were capable of. It was hard to keep his mind off an image of thirteen-year-old Nick Morgan breaking bones with a steel pipe. *"One lost an eye."*

He was itching to make a move on this elder scam. "Anything yet on George Adams?" he asked. That was the name listed with Iris Larson's on the joint tenancy agreement. David and Lip figured Adams had to be the male half of the live-in gypsy team.

Lip shook his head as he blew out smoke. "Nada. Maybe it's a new alias, still clean. But I got something else, Counselor." His eyes almost twinkled. "Last night a guy parked in front of Larson's in a gold Cadillac. Alabama plates. Car's still there."

For what it's worth, David thought. Alabama mailed plates and registration to anyone upon receipt of a money order. "And?"

"Registration's under a Danny Rogers."

"With a bogus address, right?"

"Natch. But I ran the name. AKA Stefan Marks, also Danny Roman."

David's breath caught. "Marks?"

"Gives us more to go on."

Yeah. Like Rajko Marks, AKA Roman Mitchell, *rom baro* of his clan in Queens. Alana's dad. Maybe just a coincidence, David told himself. Marks was a common gypsy name. On the other hand, could Alana's father be running the whole elder scam? Keeping his apprehension to himself, he said he'd request authorization for Lip to do surveillance on the driver.

"Good," Lip said. "Let's hope we can help this lady *before* the funeral."

"You brought lunch, I hope." The gravel voice made the ironic statement sound like a threat.

In answer, Knelman nervously lifted the brown paper bag. Five thousand dollars cash was inside. The instructions last night on the phone had been plain: half the payment now, nonrefundable. He felt a chill, remembering the rest. *"Second half when the job's done."*

"Address and description," the black man said now, same gravel voice as on the phone. They stood side by side in Washington Square Park, their eyes on a scruffy trio of long-haired rock musicians who were testing an amplifier with much jarring feedback. In his nervous state, Knelman tensed at each electronic squawk. It was unnerving to be standing here beside a professional murderer. "Give me the info, then go," the man went on. "Drop the lunch bag in that trash bin over there, the one beside the lamppost with the kite stuck on top. I'll pick up the bag when you're gone."

Knelman looked at him. Early thirties, he guessed. Rangy like a basketball player, neatly barbered, dressed all in khaki, the work shirt and slacks starched and pressed. He had dark black skin that was deeply pocked, a carriage that was faintly military—hands behind his back, legs spread "at ease"—and an aura of stillness that both disquieted and reassured Knelman. "Python," he said—but using the code name felt faintly ridiculous. "May I know your real name?"

A sharp glance. "No."

The whites of his eyes, Knelman noticed, were yellowish. And the khaki shirt sleeves were buttoned at the wrists despite the sultry day. Knelman wondered if the man was concealing something. Like the tattooed Jewish survivor he himself pretended to be, he too always wore long sleeves. A theory sprang to mind: that "Python" had just been in Vietnam, perhaps as an expert sniper, hence his present skill, and while there had become addicted to heroin, a habit that left injection bruises. If so, it explained both the sleeves and his need for large amounts of cash. None of that concerned Knelman. He knew a competent surgeon named Farrell who was an addict. A well-maintained habit did not necessarily hinder performance. "You remind me of a colleague. I shall call you Farrell."

The man ignored the comment. "The payment's enough to cover both targets?"

Knelman's stomach lurched. Both: mother and son. It appalled him. But what choice did he have after David's declaration that he meant to marry the gypsy girl? Their argument after the gala had left Knelman literally shaking. The thought of David having children with this girl made him ill. Five days ago—an eternity, it seemed—he had hoped his mission would be over once she agreed to sterilization, but now, not only was there her son to deal with, but David had pushed matters so far, and the situation had become so precarious, that Knelman could see no option. The girl, too, had to go. The moment David had left his bedroom, he'd pulled the slip of paper from his wallet and, with trembling fingers, had dialed the number.

"Yes, both," he answered now through parched lips.

"Alana Marks, age twenty-eight. And Nick Morgan, age thirteen." He described the girl. "You will find her on City Island in the Bronx, at Beacon Marina. She lives on a sailboat there, the *Seawitch.* The boy's whereabouts I don't yet know." He still felt the shock of her phone call reporting that she'd met with the adoptive parents, only to learn that the boy had run away. Knelman had shuddered. An adolescent male carrier at large!

"I asked the Morgans to call me if they hear from him, or if the police find him," he remembered her saying on the phone. "But I'm hoping he might go home on his own. They're nice people, and he must know how worried they are. Anyway, don't worry, Dr. Knelman, I'm going to stick with this until I find Nick."

He had noted her maternal self-delusion, and her determination. He was counting on both. "You are doing the right thing," he'd assured her. "Nick has undoubtedly suffered, but once he has the benefit of your goodwill, he can make a go of his life." He had almost choked on the words. Life was not possible for the boy. Nor for her.

"They showed me his picture, Dr. Knelman, and it kind of threw me. Like looking at a lost part of myself."

"A photograph? Can you describe him?"

She had done so, at some length. Knelman passed along that description now to Farrell. "Go to the marina, find the woman, and follow her. I believe she will eventually lead you to the boy. Do not harm her until then, or we may never find Nick Morgan. Is that absolutely clear? The moment you see them together, do it."

That night, after a dinner of coq au vin at home with Esther, he was tending to his orchids on the terrace. The new *Vanda rothschildiana* showed disturbing signs of scale on several leaves' undersides, so he wiped them with a cloth soaked with methylated spirits. Moving on to his beautiful *Dendrobium* 'Stardust,' he picked up pruning scissors and snipped off two withered yellow blossoms, wondering if he really should quarantine the vanda. He would hate for the scale disease to infect all his other plants.

"Henry," Esther called from the kitchen. "Phone call for you."

He took it in his study. The gravel voice said, "I'm at the location, at a phone booth. I've seen the woman. Got a look before she went to her boat. There's a boy here too, on a bench on the dock, half asleep. Looks like he's got nowhere to go. He fits your description, but it's dark, and I can't be positive. I'll wait around until it's light. Call you when it's done."

Knelman hung up. He realized he was still gripping the pruning scissors. His knuckles were white.

As Alana loaded gear into her convertible trunk in the marina parking lot early the next morning, she couldn't shake the feeling that she was being watched. She squelched it. She had enough on her mind without inventing bogeymen.

Due on set in a little over an hour, she was at least on schedule. She'd been booked for weeks on this Sunday commercial shoot, a fantasy ad for American Express: a climb up the Flatiron Building on Fifth Avenue, including an "accidental" fall of several stories in her rope harness. She'd been up for hours checking her gear. She would need all her wits about her, which was exactly why she was looking forward to the challenge. Keep her mind off the waiting that was eating her. There was nothing she could do until she got some word from the Morgans. Or from David. His message yesterday that he had some news about Nick had excited her, but there'd been no answer at his home number when she'd called back, and the switchboard at his office was closed for the weekend. Tomorrow, first thing, she'd try him again.

It wasn't just the message that excited her. She'd been thinking about David a lot. About what a dolt she'd been to run out on him the other night at his apartment. God, she'd wanted him—but that's exactly what had freaked her, remembering Dr. Knelman's warning about her propagating a mutation that could unbalance the world. Seemed pretty far-fetched to her now, though. Because she'd also been thinking about Dr. Knelman—about his weird nervousness over the knowledge gene. The gene didn't scare her anymore. It hadn't turned *her* into a monster. In fact, if she'd only known all these years *why* she knew everything she knew, she could have used that insight, built on it. It could have given her wisdom, maybe made her a better person. That made her want all the more to explain it to Nick. Granted, Dr. Knelman was the expert on this stuff, but she was beginning to think he might have let his apprehension get the better of him. Could be he felt too close to it. Reminded her of a veteran stunt man gone gun-shy and freezing up, unable to see anything but the danger. But she knew from experience, if you handled things very carefully, you minimized the danger, aced the gag, and wowed the world.

She didn't want to be gun-shy with David. He'd gone out on a limb for her with the Morgans, and it gave her such a glow to realize he cared that much. The other night at his apartment, he'd said he loved her. It thrilled her. Her heart told her this was a man she could trust. A man who could handle the truth. There had to be some way to tell him about herself without putting his father in a bad light; she'd promised to keep Dr. Knelman's secret. But that was before she'd begun to fall in love with his son. She didn't know how to sort it out yet. All she knew was that everything in her wanted a second chance with David. Next time, she'd go for it.

"G'day, Alana."

She turned from her open trunk. It was Waldo, the marina operator, an Aussie import. His sun-leathered face and strapping build testified to a life outdoors manhandling motors and masts. "Great day for the regatta, Waldo," she said. His staff of teenage helpers was busily preparing everything from barbecues to trophy tables and the committee boat for the races. A couple of carloads of families were already drifting in, tires crunching over the gravel parking lot.

"Couldn't ask for better," he said, one eye on a young worker at a nearby slip who was struggling to make fast the dock lines of a Boston Whaler. "Say, Alana, could I ask you to move your dink a little further down? Dock space is at a premium today, with all the transients arriving. Sorry."

"No problem. I'll have the last of my gear out in a sec, then I'll move it around to C dock. That okay?"

"Super. Catch you later." He strode off, calling instructions to the ham-fisted kid.

Leaving her trunk open, Alana crossed the strip of lawn, then the dock, and stepped down into the inflatable dinghy. Only three bags left to get to the car. The morning sun just above the clubhouse struck her full in the face. Then, as she bent to hoist a bag, she felt the light slightly darken as someone stopped in front of her on the dock.

"Alana Marks?"

She looked up. A man eclipsed the sun. A boy, actually—he'd momentarily looked bigger from down where she stood at the waterline. Seeing his frozen face, something caught in her breast.

"That's your name, isn't it?" A tightness, like fear, in his voice.

Her legs felt as wobbly as the dinghy. She held the dock cleat for balance. "Nick?"

He flinched. "How do you know me? How do I know *you*?" His eyes were huge, his face white as a sail. "Holy hell, who are you?"

CHAPTER 9

KNELMAN WAS ON tenterhooks waiting for Farrell's call. He was in his study at home, the piano strains of a Chopin étude lilting through the apartment. He hoped the Sunday-morning tranquillity at least seemed routine to Esther. Coming through the living room, he'd passed her finishing her coffee in her dressing gown as she flipped through a kitchenware catalog. He'd done his best to appear normal in her presence, but here at his desk he sat stiff and tense. A pounding headache gave him no relief.

When the phone rang, he snatched it.

"I can see both subjects," the gravel voice said. "They're talking on the dock."

"Then what are you waiting for?"

"Too many people around."

"I'll add another thousand dollars. Just do it!"

"If I get the chance. I'll let you know."

The line went dead.

* * *

Alana climbed out of the dinghy and stood to face Nick. How slight he was! No taller than to her chin! He looked electrified, white-faced with wonder. The panic in his eyes tore at her, a stab within, like a birth pang.

"Nick, I've got something to tell you." She forced calmness into her voice and tried to look unthreatening, holding up her hands in reassurance. He looked as rigid as a cat poised to streak away. "It's about you . . . and me."

"Who are you?" His voice sounded strangled.

"I think, deep down, you know. What you don't know . . . what I want to explain . . . is *why* you know. It's kind of incredible, so"—she nodded to a bench—"maybe we should sit down." She took a step toward him.

He lurched back. She was terrified he was going to run. To hold him, she threw out a net of words, a Romany saying: *"Mashkar le gadiende leski shib si le Romenski zor.* What's it mean, Nick?"

He froze. Then he translated as if something compelled him, the words coming out in jerks. "Surrounded by . . . the *gadje* . . . a gypsy's tongue . . . is his only defense."

"Right. How do you know that saying?"

He shook his head, looking stunned, bewildered.

"It's Romany, the language of the gypsies," she said. "You know lots more of it too. *Feri ando payi sitsholpe te nayuas.*"

He gaped at her. Then, slowly: "It's . . . in the water that . . ." He faltered.

"That you learn to swim," she finished the proverb. "Your Romany's a little rusty, because you've never used it. But it's in your head. How about some German? *Weisst Du wer deine Mutter ist?*" Do you know who your mother is? *"Kennst Du meinen Namen?"* Do you know my name?

He was trembling. He opened his mouth as if to say "Alana," but no sound came.

She went on gently, "I know how shocking this is to you, Nick. But just hang on. Just listen. I'm going to explain everything." She decided to plunge straight in. Despite his near panic, the curiosity burning in his eyes told her that he would be satisfied by nothing but the whole truth.

"It all started twenty-nine years ago, in Germany, 1944." As calmly as she could, she went through it. That there had been a Nazi scientist who'd discovered a way to make knowledge hereditary, from mother to child, through a special gene. That he had performed an experimental operation on a gypsy woman, a prisoner in Otzenhausen, implanting the gene in her. "And I'm the gypsy's daughter. I was born knowing everything she knew. And when I was fifteen, I gave birth to a son—you, Nick—and passed on all my knowledge to you. But I was too young to take care of a baby on my own, so I gave you up for adoption. That's why you've grown up not understanding *why* you know so much . . . about me . . . and about her. Unbelievable as it sounds, it's the truth. You were born with the knowledge of two lifetimes."

There was a long moment of silence.

"That's . . . not possible," he said.

"Any ordinary person would say so. But you're not ordinary, are you, Nick? For one thing, look at how you know these languages. I'm not ordinary either. Believe me, I'm still struggling to get used to this myself. I just found it out last week. It knocked me for a loop, and yet right away it made sense. You know everything I knew when I had you, and we both know everything my mother knew. Her name was Lina. You know all about her, don't you?"

The fire in his eyes grew brighter, then it steadied. Despite his extreme shock, Alana sensed his quick brain computing. She felt she had him. His curiosity was devouring all this.

A chattering couple stopped beside them to look at a boat. Alana motioned Nick to move down the dock with her. He walked beside her as if sleepwalking, but she could tell that he'd never been more awake. His eyes stayed fixed on her. The feeling was the same for her. The connection between them was like electricity.

"I recognized you," he said in wonder. "The second I saw you."

"Because I grew up seeing my reflection. I passed that knowledge to you in my womb."

"I can't get over . . . just that you're *real.* And . . . her too. Lina." His eyes sharpened, as if to pin the facts down. "Killed in the camp, right?"

She nodded. "That's what I was told as a kid. Which is why you know it."

"So I'm not . . . not—"

"Not crazy. I know how you feel. Like the bottom of your stomach just fell out. But a fantastic relief too, right? Like, before, you were scared in the dark, seeing ghosts, and suddenly a bright light's been turned on. They're not ghosts, but real people. Weird, for sure, but such a relief."

The first hurdle was over. Alana led him to the patch of lawn by the dock, and they sat on the grass, facing each other, and talked non-stop. About Lina, Otzenhausen, the gene experiment, and how she'd learned all of this from Dr. Knelman. Or rather, Nick's questions and her answers came in bursts followed by dumbfounded silences.

A gunshot startled her. She looked out at the water and realized the shot marked the start of a sailboat race. She saw that the regatta celebrations were in full swing—activity all around them. She had blocked it out, so engrossed with Nick, but now it hit her. Cheers from the dockside crowd, squeals from kids chasing a dog on the lawn, the Lovin' Spoonful rocking from the clubhouse speakers, the whine of powerboats peeling past. Smells of hot dogs and diesel exhaust and suntan lotion. A clown in garish orange-and-purple polka dots, and out on the water, bright spinnakers billowing on the sailboats.

She checked her watch. Ten after eight! She was supposed to be on set downtown in fifty minutes. She jumped up. "Nick, I've got to go. I'll be late for work if I don't." But she couldn't leave him like this—she'd just *found* him. Uncertain, she asked, "Want to . . . come along?"

He scrambled to his feet, looking eager. "Sure."

In awkward silence they went back to her dinghy for the last of her gear. Through her tangle of feelings, Alana remembered that she had to move the dinghy for Waldo. She told Nick, and he hopped in. She started the motor and zipped around to C dock, where she found a space to tie up between two finger docks.

He asked, "So, uh . . . you live on that sailboat?"

She nodded as she tied the bowline to the dock cleat. "Been buying her in installments. Next month I'll own her, then I'm sailing to Florida."

"What'll you do in Florida?"

"Live aboard. Work from there. I'm a stunt performer in films."

"No shi—" He caught himself, blushing, and Alana almost laughed. His fascination about her seemed to blaze even brighter, and the next words burst from him as though they'd been pent up all his life. "Take me with you?"

It caught her like a trip wire. His raw plea came from a place she knew too well: the loneliness of an outcast, a misfit. It made her want to hold him. At the same time his strength of will threw her. She was astonished at how quickly he'd absorbed the shocking news, accepting the fact of the gene so much more easily than she had. For days she'd been stewing over how to break it to him, make sure he understood, guide him so that he could cope. But he seemed to be coping already. His mind moved like quicksilver.

"Nick, you've got to go home. You're just thirteen, and your parents are worried sick. And there's no question about the law on this: you belong with the Morgans."

"They're not my parents. That's not my home."

Emotions knotted up in her, all unfamiliar: protectiveness; worry for a child. "No? What is? Just where *are* you living?"

His eyes shifted off her for the first time. He looked at the water. "I get by."

"Picking pockets? Shoplifting? That's no way to live."

He looked startled that she knew. Then his mouth twitched in a smile. "Look who's talking. You were the slip-and-fall expert at—what?—age eleven?"

It took her breath away. He knew her life! The slip-and-fall, an insurance scam, was where she'd first honed her stunt skills, though she didn't know that at the time. She and her father had been a team. They'd go into a supermarket where she'd find some wet patch on the floor and go into her routine: slip, fly up in the air, and land on her back with a scream. Her father made a big terrified fuss, and when the ambulance took her to the hospital, her job was to pretend agony during the doctor's examination while her father dealt with the insurance adjuster, claiming that a lawyer wanted to sign him up. The adjuster usually advised him not to, and made him an offer. Rajko considered twenty-five hundred a good haul.

"My father was the brains behind that," she said.

"Rajko," Nick said, marveling. "Is he still alive?"

"So I hear. Haven't seen him for thirteen years."

"Jesus. He's my grandfather!" His eyes took on a new glow, almost feverish. "You're . . . my family."

It set her back. The word *family* had once meant everything—security, affection, blood bonds—but she'd been alone for so long. She said uneasily, "Yes."

"I'm a *gypsy.*"

"Half gypsy. Your father . . . wasn't."

He gaped. "Oh, man . . . that dropout loser who got you drunk? You didn't even know his name!"

A blush burned Alana's cheeks. Nick's face, too, reddened in splotches. He knew all the intimate details!

An embarrassed laugh sputtered out of her. Nick coughed a laugh as well. In a moment, they were both grinning. Alana said, "This is the damnedest mother-son relationship in the history of the world."

His feverish look intensified. "Nobody's like us. *Nobody.* That's why you've got to let me stay with you—go to Florida with you. Hey, you could teach me to do stunts! I'd be good at it. We could be a team!"

A chill flew up her spine. She hadn't searched for him with the idea of suddenly becoming a parent. She wasn't cut out for it; it didn't fit in with how she lived. She'd meant only to unlock his mental dungeon, nothing more. But here he was, wanting more, wanting a whole new life with her—and a part of her gloried at that. *Family.*

But she had no legal claim to him. In fact, they might have only this brief time together. It seemed achingly inadequate.

"Nick, we have to think responsibly. Not only about you going home. But about your future, because of the gene, and what it means. The consequences if—" She didn't know how to go on. She no longer accepted Dr. Knelman's ominous prediction, but he had made it the crux of his appeal, and she'd promised him that she would impress it on her son and bring him in for counseling. "Look, I told you about Dr. Knelman. He said there could be a danger if this gene reproduces. I mean . . . if either of *us* reproduces. So—" She broke off, looked away. How did you talk about this to a thirteen-year-old? To the son you've just met? Except, with all that Nick knew, he was more adult than child. A man in the making. She decided to plow on. "I don't exactly buy Dr. Knelman's theory, but I think you should know how seriously he takes it. He seems to think that, given enough generations, the gene could create a shift in society—that enough people born with knowledge could start controlling people *without* knowledge. He said it's like a new branch of evolution."

"Well, evolution's all about survival of the fittest, isn't it? Looks like that's us."

She felt at a loss. How could she push this when she had no intention herself of getting sterilized as Dr. Knelman had urged? When she thought of David, the last thing she wanted was to cut out the life-giving part of herself. No, if Dr. Knelman wanted to make his case to Nick, he'd just have to do it himself.

"Look, we can't sit here talking," she said, her mind churning. "I've got to get to work." Finish today's job, she told herself, then sit down with Nick and persuade him about the counseling. She climbed out of the dinghy. He did too. In strained silence, they unloaded her gear bags onto the dock.

Maybe it was her professional edge, a heightened instinct of observation—she sensed something wrong. A maroon Corvair was coming across the parking lot toward them, fast. Sun glared off the windshield, making the driver invisible. A blast from the regatta start gun made both her and Nick turn to look at the water, and at the same moment something whizzed past her ear. She didn't grasp what the *whish* was, but as she turned back she saw the Corvair stop and caught the glint of metal in a hand at the open window. Her mind stalled: a gun? Had a bullet missed her as she'd turned? It made no sense, but on instinct she pushed Nick, tumbling him backward into the dinghy's bow as another *whish* whistled past. She somersaulted over the gunnel into the stern.

"What the hell . . . ?" Nick gasped, struggling up off his back.

She scrambled onto her knees beside him, keeping low in the dinghy. "Stay down! Somebody's shooting at us!"

Her own words sounded idiotic to her. Movie talk. All around them the cheerful regatta clamor carried on. She raised her head enough to look across the dock. The Corvair had raced in a half-circle around the perimeter of the lot and was turning back, spitting gravel, heading for them again. *It's true . . . he's after us.* Fear shot through her. The driver would only have to get out and cross the dock to pick them off as they cringed down here in the dinghy.

She grabbed the pull cord to start the motor, about to tell Nick to cast off, when she saw that the narrow way out between the finger docks was blocked by a fleet of little kids' Optimist sailboats jostling into position for a race. To force her way through the kids, she'd have to go so slowly the gunman would have a clear shot right from his car. Or he might hit a child.

Only one option. Run.

"Get out!" she told Nick. They clambered onto the dock, but Alana knew they couldn't reach her Fiat. The Corvair, bearing down, was between them and her car. "Follow me!"

Bolting away from the lot, she ran for the marina's yard, where house-sized boats sat on steel cradles jammed too close for the Corvair to quickly get through. Alana zigzagged around them, glancing back to make sure Nick was keeping up. He was right behind her. But in the distance, between cradles, she spotted a man chasing them on foot. Black face, khaki clothes, a fast runner. A gun in his hand.

"Shit," Nick said, glancing back too. "A brother."

"Why the hell is he after us?"

"Not us. Me. Payback time."

With a sting of anger—what had Nick got them into?—she picked up her pace, hoping he could match it. She climbed a low chain-link fence to the adjacent boatyard, and he climbed it beside her. He was scrambling over the top as Alana jumped down on the other side. Helping him as he landed, she couldn't see the gunman among the cradles, but she heard his feet crunching fast over the gravel.

"Just through this yard," she told Nick, both of them breathing hard as they ran on. "It comes out at a chandlery on the main street." She'd brought her torn headsail to the chandlery loft last week with David, and she knew it had a side door. She hoped the shop would be full of customers. That would stop this guy.

They burst into the chandlery and found it empty. A white cat on a window seat stretched, yawning. Catching their breath, they went down the sawdust-smelling aisle, the high shelves crammed with nautical fittings. Alana saw the Open sign flipped around on the front door, and realized that the Nugents must have closed temporarily to check out the regatta. The gunman came through the side door and stopped. Alana and Nick froze. Between hanging brass lanterns she could see the man's pockmarked face. He turned and saw them. They dashed for the nearest door. It led to the sail loft. Barging in, Alana saw that it too was empty. A huge rumpled mainsail lay on the floor in the corner.

Snatching Nick's hand, she pulled him to the shallow pit in the floor where the sewing machine was recessed. The small platform with the machine and operator's chair had been left at its lowest position, leaving the top of the machine beneath floor level. "Get in," she whispered.

Doubt flashed in his eyes.

"Trust me," she said.

He hopped into the hole. He was small enough, thank God. "Don't move," she whispered. Taking hold of a corner of the rumpled sail, she ran with it, spreading it, covering him in the pit. The fabric was still settling as she sprinted for the rear door. She pushed the door wide open, leaving it that way to make it look as though she and Nick had escaped into the alley. Turning back, she dove to the floor, sliding along on her stomach into a cluster of upright bolts of sailcloth ranged like soldiers. She froze as the black man burst into the loft.

He stopped, looking around, breathing hard, gun in hand. Watching him from a crack between the bolts, Alana lay unmoving in the silence. She was afraid he must hear her hammering heart. Faint cheering washed up from the waterfront. Her eyes snapped to the center of the floor where Nick was hidden. Would the gunman know there was a pit? She prayed he wasn't a sailor.

He moved forward slowly, unconsciously walking over the sail, weapon raised, carefully looking around.

Jubilant, Alana saw that it was working: he had no idea.

And his eyes had been drawn to the open rear door. Then, sickened, she saw that the trick no longer mattered, because by sheer chance he was walking straight for the covered hole.

Two more steps, and he'd find Nick.

She had to draw the gumnan after her. With a hard shove she pushed the nearest upright bolt sideways, toppling it so that it knocked down the ones next to it like bowling pins. In the noisy clatter she scrambled to her feet and sprinted out the door to the alley.

She heard the man pounding after her as she veered onto the main street, hoping he hadn't yet noticed that Nick wasn't with her. Nick was his target; she had to lure this man away.

She slowed on the main street bustling with weekend visitors on foot and in cars. The little downtown hadn't grown much beyond its eighteenth-century layout, and traffic was moving at a crawl. She fell in among the throng on the sidewalk, looking for a police officer, planning to act the tourist and ask the cop directions—then the gunman wouldn't dare come after her. Anyway, he'd probably seen by now that he'd lost Nick, so maybe he'd give up. She could only hope he wouldn't race back to the loft—or, if he did, that Nick would have gotten out by now. Looking over her shoulder, she spotted the black face. Although he'd slowed in the crowd, he was definitely following her, looking grimly resolute. But why, if he was after Nick? Did he mean to eliminate her as a witness? She thought with a stab of fear how the crowd hid him, made him anonymous. Was she going to get a bullet in the back? Tensing, she dashed across the street, darting between cars. She had to do something to lose him. Her fear sparked an idea. She wasn't far from the bridge.

She glanced over her shoulder. The black man was dodging through the bumper-to-bumper vehicles, eyes on her, following. Alana sprinted for the end of town.

It took five minutes of hard running to reach the bridge. Her idea wasn't to get across it; he'd only keep on after her. But he couldn't follow her below, into Long Island Sound. Reaching the center of the bridge, breaths sawing her throat, she stopped. A wire mesh safety fence rose on both sides. She grappled her way to the top. The little three-lane bridge wasn't all that high off the water, and she knew the water wasn't all that deep, so she'd have to be careful not to break her neck hitting the bottom. She balanced on the top railing, then dove off.

When she hit the water, it felt like ice. Instantly breaking the surface again, gasping at the cold, she looked up over her shoulder. At the end of the bridge, where the safety fence began, the black man was leaning over the rail, arm outstretched. She saw his gun glint in the sunlight. She dove . . . a second too late. Searing pain stung her right bicep. The heat of a bullet.

The Fiat convertible wasn't hard to find. "Pretty yellow car," the maid had said yesterday on the phone. Nick's heart danced when he saw the open trunk with Alana's keys dangling in the lock. As he'd beat it out of the sail loft his plan had been to hot-wire the ignition. No need, he saw now. She'd been loading her gear here when he'd confronted her at the dinghy, and in her surprise she'd left the keys.

He got behind the wheel and saw that she'd left an open knapsack on the passenger seat. He could see a wallet in it, the edges of a few bills showing. He thought how easily he could take off, lose this black guy, hole up somewhere with the cash. This morning he would have done it without a second thought.

Not now. This was his *mother*. It still made him a bit light-headed.

Keeping his eyes peeled for the black man, he started the car and shifted into first gear. Nobody'd taught him how to drive, he just knew—because of her, he suddenly realized. As he tore out of the lot, shifting gears, tires kicking up gravel, he thought with grim glee: Beats the fucking bus. But almost immediately he had to slow in the traffic on the main street. "Shit!" How was he going to find her in this crowd? Day-trippers were rubbernecking from their crawling cars, and the ones strolling on the sidewalk gawked at store windows, licking ice cream cones, shuffling like cattle. He could have killed them. Hadn't anybody noticed a gunman on the loose?

It scared him. Was he too late? Had the guy got her?

There she was! Stepping into a bakery! Looked like her from the back, anyway—jeans, denim shirt, short dark hair—but as he drove near, he glimpsed the big-nosed face, and his heart sank. Not Alana.

He reached the intersection as the light went red, and he hit the brake. He bounced his knee in impatience, drummed his fingers on the steering wheel. Where the hell was he supposed to look, anyway? He didn't know this stupid island. He flipped open the glove compartment. Any maps? He fingered the junk inside—car manual, Kit Kat candy bar, flashlight, maps—then slammed it shut with a prick of panic at the stupid thought. What good was a map? Then, through a break between the shops, he saw the bridge. His breath stopped. The gunman stood near the end of the bridge, leaning over, his arm pointing down. Jesus Christ. *No!*

* * *

Knelman made himself chew another bite of spinach frittata. The lunch Esther had made for the two of them was delicious, but his mouth felt too dry to swallow. Yet he had to appear normal.

"Don't you like the potatoes?"

"Very good." He took a forkful. "New recipe?"

She looked pleased. "Howard's favorite. The dill was a secret of his mother's, he says."

The Chopin record ended. They ate in silence. Esther's fork clicked on the china plate.

She asked, "Will you go to the Remys' on Wednesday? Charles is showing some new oils, I hear. His trip to Sienna."

Knelman shook his head. "Hospital board meeting."

Esther absently fingered the silver salt shaker, a frown tugging her brow. "I asked David to come for lunch, you know. He said he was busy. Again. Did you two have some kind of quarrel?"

"Really, Esther, every disagreement is not a family crisis."

"I hope it wasn't over Alana. You won't budge David, you know. Anyway, I don't know why you're against the girl."

"Have I said so?"

"Oh, not in words. But I'm beginning to suspect some prejudice in you, Henry. About her gypsy—"

"It has nothing to do with that. David's conduct is inappropriate. She is a patient."

"What difference should that make?"

"Esther, I will not discuss this!"

The phone rang. He flinched. Farrell? *Was it done?* He started to his feet.

"Stay, stay, I'll get it," Esther said in exasperation, dabbing her mouth with her napkin as she got up. "My, you're jumpy today. You've been whistling all morning."

"But . . . it's likely for me."

She was closer to the kitchen door and was already on her way. She disappeared into the kitchen.

Knelman wiped his damp palms with his napkin. He was sick with tension as the moments dragged on. When she finally came back, he asked, almost in dread, "For me?"

"No."

He felt both dismay and relief. When would this purgatory be over?

"Well . . . that's that," Esther said. He saw that something was very wrong. The blood seemed to have drained from her face. She began clearing his plate and her own.

"Esther? Who was it?"

She stood still, plates in her hands, looking lost. "Howard. He had a heart attack after the gala. Taken to Roosevelt Hospital. He's coming home in a day or two, but . . . it's over between us, he said. Not right to go on, he said. Not fair to me." She was fighting tears. "Oh, Henry, what shall I do?"

Alana lay on her back, dizzy, soaking wet. She'd hauled herself up onto a private dock past the bridge. The sun-baked wood against her back was hot, but her teeth were chattering. She knew the symptoms of mild shock: dizziness, shivering, low blood pressure. But was she hallucinating as well? Her Fiat pulling up . . . Nick getting out . . .

He ran to her—not a hallucination. "Christ, he got you!" He dropped to his knees beside her, looking scared.

Alana saw that her ripped sleeve was bright pink with water-bleached blood. She remembered the fierce sting of the bullet, then a fog of frantic underwater swimming. She'd surely been carried along more by the current than by her erratic strokes. "No, I'm okay," she assured him. "It just tore off some skin." She struggled to her feet, looking around. A green boathouse, a lawn with flower beds, a big white clapboard house. No one on the dock but her and Nick. "Has he gone?"

"You bet. I saw him on the bridge, aiming at you, then a truck came by him real slow, hauling a big powerboat on a trailer, with a cop escort behind. He walked away looking pissed as hell, disappeared into that crowd on the main street. Still, I say we should beat it. Can you make it to the car?"

Her legs were unsteady. Nick opened the passenger door for her and pushed her knapsack to the floor, and she thudded down on the seat, still dizzy. He slipped behind the wheel, pulled out, and drove toward Bridge Street.

She gaped at him. "What are you doing?"

He shifted into third gear. "Getting off this island, for starters. Go get ourselves lost in the Bronx."

"But . . . you can't drive. You're thirteen!"

"Pretty good at it, though, huh? Your cousin Walter taught you when you were fourteen, remember?" He grinned at her. "I do. That's why I know how."

It knocked her back. So did his attitude, almost cheerful, as though this was some kind of adventure. Or a thrilling stunt gag, and they were a hot new team. But it was horrible to Alana. Somebody had tried to kill them. Her throbbing arm was proof.

They crossed the bridge. Nobody on it. Once off the island she closed her eyes, dizzy again.

Leaning over, Nick opened the glove compartment, pulled out the Kit Kat bar, and handed it to her. "Better eat something. You don't look so hot." When she hesitated, he gave her a sly look and said, "*Te den, xa. Te maren, de-dash!* Did I get that right?"

Despite her rockiness, she had to smile at the Romany saying. *When you're given, eat. When you're beaten, run away!* Their eyes met. "Too right. Turn left here."

"Aye, aye, Captain."

She ate half the chocolate bar as he drove on, and almost immediately she felt the shot of energy. "Follow the signs to Orchard Beach," she said. "Pull into the first gas station so I can change. I've got clothes in the back. Then *I'll* drive. We'll head into Westchester."

"That where your job is?"

Oh, God, she was supposed to be in Manhattan right now, prepping to rappel down the Flatiron Building! With a groan, she shook her head. "That's out." She wouldn't have full use of her right arm. "I'll call in, tell them I've had an accident."

"Okay. Man, that was a bitchin' trick you did back there with the sail. Outta sight." He grinned. "Literally!" He shifted into fourth. "And, hey, if we lay low for a while, then sail your boat to Florida, we'd be *gone*."

Again, he stunned her. "Nick, I've got to take you back to your parents. And first, as soon as we stop, I'm calling the police."

"Uh . . . that's not a good idea."

"That man tried to *kill* us. We have to report it."

"No. We don't."

She glared at him. "What the hell is this about? Why was he after you?"

"Hey, here we are. You can get changed." He was pulling into a burger joint. "Go on in, you're soaked."

Taking her gym bag from the trunk, she went to the washroom and peeled off her wet things. The gash on her upper arm was ugly, but not deep. She washed it but had nothing to use as a bandage; the wound would have to wait. What couldn't wait was dragging an explanation out of Nick. What kind of trouble was he in? She wondered which she felt more—anger or dread. She dashed fresh water over herself to get some of the salt off then put on the spare clothes that had been balled in her gym bag for weeks. Fresh panties, a pair of white cutoffs, kind of ragged but clean, and a wrinkled yellow cotton shirt, though no spare bra. No spare shoes, either; her wet sneakers would have to stay. At the pay phone in the hall she called the production office, told the secretary that she'd had a minor accident and asked her to contact Ian Turnbull, the stunt coordinator, to reschedule. It galled her—*never* had she missed a day of work. The production people would be furious, but they had cancellation insurance to cover things like this. They'd ride it out. She only hoped her reputation could.

The moment she got back to the car, she pulled open the driver's door. "Get out."

Looking surprised, Nick obeyed.

She stuck out her hand, palm flat. "Keys."

He handed them over.

"Now, explain to me, just why aren't we calling the police?"

"I already told you. I'm not going home, and the cops would make me. Hell, they'd *deliver* me. If you don't want me with you, fine. But no going home. I can't hack it there." He fixed her with a look that seemed part challenge, part plea. "You know why. You're the only one who does."

Alana resisted the guilt trip. "Bull. A man tried to murder us. He may try again. If you won't go to the police, it's because you're worried about something bigger than being taken back to your parents."

"They're *not* my parents! I'll never know my father's name, and I just found out you're my mother, for God's sake. Oh, and also that I'm a freak with a gene that could change the world. It's been a heavy day. What do you *want* from me?"

"Not the whine of a ten-year-old. You can do better, Nick."

His angry face was like stone. Then it cracked in a grin. "Got me."

It gave her a chill. "Like you said, we've just met, and you know what? So far I'm not too thrilled with the acquaintance. It's got me shot and almost drowned. I intend to stay alive, and to see that you do too, but I can't do that if you keep me in the dark. So either you tell me who that man was, or I'm going back inside to call the cops. You've got thirty seconds."

He looked scared. "Okay, okay." He seemed to be gauging her. "I got mixed up with the wrong guys. We cracked a few heads. The cops have to be after us. That's the deal."

"What guys? *Whose* heads?"

"Doesn't matter. I'm through with those losers."

She turned to go inside.

"Okay!" he said. She stopped. He took a deep breath as though to steel himself. "The leader calls the gang White Pride. He's into Nazi cult crap, a real head case. I joined for cover, just to disappear, because I knew my folks had the cops out looking for me. Only, then I found I had to . . . do the shit the gang did."

Alana was appalled. "White Pride?"

He looked at her with an odd smile in his eyes. "I knew the drill, see? From Lina. Staying alive among Nazis. It came in handy." His face sobered. "Then, a few days ago, for my initiation, we jumped three black kids. Not gang boys, just dumb jerks, nobodies. We left them messed up pretty bad. I think a few of the guys crippled one of them."

Alana leaned back against the car, stunned. "My God."

"Anyway, this black dude with the gun? I figure he's family. I mean, of one of the kids."

"And he's come after you . . . for revenge."

Nick nodded, kicking at the dirt. "Payback."

Avoiding her face, fists jammed in his pockets, he seemed to Alana for the first time like a mixed-up thirteen-year-old. *But he's committed an assault, hurt innocent kids.* An ache swelled in her breast. She'd abandoned him at his birth, left him prey to the awful visions, prey to Lina's poison. Guilt tore at her: *Would he have done this if I'd been there for him?* Shaped by the gene, he'd become a loner, a misfit, living by his wits, manipulating the people who loved him but didn't have a clue about his true nature. It struck her that she'd lived much the same way. Looking out for herself from such an early age, focusing on her work with near obsession—that had made her strong, ultracompetent, but it had also meant a life with no room for anyone else. Now, there was Nick. A bewildered boy pushed to the dark side, as shrewd as Lina, and aware beyond his years. Was he dangerous? He could be. But all his troubles were because of the gene . . . and because she'd deserted him. She suddenly, desperately, wished she could reverse that act of thirteen years ago. She longed to help him.

He was watching her with a new frown of concern. "Just grazed you, huh?" He nodded at her arm. "It's still bleeding."

She glanced at her sleeve and was startled at the amount of blood. And, now that she focused on it, the pain was worse.

"I should take you to a hospital," he said.

"No. I think they have to report gunshot wounds to the police. Risky for you."

He asked hesitantly, hopefully, "So . . . we're sticking together?"

It struck her that nobody had ever put Nick's needs first. She hadn't wanted him, and the Morgans had wanted a child who was normal. Well, he's my priority now, she thought. A first for us both. It made her uneasy . . . yet strangely happy. "You bet," she answered.

A smile broke from him.

"But you're right," she added, "I do need a doctor."

The intercom buzzed.

It startled Knelman. He'd been trying to comfort Esther, his arm around her on the sofa as she sobbed. It hurt him to see her so disconsolate, and yet, that she would stay with him, not marry Jaffe, brought a warm relief.

Another buzz . . .

He stiffened, remembering the call he was awaiting from Farrell. He went to the kitchen intercom. "Yes?"

"Dr. Knelman? It's Bill, downstairs. There's a woman asking to see you. A Miss Marks—and a boy with her. Should I send them up?"

CHAPTER 10

ALANA STOOD AT the open door, her good arm around Nick's shoulders. "Dr. Knelman, this is my son, Nick. We need your help."

He stood rigid, a shocked expression on his face. No wonder, she thought. Though he'd told her she could contact him at his home or office, day or night, he could hardly have expected this. "I'm sorry to barge in on you, but I hoped you'd understand."

He seemed to pull himself together. "Come in . . . come in."

It was only when they stepped in that she saw Esther, looking astonished. Alana died a little inside, knowing that her arrival out of the blue wasn't the main thing that was shocking David's aunt. Esther plainly hadn't known about Nick. "Hello, Miss Knelman," she managed.

"My dear . . . ," Esther murmured, at a loss.

Alana was aware of the marble foyer, the spacious living room and grand piano, the apartment's elegance, as she stood there in her ragged cutoffs and wet, spongy sneakers. Also, to hide her bloodstained sleeve from the doorman, she'd thrown on the ancient lime mohair shawl, blotched with oil from her car trunk. She felt like a tramp.

Esther found her manners. "Do, please, come in." She led them into the living room. Silence. No one sat.

The phone rang. As Esther went to the kitchen Knelman asked Alana in a tense whisper, "What has happened?"

She slipped the shawl off her shoulder. Knelman flinched at the bloodstain. "Dr. Knelman, Nick and I need to talk to you in private."

"Henry, it's for you." As Esther returned, Alana quickly covered her arm again. "I told him you were busy but he said it was urgent. Wouldn't give his name."

Knelman's eyes flicked between Alana and Nick. "Please, go into my study. We can discuss it there. I'll take this call and be with you in a moment. Esther, will you show them the way?"

They followed Esther down a hall lined with watercolors and etchings, all a blur to Alana as she squelched along in her shoes, clutching the shawl. As Esther led them into a cozy book-lined room, the first thing Alana noticed was the silver-framed photographs on the desk: David at five or so, hand in hand with Esther on the steps of the Lincoln Memorial in Washington; David skiing as a lanky teen; David graduating in cap and gown, his grin lit by a warmth that sent a pang through her. He'd done all he could to unite her with her son. How could she break it to him that Nick had been involved in an assault? How did she dare? David was the law.

"Please, make yourselves comfortable," Esther said, looking flustered. "I'll go and put on some coffee for . . . for when you're finished with Henry."

Alana noticed the puffy, reddened eyes. "Miss Knelman, are you all right?"

Esther gave her a stricken look. "I've just heard some bad news about a friend. Heart attack."

"Oh, no. Not Howard?"

Esther nodded.

"Will he be all right?"

"Yes, but—" Words rushed from her. "He said we can't go on. Says he doesn't want to tie me down to nurse a sick old man. But he's all alone, and I only want—" She broke off, covering her mouth with her hand. "I'm sorry." She quickly left the room.

"What's *her* problem?" Nick asked. He'd picked up a crystal paperweight from the desk and was turning it as if appraising its value.

"Howard Jaffe. Retired millionaire. She was planning to marry him."

He snorted. "A little old for marriage, isn't she?"

Alana winced. How could he be so insensitive? But it was a sharp reminder of why she'd brought him here. The gene had sent his life onto a bad track; she had to guide him in a new direction. She took the paperweight from him. "Sit down." He shrugged and flopped down in a leather easy chair.

"Nick, I didn't come here just about my arm. We've got to think about your future. I want you to know I'm going to forget about moving to Florida, so I can be here for you from now on, help you until you can legally be on your own. You can come to me anytime, with any problem. But you've got to understand one thing right now. You can't stay on the run. The only way to deal with the trouble you're in is for me to take you home, and together we'll face the police."

"But they—"

"Don't worry, I think we can get them to go easy on you. That's why we've come to Dr. Knelman. I think he might be able to get you off if he tells a judge that he's supervising you, counseling you."

The idea clearly gripped him, but his mind seemed to start computing. "Why would he go to bat for me?"

"Because he understands you—what's special about you. I'm not sure I get what makes him so nervous about the gene, but he takes it very seriously, and that's why I think he'll help. The point is, he has the professional muscle to be your advocate."

"Sounds okay. All except the part about me going home."

"There's no other way."

He cocked his head with a sly look. "Yet."

"No, Nick, that's the deal. Home to stay. Otherwise you're going to find yourself in juvenile detention. And an institution like that would be as hard for you as for—" She didn't finish.

"As for Lina?"

She'd stopped short of invoking that image. Lina had fought with every weapon, however vicious, to stay alive, and her ferocity seemed to vibrate some string in Nick. Alana didn't want to dwell on that.

Knelman came in and shut the door. He'd brought a small first-aid kit, the kind for home use. Opening it on the desk, he said, "Show me the wound. We can go to my clinic if it requires sutures." As Alana sat down in the desk chair and rolled up her sleeve, he asked her quietly, with his back to Nick, "Does he know? About the gene?"

Nick piped up, "The whole deal, Doctor. Pretty freaky, huh? I'm still getting used to the idea, but it's sure made a lot of things come clear, real fast. I gotta tell you, I like it. Knowing stuff."

Alana thought Knelman looked as strung out as she was herself. But he turned his attention to the wound, pulling a chair toward her and sitting down. "The laceration is somewhat ragged, but sutures won't be necessary."

She watched as he wetted a gauze swab with hydrogen peroxide. He hadn't asked her how it had happened, and she was wondering how best to explain it so that she could ask him to help Nick. He swabbed the wound and began rolling a gauze bandage around her arm, and in the strained silence, waiting for him to finish, she said, "I'm sorry about your sister's troubles. With Howard."

He looked at her oddly. "You know Mr. Jaffe?"

"No. David told me."

His face seemed to harden at this sign of her closeness with David, and she died a little more inside; it was so obvious he didn't approve. Could she blame him? She was hardly the ideal woman he'd want for his only son.

He tied off the bandage. "Miss Marks, would you like to tell me now what happened? If I am not mistaken, this is a gunshot wound."

She rolled down her sleeve. "At the marina a man shot at me."

"How appalling. Have you told the police?"

"Not yet. Before that, we need your support."

"I don't understand."

Alana turned to Nick. He sat in the armchair, eyeing Dr. Knelman, legs stretched out, while he toyed with a pen, slipping it over his knuckles like a magician. "Nick has something to tell you. Go ahead, Nick."

"Ground rules first, Dr. Knelman—no offense. My mother thinks you can get me out of a jam I'm in by telling the cops I'm screwy. Is that true?"

Knelman's face went pale. "What kind of trouble are you in?"

Nick hesitated. Alana said, "Tell him."

He shrugged, as though ready to take the plunge. "I got mixed up with a gang called White Pride. A few days ago we beat up some black kids pretty bad. Well, *real* bad. Anyway, the guy who came after us today was black, so I figure he's some relation, out for revenge. Real son of a bitch, if you ask me, taking it out on my mother like—"

"Wait, please." Knelman held up his hand, an expression like pain on his face. He reached for a notebook and a pen. "Go on. This . . . assault. Tell me everything. You said, White Pride?"

"Yeah. Leader's a bastard named Nardi. He's got this collection of Nazi crap—guns and flags and photos of dead Jews. He trades the stuff. Sick, if you ask me. I hung out at his ratty little bar in Bensonhurst for a while, the Tre Stelle." He gave a quick recap of his two weeks on the street before turning to the gang for cover.

Alana noticed how rigid Dr. Knelman's face had gone as he took notes of everything Nick said. It bothered her. He's afraid it's the gene at work, she thought. But why does it scare him so much? Nick needs help, sure, but he's not a lost cause.

"Dr. Knelman, what Nick did was terrible. But we both know how he got so easily led astray. If this is anybody's fault, it's mine, for abandoning him when he was born. I intend to protect him from his mistake now, if I can. Reform school would blight his life forever. You said you wanted to counsel him, and that's exactly what we want too—and, well, your taking him on as a patient might keep him out of detention."

Knelman laid down his pen. He looked shaken. "I see. Yes, the authorities can be quite open to such arrangements."

"Then you'll help us?"

"Of course. Nick, I do understand. You have borne oppressive knowledge, and done so without guidance. My only wish is to set this tragic situation to rights."

"No sweat, Doctor. Sure, it's screwed me up a bit, but finding my mother today, that changed everything. And she says she's going to be there for me from now on. Feels pretty good. So, if you can smooth things over with the cops, I guess you're my new shrink and I'm your guinea pig."

Alana felt a tug of happiness. Almost pride.

"Then it's settled," Knelman said. "Now, I suggest that the urgent priority is your safety, both of you. This gunman might still find you. Clearly you are not safe on your boat, Miss Marks. Will you allow me to arrange for you both to stay at a hotel? As my guests, of course."

Alana and Nick exchanged a look. This was unexpected.

"Meanwhile," Knelman went on, "I shall arrange a meeting with the police."

Alana gratefully agreed.

"I'll call the St. Moritz on Central Park. Will that do?"

"Great," Nick said, getting up. "Room service."

Alana and Knelman stood too. "Thank you, Doctor. I owe you."

"Not at all," he said, opening the phone book on the desk. "I'll make the reservation immediately."

Leaving him as he dialed, Alana and Nick started down the hall. When they reached the living room, she realized she'd left her shawl. She couldn't check into a fancy hotel with this dried blood all over her sleeve. Going back to the study, moving behind Dr. Knelman, she heard him softly whistling as he waited on the phone. Seemed odd in such a tense situation. Must be a nervous habit of his, she thought as she picked up her shawl. The tune was pretty, but it gave her a faintly unpleasant feeling . . . almost fearful. She recalled the German words:

Du, du liegst mir in Hertzen,
Du, du liegst mir im Sinn . . .

Silly song, really. *"You're in my heart, you're in my mind . . ."* But it wasn't the meaning that gripped her. It was a memory that seemed to hover just out of reach.

Knelman noticed her and stopped whistling. "Thank you," he said flatly into the receiver, and hung up. Their eyes locked. "It's all arranged," he said.

The eleventh-floor room was a suite. Sunny yellow drawing room with bar, two plushly carpeted bedrooms, shared gleaming bath. Alana went straight to the phone at the bar and checked her service for messages. Nick popped open a bottle of Dr Pepper, drained half in a long gulp, and flopped onto a chintz sofa, knocking a cushion to the floor. "This is the life," he said, kicking off his sneakers.

Alana hung up. Another message from David, asking her to call. She wanted to, but not now, not until things had settled down with Nick. There was also an irate message from Ian Turnbull about her no-show at the American Express shoot. Him she'd call later too, when he'd calmed down. She went to the window and looked down at the greenery of Central Park, hugging herself in the air conditioning. Her gaze fell on an officer on horseback, and she flashed on Dr. Kleist, who'd ridden every morning at Otzenhausen. The tune Dr. Knelman had been whistling crept into her head again, along with that vague anxiety she could put no name to.

She shook it off. There were enough real problems.

"That boat of yours," Nick said. "Bet you could take off on it, and nobody'd find you, huh?"

She shot him a look. "Don't get any ideas."

He said in a different tone, no more smart mouth, "Would you teach me to sail?"

The look on his face was new. Eager as a child. It touched her. "Sure. We'll have you racing in a few weeks if you're a quick study."

"You kidding? If you'd learned younger, I'd be a *commodore* by now."

"If you could reach the wheel."

They both laughed.

Nick said, "This is so amazing, huh? You know how people say, 'I feel like I've known you all my life'? The thing is . . . I have."

She nodded. "Very weird. But kind of wonderful. Hey, let's go eat. I'm starved. What do you like best? Italian? Chinese?"

"Burger and fries."

"Me too."

"I know."

They grinned again. "First," Alana said, looking down at her ragged cutoffs and bloodstained sleeve, "I've got to get something decent to wear. I saw a shop in the lobby." She grabbed her knapsack and the shawl. "Back in a bit."

The shop was so ritzy she felt like a hobo. The saleswoman's sneering glance didn't help. Looking through the merchandise, Alana figured the clientele fell into two groups: rich idle wives and high-class call girls. Sequined cocktail dresses. Pearl-buttoned cashmere cardigans. Chiffon peignoir sets. Even the jeans had bell-bottoms with panels of brocade. She finally found a plain white cotton button-down shirt and tried it on. A little tight, but okay. She came out of the change booth wearing it. "I'll take this," she told the saleswoman, whose eyes were following her as if she expected her to steal it. Putting enough cash on the counter to placate the woman, Alana turned to a rack of skirts and slacks. She was holding up a mauve suede skirt, staggered at the price, when she saw, through the glass wall to the lobby, the back of a man stepping into the elevator—a black man all in khaki. He was carrying a paper lunch bag. Her heart crammed up in her throat.

"That's not your size," the saleswoman sniffed, reaching for the skirt.

"Keep it." She dropped it over the woman's arm and hurried out.

From a house phone in the lobby she called up to the room. Her skin went clammy as the phone rang . . . rang. *Answer it, Nick.* Her eyes fixed on the elevator's lighted Up sign. The light went off at her floor. *Damn it, pick up the—*

"Yeah?"

"Nick, get out. That hood's on his way. Take the stairs. Meet me in the garage. Go *now!*"

She waited in the car in the underground garage, beside the door to the stairs. Her hands were fists around the steering wheel, and her heart was thudding. Had Nick got out or not? The Fiat's idling engine made a muffled roar in the cavernous space. When Nick burst through, she gasped in relief.

He climbed in, panting. "Nice work. Mom."

Dread knotted her stomach as she drove out of the garage. "How could that guy have known where we were?"

"Must've followed us from the Island to Knelman's. Then followed when we left."

She shook her head. "Doesn't add up. If he's been on our tail since the Island, why not come at us sooner? We stopped at that burger joint for me to change, stood around talking outside, remember? If he had us in his sights then, why wait?" So *much* of this didn't add up. "A relative of one of those kids—Nick, do you really think he'd come after you like that, just him alone? And why was he so bent on wasting *me*? It doesn't fit."

He shrugged. "Like I said, a mean son of a bitch."

She was driving down Seventh Avenue, not knowing where to go. Gus's apartment was in the East Village, and she felt sure he'd take them in, but would they be safe even there? Were they being followed right now? Stopping at a red light, she heard a Pepsodent jingle blaring from the radio of a taxi beside them. The tune Dr. Knelman had whistled came surging back. Why couldn't she get that German song out of her head? He'd warned her that her memory would be as spotty as anybody else's, but the anxiety that tune brought felt so real, she had to pin it down. "Nick, listen to this." She sang the beginning:

Du, du liegst mir in Hertzen,
Du, du liegst mir Sinn . . .

She turned to him. "Know the rest?"

He gave her a puzzled look. "Yeah." He sang:

Du, du machst mir viel Schmertzen,
Weisst nicht wie gut ich dir bin.

She stared at him, her flesh all goose bumps, not over the meaning of the two silly last lines—*You hurt me so much, you don't know what you mean to me*—but at how he'd sung it. The car behind them honked: green light. Heart thumping, she drove on with the traffic. "Why do we both know that tune?"

"From Lina. It was a popular song back then. Dumb, but popular."

"Sure, but listen to the *way* we sang it, both of us. Those little extra notes in the middle, and that long note at the end. Why did she get the tune into her head in exactly that way? I can't remember."

He brightened. "I do. She was in the clinic, stocking a phenol shipment. It was late, raining hard, lightning and stuff, and there was a leak in the roof near the doctor's offices, so the kapo sent her to mop the floor and put out a bucket. The whole time, she heard somebody whistling in the doctor's office. That was the song. Over and over."

Whistling? "Dr. Grabner's office? Kleist's?"

"Don't think it was either one. No, it was—" He shot her a sly look. "Are we having a contest?"

"It could be important."

"Yeah?" He scrunched his eyes, trying to remember. "I think the sign on the door said Schiller. Yeah, Dr. Viktor Schiller. Don't think he was around much. Lina never saw him, only heard him whistling, just that one night."

Her skin prickled with something like fear. "In my meeting last week with Dr. Knelman, he said Viktor Schiller was the Nazi scientist who created the knowledge gene. Schiller performed the operation on Lina, and ordered Knelman to assist."

"Uh . . . right." He seemed to be piecing together bits of memory. "She was sedated, though. Didn't even know what the experiment was for."

"Nick, Dr. Knelman said something else about Schiller. He was never accounted for after the war."

"Okay, good for him. Who cares?"

Alana almost sideswept a daisy-painted VW Beetle. She couldn't concentrate on driving. Pulling over into a tow-away zone in front of a bank, she stopped and shifted into neutral. "In Dr. Knelman's study, when he called the hotel, while he was waiting on hold, I heard him whistling. It was that tune. With those extra little notes, and the long one at the end."

His face went blank. "So?"

Suspicion seeped into her mind like a toxin. But it only fogged her thinking. "So . . . I don't know."

"Guess lots of Germans picked up the tune that way. Maybe a singer sang it like that on some record."

"Maybe. But the thing is, Dr. Knelman was the only person who knew we were going to that hotel. Plus, he whistled exactly the way Schiller did."

He looked fascinated, but lost. "I don't get it."

"Neither do I." She needed something to clear the fog. Details, facts, information. But who would have it? "The center?" she asked herself aloud.

"Huh?"

"The Isaac Rosenthal Center." Pulling out, she made a swift, illegal U-turn.

Nick held on. "Holy hell, and you didn't want *me* driving."

When she reached the Rosenthal Center on Eighty-second near Madison, the only parking spot was over a block away. She squeezed into the metered space.

The glass-fronted lobby of the center was bustling with a tour group in polyester and cameras. Alana thought grimly: Nick and I could give you folks a hair-raising day-in-the-life account. She took him up to the second-floor archives room. The white-haired librarian remembered Alana from her visit with Esther. "The Otzenhausen file again? Yes, of course." She gave Nick an appreciative smile. "Never too early to teach the next generation, is it? Just take a seat at the table, please."

"Man, oh, man," Nick said, his voice shaky as they looked through the photo binders. Alana knew he was reliving the horror of the camp, just as she had when she'd first seen these pictures: group shots of prisoners taken by German camp photographers, Nazi officers' mug shots from the war crimes trials, U.S. army pictures of foul inmate barrack blocks and of crematoriums. "What are we looking for?" he asked.

"Here." She found the photo that had disturbed her the last time. The prisoner with the stout peasant build and defiant scowl. "Remember this woman?"

He studied the face. "Uh . . . Wentzler."

"Right. Hilde Wentzler." They were both keeping their voices low; at the next table the librarian was quietly discussing some documents with a middle-aged couple. Alana went on, "I remember her name, and I remember her asking Lina to check out the rumor about an experiment that would bring extra rations. She asked Lina because Lina worked at the clinic. But that's all I—"

"Oh, no, she didn't just *ask*."

Alana knew that. "She paid her. Gave her shoes from a dead woman who'd heard the rumor first."

"More. She gave Lina a warning. Remember?"

It was coming back, firing her with a dark excitement. For years she'd buried these memories, appalled by her mother, and by her own mind. But now, as she summoned them, they were rising like spirits from the grave, full of secrets. "That's right, it was on the march to the factory after a dawn roll call. Hilde told Lina that she'd smothered the girl in the bunk below her, a Polish girl who'd been asking around about the rumor too."

Nick nodded. "Told her so that Lina would know she meant business—that Lina wasn't to speak of the experiment to anyone else. It was their private find."

The moment Alana had hold of that memory, another surfaced. "But there *was* someone else. Hilde didn't murder that Polish girl alone. Another woman helped her. Sarah something."

"Yeah? I forgot that. Hold on . . . flip back a few pictures."

Alana rifled through the previous photographs. She spotted it first. "That's her." Her finger touched a slight, wiry woman in the front rank of a roll call on the Appellplatz. Dirty face, small eyes, grimy uniform with rope belt. On her shaved head the hair had grown back an inch or so, like a man's brush cut. The black and white photo didn't tell it all. "She had red hair," Alana said.

"And the name's not Sarah," Nick said, eyes alight, struggling to remember. "It was Sophie something."

"Sophie—" Alana drew out the last vowel, searching her memory too.

Their eyes met.

"Sophie *Grossman*!" they exclaimed together.

The librarian and the couple looked at them. Alana and Nick quickly bent their heads over the file materials, silent, though Alana could hardly contain herself. The moment the others resumed their murmuring, she whispered, "Nick, you know why we remember these women?"

"I do now. Lina kept an eye out for those two. Tough characters."

"Exactly. Just like her. Lina was so tough she *volunteered* for this experiment, not even knowing what it was about, just hoping to get those triple rations. And so did—"

"Holy hell . . . so did *they*." His eyes were big with the thrill of a discovery.

To Alana, the thrill suddenly felt like nausea. "If Schiller implanted the gene in Hilde Wentzler and Sophie Grossman too, why didn't Dr. Knelman tell me that?"

"Knelman. We're back to him."

"I think he lied to me—or as good as lied. He made it sound like Lina was the only experimental subject."

"Maybe the Nazis had him work just on her. Maybe he didn't know about the other two."

"Maybe." But she doubted it, and she could tell that Nick did too.

"Wonder what happened to them," he said.

"Good question. And here's another. What happened to Schiller?"

They stared at each other, bewildered as they tried to dredge through memories. A connection struck Alana. "Jacob Wentzler."

"Who's he?"

"I don't know. But Wentzler isn't a common name, and when I was in Dr. Knelman's office, his receptionist told him there was a call from Jacob Wentzler's doctor. At a place called Parkview."

"A hospital?"

"Let's try and find out. I'd like to talk to Mr. Wentzler."

In the phone directory in the center's cafeteria they found a listing for a Parkview Psychiatric Institute on Amsterdam Avenue. Nick dropped a dime in the pay phone. "Hello, Parkview?" The faked maturity in his voice impressed Alana. "Listen, my wife and I are just passing through town—is this a good day to visit my nephew, Jacob Wentzler?" He waited a moment, listening, then replied, with a wink at Alana, "Oh, good. Thanks." Alana tore out a corner scrap of the yellow pages and scribbled the address.

"Family visiting hours, ten to eight," Nick said as he hung up.

"Let's go."

The seven-story building on Amsterdam was at 113th Street, just south of the Columbia campus and across from the cathedral of St. John the Divine. It looked new; the reception area's gray concrete walls and Scandinavian furniture were coldly modern. Alana signed in as "Lina Grossman-Wentzler" as the young black nurse behind the desk stifled a yawn. Nick, playing a new part, looked around like any kid brought to a hospital, with a mix of trepidation and boredom. "Haven't seen my nephew since he was a tot," Alana said, putting down the pen. She flashed a nervous smile. "Doubt if he'll recognize me." The young nurse's return smile was coolly indifferent.

A starched, gray-haired nurse built like a buffalo came to meet them, giving Alana a severe once-over. No smile. "First visit's hard for relatives—the change in him," she said, all business as she glanced over Alana's sign-in form. "Best if you have a word with Dr. Gannett first. I'll page him."

Can't risk that, Alana thought. Her gypsy training at sizing up a stranger kicked in as she noted the fleshy groove at the base of the woman's third finger—had to be left from a wedding band. Divorce? Also, the watch pinned on her chest was a locket type, and the other half displayed a tiny snapshot of a child. Grandchild? "Afraid I've only got time to nip in and out," she said sheepishly. "Dumb family feud, no love lost between Jacob's father and my hubby. Took me long enough to get the big jerk to come, and now at the last minute he says he won't come in and he's given me just twenty minutes. Men. So bullheaded, aren't they? And it's the young ones who suffer," she added, gently stroking Nick's cheek. "Couldn't I just see Jacob?"

The nurse seemed to soften. "All right, come along. Call the doctor later if you have questions."

Nick gave Alana a sly thumbs-up as they followed the nurse to the elevator. Getting out on the fourth floor, they went down a hall, then followed her through swinging doors into a gleaming white corridor. The antiseptic smell sent revulsion through Alana: her gypsy fear of hospitals. They passed the closed doors of private rooms. Through an open one she glimpsed a mattress stripped of sheets. They reached a locked door, its window encased in thick wire mesh, and the nurse pushed a wall button that buzzed on the other side, bringing a burly orderly to escort them. Alana exchanged a glance with Nick. What were they getting into?

The door opened. "Hi, Hetty," the orderly said.

"Family visit for Mr. Wentzler."

"This way, folks." *Dis* way. Brooklyn, Alana thought.

"John will take you now," the nurse told them.

"You got Dr. Knelman's number, Hetty?"

"Yes."

Alana shot her a look. "Dr. Knelman?"

"Our consulting neurosurgeon," she said. "He requested notification about everything concerning Jacob."

Alana and Nick shared a glance of alarm. But they were committed now. The big orderly ushered them in.

The ward held beds with male patients, about fifieen on each side, some of the men lying quietly, a couple sitting up and talking to nurses, one muttering to himself, two or three shuffling down the center. The windows had thick bars. The orderly led Alana and Nick to the end of the ward, where he opened the door to a small room. A muscular young man in checked pajamas sat slumped in a wheelchair, watching TV as if in a trance. *I Dream of Jeannie* was on. White walls, gray linoleum floor, a barred window. No furniture except a rumpled bed with steel restraints, and webbed straps dangling from them. "Jacob," the orderly said as if to a kindergarten child, "here's some relatives come to see you. Ain't that nice?"

Jacob didn't seem to hear. As the laugh track on the TV crested, he opened his mouth and brought out a lifeless "Ha," along with a dribble of saliva. His face was blank.

"Is he dangerous?" Nick asked, nodding at Jacob's ankles strapped to the metal footrest and his wrists to the armrests.

"Nah, he just wanders unless we tie him in. Day and night. I don't think he knows where he is."

Alana said, "Could we have a few minutes alone?"

"Don't move his chair," the orderly warned on his way out. "If he can't see the TV, he cries."

As the door closed, Alana crouched beside the wheelchair. "Jacob? Can you hear me?"

No response. Jacob's attention, such as it was, stayed fixed on the sitcom.

"Nobody home," Nick said with a nervous frown. "This guy can't tell us anything."

Alana noticed the medical chart hooked at the foot of the bed. She lifted the clipboard and scanned the top page.

"So?" Nick asked.

"Medical mumbo-jumbo. What's a cingulotomy?"

"Haven't a clue."

"Me neither, but that's an operation Jacob had." She noted the date. "Just last week. Done at—" Her breath caught in her throat. She read aloud: "Manhattan Clinic of Neuropsychiatry." She looked up. "Nick, that's Dr. Knelman's private clinic. He operated."

Jacob laughed. Drool wetted a patch of his pajama top. His eyes, locked on the TV, were dead.

Nick got up, cringing. "Holy hell, if this is Knelman's work, don't let him near *me.*"

Alana's hand was shaky as she replaced the chart. "We don't know that Jacob got like this from the operation. Maybe he's always been this way."

"You heard old Hetty. 'The change in him,' she said. I'll bet last week handsome Jake here was out dancing and wowing the girls."

"Something could have gone wrong. Accidents happen, even to brilliant surgeons."

"You don't believe that, do you? That's one serious slip of the knife! Knelman's turned this guy into a *vegetable.*"

God, yes. And it seemed she and Nick had the same horrible thought—that Knelman had botched the job on purpose. "But why?"

"Look at the build on him, and that big square face. My dad would say peasant stock. Put two and two together, and who do you think his mother is?"

Alana was already there. "Hilde." Her mouth was dry. "Which would make Jacob . . . another gene carrier."

Their eyes locked. "Yeah," Nick said. "Like us."

They fell silent. The TV characters chattered inanely. A female voice out in the ward shouted, "Mr. Forsythe, get down! *Orderly!*"

Alana was churning through memories of her first meeting with Knelman. How intensely he'd counseled her toward sterilization. How shocked he'd seemed when she'd confided she had a son. And how insistent that she bring the boy for counseling too, the moment she found him. Shaken, she said to Nick, "Knelman's obsessed with stopping the spread of the gene. I think maybe he's done this to Jacob . . .

to eliminate that chance. No more wowing the girls, like you said. It's as good as sterilization."

"But it *wouldn't* stop with him. We're carriers too."

Alana felt queasy. She didn't want to face what was taking shape.

But Nick pushed on. "You said Knelman was the only one who knew we were at that hotel. What if I was wrong about the black dude? What if there's no connection to those kids we beat up? What if the guy's working . . . for Knelman?"

Again, she was already ahead of him. "If Knelman really is his name. He whistles exactly like Schiller. He seems to know as much about the gene as if he *were* Schiller. He's *obsessed* with it as if he were Schiller, enough to ruin Jacob here. And now—"

"Now us."

They stared at each other. It was too much, too weird, Alana thought. Knelman, a Nazi? Masquerading as a Jewish survivor all these years? How could he have gotten away with such an incredible deception? She said, hesitating, "It's just guesswork. No proof."

Nick's face had gone pale. "Jacob's proof enough for me."

Alana looked at Jacob's vacant eyes and felt a stab of fear. And fury. Knelman had all but committed murder. And now he was going for broke, with her and Nick. "Me too. Let's get out of here."

Going back through the ward, they waited while the same orderly opened the locked door for them. They'd just started along the corridor when Alana saw the nurse, Hetty, striding toward them, looking anxious. The black nurse from reception hurried along at her side, clipboard in hand. They were talking in low tones, their eyes on Alana. "Miss," Hetty called to her.

With one joint instinct, Alana and Nick stopped cold.

As the nurses reached them, Hetty said in the same singsong the orderly had used to Jacob, "Come along with us now. Miss Marks, isn't it? Your doctor told me, and he's on his way."

"My doctor?"

"Dr. Knelman. He says he's very concerned that you left his clinic without authorization. You could hurt yourself, or perhaps get this boy hurt. Nobody wants that, do they? Come along now, we'll have a nice cup of coffee whilc we wait, and Dr. Knelman will be here in no time."

Alana thought: Run for it? But she could see a doctor at the far end of the hall who'd turned to look, and at the other end, behind her, she hadn't yet heard the orderly close the door, so he must be watching too. Bad odds. She reached for Nick's hand, her eyes on the nurses as she asked them, "What about my son?" Pulling Nick to her side, she turned her head and told him quietly, not moving her lips, "Run." With a flick of her eyes she indicated a fire door a few yards away.

He held her gaze for a second. Then he stepped away from her.

"Now, now, we know the boy isn't your son. That was naughty, bringing another patient with you. And one so young." As the two nurses linked their arms through hers, Nick moved away as if cowed and timid. With their attention on the balky adult, they ignored the boy. Alana watched him sidle toward the fire door, and she willed him to make it out, and escape.

But the black nurse said to him gently, "Hold on, honey."

Alana had to divert them. "I hate coffee!" she yelled, and

punched Hetty in the stomach. Hetty released her, eyes bulging in shock. The other nurse let go, too, in fright. "John!" she shouted. "Help!"

Alana turned. The big orderly was racing toward her. It seemed to give the nurses courage, and they spread out to the front and rear of Alana, their arms spread wide as if to corral a wild animal. The orderly reached her and wrenched her elbows behind her back. Pain seared her shoulder sockets. She could have handled the women, but not this big guy too. They had her.

A scream startled them all. "A-a-a!"

Nick was flying up in the air, feet out, arms akimbo. He hit the floor on his back with a sickening thud, and a bloodcurdling shriek ripped from his throat.

"Hel . . . help me . . . ," he gasped. He lay utterly still. "My back . . . please . . ."

The two nurses ran toward him. "Don't try to move, honey!" "Somebody bring a stretcher!" *"Doctor!"*

The doctor down the hall came running. A blond nurse burst from a room. The four of them surrounded Nick, all talking: "Could be spinal injury." "Don't move him!"

In the commotion Alana looked over her shoulder at the orderly holding her, and said with real enough anxiety, "It's my son. Please let me see . . ." She felt his grip become hesitant. Seizing the moment, she pulled free, twisted, and kneed him in the groin. As he doubled over, she sprinted for the cluster of people around Nick at the fire door. She kicked the blond nurse's knee from behind, felling her, creating a path for Nick. He scrambled to his feet and practically dove through to Alana. The two of them bolted out the door and raced down four flights of stairs to the ground floor.

They walked across the lobby to the front doors, pretending composure, but as soon as they were out of the place, they bolted up Amsterdam. They ducked through the open campus gates across from Columbia Law School. The grassy campus was like a Shangri-la hidden between the blare and bustle of Amsterdam and Broadway. No vehicles, just people strolling the walkways that formed quadrangles in the huge lawn enclosed by stately buildings. Catching their breath, Alana and Nick slowed down.

He grinned at her. "Fantastic, huh? We *are* a team!"

Adrenaline coursed through her, the thrill of action. It *was* fantastic, and not just the escape—Nick. When they had her pinned down and he could have taken off, he'd taken a wild risk instead, using her old slip-and-fall dodge. To save her. She'd never felt such a bond with anyone. "Yeah," she said, smiling back. "Two crazy gypsies."

They passed a crowd of students standing on the grass around an electric guitar player wailing a solo, Jimi Hendrix style, and the horror of what they'd discovered slammed into Alana again. "Thank God we found out about Knelman. To think I was going to deliver you into his hands."

Nick shrugged it off. But his smile had vanished. "Where to now?"

She could ask Gus to put them up, but Knelman's ability to track them made her shudder. Even now she found herself searching the backs of the college kids, looking for the black man in khakis. But where could she and Nick go? Not to the police; they'd never believe this story. It would come down to the word of a respected neurosurgeon against the word of his two "psychotic" patients. No contest.

As if he'd been following her thoughts, Nick said, "We should beat it. Take off on your boat. Sail south and get lost in the Florida Keys."

The idea gripped her. It would mean skipping out on the work she'd lined up, another blow to her reputation, but this was now about survival. Blake Luscombe was set to hand her the title to *Seawitch* in three weeks; she could call him and give some story, explain that she'd work out the final details with him from Florida. She already had the boat rigged for an offshore passage, and had the charts, and she felt confident single-handing.

But a new fear came over her. "Nick, he's already hired one hit man. He could hire more. He wants us dead, and if we run now, we could be on the run forever. It's no solution. No, somehow we have to try and stop him."

"How? We can't go to the law."

The law . . . It made her gasp. "David."

"Who?"

My God, she thought, David knows nothing about this! "Knelman's son," she answered shakily. Or was he? If Knelman was really Schiller, whose son was David? It made her head spin.

"I don't get it," Nick said. "You know his son?"

"I've . . . been seeing him."

He looked appalled. "Just how *well* do you know him?"

She'd tried to keep her face neutral, but she felt telltale blood warming her cheeks, and knew Nick had caught it.

His eyes widened in revulsion. "Holy hell, you're in love with him!"

It stung her. "I'm sure he's in the dark about Knelman. Look, he's an assistant district attorney, so he has the authority to stop this. I've got to go to him. I've got to tell him the truth about the man he calls his father."

CHAPTER 11

TO DAVID, IRIS Larson's death had come as a blow, a personal one. He stood in the coroner's office, impatient. It wasn't yet ten o'clock, a Monday morning at that, and Dr. Faludi's twenty-something secretary, searching for the autopsy report, was slowly poking through files on her desk as if operating on a run-down battery. Pretty girl; heavy weekend, probably. As David waited, she yawned behind her manicured hand, then glanced at him with a blush. He knew his urgency must seem odd, but when he'd got the call that Mrs. Larson was dead, he'd known that he had failed the lady. Failed to stop the gypsies.

Lipranski had told him Saturday night, when David's mind had been on Alana—on how to break the news to her about Nick Morgan. The kid had committed a vicious assault, according to the eyewitness, and that couldn't be ignored. Of course, the boy wasn't Alana's responsibility. Still, how would she take it when he told her? If, that is, she ever returned his calls. No word from her all weekend. No response to his messages. Was she really so determined never to see him again? He couldn't accept that—he would not give her up so easily. But hearing Lip's news, he'd tried to shove aside those worries about her and her son, and had gone to see the doctor who'd signed Mrs. Larson's death certificate. It had listed cause of death as "Right cerebrovascular accident, acute; arteriosclerotic vascular disease; generalized arteriosclerosis." Meaning a stroke. And hardening of the arteries. "Nothing unusual?" he'd asked.

The doctor had shrugged. "She was eighty-six. Old people die."

Still, David had got authorization from Rintoul, his boss, and ordered an autopsy.

"Here it is, Mr. Knelman," the secretary said. "Dr. Faludi rushed it through for you. Said if you have any questions to call him after one-thirty when he'll be back in the office." She smiled up at him as she handed him the file, then leaned on the desk, allowing the deep V of her filled blouse to expose a healthy cleavage that took some of the chill off David's morning. "Important case?" she asked.

"Guess they're all important, Miss Kennedy. To somebody."

Her doe eyes languidly blinked at him. "That's a nice attitude."

Reading through the report as he stood there, he noted that the toxicology analysis showed traces of digoxin, synthetic digitalis. Used as a heart regulator, but he knew its toxicity could be unpredictable, especially for a frail old person. Foul play? Possibly not—according to the files, Mrs. Larson's physician had once prescribed the drug. But it fired David's suspicion that this was the third case of what he and Lip were calling the elder scam. If Larson had been poisoned by the young gypsy couple who'd moved in to "look after" her, he felt responsible. Dosing the old lady's food with "magic salt" was what they'd been overheard saying, and now they had title to her property. He had Lip watching the gypsy driver of the gold Cadillac, but that wouldn't help Iris Larson now. Guilt fed his anger. He'd waited too long to act.

He checked his watch. He'd be late for court if he didn't hustle.

Back at Eighty Center Street he joined the flow of lawyers and clerical workers who regularly crisscrossed between these offices and the court building, the foot traffic echoing off the corridor's dark marble floor. As he passed Rudi Fielding's open door he heard, "Hey, Knelman, copies of the affidavits, remember?"

David leaned into the doorway. "Coming right up." Fielding was overseeing the paperwork for the arraignment of today's perp, a repeat insurance scammer.

Down the hall in his own office David found that his TPA, Fiona, was away from her desk. He pulled the affidavits file from among his piled dockets and headed down the corridor to the copying room to do the job himself. Behind him he heard: "David."

His heart jumped. Alana.

Before she could speak, he grabbed her hand and pulled her into the copying room, little bigger than a closet. He tossed the file on the Xerox machine, closed the door, took her in his arms, and kissed her hard.

She froze, but just for a moment. When she responded, her kiss was passionate, almost desperate, her arms tight around his neck. David was thrilled—so excited, he felt he'd be lost if he kissed her any more, and he pulled her away. Holding her at arm's length, he said, "I wanted to do that first, before things get complicated. I've got news about your son. I just want you to know that I can handle the complication if you can. *Any* complication, Alana. Remember that, okay? And don't ever run out on me again like the other night. Are we straight?"

Her smile flooded him with happiness. But then a stricken look came into her eyes, and her smile vanished. She said, "I have . . . news too."

"Mine first. It's serious." Hoping to get her over the hard part fast, he made it brief: Nick's alleged assault, with other unidentified offenders, on three innocent youths. He told her about the Morgans' confession to him of the boy's previous thefts, and his present unknown whereabouts. It wasn't a pretty picture, and at her haunted look David hastened to add, "His delinquency isn't your fault, Alana—heredity be damned. The Morgans raised him."

She was shaking her head, her face pale. "I know all about the assault. Nick told me himself."

David was astonished. "You found him?"

"He found me."

"When?"

"Sunday. He's staying with me."

It stung him. Why hadn't she at least called to tell him this? "Alana, he has to go home. He's a minor. And the police have to be notified."

She shook her head again, and her face took on a grim determination. "Nick's problems started a long time ago. Before he was born. Started with . . . your father."

"Dad? You've lost me."

She gave a humorless laugh. "Oh, you're going to have to hang on tight to keep up with this one." Her eyes darted to the clock on the wall. "Nick and I are staying with a friend. I don't want to leave him alone for long." Her glance back at him was anxious. "I bet you've heard just about everything in your line of work. But you won't be ready for this."

He leaned back against the Xerox machine, folding his arms. They couldn't stay holed up here for long, but he was prepared to listen. "Shoot."

She took a shaky breath. "It was 1944. A Nazi doctor in Berlin created a biological breakthrough—a gene that would pass along a mother's knowledge to her baby, generation after generation. He needed experimental subjects, so he went to Otzenhausen and implanted the gene in three women. One was a gypsy from Austria, named Lina. She was my mother. The experiment worked. I have all the knowledge she had. Nick has my knowledge *and* hers. I only found out the background last week, when your father told me he'd been forced to assist as a prisoner physician."

David stared at her. She seemed normal . . . except for the intense look in her eyes. It made him afraid for her.

"David, I know the name of the gray pony my mother rode when she was ten—Paprish. I know the love words my father used to her alone in their wagon the night they were married . . . and what they did together. I know the way she tied her scarf, the words she said to herself to ward off bad luck if she saw the new moon over her left shoulder, and what she ate the morning her people were rounded up for Otzenhausen, bread and bacon, the last meat she'd have for over a year. I *know* these things."

A memory jolted him of what she'd told him the night they'd met. *"I've always had a bit of a problem with reality."*

"And there's more," she went on. "I don't believe your father's real name is Knelman. I think it's Viktor Schiller. He's not a Jew. He's the Nazi scientist who created the gene."

The room was quiet except for the buzzing fluorescent light above them. Dad's words of the other night rushed back: *"She is a very troubled young woman . . . You have no idea what you are dealing with."*

"I know it seems unbelievable, David, but its true. When it came to me, it seemed so horrific that at first I didn't believe it myself. But I've taken a long hard day to think it through, and an even harder night. I looked at every fact. That's what you do, isn't it? As a prosecutor? Examine the evidence? Well, look at this." She rolled up her sleeve and showed him a gauze bandage around her upper arm. She told him that someone had tried to shoot her and Nick at the marina, that she'd been wounded, and that the would-be assassin was his father's man. "Your father's already committed *virtual* murder—on a young man named Jacob Wentzler, the son of one of the other Otzenhausen subjects, Hilde Wentzler. I remember her from the camp because my mother knew her, and Nick remembers her too. Yes, David, the knowledge gene's at work in Nick too—he knows what I know. We went to see Jacob at the Parkview Psychiatric Institute, but he couldn't talk to us. He can't talk, period, because your father operated on him last week. Messed with his brain. Turned him into a vegetable. And now, he's trying to kill me and Nick."

David forced himself to stay calm, focus on real things around him. The fluorescent buzz overhead. The whiff of print chemicals. The folder he'd tossed on the machine in his urgency to kiss her. The door that could open at any moment, a secretary or clerk walking in. It all just made him feel more off balance—and more afraid for her. One thought crowded out all others: How could he help her? Maybe, if he took her step by step through what she was claiming, used cold logic, he could deconstruct this paranoia for her. She'd spoken calmly; he made himself do the same. "Why would my father want to kill you?"

"To wipe out the gene. He's afraid it'll change the world."

"Isn't that what he meant to do by creating it?"

"I don't think so." She seemed to clutch at his interest. "It was emergent research. Besides, he probably didn't expect the subjects would survive the camp. After all, prisoners who weren't gassed were worked to death, so he figured the gene would never pass those gates. Anyway, maybe he thought if the women *did* survive, the Nazis would be running Europe by then, so he'd just go on studying the mothers and children as scientific specimens, like lab animals. Subhumans, that was the Nazis' word. Trouble was, the Nazis lost the war, and Schiller's subjects went free. Except my mother. She was killed in the camp. I think he's been tracking down the other two ever since. And us. The next generations."

David couldn't speak. She'd crafted a logic all her own—tortuous, but coherent and consistent—arguing as nimbly as a defense opponent. He swallowed, and found his voice. "If my father isn't who he says he is, then how do you explain the twenty-eight years his sister's lived with him? How do you explain *me*?"

Her shoulders slumped. "I don't know. But my people have a saying. *Si khohaimo may patshivalo sar o tshatshimo.* It means, There are lies more believable than the truth."

Her delusion pained him as though he were watching someone physically hurting her.

"Look," she went on, "I don't know all the answers yet. We can't *see* the answers, because Dr. Knelman—Schiller—has lived the perfect lie. David, I came here because you can use the law to stop him from killing Nick and me. If you don't believe me, then find out for yourself. Get the truth."

His mind groped. "The law . . . requires evidence."

Her face darkened, like a door closing. As though she'd decided he was against her. "You know what? I'm not all that interested in courtroom rules when I know somebody's trying to blow my head off. I'm a gypsy, and I trust my instincts. Coming here was a big mistake." She started for the door.

"Alana, don't do this. Don't walk out again. There's some kind of terrible misunderstanding. Stay. We'll work it out."

She met his gaze. "I've got to protect my son, David. I'm not waiting around for Knelman's hit man to find us. I'm leaving town, and I'm taking Nick with me."

"Don't. It'd be kidnapping. That's the law."

"Your law. It would let Knelman kill us."

"It's a law with teeth. Steel bars. You'd do time."

"They'll have to catch me first."

The door opened. Rudi Fielding. "Knelman, have you got . . . Oh, excuse me, miss."

David's stomach clenched. Alana looked ready to bolt. Fielding said, "Knelman? Affidavits?"

"Yeah, give me a minute to finish the copying." Fielding eyed Alana, making no move to go. David grabbed the file and said tightly to her, "Wait. Please."

They all stood in silence as he copied seven pages as fast as he could. His mind locked on one thought: How to stall her, keep her in town. He couldn't let her commit a kidnapping that would ruin her life. *"Get the truth,"* she'd said. Watching the last copy slide out, he suddenly thought: Documents. Would that satisfy her?

"Thanks," Fielding said as David handed him the pages. He left, and David shut the door.

"What if I *did* get you evidence?" he said to Alana. "Proof that your theory is groundless."

"That's not what you'll find."

They regarded each other in a kind of standoff, both ready to trust a search for the truth, but with opposite expectations of what that search would yield. Still, David knew her quick intelligence, despite this paranoid fantasy. She would accept irrefutable documentation. "Let me make a call. I have a friend at the Department of Defense. They have records on the camps liberated by U.S. troops, and Otzenhausen was one. Survivor names and numbers. Facts, Alana. We can clear this up in no time. But you've got to stay where you are until I get some answers. Okay? Will you let me do that?"

She studied him as if weighing a risk. "I should get out right now, with Nick."

"Look, I love you. I don't want it to end this way. Let me get you proof."

She turned her face away. Grabbing a sheet of copy paper from the tray in the machine, she asked, "Got a pen?" He pulled one from his inside jacket pocket and gave it to her. "These are the names of the two other subjects," she said, writing. "Find out what happened to them too, if you can. You know my message service number. Call there when you have something."

When she looked up at him, he saw the glint of tears in her eyes. "I'd give anything for it *not* to end, David. It's up to you."

During the arraignment David found it hard to concentrate. At one point, as he shuffled through his notes in the noisy courtroom, the judge made a remark that was close to a reprimand about his wandering attention. On their way back to the office Rudi Fielding said to him with a knowing look, "Can't blame you. She's a looker."

The moment he reached his desk, David put in the call to Washington.

"David! How's it going?" Toby DeVrey's bonhomie was as breezy as the day they'd graduated Columbia Law, though they'd gotten together only a few times since, catching up over a beer now and then when the DoD sent Toby, one of their junior litigation specialists, to New York. Toby always swore that David's help during several late-night study sessions had got him through second year. "Hey, when am I going to read about you taking the executive ADA's chair?"

"Don't hold your breath. The guy sitting in it isn't doing too shabby a job."

"We could pray he's dirty with Watergate. Look what it's doing to Nixon. What's up? You coming to D.C.?"

David said he had a favor to ask, a little archive digging. Telling Toby he was putting together a family history, he asked if he would check the army's records on the liberation of Otzenhausen for information concerning his father, a former prisoner. "Heinrich Knelmann, with two N's." Dad never talked about those days, but Aunt Es had once mentioned the original form of the name, and how she and Dad had each dropped an N—more American—when they came, independently, to the States. From his pocket he pulled the paper Alana had given him with the names of the two women. "Toby, could you also check out a Hilde Wentzler and a Sophie Grossman in the same camp?" He felt foolish asking—Jesus, a "knowledge gene"—but he plowed on. Only facts on paper would keep Alana from running. He said to Toby, "Sorry to put you out."

"Not me, I'll have a clerk do the legwork. What's a big office for?"

"Thanks. I owe you."

"Forget it. Buy me a beer next time. I'll get back to you, pal."

David hashed through paperwork on the insurance case until almost six. Fiona had gone home, and the office typewriters and phones had quieted. Lipranski walked in.

"Had dinner, Counselor?"

"Not hungry."

"This'll perk up your appetite. Remember the gold Cadillac gypsy?"

"George Adams." David thought of the male half of the scam team claiming title to Iris Larson's property, all perfectly legit. At this very moment the creep was probably making plans to change the locks.

"Yeah, but remember his aliases? Danny Rogers, Stefan Marks, Danny Roman. Told you that would pay off. My source has just confirmed a connection to the clan of Rajko Marks. Looks like our man George is the nephew of the *rom baro* himself."

David had dreaded this. Alana's father. He told Lip about the coroner's tox report.

Lip's grin was wolfish. "Bet you ten to one we're gonna find this wily bastard Rajko's running the whole fucking scam."

"Yeah." Three poisonings. Maybe more going on right now. Something inside David hardened. Alana had a psychological problem that he was more than willing to help her deal with, but she also had a shady family, and his liberality didn't extend to a man who was masterminding murder. Anger cut through him as he remembered the frail old lady isolated from friends and neighbors, dependent on these parasites who'd pushed her into her grave.

"The Cadillac nephew," he told Lip. "Pick him up for questioning."

At six-thirty Knelman was sorting through patients' histories in his study at home, his mind in turmoil. For two days Farrell had not been able to find Alana Marks and Nick Morgan. Two hellish days. A Beethoven piano sonata drifted from the living room through the open door, and despite his anxiety, he forced himself not to whistle along. On Sunday that had been his great mistake. How shocked she'd looked when she'd heard him—almost certainly a tune she'd recognized from Otzenhausen. Stupid! Later, she and the boy had evaded Farrell at the hotel. They'd even gone to see Jacob in Parkview! Then they'd disappeared. How could he ever find them now? A cold fear swept him. They knew so much. Had they pieced together the whole truth? If so, what would they *do* with it? Sitting at his desk, he buried his face in his hands with a shudder.

Voices in the living room reached him. Esther, greeting David. He felt a pang. He and David hadn't spoken since their argument about the girl four days ago. He turned in his chair. David stood in the doorway, still in suit and tie from the office.

"Aunt Es says you're off to Philadelphia in the morning. Another speech?"

"For an association of support families. Poor souls." Knelman indicated the scattered notes. "I'm structuring my talk around these case histories."

"You're a great guy, Dad." David's tone made it clear that this was his olive branch. It moved Knelman.

"It's good to see you, son."

"Listen, I know you're busy, but . . . could I bend your ear for a minute?" Hands in his pockets, his expression unsure, David moved to the bookcase where the antique clock ticked softly. Knelman remembered him as a child so often drawn to its gleaming, efficient pendulum. Such a tenacious young mind. The warm memory collided with his anxiety: he was sure this visit was about Alana Marks.

"You'll stay for supper, won't you, David?" Esther asked from the doorway. "Though I'm afraid I was only going to open a can of soup for Henry. Can't seem to get myself going these days."

"What's wrong?" David asked.

She heaved a sigh and sat down in the leather easy chair, and as she told David about Howard Jaffe's heart attack and his subsequent decision, Knelman felt grateful for her interruption—a reprieve.

"That's a bad break," David commiserated, sitting down on the leather footstool beside her. "He'll have second thoughts, though, once you visit him."

She shook her head. "I called his home this afternoon, talked to his daughter, in from Minneapolis, his only child. She said Howard wouldn't speak to me. I don't know who was more mortified, her or me. She said she has to go home tomorrow, which means poor Howard will be all alone. I told her I wanted to come and see him, take care of him, but she said he wouldn't hear of it—he's insisting he'll be fine."

David squeezed her hand. "He's a knucklehead."

"A stubborn old mule."

The scene touched Knelman. His kind son, his gentle sister. They were not really his blood, but they filled his heart. Yet Alana Marks could turn them against him, destroy his world. The very thought shook him: Esther's revulsion, David's hatred.

"Well," Esther said, getting up, smoothing her skirt. "I do have eggs and some mushrooms. You'll stay for an omelet, won't you?"

"I've got a better idea. Dad and I'll take you out for dinner. Or just you and me if he's too busy. How about that French place on Harrison you like, the one with the great pastry chef?"

She brightened. "Well . . ."

"A fine idea," Knelman said. "We'll all go."

"Aunt Es, why don't you book a table. Give me a minute with Dad."

Alone with his son, Knelman said, "It's for the best, about Jaffe. This is her home."

David nodded, looking edgy. "But I know how she feels." Still on the footstool, he leaned over, elbows on his spread knees, hands clasped. "Dad, I came to ask your advice about Alana. I know it's putting you on the spot, that you feel you shouldn't discuss her case, but . . . boy, I really need some help. She came to me today with a story."

"The knowledge gene?"

David looked amazed. "You know?"

"Oh, yes." Knelman had made a quick, desperate calculation: to keep David from digging, he had to appear in control. "A Nazi experiment? A gene that passed to Miss Marks her mother's knowledge? She told me all about it in our session. It is an ingenious construct—a delusional variation that I have not encountered in any other patient. But I fear it could lead her to cause harm to herself. Or to others."

David's face creased in worry. "She's found her son—did you know? He's with her now. Nick Morgan, just thirteen, but already in trouble with the law. She wants to leave town with him. I warned her she'd be kidnapping, but she's in such a state she doesn't care. She's convinced herself that you—" He stopped, as though overwhelmed.

"Go on, son." Hope gripped Knelman. Since she'd gone to see David, did that mean he knew where she was?

Looking him in the eye, David said quickly, as though to get it over with, "She thinks you're the Nazi scientist behind the thing, that you've turned some guy named Wentzler into a vegetable, and that now you've hired a hit man to kill her and her son."

Knelman forced himself to not blink. "Extraordinary. I do so wish she would allow me to help her. But I don't know where she is. Do you?"

"Staying with some friend, wouldn't say where. She's really afraid."

Knelman's hope withered. "When she told you all this, what did you say?"

"Told her I'd show her that you can't be who she says you are. I've got a call in to Toby DeVrey at the DoD, and he's going to get back to me with facts about Otzenhausen from the army archives. That'll convince her. She's very bright—I'm almost sure she'll accept documented evidence." He paused, and shook his head in frustration. "Dad, I told you how I feel about Alana, and that hasn't changed. But I know now you were right about her problem. All I want to do is help her. Trouble is, I don't understand what her problem *is*. Won't you tell me? What exactly is wrong with her?"

The sides of Knelman's throat felt stuck together. David . . . *investigating* him. He sat back, and forced himself to sound calm and professional. "Miss Marks suffers from a controversial syndrome known as multiple personality disorder. An extreme case."

David looked surprised. "Split personality? Isn't that just in B movies?"

"Not at all. The mind is constantly struggling to create a coherent belief system from a multiplicity of life experiences. When there are minor discrepancies, a person usually adjusts his beliefs, or engages in the denials and rationalizations that Freud wrote about. However, should a person hold two sets of beliefs that conflict—though each may be internally consistent—a solution is to balkanize the beliefs, to wall them off from each other by creating two personalities." He was recovering his balance, spinning facts as he went. "Miss Marks's case, as I said, is extreme, yet the roots are not so difficult to see. Consider her upbringing among gypsies—illiterate, immoral, opportunistic. Then consider, if I may say so, her intimacy with you, educated and cultured, a man she must surely feel is above her. Consider further the guilt that she suffers from having abandoned her illegitimate child. Result? An unbearable war of emotions."

"But until this fantasy took hold of her she was so grounded. Great at her work, capable, conscientious." He raked a hand through his hair. "Not exactly conventional, but . . . wonderful."

A thought propelled Knelman to his feet. It exhilarated him. Mind racing, he couldn't trust himself to appear composed, and he moved to the bookcase. *David has the authority to capture this woman and her son.* And he might do it, if he believed it was in their best interest. Knelman saw that everything depended on the foundation he laid down now. He had to confirm David's unspoken fear. He had to paint the girl as insane.

"Your distress reminds me of the grieving father of one of my patients, an NYU student with Capgras syndrome. He suffers from the cruel delusion that his parents are impostors." Since he did have such a patient, this much was easy. He took a silver-framed photograph of Esther from the bookcase and sat again as if he'd gone for it to illustrate his point. "The young man was in a car accident that left him in a coma, and though he eventually made a full physical recovery, he has this one extraordinary delusion that his father and mother are not his real parents. Nothing can convince him otherwise. I'm certain it's because neural pathways were damaged—pathways that connect the signals between face recognition and emotional response. He recognizes his parents, but experiences no emotion for them." He held up the photo of Esther for them both to look at. "He says to himself, 'If this is my mother, why doesn't her presence make me *feel* like I'm with my mother?" His only way of making sense of it is to assume that these people merely *resemble* his father and mother—they must be impostors." He set down the photo. "Miss Marks's disorder, while its root cause is different, is just as debilitating."

David was clearly struggling to follow. "Alana wasn't in an accident."

"Oh? Consider the work she does. And it's not uncommon for patients with a disorder of this type to have paranoid delusions about their doctor. Sometimes they demonize him, even to the point of believing him to be a threat. As I have said, her psychosis is severe. I only hope it does not drive her to an irrational act—to become a danger to herself."

David's alarm was evident. "You think that's possible?"

Knelman's heart beat faster. "There might be a way we can help her, together. With the aid of the police. If she could be brought in and committed to my care, I could see that she receives the special treatment she needs."

David got up and paced. "Protective custody—a court

order. For her own good. And Nick could be sent home. He may have taken part in an assault, but I'm sure a judge would be lenient, since the boy's so young."

"Can it be done? Can you arrest her?"

"Yes. Technically, she's already guilty of kidnapping."

"But how will you find her?"

"Don't need to. I'll get her to come to me. She's waiting for my call." He gave Knelman a look that was both agonized and determined. "All I have to do is lie to her."

CHAPTER 12

"BUT HE *WANTS* to talk to me—I'm returning his call." *Again.* Alana seethed with frustration. David had left a brief message with her service at nine A.M., but it was after ten now, and this was her second exchange with his secretary, and she still had no idea what he'd called about. His four words, "I have some news," had been enough to fire her hopes, though. The right news could send Knelman to prison.

"Don't you give him his messages?" she pressed the secretary. "Doesn't he check in with you?"

"When he can, but he's been in court all—"

"Pardon?" It was hard to hear above the Sam Cooke album Gus and his lady friend had on in the next room. She plugged her other ear. "I'm sorry, could you speak up?"

"I said Mr. Knelman has been in court all morning. But I'll give him your message as soon as he gets back."

"The *moment* he gets in. Tell him it's urgent. Thanks."

She hung up. She was sitting on the mattress on the floor in Gus's spare room in his cramped East Village apartment, and as she got up, she kicked aside the long phone cord that snaked out under the door. Strewn with his stunt gear and a pile of dirty laundry, the room had the mildewy whiff of old shoes and even older shag carpet. She'd slept here for two nights; Nick on the couch in the living room. The place was overcrowded with them here. Alana hated imposing, especially since Gus had a new live-in lady, but she and Nick couldn't go back to the boat, not with Knelman's gunman out there, and after the St. Moritz she felt that even a hotel wouldn't be safe. She doubted Nick had been getting much sleep, though. Join the club, she thought as she watched a cockroach skitter over the dingy sheet and onto the orange shag. She stomped on it.

"Who were you calling?" Nick stood in the doorway, glowering. "Not him again?"

Alana bit back her annoyance. They'd had a fierce argument yesterday after her visit to David. Nick had been dead set against her going to him.

"It's not too late for us to get the hell out, you know," he said now. "We could sail away today. We could be *gone*."

"And be on the run for the rest of our lives."

"Gypsies always run. That's how we survive."

"Don't start with the gypsy stuff, Nick. David's our best hope. He can stop this."

"Stop *us*, you mean. He's the law, for God's sake."

"He's my friend," she flared. "His message said he had news. And until I speak to him and find out where we stand, I don't want to hear another word against him. Got that?"

"Yeah, I got it," he said sullenly. "You're dreaming of you and your *friend* happy ever after in a little house with a picket fence. You're not thinking."

He sounded jealous. She felt at a loss. "I'm just trying to keep us alive," she said, and pushed past him.

The music was loud in the living room, and Gus and

Crystal, his bleached blond girlfriend, sat on the floor at the coffee table, chuckling over a Monopoly game. The pie-tin ashtray between them was full of butts, the air still stale with last night's smoke. Cans of Coors littered the table; Alana figured most of a twelve-pack had been their breakfast. She felt horrible about being in their way, but she didn't dare even step outside in case David called. She hadn't been out since a quick trip yesterday to a neighborhood store to buy something decent to wear after those ragged cutoffs and old sneakers. All her stuff was on the boat. The new white Levis and blue jersey top still felt stiff, and she hadn't yet broken in the sandals.

She sat on the couch, trying to make herself unobtrusive. Sam Cooke's sad-sweet music took her back thirteen years, when Gus had first taken her under his wing. She'd picked up her love of R&B from him. Poor Gus, she thought, looking at him. No spring chicken now, he wasn't attracting the girls the way he had in his hell-raising days, and the alcohol had taken its toll. Puffy eyes, spider-veined cheeks, sagging muscles. He sat in an open bathrobe, his gut hanging over the waistband of his boxers. Crystal was in a tight purple polyester catsuit that showed off what must have been a knockout figure fifteen years and a few cases of vodka ago. Alana told herself not to be such a judgmental bitch. Gus had been a good friend to let her and Nick crash here, no questions asked, and Crystal, despite smiles and winks at Nick that were weirdly close to flirting, couldn't be too thrilled with the extra company. Alana longed to get out and leave them in peace, but first she had to know where she stood. If she found there was no hope through David, she'd be out the door with Nick, and by nightfall they'd be sailing out of New York. If only David would call!

Nick slouched past her on his way to the kitchen.

Crystal called to him, "Hey, hon, get us a little ice, would you?" She lifted a bottle of Southern Comfort from the floor. "Like, in some cups?"

"Some peanuts, too," Gus said.

Crystal snorted. "Jeez, Gus, you think the kid's a freakin' waiter? I'll go."

Alana swung her legs up on the couch to let her get past. Crystal's beery-eyed gaze was on Nick as she headed for the kitchen, primping her poodle-curly hair. On the way she turned up the stereo even louder. Alana could see Nick in the kitchen, standing at the open fridge, pulling out a Coke can. Crystal went right to him, and as he turned, she pressed up against him, pushing him back against the fridge racks. He froze, wide-eyed. Her tongue flicked at his mouth.

Alana was stunned. "Hey!" Nobody heard her above the music.

Crystal's hand slid to Nick's crotch. He jumped. She took the Coke from him and tossed it in the sink, then took his hand and clamped it on her breast. She rubbed his crotch. His eyes went glassy.

Alana leaped up. *"Hey!"*

Gus looked at her, oblivious. "Huh?"

By the time Alana got to the kitchen, Crystal had taken two glasses from the dish rack and was starting back out. Alana stepped in her way and said in her face, "He's *thirteen.* You come on to him again, I'll break your arm."

Crystal's eyes were hard. "Then where would you sleep, hon?" She threw a glance at Nick. "*He's* not complaining."

Alana could see that. His glazed eyes were locked on Crystal's rump as she walked out. Alana slapped his face. "Smarten up!"

"Holy hell." He rubbed his cheek, blinking. "What's it to *you*?"

"This is Gus's place, and that woman is his! And you're just a boy!"

"About a year younger than you when you got knocked up. Remember? I do."

It threw her. That he knew so much, had sexual knowledge—her knowledge. And Lina's. All he didn't have was experience. So far.

"Take it easy," he said. "We're gypsies. We make out young."

"You mean *marry* young."

His gaze slid back to where Crystal had been, and his look turned sly. "I've been thinking, we might make ourselves some cash out of this gene thing. I mean, if people knew about it, they'd want their kids to have it, wouldn't they? You bet they would. Kids born knowing stuff? Give them a fantastic edge. I heard on TV that doctors are gonna be growing babies in test tubes soon. With sperm from donors, like deposits in a bank. Women are gonna come in and *buy* the stuff, pick the kind they want. I bet we could sell mine for a bundle. Once we leave this dump, I mean, and head down south, use new names; and all that." Alana wasn't sure whether to laugh or cry. She knew him well enough by now to know he was jazzing on like this to cover his embarrassment. "Hey, we could even run the operation ourselves. Pitch it to lady doctors and lawyers, maybe women with companies who want an heir. Bet they'd jump at the chance to pass on their smarts. 'Want Junior to be a genius? Sign up here.'" He grinned. "Or I could always service them the old-fashioned way."

"Nick, shut up."

He shrugged. "Just trying to help."

The phone rang. She heard Gus answer it. Then he called, "Alana, it's for you."

She dashed to the spare room, shutting the door. She'd left this number only with David's secretary. "Hello?"

"Alana?"

"David, thank God."

"I've discovered . . . discrepancies. About my father."

His voice sounded so different. Flat and strained. No wonder, if he'd learned Knelman was Schiller! She felt a rush of sympathy for him. "What have you found out?"

"Look . . . this is hard. I'm at the office, can't go into it here. Can I meet you? You and Nick? There are some photostats I need you to look at. Then, after, I'll need statements from both of you. For a possible investigation."

Finally! "Yes, of course. When?"

"Now. Where are you?"

The door opened. Nick stood watching her.

"No, here's not good," she said to David. She named a café on St. Mark's Place near Third Avenue, just a few blocks away; she and Nick could walk. David suggested meeting in half an hour, and she said fine. "David, I know this must be hell for you. I just want to say . . . thank you."

No reply. He hung up.

Nick was scowling. "Was that him? The DA?"

"Yes, and he's got some evidence he needs us to see. Couldn't go into it on the phone, but he mentioned a possible investigation. Just what we hoped for." She grabbed her knapsack. "Come on. He's meeting us in thirty minutes."

"Me? Go meet the law? No way."

"Look, we can trust David. And he has the power to put Knelman behind bars."

"Are you nuts? Knelman's his *father*. That's what he's believed all his life. He can't have got enough overnight to change his mind—not just like that. It's a setup. I can smell it. And so could you if you weren't so gaga about the guy."

"Nick, he's a prosecutor. His whole life is facts and evidence. Now the facts are proving I was right. It's killing him, I could hear it in his voice, but he's ready to get to the bottom of this. We've got to go see him and tell him what we know."

"*You* go. Call me from jail."

What a damn mule he was! "All right, I'll see him myself. Just hang tight, and I'll bring you back the news."

His eyes narrowed. "If you're not back in two hours, save that call from jail for a lawyer. I'll be gone."

She arrived at Luba's Café early. It was a Ukrainian diner with Old World prices and honest food. The twenty-four-hour breakfast was popular enough that the mom-and-pop owners had expanded the small, one-room operation by knocking an arch into a bearing brick wall, making it two small rooms, side by side. There were faded posters of girls in peasant dresses, painted wooden Easter eggs on shelves, ferns hanging in the window, plastic menus. Alana had once had a great bowl of borscht here with Gus. Coming in, she saw that the first room wasn't exactly full: two young guys at the counter, and at the tables a scatter of people—a red-nosed man sniffling as he read the *Daily News*, a couple of matronly women chatting over a shared plate of pirogies, a long-haired hippie wolfing bacon and eggs, with a battered guitar case at his feet. But Alana wanted privacy with David, and decided to go on through to the next room. As she approached the arch she heard the front door open behind her. David? She turned, but it was just a guy delivering produce. Arms full with a box of lettuces, he passed her and disappeared into the kitchen. Alana went through the arch and found the little room deserted, as she'd hoped.

She picked a table at the back and sat so she could see

David when he came in. The waitress arrived, and she ordered tea. After the woman walked away, Alana caught a faint whiff of the hippie's bacon, and her stomach grumbled with hunger. But she couldn't eat. Too nervous. Nick's behavior had knocked her back. His hormonal response when that female predator had put the moves on him. His blather about selling the gene. His smart-ass hustle could be seen as comical if she didn't so vividly recall Knelman's warning: *"Sterilization is the only responsible option."* It was hard to get her mind around it. Knelman was the enemy, out to kill them . . . yet was he partly right? Was it irresponsible to let Nick walk around horny and reckless?

The waitress came back with a metal teapot and a thick mug. "Milk with that?" she asked, stifling a yawn. Alana shook her head. As the waitress was leaving, Alana looked over and saw David standing in the arch. At the sight of his drawn face, her heart went out to him.

He reached the table but didn't sit. "Where's Nick?"

"It's okay, David, I'll take care of Nick. Sit down. Please." He looked so horribly anxious, she tried to make light of it. "Relax. I'm freaked out enough for us both."

He couldn't even crack a smile. God, this was going to be hard.

When he finally sat, she followed an impulse and reached across the table to him, her hand palm-up, inviting. He stared at it a moment, then lifted her hand and kissed her palm. A kiss so tender it made her want to cry.

"Alana Marks?"

She looked up at the waitress.

"There's a call for you."

"Me? Are you sure?"

"Blue top, dark hair, knapsack. Alana Marks."

Didn't make sense. David's frown showed he thought the same.

"My friend probably wants me to bring back pirogies," she told him. "Back in a sec." She followed the waitress through to the other room, to a wall phone behind the counter, and picked up the receiver. "Hello?"

"I'm at a pay phone down the block," Nick said. "Two cop cruisers just pulled up in front of the joint you're in. Get out now."

"What? How—"

"He *set you up.*"

Her breath caught. "You're imagining things."

"You'll see how real it is when they slap the cuffs on you!"

"No, he wouldn't do—"

"It's his *job!* But I'll bet you anything Knelman's behind it. Jesus, are you going to trust me—your own flesh and blood—or a DA raised by a Nazi?"

Her eyes snapped to the arch, but of course she couldn't see David from here.

"Alana?" Nick's voice was strained. "I can't stick around. You see that, don't you? I gotta take off. And you'd better too, fast. Because if that DA brings you in, Knelman's gonna get to you. Please, *please,* find a way out. Oh, shit, the cop riding shotgun is looking my way. I gotta go."

"Nick, wait—"

"I wish . . . wish you . . . *baxt.*" He hung up.

Baxt. Gypsy luck.

A metal taste like sickness came into Alana's mouth. Replacing the receiver, she looked out the window to the street. She couldn't see either of the cruisers, just a delivery truck right at the door, "Garibaldi's Fresh Produce." Turning back, she saw the deliveryman at the far end of the counter sliding a box of bananas under the sink—a stocky guy in a Dodgers baseball cap and baggy pants. At this end of the counter was another box of his stuff. Potatoes, carrots, onions. He'd likely take it to the kitchen next. Her eyes snapped back to his truck. Would he have left the keys in the ignition? She decided no, not in this neighborhood.

Wiping her slick palms on her pant legs, she waited as the delivery man jostled the bananas in place. He was taking forever. She was sure David would come through the arch in a second, wondering what was up. She watched the man. Come on, come on!

He straightened, and when he started for his box on the counter, coming her way, she moved fast. She collided with him, her hands fluttering as she made embarrassed apologies and staggered a bit to regain her balance. He reddened and chuckled as he steadied her. "My fault, ma'am."

"No, no, my fault. I'm so sorry."

Her fingers closed around the keys that she'd slipped from his pocket. Oblivious, he picked up his box and walked on to the kitchen.

She glanced at the arch. She'd have to go past it. What if David was getting up, coming for her? She was so tense she couldn't move. She felt blood pumping in her ears. She told herself, *Go*.

She walked out the door, went straight to the truck, walking around the front to the driver's side. Opening the door she caught a glimpse in its mirror of a parked cruiser. Her heart kicked with fear. Thank God, the truck had blocked her as she'd come out. *Baxt*. As she climbed up into the seat, she saw the other cruiser parked across the street. She told herself their attention wouldn't be on a produce truck. She started the engine, keeping her face turned away, the way she played away from a camera when she was working.

Shifting into gear, she pulled out slowly, as the deliveryman would if he were leaving. Her head start might give her only a minute or two. The driver would come out yelling, then the cops would be hot after her.

She went east three blocks, not attracting attention, driving carefully—and fighting back tears. At Tompkins Square Park she pulled up onto the curb and stopped. Climbing out, she spotted a teenager who'd stopped for a drink from the water fountain. He'd rested his bike against the statue of Chastity, Temperance, and Faith. She grabbed the bike and cycled away fast, the kid yelling after her. She pumped hard across the park, thigh muscles burning. At the other side she ditched the bike, walked out onto the avenue at East Eighth Street, and flagged a taxi. As it pulled up, she realized she didn't have her wallet—she'd had to leave her knapsack at the table. She dug into her pockets. Some change. And a ten, thank God.

"Grand Central," she told the driver, the first place that came into her head. Her shaky voice sounded like it belonged to a different person. She looked out the rear window as the driver pulled into the traffic. Now that she'd stopped moving, she realized she was trembling all over. She *felt* like a different person . . . someone David had betrayed. How could he? What had made him change? It could only be Knelman.

And Nick . . . it felt like he'd been torn from her. Where would he go?

She'd never been so afraid. Knelman wouldn't give up until she and Nick were dead. She hugged herself to control the shaking. She had to stop this man.

Pushing open the phone booth door, Nick felt the cop's gaze on him from the cruiser. He walked away as fast as he could without looking suspicious. The moment he turned the corner, he ran. He didn't know where he was going. *They'll have her by now.* He felt a hot scratchiness in his throat, an urge to cry. For three days he'd been over the moon, thrilled to have found her, so happy just to be with her. But now she'd turned out to be as gullible as any *gadjo*. Trust a lawman? *How could she believe him instead of me?* He swallowed and ran on faster. He'd be damned if he was going to cry. As if tears would help her. And they sure as hell wouldn't help him.

He needed to think straight. One thing was clear: he had to get off the street, fast. That DA would have the cops looking for him. Reaching Third Avenue, he ducked into a recessed store doorway to catch his breath and scan for cruisers. Shit, a new one had pulled over right across the street. He turned to go into the store, but the door was locked—he hadn't noticed the For Sale sign in the window. Where could he run without those cops seeing him? And even if he got past them, then where? Not back to Gus's: not without Alana. Not home to Glen Cove: more cops there. Not back to Nardi and his goons. Kuelman knew all about the Tre Stelle; Nick had told him everything. He felt panicky, shivery. The whole world was after him.

He saw a bus coming. Saw that the stop was right here in front of the store—so the bus would come between him and the cop car. When it pulled up, he dashed out and got on. Taking a seat, he thought in relief: *Baxt.*

The gypsy word ignited an idea. Maybe there *was* someone he could turn to. They'd never met, but they were blood kin. Rajko Marks.

What would he do if I showed up on his doorstep?

Stupid—what would *anybody* do if some stranger showed up, on the run from the cops? Slam the door in my face. Yeah, except gypsies weren't like that. Blood was supposed to mean everything. He remembered a thing from when Alana was about eight, a relative from out of town showing up, in trouble with the law. The whole clan had closed ranks, hiding the guy, moving him from house to house, blowing a wall of smoke to confuse the *gadje* police. That was the very smokescreen he needed now.

He dug into his memory for the address. Queens. Sunnyside. Yeah, Van Dam Street—if Rajko hadn't moved since Alana left home. The bus was going north. At Sixtieth he could take the subway across the Queensboro Bridge. Right into his grandfather's territory.

He felt a crazy kind of thrill. This was meant to be.

Pink neon rimmed the dumb little storefront picture window wedged between Curry's Hardware and the Van Dam Laundromat. The backdrop inside was a curtain of sun-faded red satin in thick folds, hiding the room behind. Nick stood close up, out of the way of people walking by, traffic passing beyond. He couldn't get over how he'd arrived like a homing pigeon right at the *ofisa,* the fortune-telling parlor where Alana had grown up. "Card & Palm Reading," the black-lettered sign on the glass said. Three tarot cards were painted on the top right corner, and a crystal ball on the left, and on a stand in the center of the window a mechanical doll in long skirts beckoned jerkily. Nick shook his head with a small smile, thinking, Only losers could fall for this—and, luckily for gypsies, there's a never-ending supply. As he pushed open the door, a little bell on it tinkled.

"Hi," a young man said. He sat in the only chair in the small front room, a cigarette in his mouth. Two kids, a boy and a girl of about seven or eight, looked up from the floor at his feet where they were sorting artificial flowers. The man put down his cigarette and got up. He looked in his early twenties, with thick black hair in an Elvis pompadour and chunky sideburns. He wore a checked tank top and red bell-bottoms with a red plastic belt and yellow suede shoes. His eyes flicked over Nick in a quick assessment. "We're closed. Family function." His tone was friendly but distant. "Come back tomorrow."

"I'm not here for a reading."

"Oh?"

Nick's heart was in his throat as he switched to Romany. "I'm visiting town. Came to pay my family's respects to the *rom baro*." He knew that a formal visit for anyone passing through was required among gypsies, but he was terrified he hadn't got the words right.

The man's whole expression changed. Grinning, he said in Romany, "Why didn't you say so? Baby, this *pomana*'s got me jumping so I can't tell real people from the *gadje*." He stuck out his hand. "I'm welcoming folks. The name's Vesh. Vesh Marks."

Nick stared. *Alana's half-brother.* His mind was whirring. Vesh's slangy Romany had been hard to follow, but Nick had caught *pomana,* and remembered that was a sociable feast held a few days after a funeral. Gypsies visiting from all over would be expected; Vesh was accepting him as just one more. "Nick," he replied, shaking hands. "Nick Marks." He knew his last name was common.

"Where you from, Nicky?"

"Austin." Far enough away to be safe, he hoped.

Vesh nodded, looking proud. "May I die as respected as my mother's uncle was."

Nick figured that had to be the dead guy. "I hear he was a great man."

Vesh grinned. "When he wasn't being a jerk." He looked past Nick. "Not by yourself, are you?"

That tripped him. No gypsy traveled alone. "Uh, my brothers and cousins arc finishing some business at the hotel. I thought I'd come ahead." Nervous though he was, he was amazed at how the Romany words were rolling off his tongue once he'd got going. Just like Alana said.

"Okay, we'll look out for them. Come on in, I'll show you around."

The two kids had hopped up and crowded close to Nick, not at all shy. He remembered that gypsy kids past about nine or ten got treated pretty much as adults. It struck him, too, how Vesh talked to him like an equal, none of the "you're just a child" shit he got everywhere else. It felt terrific.

Vesh opened the rear door, beckoning him with a smile. The kids came with them down a narrow hall with dinky fortune-telling rooms on either side, the doors open, nobody in them. Passing one, Nick glimpsed a gaudy painting of the Virgin Mary and a big crucifix. "That one's for the Italians," Vesh said. "At our *ofisa* on Canal Street in the city we got a room like that and another for the Chinese, with no religious junk."

Nick thought of Canal Street passing right between Little Italy and Chinatown. Smart location: heavy foot traffic, and immigrants were attracted to fortune-telling, Asians most of all. The nuts and bolts of the business that Alana had learned as a kid were coming back to him. He said to Vesh, "You've got a big territory."

"Prime. Here we got three *ofisas* in ten blocks of Sunnyside alone. A bunch more in Manhattan. All paying good. Had a scuff-up last month with some Kuneshti guys from

Jersey trying to muscle in, but after the *kris* called the shots our way, we ran those shits out of town."

Nick nodded, glad that he could recall the big picture: the system. State and city boundaries didn't mean a thing to gypsies, but they'd carved up the whole country into clearly drawn business territories, and any clan that tried to encroach on another's zone would have to defend itself at a gypsy trial.

Leaving the cubicles behind, Vesh opened another door, and Nick's mouth opened in awe as they stepped into a different world. A big open room, every wall covered with colorful fabrics, partying people coming and going. Music, laughter, kids running around, the smells of spicy cabbage rolls and strong coffee. He heard female voices and turned to see a kitchen crowded with women and girls cooking amid clouds of steam and nonstop chatter. In the midst of it all a scrawny old man in a black suit stood strumming a guitar as if he was alone, singing a Romany lament, his voice sad and soulful. Nick's pulse was doing a dance. His mouth watered at the aromas, and his heart vibrated to the guitar chords. A sense of belonging welled up in him. He thought, *I'm home.*

Vesh said to the boy, "Go get Nicu to take over for me." The kid nodded and took off, the little girl skipping after. Vesh said to Nick, "Come on, the old man's out back. Mad as hell, though, I hear. There's talk that my cousin just fucked up a business deal."

They stepped outside into a yard bustling with dozens more people. A dizzy happiness swept Nick as he thought, Not much has changed. Washing hung on crisscrossed clotheslines, and the yard ran to the back of the building on the next street, where four stories of apartments, plus the three stories above the *ofisa* they'd just come through, housed the bulk of Rajko's clan. A sprawling, noisy enclave. To the left it spilled into a crummy-looking scrap-metal yard, a clan enterprise, that faced the side street. To the right was a concrete wall with a car-wide gated arch to the alley. The asphalted area leading to the scrap-metal yard was littered with the clan's other stock-in-trade: broken-down cars. Nick counted five, including a rusty gray Pinto, a graffiti-covered Dodge pickup with no fenders, and a dented blue Thunderbird. He knew the men would fix them up and sell them on the fly at out-of-town fairs, concert parking lots, roadsides: no sales license, all cash deals.

As he followed Vesh through the throng, he was hungrily taking it all in. Men in small groups idly inspected the vehicles, talking and joking, beer cans in hands. Their clothes ranged from well-cut suits with flashy shirts to jeans with undershirts. Women carried out food platters to a long table, their bright print dresses all variations on the same style: sleeveless, V neck, full skirt to the knee or ankle, worn with lots of movable gold: earrings, necklaces, wrist bangles. Little kids ran everywhere, some half naked, some in party ruffles. Men and women mostly moved within their own groups. Near the kitchen door a half-dozen aproned women on a cigarette break were taking turns dancing to a music tape—it looked to Nick like a private contest. As each one did a flamenco-like turn, the other women clapped and grinned, egging her on. A bored-looking girl watched from a lawn chair as she breast-fed her baby. And all this congregating and cooking, Nick knew, was just in preparation for the *pomana* to be held in some restaurant banquet hall; there, several hundred gypsies visiting from around the country would come to feast and remember the dead man.

A sallow-faced guy approached him and held out a bread

basket lined with red satin scattered with twenties and fifties. "Make a contribution, my friend?"

Nick shot a look at Vesh.

"We're trying to raise a bride-price for my brother Jimmy," Vesh explained. "The girl's dad is driving a hard bargain."

"Oh, sure thing." Nick dug into his pocket and pulled out a crumpled five. It was almost the last of his cash, but he was glad to hand it over—anything to be accepted here. It gave him a giddy feeling as stuff was coming back to him, like this deal about buying a bride: an expensive one would bring honor to the whole clan, he remembered. Everyone would chip in, even the little kids, handing over what they made selling flowers or shining shoes. Catching the bagman's faint look of scorn, though, he realized his fiver was too measly, and his face burned with shame.

"Don't mind my uncle," Vesh said as they walked on. "He's a pushy bugger. The girl's worth it, though—her dad's a *rom baro* in Atlantic City. Six grand for her, but my old man's made up his mind she's the *bori* he wants."

Bori. Nick racked his memory for the meaning. Daughter-in-law, but more like "woman who marries into my family." A *bori* cooked and cleaned for her husband's family, and also got trained in her mother-in-law's fortune-telling business so she'd bring in steady cash. Man, he loved remembering all this stuff.

A big-boned woman wearing a long skirt and lots of gold came up to them, her leathery hands gripping the handles of a cooking pot of stew, the cigarette in her mouth spilling ash. "Vesh, get them kids down from the wall. One's gonna break his neck."

"Sure, Ma. This here's Nicky from Austin."

"How you doing, Nicky?"

He couldn't speak. This was Yanka, the stepmother Alana had grown up with. He knew those sharp blue eyes, that hawk nose, the tobacco-harsh voice. Remembered what a haul she made telling fortunes, a savvy breadwinner. Even remembered how she stashed her cigarette pack and spare cash in her bra. "Pretty good," he managed.

"Catch you later," she said, and hustled on with her burden of stew to the table.

Nick noticed a new group of visitors coming out from the kitchen: a bearish man in a powder-blue suit with three teenage boys, an old lady, and a pretty girl of about fifteen. The girl wore a modest pink party dress, her slim bare arms silky brown against it. She was giggling at something, and had the whitest teeth Nick had ever seen.

"That's her," Vesh said, following his gaze. "The *bori* my dad wants. Kind of cute, huh? Mimi Toma."

Nick couldn't take his eyes off her.

Vesh turned and pointed. "There's my dad. The *rom baro*. Come on."

At first, looking toward the wall, all Nick saw was a gleaming gold Cadillac under a jutting little roof. But as he and Vesh got closer, he saw a bunch of men beyond the car—fifteen or so, from teenagers to old men, some standing, some sitting in lawn chairs, their attention all on one man. He sat in an upholstered easy chair, shaded by an awning of black plastic stretched with twine between a clothesline post and the wall. As they reached the edge of the group, Vesh stopped and put his finger to his lips to warn Nick to keep quiet. Nick finally got a good look, and it sent a shiver through him. Rajko Marks was a little paunchier, a little grayer, but the same iron-eyed patriarch who'd dragged Alana to the *kris,* got a *marimé* verdict against her, and disowned her. *Rom baro* meant "big man," and Rajko was big in every way—tall and beefy, with a bull neck and long, thick legs. Black, bushy eyebrows bristled on his craggy face. Under a green felt fedora, salt-and-pepper hair curled over his collar. He wore shiny pearl gray pants and a cowboy shirt that was bright white except for the gaudily red-flowered yoke, with sparkling rhinestone buttons. He even had a big voice. Not that he was raising it. No need; the men around him were listening in silence. But the voice was deep and rich, and he used it like an actor. "And I thank you all for your counsel," he was saying.

Vesh whispered, "Holy shit, he's mad."

Next to them a skinny guy with a gray goatee said quietly, "Yeah, we just got a tip the heat's coming."

Nick felt a ripple of fear. "Police?"

Vesh asked the man, "Coming for Stefan?"

He nodded. "The fool's been driving around in Rajko's Cadillac. Rajko figures that's what's drawn them."

Vesh groaned and turned to Nick. "My cousin Stefan, the dumb-ass."

Nick saw a man of about twenty-five standing near Rajko, his head lowered as if in shame. He was smooth-faced, good looking. "That him?"

"Yeah. He's been working a deal for my dad, something about an old lady's brownstone, I don't know the details. He should've laid low, though."

"How do we know the cops are coming?" Nick asked.

The goatee guy nodded toward a chubby man chatting at the food table. "Ion Stanley. Sells info to the cops downtown. We use him sometimes to blow smoke their way. He says a detective name of Lipranski just came asking about the Caddy. Rajko can add."

Rajko was getting to his feet. "All right, my friends,

what's done is done," he declared. "Now *we* got to do something, because the law's on its way for Stefan."

Nick noticed that the men around Rajko weren't the only ones riveted by this potential disaster. More people were drifting over. Nick felt the press of bodies behind him and heard whispers as men and women craned to see around him.

Rajko took a young woman by the hand and drew her forward. She was crying as he joined her hand to Stefan's. Stefan had tears in his eyes now too, so Nick figured the woman was Stefan's wife. Rajko beckoned some kids forward, a half dozen, one after another, and the crying woman pulled them to her, and the kids stood still, their eyes big with fright. Nick looked around. All through the yard the party atmosphere had gotten quieter. He caught sight of Yanka. Steely-eyed, she was following Rajko's every word, her arm around the shoulders of a fleshy woman who was sobbing. Again, Nick felt a jolt of recognition: this was Yanka's sister, Stefan's mother.

Rajko stood behind Stefan's stricken family group, his arms raised like protective wings, and addressed the whole gathering. "Now, they can hold him for questioning, and then maybe they'll send him home. But I just talked to my lawyer, and he says if the DA thinks he's got a case and takes it to trial, they could convict Stefan for extortion, and he could be looking at a year, minimum."

Stefan's wife cried out and threw her arms around her husband, and his mother wailed. Stefan swiped away tears and stared at the ground. Scared voices rose up all through the crowd. Nick figured the young couple had to be related to over half the people here.

Rajko moved around in front of the little family. "Okay, we got ourselves a hell of a problem. Stefan's married to

Rosa here, Stoika Mitchell's daughter, and they got seven little kids. Stefan doing time in a *gadje* cell is going to go real hard on these kids." Rajko clamped a hand on the ragged-haired youngest boy and gruffly hugged the child to his belly. "Another man, now, jail wouldn't be so bad. Say, a man like Stefan's brother here, Emilian. He's not married."

He beckoned forward Emilian, who looked about eighteen and in awe of Rajko. Rajko stood between the two brothers, his arms around them both.

"So here's my decision. Stefan leaves town today, and Emilian faces the cops in his place as George Adams. That's who they're coming for, George Adams, and they won't know the difference so long as we all keep our story straight. If he has to, Emilian will do the jail time. Stefan will lay low for a couple months, then come home, keep his head down, and take care of his family. And Emilian"—Rajko winked at him—"the day he gets out of jail, we're going to give him the best bride money can buy."

There was silence.

Rajko turned to the dumbfounded brothers. "That sit okay with you two?"

They stared at each other, then at Rajko.

"Speak up," he said.

Emilian said, "Yes, sir."

Nick couldn't believe it: Emilian was smiling. Then he realized why. The guy was now a goddamn hero. Stefan was gratefully shaking his brother's hand, and Stefan's wife was kissing her brother-in-law's cheek, and their kids were tugging at his sleeves, and all the people were gazing at him with big smiles, some moving closer to be near him, touch him. It amazed Nick: Rajko had made this happen. Solved the crisis, and made the whole clan feel close, all in one stroke. In a heartbeat he understood the core of gypsy life.

He said to Vesh, in awe, "Mess with one of us, you mess with all of us."

Vesh said proudly, "That's why he's the *rom baro*."

Rajko organized a plan on the spot. Almost everyone had a part to play, some to help Stefan get cleanly out of town to stay with relatives in Cincinnati; some to help Emilian make last-minute arrangements; some, including Vesh, heading in to the *ofisa* to deal with the police when they arrived. As Emilian, with a small throng, was led inside, Rajko called to him, "When they come, make a run for it, let them chase you a bit. More realistic."

Someone piped up, "Make them work for their pay-check."

A few people laughed, but Nick saw that Rajko didn't.

Things were quiet and tense as everyone waited. Rajko walked through the crowd, his big green fedora above everyone, and Nick noticed the way he touched people as he passed—patting shoulders, heads, backs—moving among his people like a king. Finally, word filtered out from the *ofisa* that the police had come, asked for George Adams, taken Emilian, and gone.

Right away Rajko called together a couple of men with guitars. People brightened up. Rajko went to his red-eyed sister-in-law, the mother of Stefan and Emilian. She was still sniffling, and as he took her by the hand, people crowded around. Rajko led her in a dignified Old World dance, and she seemed to grow in stature. She smiled. People clapped rhythmically. The music got livelier, and others started dancing. The party was on again—not quite as though nothing had happened, but as though everyone was more alive than before. Nick was mesmerized by this show of his grandfather's power. He thought, That's how I'd like to be.

He watched Rajko take to his easy chair under the

awning again as everyone went back to eating and drinking and socializing. People came and went around the *rom baro,* talking to him and then walking away, while two young women—his *boris,* Nick figured—brought him things: a plate of food, a beer, a baby to sit on his lap. Nick took a deep breath, thinking, Now or never. The only hope for him, and for Alana, lay in the hands of this man. Walking over, he stood in front of the patriarch. "Thank you for your hospitality, sir. I'm Nick Marks."

"Hello, Nicky." Rajko took a swig of beer. "Do I know your father?"

"You know my mother."

"Oh?" Idly, he glanced at a card game some men had begun. "Where you from, Nicky?"

"I told Vesh I was from Austin. But I lied."

Rajko shot him a look. Then a twinkle came into his eye. "Sure, you're a gypsy." He called to the card players, "Hey, Jimmy, how do you make a gypsy omelet?"

The man dealing cards answered, "First you steal some eggs, then you steal some butter—"

Rajko laughed, a deep baritone guffaw.

"Actually," Nick said, "I'm only half gypsy. But I make up for it with something better."

Rajko's eyes snapped to him. His face darkened, and he almost seemed to recoil, and Nick suddenly knew what it felt like to be considered *marimé,* unclean: to Rajko, anyone with *gadje* blood was. "Your Romany's real good for a *gadjo*, I'll give you that. How'd you get in here?"

Nick figured he had only a minute before he'd be thrown out, because Rajko strictly held to all the traditions; no one *marimé* would be allowed to pollute his home. Nick had to go for broke. "My memory's real good too. In fact, it's kind of special. That was a terrible thing, back in the spring of

’42, how Lina’s brother Milosh got his foot crushed by the wagon wheel. Right after the river flooded so bad, wasn’t it? Late in May? Yeah, the same month you and Lina got married. Remember, that summer, how she wanted to name the baby after you if it had been a boy? So sad, her miscarriage.”

Rajko stared at him, dumbfounded. “How did you—? No one but me and her knew about that baby.”

“Probably a good thing she did lose it, since you were all rounded up for Otzenhausen that winter. Not many kids made it out of that hellhole. By the way, those extra rations Lina brought you and your brothers in the camp—the cabbage and hunks of salami, all those months? And the fantastic ham and potato pancakes left over from the guards’ dinner the day after Christmas? Ever wonder how she got that food? You didn’t really believe she stole it, did you?”

Rajko’s face had gone pale, as if in fear. With his eyes still on Nick, he lifted the baby from his lap and called, “Liza.” A pudgy girl hurried over and took the baby. “You want another beer?” she asked him.

“Leave us.”

When she left, Rajko asked, his voice so strained it sounded hoarse, “Who are you? How can you know . . . such things? What do you want?”

Nick pulled up a lawn chair and sat down so they were knee to knee. Around them, people carried on chattering and laughing and dancing. “I’m your grandson. I want to join your family. And when I tell you what’s special about me, and why, you’re going to see how valuable I can be to you. In fact, that girl Mimi you’re planning to marry to your son, Jimmy? You’re going to want to think instead about buying her for me.”

* * *

It was dark when Knelman unlocked the door of his Park Avenue office that night. Groping for the light switch, he felt unwell, disoriented. The clamminess of his skin was almost like a fever. He'd come straight from the airport. As he'd looked through the Philadelphia taxi's window, then from the taxi coming in from LaGuardia, the two cities had blurred into one. He flashed back to that sense of a doubled self the day he'd walked out of Otzenhausen: that sense of being two people. Just hours ago, his other self had been walking up to the podium to address the support families association. The banquet room had burst into applause, and he'd launched into his speech, his ears still ringing with David's words on the phone moments before. "Dad, the stakeout failed. Alana bolted. Nick never even showed. I have no idea where they are." Addressing the audience, Knelman had fought his sense of panic. *Both gene carriers at large . . . preparing to expose me.* Yet by the end of his speech a thought had broken through: maybe he did know where Alana Marks was.

He switched on the desk light, opened the filing cabinet, and found her file. Laying it on the desk, he turned pages, searching. . . . Yes, here it was. Gus Yuill. In his session with her here Knelman had begun in the usual way, by taking a history, and she had mentioned her mentor and friend, a veteran stuntman. Might she be hiding with this man? He flipped open the phone directory and found a G. Yuill. Not a common name. Address in the East Village. East Sixth Street. He took a deep breath as he dialed.

"Hello, Mr. Yuill? I'm very sorry to call so late. I'm a friend of Alana's. Is she there?"

"This about the kid? You got some information?"

"Do you mean Nick? Is there . . . a problem?"

"Yeah, he split. Look, Alana's lying down. She came in pretty broken up. But if it's about Nick, I'll go get her."

She's there . . . but the boy is not. "No, no need to wake her, I'll call back tomorrow." He hung up, telling himself not to despair. He knew this woman. At dawn she would be searching for her son. If anyone could find him, she could.

He picked up the phone again and dialed Farrell's number to tell him to watch Yuill's place and follow her. But as he listened to it ring and ring, he remembered that Farrell had told him never to call. The instructions had been clear: Farrell called every day at noon; updates or changes were to be arranged at that scheduled time; there was to be no other contact. Knelman hung up and looked at the clock, sick with anxiety. He would have to wait thirteen hours.

CHAPTER 13

DAWN WAS BRIGHTENING the threadbare batik bedspread tacked up as a curtain in Gus's spare room as Alana sat writing, cross-legged on the mattress on the floor. She was already dressed, and the mug of black coffee by her side was getting cold as she concentrated on her list. An indictment. Hardly in the form David was used to—handwritten on raggedy-edged pages of a spiral-bound pad from Gus's gear kit. And certainly not in legalese. But it would have to do. Her life and Nick's depended on it.

It took her over an hour, and when she was finished, it ran to five pages. She folded them and slipped them into a smudged white envelope, licked the flap, and sealed it. Now came the hard part, waiting: offices wouldn't be open until nine. She moved the phone closer so it was at her feet, sipped cold coffee, and carefully thought through every step of what she was about to do. This would be the most crucial stunt she'd ever planned. She couldn't run; she wouldn't without Nick, and she didn't know where he was. She clamped down her anxiety about him and focused on this, her only option. Knelman wouldn't stop until he'd found them both—so she had to stop *him*. Through David. But this time, on her terms.

At nine she began. Her first call was to Knelman's receptionist. "This is Mr. Knelman's assistant at the district attorney's office," she said in her best secretarial tone. "Could Dr. Knelman please meet his son today for lunch? It's rather urgent, Mr. Knelman says." She waited nervously as the woman went to check with the doctor. When she came back on the line to say that would be fine, Alana plowed ahead. "Please ask the doctor to come to the London Grill on Madison at Thirty-seventh Street, twelve-thirty." Hanging up, she called David's secretary and went through the same routine. She almost didn't believe it would work twice—David either would be scheduled in court for noon, or would suddenly come on the line himself. If he did, she was ready to hang up. But he didn't, and again the magic word "urgent" brought back the response she'd hoped for from the secretary. David could make it. The father-son lunch date was on.

Her third call was to Don Grimes, a reporter at the *Daily News* who'd interviewed her in June for a feature article about the film business in New York. He hadn't come in to work yet, and she had to wait another forty minutes, but when she reached him, things went well. He chuckled at the favor she requested and waived her offer to pay for his meal, saying he'd planned to take a contact to lunch anyway and could easily make it the London Grill.

More waiting. When the restaurant opened at around ten, she called and reserved for three under Knelman, asking for a table in the center. A little before noon she went to borrow some cash from Gus. She hated to tap him, but she had no choice: her knapsack, left at the café yesterday, had everything in it. When she'd called them later, they'd said they had it, but she didn't want to go pick it up in case David still had the police watching the place; he might even have left it there on purpose, hoping it would draw her back. Gus had offered to go and get it for her today, but meanwhile she was without wallet, checkbook, even car keys. Her car—another blow. By the time she'd got back yesterday, her Fiat had been towed. She couldn't even go to pay the fine and pick it up until she had her wallet and keys. It felt as though parts of her life were being severed from her, one by one. Boat, car. David. And Nick.

She found Gus at the kitchen table with a cigarette and a can of Bud, circling items on the racing sheet. Crystal had gone shopping. On the radio the laid-back DJ was introducing the next track: "Bad, Bad Leroy Brown." Alana hated asking Gus for money, and apologized twice.

"No sweat," he said as he dug in his jeans for his wallet. "Hey, a guy called for you late last night. I didn't want to wake you up. Didn't give his name, said he'd call back. Polite as hell, sounded foreign."

It stunned her. Knelman had tracked her. *Can't stay here anymore.*

Gus sat back, concern on his stubbled face. "Alana, what's going on?"

She leaned against the counter, wondering how she could explain. Where would she start?

He butted out his smoke. "Remember how we met? You were scamming a guy on West Twenty-fourth for bumping you with his Mercedes. I saw the whole thing from the curb." He chuckled. "Saw you wait until he was about to make a right turn, then you stepped out and did this fantastic, perfect flip. Scared the bejesus out of that guy. You did your sob story to him, and he forked over everything in his wallet, then took off. Remember?"

She had to smile. "I thought I had talent."

"Under layers of crud and attitude, yeah."

They both laughed.

"Criminy, you looked liked something the cat dragged in," he said. "Had my work cut out for me."

She remembered as if it were last week how he'd told her he could train her for film stunts, told her she could stay with him until she got work, how she'd almost cried in relief—no more sleeping in bus stations and parks. At the time, he was living with a skinny blond who worked wardrobe. "Your girlfriend sure cleared out fast when she saw me."

"Ignorant broad. Said I was a dirty old man, picking you up."

Ignorant is right, Alana thought. Gus had never laid a hand on her that way, only as a coach.

"We got right to work, didn't we?" He jabbed the air like a boxer. "Shoulder rolls, how to fall, how to fight. Judo, karate. A natural, you were. But so damned jumpy." He shook his head. "Took a month before you told me your secret, that you were pregnant. Well, we got you through that, the adoption and all. And now look at you, you've made it right up there." He settled back, folding his arms. "But I can see that old look in your eyes, like you're set to do a scam—and like you've got a new secret. Alana, I don't know what's going on with your son, and I don't know what you're running from, but if you're in trouble, maybe you oughta tell me. If I can help, you know I will."

She came over and hugged him. "You already have, Gus, just letting me crash here. You're a true-blue friend. I think the trouble's almost over. I'll know today. Wish me luck."

At twelve, with the envelope in her pocket, she walked down the three flights of stairs, where a smell of burned garlic filled the shabby stairwell. She got on the subway at Bleeker Street, on her way to the London Grill.

Nick was doing all he could to please his grandfather, buffing the gold Cadillac with a chamois, even working up a sweat, but all the while he was watching Rajko's face for a sign. Nick was planning a move, but he needed the right moment. Nearby, Rajko stood in his undershirt and trousers, shaving at an outdoor washstand that his *boris* had set up for him, with a mirror on a frame, his straight razor, a white porcelain bowl of water, and a fresh striped towel. The enclave yard rang with morning sounds: squealing little kids playing around the broken-down cars, three women chattering as they hung up wet laundry, a couple of men with mallets tapping at the dented door panel of a blue Thunderbird. A tape of gypsy guitar music drifted from an upstairs window, and the smell of coffee was strong in the air. Nick loved it here. He'd never felt so at home.

"Damnedest thing I ever heard," Rajko mused, scraping at his whiskers around the thick black sideburns. His salt-and-pepper hair was combed straight back. His craggy face was grave. "Tell you the truth, Nicky, I don't know what to make of you."

"Make me one of *you*. That's all I want."

Rajko turned to him, razor in hand, a faint smile on his lips. He had the look of a man who'd picked up a stone from the mud and wondered if it might be a gemstone. "I'll say one thing. You're an original. Looks like there's no kid like you on this earth."

"You got that right, *Kirvo*." They were speaking in Romany and Nick was carefully addressing him as "godfather," a respectful term. To use *papio*, "grandfather," might be like rubbing salt in a wound, because the subject of

Alana, he knew, was dangerous territory. Since her *marimé* sentence thirteen years ago, she'd been dead to her family. Nick was hoping to eventually bring Rajko around about her. If she was in the DA's custody, which Nick figured she had to be—and if, he thought with a sick feeling, Knelman hadn't got to her yet—then the clan might do something to get her out, maybe through Rajko's hotshot lawyer. But one step at a time. First, he had to get Rajko's trust, and since Rajko hadn't fully accepted him yet, mentioning Alana could be a stupid move. Besides, if he explained the trouble she was in, he'd have to explain Knelman's gunman too, and Rajko's response to a threat like that being brought to his door could be to toss Nick out, case closed.

What he *had* told his grandfather was all about the gene; Nick knew that's where his value lay. After a knee-jerk reaction of shock yesterday, Rajko had become enthralled, hungry for detail. Just what Nick had hoped. He'd explained the Nazi experiment on Lina, then dazzled the old guy with his memories of Lina's whole life, including their time in Otzenhausen. Yet all through it Rajko had kept quiet, guarded, and unreadable, even when it got late and he'd sent Nick inside to bunk down. Nick had spent a mostly sleepless night in the big room with the wall coverings, where thin mattresses, stacked in corners in the day, were spread out for everybody to sleep on, men and boys on one side, girls and women on the other, with Rajko and Yanka in the only bed. Nick had settled into the cozy communality right away, yet all night he'd worried about Rajko's decision, and this morning he still didn't know where he stood. Being Alana's son went against him. So did his half-*gadje* blood. To win over the *rom baro,* he decided he'd have to take a gamble now.

"There's no kid on earth like me *yet.*" He leaned back

against the Cadillac, folding the chamois. "You and me, we can change that. And we should. With what I've got, I can give this family a fantastic edge."

Toweling soap off his face, Rajko cast him a frown. But he looked intrigued. "What are you talking about? What edge?"

Nick jammed the chamois in his pocket and came closer. "I may be just thirteen, but because of this gene I know a hell of a lot. And here's the thing. Every kid of mine is going to have the same edge. See, I pass on the gene, and when the kid's in his mother's belly, he's sucking in everything she knows—it's some hookup with the mother's system. So think about it—I marry a gypsy girl, all my kids are born with gypsy smarts! It could make this family so strong, so powerful, it would put us right on top. We'll become the most respected *kris* judges, the biggest of the *rom baros,* the richest clan around. Okay, that'll take a few years, but right away this thing gives us bargaining power. When word gets around about what we've got, every family is going to want to join with us. Take that Atlantic City *rom baro,* Toma—the one whose daughter you want to marry to Jimmy. Toma's asking a huge bride price, right? Well, switch me for Jimmy, and once we tell Toma about the gene, about the chance we're offering him to get in on the ground floor, an alliance with a family that's going to be as strong as we are, I bet he'll drop his price fast. Hell, he'll pay *us* to take his daughter. See what I mean? One day you'll be making deals for territory up and down the coast. In a dozen years or so my kids can start running whole areas for us, and we could be controlling half the country. Sky's the limit, *Kirvo*."

Rajko watched him with no expression but the faintest shrewd smile, noncommittal as ever. But Nick thought he could see a flame kindle deep in his eyes. "You think big,

Nicky. I like that." Tossing down the towel, he lifted his green fedora from its peg on the mirror frame, smoothed his hair back with one big hand, and put on the hat at a tilt. His eyes hadn't left Nick's face. "Thing is, I don't know you from Adam."

That took Nick by surprise. It sounded like a challenge. "Sure, sure, I understand, *Kirvo*. You need to get to know me. See that you can trust me."

"Exactly. So let's talk." Rajko reached across Nick to a chair where his shirt lay, a faded red cotton with tiny blue flowers all over, and put it on. "I got a couple deals on the go. You lend a hand there, I'll see how you work out." He was buttoning the shirt as he added, " 'Course, you breathe a word outside this family, we'll make you one sorry *gadje* kid."

Nick didn't doubt the threat. "Okay. What deals?"

"One goes like this. We check the obits for fat cats. Doctors, lawyers, business big shots. Lots of times they print the funeral details. Practically an invitation, you know? Because what it tells me is that at such-and-such a time the family's all going to be at the funeral, nobody home. Good time to get into that house and clear out a few valuables. It's not perfect—we always gotta be careful, Nicky. But so far, it's working pretty good."

"Smart." But thieving wasn't how Nick saw himself making a big impression on this man. "And the other deal?"

"Bit trickier. Takes time to set up." He beckoned Nick to come with him, and as he sat down in his upholstered easy chair under the black plastic awning, he motioned for Nick to pull up a lawn chair. Almost instantly a *bori* came out and brought the *rom baro* a mug of steaming coffee—Nick knew now that she was Ruby, the wife of Rajko's oldest son, Boldor. Rajko settled back with his coffee and went on to explain the scam. First, his people would pick the mark, which took time because of the criteria: an ailing old person who owned a valuable property and lived alone. The family would case out stores and doctors' offices where old folks with money were regular customers. Once they'd picked out a likely mark, they decided who in the clan would work it. A "chance" meeting would be maneuvered with the old person, usually an offer to help with grocery shopping or odd jobs in their home, and after a while carefully building a friendship, the gypsy would ask to rent a room. The gist of it was, they got the mark to sign a joint tenancy agreement, which, once the old person died, gave the gypsy title. "It's worked out real good for us, three deals in the last two years," Rajko said. "We sell up right away, before the relatives start calling lawyers."

"Cash in and lay low, huh? Fantastic." A thought jumped into Nick's head—that old guy that Knelman's sister had been choked up about. Retired millionaire, Alana had said. Heart attack. A perfect mark. Old, rich, and sick.

"Yeah, as long as everybody uses their head," Rajko said. "My nephew made a big fucking mistake. I can't afford anybody else doing the same." He added pointedly "*Wunderkind* or not."

"Stefan? The one the cops came for?"

Rajko nodded. "Went tooling around in my car. Parked right outside the old dame's place he was scamming, the dumb-ass. Anyway, we got that under control with Emilian. He kept his mouth shut—didn't know much anyway. The cops got nothing." Nick knew that Emilian had been questioned, then let go. The young family hero had come in late last night and regaled the household with his success.

Rajko swished his coffee, looking satisfied. "Important thing is, the deal wrapped up real good. Old lady died on the weekend, left a fancy old brownstone apartment. We'll sell up quick, make a bundle." He gave Nick a sly look. "And I'll need a good whack of it to meet Toma's bride price."

"For Jimmy?" He held his breath. "Or for me?"

Rajko's look became stem. "Kid, we play this by the book. It's hard enough arranging decent marriages. Lots of families won't come near us, because of the *marimé* taint my daughter brought on us. It's been hell."

Nick heard his grandfather's bitterness, but it didn't deflate his own swelling confidence. Rajko hadn't cut him out of the running. "Like I said, we can soon change that."

"Now you listen to me. Nobody hears about this gene thing, not until I say so. You got that?"

"Got it."

"Okay. Now, back to a job for you. There's a funeral on tomorrow, one we got from the obits. We'll send you out with Vesh and the boys. See how you do."

But Nick hated the thought of being an underling in a house theft, taking orders, scurrying out with the silverware. He wanted to score in a big enough way to make Rajko sit up and take notice. And thanks to Esther Knelman, he might be able to. "I got a better idea. What if I delivered you a prime mark—sick old guy, plenty of dough. Would you let me work it?"

Rajko shot him a fierce look. "You are one pushy gypsy."

"Lina called you the same thing once. When you muscled out that jerk set to marry her. Gyorgy—wasn't that his name? She got her father to give her to you instead. See, Lina never thought pushy was bad."

Rajko's mouth fell open. Nick was scared he might hit him. But Rajko suddenly let out a laugh. "You got *her* right." He shook his head in wonder. "Damnedest thing." His gaze lasered on Nick. "Who's this mark?"

Nick felt a rush of excitement. "Name's Howard Jaffe. Just had a heart attack. Lives alone, that much I'm pretty sure of. Exactly where, I'd have to find out."

"Finding out's easy."

"*Kirvo,* let me work this. Let me prove myself to you. I'm quicker and smarter than anybody you've ever seen. At least, not since Alana."

Rajko's eyes flashed. "Pushy and fresh," he growled.

Nick shot back a Romany saying, one of Lina's favorites. "Without wood the fire would die."

Rajko swished his coffee. Slowly, his face spread in a grin. "Let's get to work."

The London Grill was a popular spot, with mirrored walls, black leather banquettes, an ornate pressed-tin ceiling, and a floor tiled in white and green. Packed with lunch-hour diners, it rang with the chatter of businesspeople and the clatter of cutlery. Alana stood by a wall near the entrance, feeling a flurry of nerves as she watched Knelman following the hostess to a table near a central pillar where David sat. Knelman took a seat, talking to David, and the puzzled expressions on both their faces told her they were just discovering that neither had asked for the meeting. Good. She had them off balance.

Steadying herself, she started for their table, and caught sight of Don Grimes at a booth with fresh martinis in front of him and his guest. On the phone she'd told him she wanted to impress an action film director she was lunching with, and the favor she'd asked was for him to visit her table and give her a boost. As she passed, Grimes winked at her, but she was too keyed-up to smile back.

She reached David and Knelman's table. "Glad you both could make it. Mind if I join you?"

They gaped at her.

She sat down. "This shouldn't take long. We're not here to eat. I've learned something about both of you. Helpful facts." She looked at David. "I found out that I can't trust you to help me and Nick. But I can trust you to do your job."

"Alana—"

"No, just *do* your job. That's all I want from you." She turned to Knelman, folding her hands on the table. "And you, Doctor, I've figured out your worst nightmare. It's for the gene to become public knowledge. That would blow open your past, and guarantee the gene a future. Am I right?"

Rigid, he didn't move a muscle.

David said, "Alana, about yesterday, let me explain—"

"No. You brought the police to collar me and Nick. I don't know why. Maybe the good doctor here convinced you it was somehow for the best—to save me from myself, my so-called mental condition. But for all I know, you've been his accomplice from the start. Tracking me down on that film set. Making me fall for you."

He gripped her hand on the table. "I'm the one who fell."

She swallowed and pulled her hand out from under his. She couldn't let herself go soft. "I'm hoping I can trust you as a prosecutor, but that's all about you I *will* trust. It's my gamble—and why this meeting had to be a surprise. No cops outside today."

He looked stricken. "You're entitled."

She took the envelope from her pocket and set it down on the table. She went on to David, "Until now, you haven't believed me. We're here to change that. I'm presenting a formal complaint. But with a twist, gypsy style."

Knelman said in a strained voice, "Miss Marks, I suggest we discuss this in private so that—"

"Gypsies don't believe in privacy, Doctor." She wasn't expecting a miracle; she didn't think he would crack. But she had to plant enough doubt about him in David's mind to make David act. "At a *kris* the idea is to air grievances in front of everybody, so the judge and the people can see how the battling parties react. That's how gypsies root out the truth. No rules of evidence, no rights of the accused, just a face-to-face test for everyone to witness. Today, we'll forgo the onlookers." She looked at David. "And you're the judge."

His face clouded. "Alana, this is a bad idea."

"Better keep an open mind, Judge."

"Can I get you folks something from the bar?" the waiter asked, arriving with menus.

"Scotch for these two gentlemen," Alana said. "Better makes it doubles. And I'll have a Virgin Mary."

When the waiter left, she said to them both, "There are three things you need to know. First, in this envelope is an account of everything that's happened, going back to the beginning. A full and complete indictment with names, dates, and locations—more than enough for David to act on. Your Nazi past, Doctor, and how you entered the country illegally under an assumed name. How you implanted the gene in my mother and two other women. Its effects on me and my son. What you did to Jacob Wentzler. And your attempts to kill me and Nick through a hit man." The thought of those close escapes made her shudder, and so did saying all of this to Knelman's face. God only knew what he'd do. But it felt good to finally come out swinging. "Second, that balding man in the booth over there with a martini is a staff reporter with the *Daily News*. A friend of mine, Don Grimes. Third, this envelope is going to leave the restaurant in the hands of either David or the reporter. Grimes may not believe the whole story right off, but he'll certainly check it out. Your prestige guarantees that, Doctor—the media love to see the mighty fall. He'll look into records, German university transcripts and whatnot, and he'll dig up enough of the truth about you to turn us all into front-page stop-the-press news. You, me, Nick. Your worst nightmare come true."

Knelman's face was blanched as bone. David looked appalled.

"Believe me, I don't *want* to go public," she went on. "It would turn me and Nick into freak celebrities. Everybody would want a piece of us. Grief all around. But if I have to choose between that and getting killed by your hit man—if it's the only way I can protect Nick and myself from you—I'll do it. We could survive the ordeal. Eventually, we'd disappear. Gypsies are good at disappearing—ask David. But you? Once the world knows you're a Nazi war criminal masquerading as a Jew, the media would crucify you. Everyone from the FBI to the German government to the Israelis would want your head, to say nothing of organizations like the Isaac Rosenthal Center, and finally you'd be taken down like a dog. I'm betting you don't want that. In David's custody you can go quietly. He can take you in for whatever charge will put you behind bars until you're an old, old man. That's all I want."

Knelman's eyes hadn't left her, and he was so still, he seemed to have stopped breathing. David's eyes flicked from her to the envelope to Knelman.

"Hi, Alana." It was Grimes. "Say, my paper would really love to do a follow-up feature on you. My editor raved about the June interview—agreed with me you're the best in the business. Could I call you and discuss it?"

"Sure, Don. Love to. Thanks for stopping by."

He grinned and walked away. Alana noticed a sheen of sweat on Knelman's forehead as his eyes followed Grimes back to his table. "The masquerade's over, Doctor. It's only a question of whether David takes you in, or the world tears you to pieces." She turned to David. "Which puts the burden on you, Judge. So let's get started, gypsy style. Let this man defend himself before you." She turned to Knelman. "I accuse you of—"

"David," he cut in shakily, "I must confess that I . . . misrepresented Miss Marks's case to you. That is, about the gene she refers to. It exists."

David's blinked. "What?"

A thrill shot through Alana. She'd never expected a confession! Then a red flag sprang up in her mind. *Why* was he confessing?

"Two double scotches, one Virgin Mary," the waiter said, setting down the drinks from his tray. "You folks ready to order?"

"Not yet, thanks," Alana said. The waiter left.

Knelman went on to David, his voice flat with strain, "It was a breakthrough research project at the Kaiser Wilholm Institute of Human Heredity and Eugenics. It became a pet project of Himmler's, Hitler's right-hand man. The research goals fit the Nazi philosophy, you see. A gene to produce a master race."

"Are you saying—" David faltered. His eyes flicked between the two of them. "Are you telling me that Alana truly has some . . . genetic superiority? Because of a Nazi experiment?"

"The science is complicated. Too much so to explain now. Suffice it to say that during the course of the project a specially engineered gene was implanted in Miss Marks's mother in Otzenhausen, just as she claims. The result was successful—alarmingly so. Miss Marks was indeed born with her mother's knowledge, which she then passed to her son, along with all her own knowledge. Since offspring of both sexes inherit the gene, it would thereafter be passed along by either sex, in perpetuity, every fetus inheriting all its mother knows. A never-ending chain." He glanced at Alana. "Unless the first links can be broken."

Hope cut into her like pain. Was he actually going to make it so easy and hang himself?

David took hold of her hand on the envelope as if to steady himself. "Alana, I'm sorry that I . . . didn't believe you. This . . . gene."

"Well, you know now. Go on, Doctor, tell him the rest. Who you really are. Tell it all."

"Miss Marks, it pains me deeply that the legacy of this experiment has unbalanced your judgment. Such unstable brain function is the very reason I have devoted myself to preventing the gene's further propagation. I hoped to persuade you and Nick to accept sterilization as the safest and fastest way to close the book on this abominable experiment." He looked at David. "Forgive me, son, that was the reason I objected to your developing an intimate relationship with Miss Marks."

Son. She felt a pang of dread. He was sticking to his basic lie. She had to make David see. "David, let me make my charge crystal clear. He's Viktor Schiller. He's the Nazi scientist who *created* the gene. He's terrified this will all come out and ruin him. If not, ask him how come he knows every detail about the experiment."

David turned to Knelman.

Knelman suddenly buried his face in his hands with a moan. Elbows on the table, his face masked, he seemed to shudder. "So painful."

"Dad?" David's voice was hoarse.

Knelman dropped his hands. His face was ashen as he

spoke straight to David. "Six days we were on the boxcar to Otzenhausen. Hundreds of starving Berlin Jews. Your mother and I, and you, just fourteen months old. Hannah held you in her arms the whole way, would only let me take you when she snatched a few moments of sleep in that foul car. The dead fell where they stood—the sick, the old, the very young. When the door rolled open, we saw guards with rifles and dogs. Right there at the unloading ramp is where the doctors made their selections—their word, every arrival selected for work or for death." His eyes snapped to Alana. "Miss Marks herself, with her abnormally enhanced memory, recounted the horror of it at our first meeting. Remember, Miss Marks? *Rechts! Links!* Right, to work. Left, to the gas."

Her thoughts were skidding. Where could he hope to go with this lie? The horrible thing was, David looked riveted.

"All women with children were sent left. Illogical," Knelman went on hollowly, "since many young mothers would have made strong workers. But to Nazis the most vile creature was a breeding Jewess, so the regulation had a logic of its own. Hannah, holding you, was put with the mothers and children to go to the gas. I fought to reach her, and got a rifle stock in the groin."

Then it hit her: *He just can't bear to have David know.*

"What happened next, David, I hoped I would never have to tell you. A doctor approached me. His name was Schiller. He referred to my neurosurgical research and said that he'd requested that I be shipped to Otzenhausen instead of another camp. He told the guards to take Hannah and you to his quarters. He showed me his laboratory and gave me tea in his office, and outlined the genetic project he was developing and said that my expertise would be invaluable. I was horrified. Told him I would rather die than assist Nazis. He brought in Hannah. She was holding you. He shot her between the eyes. She fell dead at his feet, still clutching you. I was in shock. About to shoot you too, he said that he would spare you if I agreed to assist him. I—" His voice broke. "They sent you to Switzerland with the Red Cross. I thanked God you were safe." His face creased as if in pain. "I had to work with him."

Alana saw that the phony tale had gone straight to David's heart. He had the raw look of a man unused to feeling tears. "My God—," he whispered.

"David, it's all lies!" She held up the envelope. "The truth is in here. He's manipulating you, playing you. None of that happened."

David's hand shot up for her silence. "Please, Alana." His pained expression showed his struggle to grapple with the facts. "My father *did* get me out to Switzerland with the Red Cross. My aunt will tell you that. And my mother was murdered in the camp."

"But not like that! She was probably one of those poor millions who were gassed." She turned on Knelman. "What happened to Schiller?"

"I have no idea, Miss Marks. Many people, officers and prisoners alike, went unaccounted for in the chaos of liberation. I only thanked God that I could join my sister here, where I was overjoyed to find my son."

"Why did you operate on Jacob Wentzler and leave him brain dead?"

His puzzled expression looked eerily convincing. "I did recently perform a cingulotomy on a patient named Wentzler. He is experiencing temporary postoperative side effects, but I expect a full recovery. In any case, I see no connection to the events we are discussing."

"David, he hired a gunman to kill me and Nick. The man

shot at me on the City Island Bridge. I have the scar to prove it. He followed us to the St. Moritz Hotel, and we had to run from him. We're *still* running from him."

Knelman's look became indulgent, as though he pitied her. "Such hallucinations are the tragic effect of the gene, Miss Marks. The very mental imbalance I warned you about."

His act infuriated her. "I heard you in your study whistling exactly the way Schiller did. David, I *remember* how Schiller whistled, because my mother heard him in his office."

"As I believe I have made clear, I was forced to work as a prisoner physician, and I often worked in Schiller's office on his research data. My whistling there must be the memory you refer to—it was me your mother heard, not him. Had I refused to cooperate on his research, I would have blasted my only chance to save my baby son."

He had an answer for everything. David's agonized gaze moved back and forth between them. Alana couldn't take any more. Though David was clearly shaken, his belief in Knelman was not. She couldn't crack a lifetime of father-son bonding. "So it's Plan B, then. Don Grimes breaks the story in the *Daily News*. You brought this on yourself, Doctor. God help us all."

Envelope in hand, she got to her feet.

"Stop." His face was white. "There is something you do not know about the gene. A negative characteristic—a *perilous* characteristic. Miss Marks, let me explain the danger. It expressly concerns your son."

"What are you trying to pull now?"

"Only the awful truth. Please, sit down."

A danger? To Nick? Wary, she sat.

Knelman took a sip of scotch as if to brace himself. "I

was working at the lab in the camp, late April of 'forty-five, just before liberation, and I discovered something in the research data that horrified me. It suggested that the gene might suppress the system of the brain that regulates a sense of right and wrong. I could explain more precisely, but the terminology would be abstruse for the layperson—a complicated synchronicity of hormones, chromosomes, and electrical brain function. The result, baldly put, is that the sensory areas in the brain are disconnected from the limbic system, leading to a complete lack of emotional contact with the world. In other words, while this gene enables the transfer of knowledge, it switches off conscience. It could unleash a dangerous mutation, men with no compunction against doing harm. Born killers."

Alana met his gaze. "Bullshit."

"Dad, that makes no sense. Look at Alana. You've admitted she carries the gene, but it hasn't had this terrible effect on her."

"I said *men*. We are dealing with a peculiarity of heredity in which, as with hemophilia, the mutation presents only in *males*. The mother is the carrier of the gene, which enables her sons and daughters to inherit her knowledge, but in a son the male chromosome, in combination with sex hormones in the brain, mutates the genetic material, switching off conscience."

He let out a tight breath. "This, Miss Marks, has been the reason for my vigilance, and the reason I now bring David into our confidence. The peril must be faced. Make no mistake, this mutation could alter the course of humanity. And it would not take long. Once the phenomenon became known, people would *want* enhanced children. They would seek out marriage partners who carry the gene. Their gifted offspring would gain positions of power in industry, government, the military, academia. A fundamental shift in society could take hold within a single generation. After that, the evolutionary drift would be biologically unstoppable, like an ever-spreading virus. It would be a case of natural selection speeded up—the strong not just weeding out the weak, but *dominating* them. The Nazis' dream come true."

"But . . . surely that would take a population of millions," David said. "Some kind of critical mass."

"History shows us otherwise. Ancient Rome, a city of a few thousand, subjugated the entire known world. A mere three dozen Spanish conquistadors, with guns and a will to conquer, took control of the immense kingdom of the Incas. In South Africa a small minority maintained apartheid to bar the vast majority from power. And a handful of Nazis running Germany took just five years to exterminate almost a whole people. Small numbers, wielding superior advantage. And the groups I just cited only *believed* they were superior—the inheritors of the knowledge gene truly *are*. Once the gene produces enough enhanced people, will the unenhanced stand a chance? How long before they are considered inferior, even defective? Eventually, subhuman. Enhanced males would virtually guarantee this outcome. With no conscience, they would be not only intolerant in their superiority but vicious. They would accept no responsibility, make no sacrifices, because they would care nothing about mankind."

Alana felt almost paralyzed. She sensed David was too.

Knelman plowed on. "Since those final days in Otzenhausen I have been tormented by what this mutation could unleash. I searched for you, Miss Marks—I frankly and fully confess that. I hoped to persuade you to be sterilized, hoped that solution would end the nightmare. But after David found you, you brought me face to face with your son. By his own admission, Nick has already carried out at least one brutal assault. Who knows if there have been others? Or what even worse attacks he *will* commit? Nick is no mere disturbed boy. He is the Nazis' biological time bomb. A killer in waiting. And, left unchecked, he could become the father of killers for endless generations to come."

Alana could hardly breathe. When David spoke to her, he sounded like someone still in shock. "Is Nick staying with you?"

She tried not to move a muscle, but she knew her anxious hesitation told them: she didn't know where Nick was. She found her voice, though the sides of her throat felt stuck together. "You said yourself this is only theory . . . about the males. You don't know if it's true."

"It is a hypothesis, yes, but it is based on my lifetime of experience with the workings of the brain, and firsthand knowledge of the gene's implantation. Please, do not gamble that I have made an error. I have not."

Every instinct drove her to call his bluff, go public, hang the bastard. But he froze her with a faint horror that he might be right. Nick's callousness had sometimes worried her, even scared her. She didn't trust Knelman—but did she dare not trust his expertise?

She stood up stiffly, catching both men off guard. "I'm leaving this envelope with you," she told David. "My life and my son's life are in your hands. You've got half the truth, you know the gene is real. Find out the other half, investigate this man. Do your job."

Knelman didn't even crack, she thought, going almost blindly down the steps to the subway at Forty-second Street. Approaching the turnstile, she stopped. Where to? She had to find Nick, but how? Where could he have gone?

And where can I go? Can't stay at Gus's any more; Knelman has the address. *Where to?*

Aimlessly, she stepped onto the 6 train and found a seat, her thoughts churning. What was she to believe? When Knelman had admitted the gene to David, she'd wondered why, but now she thought she knew. He'd done it to stun them both. How deftly he'd woven that one truth into his lies, all to undercut her. Since David had bought the heart-wrenching wartime tale, he wouldn't be rushing off to investigate—and given Knelman's frightening prediction, neither could Alana go rushing off to the press. Knelman had cleverly withered both her options.

Yet she'd seen desperation in his eyes. He must know that, eventually, David would *have* to investigate. Discreetly—reluctantly, even. But no DA, not even a loving son, could leave such charges unexamined. And one crack in the story would bring down the whole house of cards. It was inevitable, and Knelman had to know it.

So all he'd done was buy himself a little time. Time, she realized, to finish what he'd set out to do. Kill her and Nick.

She was facing a man whose goal now was to finish them off before he was caught. A man who'd already accepted his own end.

The time he'd just gained, she had lost.

She felt so shaken, it seemed that the people sitting across the aisle were staring at her as if to demand, What are you going to do?

First things first, she told herself. Find Nick.

Think like he would think. Knowing the police were after him, he wouldn't stay on the street. But he'd never go back to the Morgans, and he couldn't go back to White Pride. He had no friends and he was low on cash. Where could he go to be safe?

The train pulled into Fifty-first Street, and a mustachioed hippie strolled into the car, holding the hand of a smiling little girl. Both blond, they wore matching tie-dyed headbands. Father and daughter. An idea stole over Alana, as magnetic as the little girl's smile. Where do you go when there's nowhere else to go? *Home.*

Nick knew the place because *she* knew it. And she'd seen how enthralled he was about his gypsy roots. Had he gone there, seeking refuge? The certainty of it made her shiver: she and Nick thought so much alike.

The difference was, home was no refuge for her.

CHAPTER 14

THEY WAITED UNTIL three-thirty to leave the Van Dam Street enclave. For this job Nick knew it wouldn't look right for him to be out during school hours. They drove out in an old green Dart, Rajko at the wheel. As they crossed into Manhattan, heading for the Upper West Side, Nick looked back at Boldor's pudgy wife Ruby in the backseat, painting her nails. He'd asked Rajko for her. She looked kind of frumpy in a brown skirt and beige blouse, and the glasses and lack of makeup, plus her hair pulled back in a bun, didn't do her plain features any favors, but she had the kind of open face the *gadje* trusted, and she was quick. More important, she knew the ropes; she'd been Stefan's partner in working the old lady who'd just died. She would be following Nick's plan for this job—Rajko had okayed it, and Nick had coached her. Still, he was glad of her experience.

"Got the pepper?" he asked her.

She opened her old-lady-style handbag and handed him a tiny rigid package of black pepper, the takeout kind from a burger joint. Nick put it in his right pants pocket.

Rajko let them out on West End Avenue, around the corner from Howard Jaffe's brownstone on West Eighty-fourth. They walked to his place, a narrow, spick-and-span building with purple petunias spilling from first-floor window boxes, and Ruby rang the bell. They waited so long, Nick was afraid no one was home. Then a voice came over the speaker. "Yes?"

"Mr. Jaffe?" Ruby asked.

"Yes?"

"Hi, it's Mrs. Livingstone from the Roosevelt Hospital's Outpatient Outreach Services. The department wants to be sure you're making out okay, all on your own. Could I have a word?"

When the second-floor apartment door opened, Nick took the measure of the bald old man who stood there. He looked tired, worn out. Good sign. But he'd taken the care to dress well, actually looked pretty sharp for an old guy. Gray wool slacks, a fawn-colored suede jacket, pale blue shirt, blue knit tie. As he glanced at Nick, who wore a school jacket and tie bought secondhand for this job, there was a faint smile of approval in Jaffe's eyes. Another good sign.

Ruby held up a laminated ID card just long enough to look official, and smiled. "The outpatient department called earlier, but they couldn't get through," she said. "Is there a problem with your phone?"

Jaffe looked perplexed. "No, I . . . didn't think so."

Nick felt for the tiny rigid package of pepper, broke it open in his pocket, and ground the pepper between his right fingers. His eyes hadn't left Jaffe.

"Well, I've just come along to ask if there's anything you need," Ruby went on pleasantly. "Sometimes we find that our senior patients could use some help with a little light cooking or cleaning. You know, just an hour here and there, to lend a hand. It's covered by your insurance."

Nick coughed.

Glancing at him, Ruby said, "I hope you don't mind my son tagging along. The fact is, I have a bit of a disability, I'm losing my hearing, and Joey's a big help." She added with a small laugh, "I call him my hearing-ear dog."

Nick smiled at the old man. "Woof."

Jaffe chuckled. "Smart pup. Can't say I need any help, though."

"Oh? Is there some family member staying with you while you get back on your feet?"

"No, no, I'm alone. But a cleaning woman comes every Wednesday."

"Oh, good."

Nick deliberately rubbed his eyes with his right fingers. The pepper stung like hell.

Ruby went on, "Still, no daily chores you're finding a bit of a challenge? We know you independent gentlemen don't like asking for help, and that's why we make the offer first."

"No, I get by fine."

"Well, good, I'm glad to hear you're feeling so well. I won't keep you any longer. It was nice to meet you, Mr. Jaffe. You have a lovely day, now. Good-bye." She turned to go.

"Good-bye." Jaffe started to close the door.

Nick coughed several times fast and harsh, as though he was having trouble breathing. Jaffe stopped, looking concerned. Nick's eyes were watering now, and he figured they had to be red. He sniffed hard between coughs.

"Joey?" Ruby took him by the shoulders. "Are you okay?" She glanced at Jaffe. "Hay fever. This season's terrible for him. Sometimes it gets so bad, he can hardly breathe."

"Want a glass of water young fella? Would that help?"

Coughing and sniffing, Nick nodded.

"Oh, we don't want to trouble you," Ruby said.

"No trouble." Jaffe opened the door. "Come on in to the kitchen. I was just getting a sandwich."

"Now, you let *me* fix that sandwich, Mr. Jaffe," Ruby said, walking in, Nick behind her. "Let me guess, I bet you'd like it with a big slice of pickle."

Rajko picked them up in the Dart two hours later, again around the corner. They'd washed Jaffe's dishes, vacuumed his front room, changed a burned-out overhead lightbulb, and taken out the garbage, and when they left him, he was sitting in his favorite chair with a cup of coffee and the *New York Times*, his calico cat on his lap and a tired but grateful look on his face. "Now, I'll check back day after tomorrow, Mr. Jaffe, but if you need to get in touch in the meantime, just call me," Ruby had told him, handing him her number. "I don't recommend calling the hospital, because they take forever getting messages to me—they're swamped. Easier to call me at home. I don't mind." Jaffe had tried to give Nick five dollars, but Nick turned it down, saying he was glad to help his mother. "She's having a hard time since my dad walked out on us," he'd confided, petting the cat in Jaffe's lap. "Anyway, I do chores like this at the church hall. Nice cat. 'Bye."

On the drive back to Sunnyside they relayed the details to Rajko, and he nodded in approval. On Van Dam he pulled into the scrap-metal yard and drove on through into the enclave. As Ruby got out, Rajko motioned Nick to stay. He reached over and ruffled his hair. "Nicky, you did real good today. You weren't fooling, you *are* smart." He laughed. "Smarter than my sons—bunch of thick-heads."

Nick felt a glow of pride. He settled back in the late-afternoon sun streaming into the car. "In a week or so we'll tell Jaffe my dad's debts have forced us to look for a room to rent until we get back on our feet. I checked out his lay-out. Tons of space. He owns the whole second floor."

Rajko nodded. "Great, great." He threw his arm along the seatback. "Now I'm gonna tell you something, Nicky. Know why we've had three good deals on this scam in two years?"

"Because you picked good marks."

"Sure, but something else too. See, we hurry these old folks along. To the other side. You get me?"

Nick didn't move. The sun on him had suddenly lost its warmth. "How?"

"Stuff in their food. Magic salt. Good results, no pain. They're at death's door anyway. Let's just say, I open the door." He looked hard at Nick. "This Jaffe, he's all yours. Think you can handle it?"

Murder. Nick felt his body slowing down—his breathing, his heart. It wasn't shock, more like settling into the idea. Remembering. Lina had done it, helped the Nazi doctors. She'd sat women down, one by one, and got them to put their arms behind their head so the doctor could inject phe-nol into their heart. Then she and another prisoner tossed the bodies in the storeroom. A roomful of pink corpses, that was a day's work. When it came to the kids, she'd sometimes in-jected them herself. Nick looked out at the enclave yard. The men fixing the blue Thunderbird had knocked off for the day and sat gabbing over beers, Vesh among them. Women were already setting out plates and bowls on the long table. A chunky girl of about seventeen was strolling by the wall, breast-feeding her baby and crooning to it, it looked like.

Vesh caught Nick's eye and waved. Nick longed to join them. "Yeah," he answered his grandfather. "I can handle it." It would make the family stronger. And so would the gene he carried, if he could just get Rajko to come around. *Once I'm married. I'll be one of them forever.* "If you can handle thinking again about giving the Toma girl to me."

He turned, expecting an argument, but Rajko, looking straight ahead, didn't seem to be listening. His face had clouded over, and when he spoke, there was ice in his voice. "Who the fuck let her in?"

As Nick followed his grandfather's gaze, his heart jumped. Standing at the kitchen door was Alana.

David was already late for a meeting upstairs with Jack Rintoul, his boss, but he felt glued to the chair at his desk. He was reading through Alana's five-page handwritten indictment for the second time since coming back from her ambush at the London Grill. Or maybe the third time. Hard to concentrate. The legal pad he'd gotten out to jot notes on lay unmarked. He felt sick, remembering how she'd said she couldn't trust him after yesterday, except to do his job. Yet what was he to make of these wild charges she'd listed here? And he was still reeling from Dad's admission about the knowledge gene, that Alana truly was . . . enhanced. He could barely grasp the fact of that. And the opposing claims that she and Dad had made threw up a kaleidoscope of images he couldn't make any sense of. A Nazi doctor shot my mother, Dad said. . . . Dad *himself* is a Nazi, Alana said. He's trying to kill her and Nick, Alana said. . . . She's unbalanced, Dad said. And Nick—what in God's name lay ahead there? The whole thing overwhelmed him. There was only one fact that he clearly understood, and it was burrowing into his mind like a tick into his skin: Dad had lied to him for weeks about Alana's "condition."

The phone rang. He grabbed the receiver before it rang again. "Assistant District Attorney Knelman."

It was Toby DeVrey, returning the call David had put in to Washington after the first read-through of Alana's charges. Barging through the pleasantries now, David asked Toby if he could put a rush on the search of the army archives he'd requested two days ago. He threw in a lame comment that the family history he was compiling was to be a gift for his aunt's birthday.

"Actually," Toby said, "I've got the results right in front of me. Thought it might be what you were calling about."

"That's fast work."

"Maybe too fast. Fast can mean sloppy, which I'm afraid is what my clerk has handed me. Her report doesn't make sense."

David asked, uneasy, "What did she find?"

He heard Toby rustling pages. "It's a bit complicated. Got a few minutes?"

David glanced at his watch. Rintoul was expecting him. Already late. "Shoot."

"Well, first off, the surviving records of the Germans are impeccable, no problem there. They list Heinrich Knelmann and his wife Hannah, from Berlin, inducted into the camp on August 7, 1943." More rustling pages. "Here's a photostat of the German clerk's notation that Knelmann was deloused, tattooed, issued inmate clothing, and installed as a prisoner physician. His number was 17233."

Something in David gave way, like sinking into a chair in relief. He hadn't realized how anxiously he'd wanted to hear that number read out—the five digits that purpled Dad's forearm, tattooed on David's mind since he was a child.

Toby cleared his throat. "The next bit may be tough to take, my friend. The German clerk made an entry that a little over two months later, October twenty-third, Hannah Knelmann died of heart failure. That was how the camp doctors wrote up death certificates for prisoners who were worked to death, you know—as heart failure, pneumonia, dysentery, that kind of thing. They were sticklers at these bureaucratic cover-ups. They didn't bother with death certificates for anyone sent straight to the gas, because those people never officially entered the camp. Ingenious bookkeepers, the Nazis. Mrs. Knelmann entered, but we'll never know her actual cause of death. Likely the slave labor conditions, or starvation."

Or a bullet in the head, David thought with a fleeting pang for the mother he'd never known. "So what doesn't make sense?"

"The problem crops up in the record made by our troops. Don't get me wrong, there's a mountain of official on-the-spot data." More rustling of pages. "The 1945 spring push into Germany was led by General Jacob Devers's Sixth Army Group, which consisted of the French First Army and the American Seventh Army under General Alexander Patch. By April, the Seventh Army was strung out on an east-west axis just south of the Danube, poised for an advance into southern Germany. Otzenhausen was in their path, and on the thirtieth of April they went in and liberated the place. There are several official accounts—called After-Action Reports—and in one of them my clerk did find a reference to Heinrich Knelmann. It's in the report of a Captain Crothers of the 180th regiment of the Forty-fifth Division, one of six divisions making up the Seventh Army. Crothers writes that Knelmann was found dead on the day of liberation. The reference is quite specific. Prisoner number 17233, shot in the head, apparently on that very day, his body found in a closet in the office of a Dr. Viktor Schiller. Now, since your dad is hale and hearty and ministering to his patients in the Big Apple as we speak, obviously the good Captain Crothers made an error."

"Did you say . . . Schiller?"

"Don't bother trying to pin this down, David. There are all sorts of reasons why the error could have happened. There was chaos that day. As the tanks were rolling in, some inmates settled scores against the brutal prisoner kapos—a few got the chop in dark corners—so this body in the closet might have been one of them, and the ID got mixed up. Also, the Nazis managed to burn some records. And then, the Allies let out prisoners in waves of several hundred each day—hard to keep perfect records in that upheaval. All in all, we're talking a bureaucratic mess. My clerk wrote up that this indicates Heinrich Knelmann never left the camp alive. Obviously, that's not true. Like I said, sloppy work."

David found his voice. "She include anything about the two women prisoners? Hilde Wentzler and Sophie Grossman?"

"Actually, the gal's quite a sleuth. I've got to hand it to her, she ran with this. Didn't find anything about Grossman, but she did track Wentzler's trail to Amsterdam. Hilde Wentzler, a Jewish German immigrant, found dead in a waterfront slum flat, March 1958. An unsolved homicide. Her camp tattoo showed she'd been in Otzenhausen."

"Mr. Knelman?" Fiona poked her head in the doorway. "Mr. Rintoul just buzzed. Shall I tell him you've been held up?"

"No. I'm on my way." He said to Toby, "I'd be grateful if you could send me your clerk's report."

"Sure, for what it's worth."

Walking up the marble stairs, David's legs felt leaden. *"A bureaucratic mess"* . . . that had to be the explanation. But each thud of his shoes on the steps brought back Alana's words. *"He's Dr. Viktor Schiller . . . he's the Nazi scientist who created the gene . . ."* Eyes on the veined marble underfoot, David saw the purple-black 17233 etched on his father's skin, and he narrowed his mind onto it like a talisman rooting his faith. A tattoo couldn't lie.

Alana walked across the yard toward the Dart, feeling so incredibly relieved to see Nick in the car: she'd been right to come here. But the sight of Rajko getting out from behind the wheel rocked her. *Taté* . . . father. He looked the same; older, with a paunch, but still every inch the "big man." And he was coming straight for her, a storm in his eyes. She dreaded this. Arriving at the *ofisa,* she'd so surprised her cousin Liza, her best friend when they were kids, that Liza had let her in, and they'd passed through the house leaving shocked whispers in their wake: "It's *Alana. . . .*" Now, as she and Rajko approached each other, people were drifting out, sniffing a fight—coming from the kitchen, from across the enclave, from everywhere, it seemed. Women chattering, men muttering, kids crowding near, everyone asking what was up. Life here was one long communal drama, privacy unheard of, and Alana knew, with a knot tightening her stomach, that this face-off would be no different.

She and Rajko met on the spot where the asphalt met the earth. Behind him, and behind the forming ring of people, she could see Nick get out and stand by the car, stony-faced. Reaching her father, Alana chose English, like a weapon. "Don't worry, I'm not staying. I only came for Nick."

"You came for nothing. Get the hell out."

"Let me talk to him."

"He's one of us now, and we don't talk to whores."

He made all the old anger boil up in her again. "One of you? Never. He's *my* son. My *marimé* blood. You have no rights in this. You gave them up when you washed your hands of me."

"Not me—the *kris*'s judgment. I arranged a marriage to redeem you. It was *you* who disobeyed and took off."

"A marriage in hell."

"Where you belonged!" he shouted. "I hoped I'd never see you again. How do you have the nerve to come and pollute my home?"

"Your goddamned pure home," she snapped. "You wouldn't even be here, wouldn't be *alive,* if Lina hadn't broken every Romany rule there is. She volunteered to be a Nazi doctor's guinea pig to get extra food, and she took most of it back to you. You have no idea what she did to save your pure gypsy skin."

"Yeah, Nicky's told me all about that. Question is, why didn't *you?* All those years ago, Jesus, I thought you were *crazy*. I had to protect my people from you. And what you put us through at that *kris* set us back for years. Decent families wouldn't come near us. We're *still* paying the price."

"I didn't *know* the truth then," she yelled. "I thought I was crazy too! And believe me, it hasn't been any picnic since. On the street at fifteen, thanks to you. And the next thirteen years alone. I didn't even have my son."

"And you still won't! He came here to be with *us*."

That was the last straw. Her fury burst. "This isn't your business, you old crook. I've come for my son. I'm going to take him away, and I swear I'll break your goddamned back if you come between us."

"You'd raise your hand against you own father?" he

raged. "It's not enough, all the hell you've caused as a troublemaker and a whore?"

She took a judo stance. "And a fighter, part of my job. I can take down a sack of lard like you without breaking a sweat. Come on, try me. Take me on!"

Red-faced, he raised his fist high as if to strike her. "Bitch!"

"Hold it!" Nick called out, coming between them. "Hold it, both of you!" He went up to Rajko. "Some big man you are. Big jerk is more like it." He snatched the fedora right off Rajko's head.

People gasped. Rajko looked stunned.

Alana stared at Nick in amazement. She'd heard Lina in his voice, could almost see Lina in the way he was pushing his face right up to Rajko's. At least, as close as he could, being so much shorter. It knocked her back as she realized he was playing this role from memory. The hard-nosed peacemaker. Lina had maneuvered Rajko with the act more than once.

"This is Lina's only child," Nick went on, chewing him out. "She'd cuff you good if she could see you cursing her baby. She never had a *pomana* to put her soul to rest, and her spirit's been wandering for twenty-eight years, looking for her child. You want her to come haunting this *kumpania* night and day? To bring us nothing but bad luck, never leave us in peace, all because you're too proud? Is that how you lead your people? Look at her!" he yelled, pointing to Alana. "You two used to be partners. *That's* what Lina wants." He swatted Rajko's arm hard with the hat. The gesture was pure Lina, and Rajko blinked in astonishment.

Nick stomped over to Alana. "And you," he said, scowling in her face. "I thought you were smart, but you're acting dumb as a *gadje* mark. You're more alone than ever, and if you weren't so mad at him, you'd see that. You need *friends,* woman. So you'd better get wise, because barging in where you're not wanted and yelling at the *rom baro* is no way to make friends." He lowered his voice so that only she could hear. "Don't make him lose face. You need this man." Their eyes locked. They both knew he was doing Lina. She could see that it gave him a kind of high, and she felt it too: it was weird, but a thrill.

He grabbed her arm and pulled her over to Rajko, whose look was still fierce. Rajko raised both arms, and Alana steeled herself for the blows. But when the weight of his arms fell on her, it wasn't in blows. He crushed her in a hug that took her breath away.

"My daughter . . . daughter . . . *shori, shori . . .*" She was stunned—he was crying! His chest heaved against her. "You were the smartest of the bunch," he cried out, then groaned, "Smart as Lina. Alana . . . *shori.*"

Suddenly she was a child again, with no thought, just need and awe. Tears blurred her vision. She held him. *"Taté . . . Taté."*

He circled on the spot, still holding her tight, moving in a clumsy dance motion like a bear. He raised his voice so that all the people gaping in the yard could hear, declaring to her in Romany, "I forgive you, I forgive you, and may God forgive you as I do."

Voices burst out all around them, gabbling and laughing. Through her tears, Alana saw Nick. He was putting on Rajko's fedora, way too big for him, and grinning.

The moment her father lifted her exile, she was caught up in a noisy, boisterous reunion with dozens of relatives. Yanka, her stepmother, ever aloof, turned and went back into the kitchen, but the younger women and girls crowded round, led by her cousin Liza, bursting with questions about her work in films and how she lived. They pulled her over to the yard table and sat her down and served her coffee, and their faces lit up at her talk of movie stars and adventure.

"Paul *Newman*?"

"He *spoke* to you?"

"Is he really as good-looking as in the movies?"

"Better," Alana said.

They squealed.

But they all looked puzzled at her answers about her solitary life, alone on a boat. She knew it didn't make sense to them. They didn't see it as self-sufficiency, but as loneliness and emptiness: how the *gadje* lived. Asking about her half-brothers, she was told that Jimmy and Nicu were on the road, but she hugged Vesh and Boldor as they came to greet her, amazed at how they'd grown into men. She met their wives and children: eleven kids altogether, whose jostling and giggling and big curious eyes tickled and delighted her. She felt a pang at seeing one of her half-sisters, though—shy, nineteen-year-old Nadja. The other two were long married and gone to their in-laws' *kumpanias* in San Francisco and Minneapolis. Later, Alana heard Nadja's story from the other women. They were preparing the evening meal, with Nadja right there, peeling potatoes.

"Sent home," Liza said, cutting chunks of stewing pork. "That ugly husband of hers divorced her."

"Well, what else?" Vesh's wife reasonably pointed out. "No kids after three years."

Nadja lowered her eyes at her shame.

The others told Alana how the *kris* divorce settlement had demanded that Rajko return three-quarters of the bride price to the husband's family, and how Rajko was going to marry her again to a Machwaya family in Dallas, at a much-reduced price. When Alana asked Nadja how she felt about it, Nadja shrugged; it was the gypsy way. It made Alana shudder. She'd been living on the outside too long to accept all this.

That evening, Rajko sent the others inside, and Alana sat with him and Nick in the yard around a small campfire, under stars that were invisible above the city's glow. When she was growing up, a big pot of stew hung over coals here all day, and people helped themselves whenever they got hungry. These days there was a casual evening meal instead, but the campfire was still set at night, just for sitting around and talking and playing music. No music now, just the crackle of the flames. Alana felt profoundly out of place. She'd changed in thirteen years, but life here had hardly changed at all, and the smells of wood smoke and pork fat, of tobacco and coffee and earth, brought back achingly familiar flashes of childhood. But the clan's nasty gossip and bickering all evening had been familiar too. She'd felt it like some heavy blanket, restricting her, dulling her energy. She wasn't sorry she'd soon be leaving.

She said to Rajko, "I gather Nick's told you about the gene, but not about Knelman."

"I didn't want to get into that," Nick said quickly. "Thought I'd get tossed out."

"Not a bad call," she said with a wry smile.

Rajko asked, "Who's Knelman?"

She brought him up to date. How, after implanting the gene in Lina, Viktor Schiller escaped a war crimes tribunal by impersonating a Jew, and later established himself here as Dr. Henry Knelman. How he'd spent years tracking down Alana, then waited until she'd found Nick and sent a hit man to kill them.

She watched them—Rajko shaking his head in amazement, Nick staring into the flames. She hadn't told them

Knelman's theory that males with the gene had an inherently amoral and violent nature, that they threatened an evolutionary disaster. It had shocked her when Knelman had sprung it on her, but now she knew she didn't believe it. He had to be wrong. Nick was a troubled kid, but he was no killer. What she *did* believe was that the horror of the theory was driving Knelman. Maybe it had driven him crazy.

Rajko said, "So, this Nazi bastard's trying to kill you both before you blow his cover and send him to prison."

"For sure, but it goes even deeper," she said. "It's the gene itself he wants to kill. A week ago neither Nick or I even knew about Schiller. We had no memory of him because Lina was sedated for the operation, and never even knew what it was about. I wouldn't have known any of it if Knelman hadn't told me himself and insisted I get sterilized. Then I told him about Nick. It was only after the bullets came at us that Nick and I pieced it together. Knelman's doing this to wipe out the thing he created. He thinks it's evil."

Rajko sat forward in his chair. There was a new look in his eyes, hotly alert. "This Knelman—Schiller. Makes me wonder. That day the Yanks freed the camp, it was a Nazi doctor killed Lina. There was craziness that day, tanks rolling in, loudspeakers squawking, people wandering like zombies. Me and my brothers, we went to the hospital block to get Lina and her baby—you. I saw this doctor standing at Lina's bed with a gun. He shot her—*bang,* straight into her heart. I couldn't believe it. He was fixing to shoot you next, but I charged him. Then the Yanks were at the door, so I grabbed you and ran." His eyes glinted in the firelight. "I sure would like to get a look at this Knelman. If he's the one, I wouldn't kill him. Not right off. I'd rip out his liver and make him eat it."

His story sent a shiver through Alana: *Knelman* had shot her mother, his first murderous step on the road that had led him to her and Nick. Seeing the spark of revenge in her father's eyes, she felt it kindle inside her too. But there was no time for that, only time for escape. "You're probably right—he's the one. But Nick and I can't risk hanging around to find out."

Nick's eyes snapped up from the fire. "What?"

"I know I've been telling you we should stay and beat him. But I don't think that's possible anymore." Today, when she'd threatened Knelman at the restaurant, he hadn't even cracked. And even if David did move on her charges, his action could come too late—after she and Nick were dead. As for going public, that had only been to goad Knelman; it was the last thing she wanted for Nick or herself. "No, we've got to get out of town tonight. Get away from him. It's the only way." She turned to Rajko. "*Taté,* I never thought I'd have to ask your help, but I sure need it now. Could you give us a car? And a little cash? And maybe some alias IDs? You can see why we have to take off."

Nick got to his feet. The campfire was between him and Alana. "I'm not going," he said flatly.

The trick of firelight and shadow on his face startled her—she could be looking at Lina. "Don't you get it?" she said. "Knelman won't stop until we're dead. We *have* to go."

"We're with our own people now, and here he can't touch us. I'm not running."

"We can't hide here forever. That's no life."

"It's all the life I want. All I've ever wanted. This is where I belong. I'm *home*."

Dismayed, she turned to Rajko. "Tell him how it is. Tell him we'd never be able to step outside without a bodyguard.

Tell him you don't want this kind of trouble brought on the *kumpania*. Tell him he's *got* to come with me."

Rajko stood up. "Tell you the truth, I'm not so sure. Nicky, he's special—I'd hate to lose him. He's got what it takes to be *rom baro* one day, which God knows my own sons don't." He moved to Nick and put his arm around him. "You been away too long, Alana. You forget how we take care of our own. No *gadje* hit man's going to touch me or mine. Besides, I have plans for Nicky. This special knowledge he can pass on, it's like a kind of magic, isn't it? A magic to make this *kumpania* strong."

She was on her feet now too. She felt the fire's heat, and the distance from Nick, and a needle of alarm. "What plans?"

Nick and Rajko exchanged a look. When Rajko nodded, Nick turned to her, smiling and defiant. "This time next year, you just might be a grandmother. I'm going to get married."

CHAPTER 15

DAVID STOOD IN the rain trying to hail a taxi. Impossible. Half of lower Manhattan had the same idea, what with the downpour, plus the Broadway subway line temporarily out of commission. But he felt he had to do this before he had time to reconsider. He'd made the decision as he'd arrived at Eighty Center Street minutes ago, his trench coat dripping, his hair soaked after walking in the rain from the Prince Street stop when the subway had broken down. He'd hardly slept all night, tormented by DeVrey's report. As soon as he'd reached his office door, he knew he wouldn't get through the day if he didn't go straight to Dad.

As traffic stopped for a red light, he strode out to a cab and opened the door, then saw a passenger inside. Slamming the door, he splashed through puddles toward the next cab several cars back. Half the time this damn city didn't work, he thought. Maybe the whole damn country. Last night Vice President Agnew had resigned, admitting income tax evasion, and there was talk that the president himself might be impeached over Watergate. Liars, both of them. No wonder people had lost faith in government.

And Dad? he thought with a pang. What's the truth there?

Seeing the taxi was free, he picked up his pace to get it.

"Hey, Counselor, wait up!"

David turned to see Lipranski running toward him, shoulders hunched against the rain. "I got something you're gonna like," Lip said as he reached him. He jerked his chin toward the curb. "Got a minute for a coffee?"

"No. What is it?"

"I followed him yesterday afternoon. The *rom baro* himself, with a woman and a kid."

"A woman?" David had the weird thought it might be Alana. "What did she look like?"

"Early twenties, glasses, nothing to write home about."

Not Alana. The taxi splashed him as it drove past. He looked for another.

"Thing is," Lip went on, "she matches the witness's description of George Adams's partner on the team that worked Mrs. Larson. That's what I twigged to when I followed her and Marks yesterday. Marks drove out of his place at three-thirty, and when he dropped the woman and kid on West End Avenue, I followed her. She and the kid went around the corner to a brownstone on West Eighty-fourth, and they were inside almost two hours. Owner's a sick old man, it turns out, and loaded. So you know what I bet happens next? She gets to be this geezer's friend, rents a room, begins to take over his life. Cancels his phone, won't let neighbors visit, pretty soon he's putty in her hands. Then dead putty. What do you say I talk to her, next time she visits him? With that tox report on Larson, we got more this time than just a car."

The Cadillac. Two days ago they'd had to release George Adams, aka Stefan Marks, after a futile interrogation. He'd given them nothing, and David suspected he wasn't even the one they were after. He'd outlined to his boss the weight of circumstantial evidence and suggested they bring in Rajko Marks himself for questioning, but Rintoul had called it premature and opted for more surveillance. "What's the old man's name?" he asked Lip as he spotted a free taxi. He raised his arm and whistled, and started out to meet it.

"Daniel H. Jaffe."

David stopped cold. "*Howard* Jaffe?"

"That's what he goes by, yeah. Retired entrepreneur, retail clothing. You know him?"

It unnerved David, this convergence of two streams of his life: Alana's father running the scam, now his aunt's friend a potential victim. When he thought of Rajko Marks planning to poison Howard Jaffe, his frustration and anger after months on this investigation gripped him. To hell with surveillance he wanted the murdering *rom baro*. Opening the cab door, he said to Lip, "Go pick up the woman."

He slid into the lumpy back seat. Change of plans. "Seventy-third and Park," he told the driver. He had to see if Aunt Es knew anything about the gypsies moving in on Howard. He felt a disquieting rush of relief that his talk with Dad would have to wait.

He smelled cinnamon the moment he opened the penthouse door. He found her in the kitchen, making strudel.

"David, what a lovely surprise." She held a rolling pin in her floured hands and went on working as she spoke, rolling pastry on a gray marble slab. Beside it some paper-thin layers already lay between sheets of waxed paper. "Did your Mr. Rintoul finally admit he's working you too hard, or are you playing hooky? Oh, but you're *soaked!* Take off that wet coat and sit down and have a cup of coffee. I've just made a fresh pot.

I'll have this strudel in the oven in a few minutes, and then I'll join you."

"Can't stay, Aunt Es."

"No? Well, actually, I'm going out myself soon—lunch and a movie with Miriam Goldhar. Enough moping, I've decided." Her powdered cheeks were slightly flushed as she worked. The air was humid from a bowl of steaming poached apples dotted with raisins, and golden with cinnamon. The small TV on the counter was on, the volume tuned low, showing a preview of *The Edge of Night.* David knew that when his father wasn't home, filling the apartment with Beethoven, Aunt Es liked to watch the soaps. She asked, "Have you seen this new picture we're going to, *The Way We Were*? Not too racy, I hope." Her smile was playful as she dipped a little brush into a dish of melted butter, then brushed the pastry sheet in quick strokes. "That young Robert Redford is such a dreamboat."

"Aunt Es, have you heard anything from Howard?"

Her hands stilled. "No. Why?"

"Did he ever mention a man named George Adams? Or Stefan Marks?"

"Not that I recall." She wiped her hands on her apron. "David, has something happened? Who are these people? Is Howard all right?"

"As far as I know, he's fine. But he might be a target in a swindle I'm investigating."

Her eyes widened with anxiety. "What kind of swindle?"

He didn't want to worry her by describing the deadly scam. "Sorry, I can't give out any details, but if you do hear from him, would you call me right away?"

"Yes, of course. Oh, poor Howard. If only he *would* call."

She looked so forlorn, David got her to sit down at the kitchen table and poured her a cup of coffee. He went to the fridge for the heavy cream she liked, and as he set down the little Delft china pitcher in front of her, he felt her watching him. "How's Alana?" she asked.

It caught him off guard. She knew nothing about the seismic shifts that were rocking him. He gave the only answer he could truthfully make. "I don't know."

She poured cream, sadly shaking her head. "I could tell something was very wrong that day she came here to see Henry. She looked so upset."

"Alana came here?" He remembered yesterday at the London Grill she'd said something about Dad whistling in his study. The detail had got buried in the avalanche of her claims, and Dad's, but now David was digging for details.

"Perhaps I shouldn't have said. She is Henry's patient, after all. He says she needs special care." Esther sipped her coffee, then looked up at him. "She had . . . someone with her that day. A boy."

"Nick?"

"So you know." She went on, gently probing, "Does it make a difference, her having a son?"

"Not to me. But to her . . ." He didn't finish. There was so much more that did make a difference. *Not to me. To her.*

"David, I haven't accomplished great things in my life. Not like your father, so brilliant, so committed to helping people. But I am very good at one thing, and that is seeing a person's heart. Their real worth. I know Alana is in some kind of difficulty, and I can see it's demanding a lot of you. But, believe me, this girl is worth it. Unless . . . oh, dear, have you already lost her?"

That he couldn't answer.

She cupped her hands around her coffee as if for warmth. "You and I, we're not having have much luck in the love department, are we?"

Still standing, he'd rested his forearms on a chair back,

hands clasped, and as he now watched her finger trace the rim of her cup, the familiarity of it brought a surge of comfort—the answer he'd craved. Dad couldn't possibly be what Alana accused him of being, because an essential piece of the puzzle didn't fit: his sister. "Aunt Es, what you said just now, about Dad helping people. Was he always like that? I mean, when you were kids? Or did the war make him what he is?"

"Oh, I'm sure Henry's always been that way."

"You don't remember?"

She got up and went back to her pastry. "Well, as you know, we grew up apart."

He did know. It had never seemed important, until now. "Must have been quite a reunion, after the war."

"I don't suppose you could really call it a reunion," she said, laying a fragile buttered sheet in the strudel pan. "I never knew him before."

Hairs lifted on the back of David's neck. He straightened at the chair back. "What do you mean? You *are* brother and sister?"

"Yes, of course. But when our parents divorced, they each took one of us, so—" She shrugged, the rest self-evident, then lifted the next sheet from between the waxed paper and brushed it.

"I guess I'd always imagined you playing together as kids. Or at least getting in touch as adults, before the war. I mean . . . you did *know* him."

She shook her head. "I was just a baby at the time of the divorce, and Henry was only four. My mother stayed in Dusseldorf, and Henry went with our father to Berlin. A complete break." She continued buttering pastry layers and draping them in the pan. "I moved to New York before the war. Then came the Holocaust—I lost everyone. But you were sent to me out of the blue, for which I thanked God. And after the war I was thrilled when Henry arrived and introduced himself. He'd come to claim you, but he stayed to take care of us both."

Cold sweat prickled under David's clothes. The core of him seemed to have frozen, but his thoughts kept working, and a file opened in his mind—the two women Alana had named as experimental subjects with her mother. Hilde Wentzler had been found murdered in Amsterdam in March 1958—"an unsolved homicide." When Toby had reported that, David had flashed on himself as a fourteen-year-old, his memory of that spring quite clear because he'd been stricken with appendicitis. His father had been away. "Aunt Es, remember when I had my appendix out? Nineteen-fifty-eight, wasn't it?"

She looked mildly surprised at the off-topic question. "March. How could I ever forget? We almost lost you."

"I remember Dad was in Europe for some conference."

She nodded. "He rushed home to be with you."

"Was it Holland?"

"That's right. Amsterdam."

David was gripping the chair back so tightly his knuckles were white. Alana's indictment . . . too many parts were fitting. And they were killing him.

Nick was prowling old man Jaffe's den. He scanned the bookshelf for photo albums, then went to the desk and poked through the drawers. He was looking for photographs, letters, postcards, phone messages, anything that would tell him whether Jaffe had family, and if so, whether they lived close enough to make trouble. He wasn't in a hurry; down the hall, Ruby had things under control. He could hear her in the living room, talking to the old guy:

"There's your phone on the blink again, Mr. Jaffe, no dial tone. No, no, don't get up, finish your soup. Sometimes the darn thing works, sometimes it doesn't. I'm going to report it to the phone company when Joey and I leave. Wasn't it lucky that Joey had no school today? Lets us have an early visit with you. Mr. Jaffe? My, what a big yawn! I'll just go turn down your bed—after that hot broth you're going to want a nice long nap."

No wonder, Nick thought, after the sleeping pill she'd put in his soup. He and Ruby planned to use this time to case the place, check out Jaffe's bank books, any financial documents. At the very least they'd come away with an example of his signature; at best, some overview of what he owned. Running his finger over upright file folders packed in a drawer, Nick had never felt so alive. Rajko's words last night at the campfire warmed him now like glowing embers. To be *rom baro* one day in his grandfather's place—it thrilled him. Rajko's confidence in him was like a rare food he'd hungered for all his life but never knew where to find. Now, he was in the place where it grew, his grandfather's world, and he couldn't get enough of it. It had made him so much stronger already: he wasn't afraid of Knelman. Working together, his clan could take out that Nazi one day. It just took planning. Nick could do that, now that he was safe.

If only Alana understood, he thought, peering into an envelope of snapshots. But she would, sooner or later. She was just shaken up right now by his decision to stay, but she'd come 'round. She'd grown up in this world, so she must know it was where she belonged, just like he did. She'd soon get back into the swing of it, going out with Yanka and the women on some job, and she'd feel the old excitement, using her smarts to put one over on the *gadje*. After all, they both had Lina's knowledge, Lina's blood. Her home was with her people, and Nick wanted so much to help her see that. Once things settled down, maybe Rajko could find her a good husband. That would do it; no turning back then. But she wouldn't be sent away to her husband's family; Nick would somehow stop that. Finding his mother had changed his whole life. He felt closer to her than to anyone, and he couldn't stand having her packed off to be some distant family's *bori*. He wanted her near from now on. When she married, he'd find a way to get around Rajko, just like Lina used to—get him to bend the rule and keep Alana in the enclave. Maybe point out how valuable she was as a gene carrier, and how Rajko had to control its reproduction to get the most mileage out of it. Yeah, that should do it. Then they'd all be together, him and his mother and grandfather, three kingpins of a powerful clan. As he flipped through the snapshots, he'd never felt so happy.

Snapshots of Esther Knelman, he realized. Some party at that Jewish Center where he and Alana had seen the camp files. Dressed to kill, and that funny eye of hers. Dumb, lonely old broad.

A sound made him look up. Tires splashing through puddles—a car pulling up right below. He felt a prickle of caution: there was no parking this side of the street. He went to the window and looked down through the rain. His heart thudded. A cop cruiser.

He'd only had time to start for the doorway when he heard the front door buzzer. *No time to warn Ruby.* He was already searching for a way out . . .

He scrambled up the fire escape in the rain. Reaching the flat roof, he scurried to the front, keeping low. At the edge he got down on his belly, his pants and shirt soaked in the puddle on the gravel, and looked down at the street. His heart was banging as he watched two cops lead Ruby out of the building to the cruiser. One opened the rear door, the other guided her into the backseat. Then they got in and drove off.

Nick climbed back down the fire escape. Wet and cold and

shaking, he went straight through Jaffe's apartment and out the front door. He forced himself to walk slowly east to Broadway—*walk, don't run*—then two blocks north to the Eighty-sixth Street subway.

By the time he got out at Sunnyside, the rain had let up, but he was still shivering wet, and so edgy he kept eyeing Van Dam Street for cops.

Reaching the enclave, he went right out to the yard. Rajko was with Vesh and Uncle Boldor, looking over their finished bodywork on the blue Thunderbird. As he approached his grandfather, Nick couldn't hide how tense he was. Rajko noticed, and motioned him to the far side of the T-bird, away from the others.

"Where's Ruby?"

"The cops got her. Came to the door for her."

"What went wrong?"

"I don't know."

Rajko seemed calm as he leaned back against the driver's window, folding his arms as though he was thinking. "Jaffe call them?"

"No way. He was nodding off in his soup. Somebody must've tipped them." Nick was nervous as hell, and he saw that Rajko was too, despite his stillness. No, not nervous. Mad.

"Fuck that. Nobody in my family talks. Even Alana wouldn't—she's one of us again. Anyway, she doesn't even know about this job. No, there's something weird going down," he said, his voice a growl. It started to rain again, and Vesh and Boldor started inside. Rajko didn't move. "My lawyer called this morning, told me he got the dope on the DA who's been breathing down our necks. Turns out the guy's not only hot to hunt gypsies, his name's Knelman." He looked at Nick. "Quite the coincidence, huh?"

Nick's nervousness drained, and in its place anger surged,

like his grandfather's. "He's the doctor's son. Thinks he is, anyway. His real father's probably the dead Jew that Knelman passes himself off as. His name's David. And Alana knows him."

"What?"

"It's worse. She's in love with him."

"What?"

"She trusted him once before, and he set us up. Almost got us. She should know he's poison, but I bet she just blames the doc for putting him up to it. You're right, there's no way she's behind the cops picking up Ruby, but if this pushy prosecutor gets to her, it could be bad news. She's not herself when it comes to him."

With sudden fury Rajko whacked the window with the flat of his hand. "*Fuck* this. The Nazi's out to kill my family, and his Yid son wants to put us behind bars. And use my daughter to do it."

Nick kept his fury inside. All he wanted was to help the clan and keep his mother safe at home. But this DA creep was ruining everything. "We need to teach this jerk a lesson. Give me a few guys and let me take care of him. Today."

Rajko shot him a look. His frown relaxed into a slow smile of respect. "You think big, Nicky. I like that."

CHAPTER 16

KNELMAN WAS SEEING out five-year-old Myrna Iskander, passing his receptionist's desk with the child's parents, when David walked in. At the sight of his son's haggard face, dread reared up in Knelman.

"Pollipop," Myrna said.

A flustered look crossed David's features as he noticed the child, her head bald and bandaged.

"Yes, of course, Myrna, your lollipop." Knelman reached into his pocket and handed her the yellow, cellophane-wrapped sucker.

The father said, "Hardly know how to thank you, Doctor. Since you operated, she talks, she laughs—she's ours again. It's like a miracle."

"Miracles and medicine are surprisingly compatible, Mr. Iskander. No thanks are necessary." Iskander's wife suddenly reached for Knelman's wrist, and before he could react, she kissed his hand. He awkwardly withdrew his arm.

"Same time next week, Doctor?" Iskander asked, hoisting up his daughter to sit in the crook of his arm.

Knelman looked at David, and his dread turned to despair. He was gripped by the certainty that this child was the last patient he would ever treat. "No, I don't think I'll need to see Myrna again," he said, feeling deeply gratified that he had been able to help her. "Your family doctor is well qualified to take over from here. I shall see that he is brought up to date. Good-bye. Good-bye, Myrna."

Iskander started to go, but David stiffly stood in his way. Realizing it, David stepped aside, muttering, "Sorry . . ."

Mrs. Iskander was smiling and crying softly as she followed her husband and daughter out.

"Mrs. Lowell," Knelman said to his receptionist, "No calls, please. No one."

David followed him into his office and closed the door. When Knelman turned, David looked so torn, so reluctant to believe what he must now know, that it hurt more than if he'd physically attacked. *My son . . . lover of justice.* Knelman couldn't bear to face him. He went to the window where his orchids were ranged on glass shelves, took up a pair of pruning scissors and forced himself to examine the foliage of his lovely *Aerangis citrata* for signs of decay. He felt a queasy shortness of breath. He knew he could no longer avoid the death blows to come; he could only try to make the ritual more civilized. "You've come for the truth," he managed to say.

David came beside him. "Sometimes, evidence can lead a prosecutor off course. Please . . . give me a defense."

Knelman snipped off a browning pink blossom. He was vaguely aware of rain needling the window, and water dripping off David's trench coat onto the carpet . . . and that David seemed almost as tense as himself. "Let me hear your evidence."

"On April thirtieth, 1945, Heinrich Knelmann was found

shot dead in Viktor Schiller's office. In 1958 Hilde Wentzler was murdered in Amsterdam, the same week you were there. And then there's Esther. She never knew the brother she'd been separated from as a baby."

A phone rang in reception. A second ring, then the phone stopped. David's tight breathing was the only sound.

Finally, he asked it. "Are you Viktor Schiller?"

Knelman turned. Their eyes locked. "Yes."

David's hands hung at his sides, rigid as rocks. His voice, when it came, was raw. "You're a Nazi."

"In my soul, never. I abhorred everything they stood for. I am a scientist."

"Did you kill my father?"

"No! Dear God, no, Heinrich was my friend. I tried to save him."

At David's unbelieving stare, Knelman said, "It's true, we were close. In Berlin, at medical school, we studied together, worked in the lab together, went to the Biergarten, rowed on the lake. David, I was a guest at his wedding. That was the day he told me he had a sister in New York he'd never met. Then, the racial laws against Jews became so harsh we could no longer openly be friends. Then, the war. I was so engrossed in my research I blinkered myself about politics, told myself the war could not last. When my family were killed in the bombing, I buried myself in my work. It was all I had."

"Your . . . family?"

Gone so long. What could he say about them now? While David's love, the wellspring of his life, was dying before his eyes . . . and he felt himself dying with it. But he would not die in silence. He had to make David understand. "When my research came to Himmler's attention, he decided it might further his goal of entrenching a master race. He suggested making Otzenhausen available to me, and I agreed. Yes, to experiment on prisoners. Other experiments were performed there too—barbaric, unspeakable things—but mine was a benign undertaking. How could the gift of knowledge be otherwise? At least, that's what I then believed. I sinned, David. Sinned grievously. Please, please understand how—"

"The lie you told—my mother being shot. What really happened?"

Knelman's throat felt parched. "I was in the camp the August day the transport rolled in with Heinrich and his wife and baby—you. I could do nothing for his wife. She was selected for work, and later perished. But on the pretext of needing infants for my research, I had you brought to my lab, then arranged to have you smuggled out to a Swiss Zionist group who had ties to the Red Cross, with a note sewed into your clothing asking them to send you to Heinrich's sister in America. As for my friend Heinrich, I knew the Nazis used some prisoner physicians to keep the inmates on their feet as long as possible for labor, so I requested that he be consigned to assist with my work—I assured Himmler that his brilliance as a researcher was essential. Heinrich became my personal assistant, and it kept him alive for almost two years. Until the last day, when a doctor shot all the prisoner physicians who'd witnessed his depravity. I couldn't save Heinrich from him."

David winced as though the truth had lashed him. "And you. To evade indictment yourself, you assumed my father's identity."

"Yes."

"The tattoo?"

"I did it myself. Heinrich's number. Took his inmate clothes as well, and walked out of the camp."

"Incredible," David said hollowly. "And then, you must have seen that I could be your ticket to get here."

"You and Esther . . . you have been my life." The declaration brought such an ache, he reached to touch David's shoulder.

David jerked away. Knelman saw horror in his eyes. "And all these years later," David said, "you asked me to find Alana."

Knelman felt a rising despair. "You have to understand . . . I believed I was conducting pure research on subjects who were under a death sentence and would never leave that camp. When I saw them being liberated, it struck me like a thunderbolt—the seed of an evolutionary shift had been let loose. I *had* to stop that seed from generating. Because what I told you about the mutation is true. Males with the gene are psychopaths. They will produce psychopaths for endless generations to come. It was *my* fault. My *sin*. What could I do but try to set it right?"

"Hilde Wentzler and Sophie Grossman. What happened to them?"

Knelman saw the danger in making a confession that could lead to his arrest. But he felt such a raw need to make David comprehend . . . and forgive. "I located Sophie Grossman a few months after the war in a French coastal town. She was pregnant. I had to terminate the gene before she could reproduce. Then I came to America, so it was years before I traced Hilde Wentzler to Amsterdam, and by then she'd already had a son, taken away by his father. At that point the best I could do was ensure that she never gave birth again. Yet when I went to her and explained, exactly as I did to Miss Marks, she refused sterilization. I did what was necessary."

"You murdered those women, didn't you? And lobotomized Wentzler's son."

"I did what was necessary. Jacob Wentzler has been brought under control through a surgical procedure. He will never beget a child."

David whispered, "My God . . ."

A blade of anger cut into Knelman. "Should I have simply washed my hands of this? Let the gene breed a brutal new race to dominate the world exactly as the Nazis dreamed of doing? Loose such evil, when I could prevent it through the removal of the few infected individuals?"

"So now," David said quietly, "Alana and her son are the only ones left."

A voice of caution warned Knelman: *Tread carefully here.* "Yes." He set down his pruning scissors. "And my goal from the beginning has been containment by sterilization." *Please, let that satisfy him.*

He turned to his desk and pressed the button on his intercom. "Mrs. Lowell, could you step in, please?"

He went to the louvered closet behind his desk, opened the door, and slipped his raincoat off the hanger. "David, I created the gene because I *could.* I implanted it because I could. I played God . . . because I could. But there is only one God, for Jew and Christian alike, and all others too, and He brought me out of that camp for one reason only—to remedy the terrible result of my sin."

"It ends now. It's over."

"I am afraid that cannot be." Something like a sob caught in Knelman's chest. "You hate me, and from that I shall never recover. And, of course, the truth about me will eventually become public." He added bitterly, "Miss Marks has the measure of you there—you'll do your job. Ruin and prison await me. My life is over." He was putting on his raincoat. "But the gene is my responsibility, and I will not walk away from that."

David stepped in his path, blocking his way. "Dad—" The word that had slipped out by habit made David flinch. "I don't hate you. Like you said, you did all you could. Saved my life. Saved my father right until the end. But the experiment pushed you over an edge. And you're still falling. There's a defense for you—insanity. I recommend you use it. But I can't let you leave."

"Don't try to stop me, David. I have a moral duty to perform." He moved around to the other side of the desk, about to go.

David again stepped in his way. His face was pale. "Alana said you have a gunman hunting her and Nick. Is that true?"

Knelman knew this was the line that could not be crossed. He answered evenly, "No. I swear it. There is no gunman."

"You've perjured yourself so often. How can I believe a man whose whole life has been a lie?"

"Believe the father who brought you up, gave you your values, and who loves you more than life itself."

David's struggle showed on his face. "I have to believe Alana this time. I can't let you leave."

"How will you prevent me? You have no grounds on which to call in the police."

"I could hold you myself."

"Of course, you are a young man, far stronger than I. The question is, do you have the will? Because I shall struggle with all my might. If you knock me down, I shall get up. If you knock me down again and kick me, I shall crawl. No, David, the only way to stop me is to kill me. Can you do that?"

The door opened. His receptionist. "Yes, Doctor?"

"Something has come up. Please cancel my afternoon appointments." He walked to the door. His heart was breaking. "Good-bye, David."

David walked along Park Avenue in the rain, going nowhere. A woman jostled him, oblivious under her umbrella. He couldn't marshal any identity to his feelings. Horror, sorrow, rage—he was at the edge of panic. What could he do? Take this to the precinct? The cops he worked with would think he was nuts. A knowledge gene . . . a Nazi masquerading as a Jew for almost thirty years . . . committing serial murders in the insane belief that he was saving the world. And the Nazi is Dad.

Sickness rose in his throat. He lurched toward a wire-mesh trash bin, sure he was going to vomit. Gripping the rim, a cold sweat on his forehead, he forced the nausea to subside.

He was aware of a car pulling over beside him. Some good Samaritan seeing if he needed help? The car stopped. He glanced at it, getting his bearings. Blue Thunderbird. Don't need help, he thought, walking on, picking up his pace. Need to decide what to do. No evidence of any crime, no witnesses, no grounds even for asking a judge for a restraining order. Restrain the eminent Dr. Knelman? From doing what?

Then the real horror hit, not in his gut but in his mind. Dad had sworn there was no assassin, but he'd flatly said "containment" was his goal—and what better containment was there than death? Which meant Dad would do it himself. He was out to kill Alana and her son.

Got to find her. Get them to safety.

First priority: warn her. He went to a phone booth at the

corner, stepped in, and closed the door. With cold wet fingers he dug in his jacket breast pocket and pulled out the pink memo slip where his secretary had written the number Alana had left. Staying at a friend's place, she'd said. He'd called her there two days ago. As the phone rang, he closed his eyes in revulsion, remembering how he'd set her up for the meeting at that East Village café. *I almost delivered her into his hands.* More ringing; no answer. He hung up and called her message service. That number he'd memorized. As it rang he planned his message—that she'd been right about everything, and that wherever she was, she had to get out now, get away.

The door opened. What the hell?

"Mr. Knelman?"

It was a kid, maybe twelve. Friendly smile. Something familiar about him.

"My name's Nick Morgan. I hear you've been looking for me. And for my mother."

It rocked David—like an answered prayer. Weird, the kid showing up like this, but still an answered prayer. The phone was still ringing at the other end as he hung up. "Nick, you don't know how glad I am to see you." He stepped out of the booth. "Look, I don't know what you've heard about me, but believe me, all I want to do is help you and Alana. I've got to reach her. Do you know where she is?"

The boy's smile widened. "Sure. That's what I came to tell you. She wants a meeting." He indicated the waiting blue Thunderbird. "Want to come along? I'll take you to her."

There were three men in the car—a driver and two in the back seat. One stepped out to let David in, then slid back in himself so that David was in the middle. All three were swarthy and silent. Nick got in front, and the driver pulled smoothly into the traffic. By the time David took in the fact that they were gypsies, they'd locked the doors. By the time he knew he'd made the stupidest mistake of his life, they had a knife at his ribs and were tying his hands behind his back.

"You should've kept your nose out of other people's business," Nick said, not turning around. The others sat quietly. David was amazed: Nick seemed to be their leader.

They crossed the Queensboro Bridge, the windshield wipers beating back and forth in the rain, and David tried to deal with his fear. Since they'd let him see their faces, were they were going to kill him? But murder didn't fit the gypsy MO. Maybe they felt confident they could melt into their underground, so he'd never ID them. He grabbed hold of that hope—it made some sense. What threw him was Nick's power here. A boy. Unruly hair, ears that could use a wash, a cheek as smooth as Alana's. But the boy was clearly in charge. Was he truly a genetic mutation that could change the course of the world?

They pulled into a vacant parking lot behind a boarded-up factory. Nick stayed in the front seat as the men dragged David out. The first blow to his jaw sent him staggering back against the car door. One man held him up and the other two took turns punching his face, jabbing his stomach. Guts on fire, he fell, his shoulder hitting the ground, the asphalt grating skin off his cheek. He curled up in pain as the men kicked him. The blows stopped. The men got back in the car.

Nick got out. "Lay off Rajko Marks's business." His single, savage kick to David's ribs jerked him onto his back with a gasp. "And stay away from my mother."

"She's . . . with him?" David managed.

"Where she belongs."

Then he saw nothing but leaden sky. Heard tires splashing away. Then silence. Breathing was agony. Rain and blood in his open mouth gagged him. Darkness engulfed him. And the pain stopped.

The bells were ringing. Knelman blinked up at the glorious twin spires of St. Patrick's Cathedral rising from Fifth Avenue. His spirit was too numb to feel the rain. He knew only that he craved to be inside. He went in to the right of the great bronze doors, and immediately heard the far-off priest saying mass. Knelman moved through the comforting gloom of the broad narthex, where banks of candles flickered and a residue of incense spiced the air, and as he reached the back of the nave, where pillars rose on either side of him in that immense vault of space, he felt as though he'd been grimly crossing a desert for years and had reached a verdant oasis. Standing still, he filled his lungs with the holy air. For so many parched years he had not dared to enter; living as a Jew, he had no business here. But now that all was lost, and grief confounded him—his mask stripped off, nothing left to pretend—the sacred air was balm.

He genuflected to the cross, then entered a rear pew and kneeled. Silent worshipers sat scattered throughout the cathedral, and tourists with dripping umbrellas tiptoed down the aisles, whispering. Even against the gray light outside, the stained-glass windows dazzled Knelman. Their beauty, and the incense, the bells, the priest's intonations—the heady effect intoxicated him. He looked with longing at the line of people waiting to enter the confessional by the altar of Saint John Baptist de la Salle. Watching a young man go in, Knelman hungered for the rite, "Father, forgive me . . ."

No. That balm could not be his. It was hard to bear. And yet, he had an odd sensation of being lightened. No longer was he burdened with the terrible fear of being found out. David knew. Soon Esther would know too. *Their love is lost to me.* His life was now reduced to the fundamental task: extermination of the gene. *"It ends now. It's over,"* David had said. But that would make the deaths of the three original subjects mere pointless murder. Wicked. Depraved. No, he was not a murderer; he was carrying out a sacred mission. And he had no time left. David would soon be on his heels. He had to act before David could stop him.

But how? He had not lied about the assassin. That chapter had closed today, just before he'd seen Myrna Iskander. At noon, with the child and her parents waiting in reception, he had taken Farrell's call.

"You're alone?" the gravel voice had asked.

"Yes, and I have news. I know where the woman is. But the boy—"

"You haven't been there for my noon call in two days. I don't like changes."

"Impossible yesterday." That lunchtime ambush at the London Grill. "And the day before, I was in Philadelphia. I'd been attempting another plan, but the police botched it. But I know now that she's staying with a friend in the East Village, so take down his address and—"

"You called in the law? No, I don't work when the police are involved. This mission is terminated. I'm out."

"But . . . you can't! I gave you the money!"

"Half. I earned it. Don't call this number again. It won't be in service." The line went dead.

Then the Iskanders had come in. Then David.

Looking up at the stained glass now, Knelman felt a sharp constriction in his chest. With Farrell gone, who would carry out the *Sonderbehandlung?* That German word coming unbidden startled him. The Nazis at the death camps had insisted on using it: "special treatment." Never "killing." As the cathedral organ thundered into a hymn, he felt the vibrations rise into his bones, and he knew the answer: *I must conclude this myself.*

But how? He could not manage it alone.

The solution came to him like a dismally inevitable final chord. *Nazis.*

Arriving home, he was relieved to find that Esther was out. He went straight to his study. In this very room Nick had confessed his involvement with the White Pride gang, and Knelman had taken notes. Rifling through the pages at his desk, he found what he was looking for in Nick's own words. The gang's location in Bensonhurst: the Tre Stelle bar. The leader's name: Nardi.

The notes even pointed to a way to gain access. Nick had made reference to Nardi's penchant for collecting and trading Nazi memorabilia.

Knelman thought: I'll need Esther's keys.

She came home a little before six. He watched her put her purse on the kitchen counter as she talked about the film she'd just seen, then began to prepare supper. Knelman emptied his mind of everything except his mission. They ate veal cutlets and rösti and green salad, with fresh apple strudel for desert, the food all tasting like paste in his mouth. As he cleared the dishes, she brought her purse from the kitchen to the living room and took out her reading glasses and sat down to read a novel, *The Odessa File*, setting her purse on the table beside her. Knelman put on a Schubert string quartet recording and pretended to read the latest *JAMA* issue, the medical articles a blur as he waited for her to go to bed. At eight-forty she put down her book, took her sewing basket from the side table, and started on her embroidery.

After half an hour he finally said, "You must be tired after your long day."

"I don't think I could sleep," she said with a troubled sigh. She put down her sewing. "I didn't mention it before, didn't want to upset you, but David says some people might be planning to swindle Howard."

Knelman fleetingly wondered what she was talking about. It didn't matter. "Let me get you something to help you sleep."

She swallowed the tranquilizers, then went to her room. He listened to twenty minutes of Bach, the *Goldberg Variations*, then went down the hall and softly opened her bedroom door. She was asleep. He came back to her purse in the living room and took her keys.

The Memorial Museum was dark and silent, and Knelman's heart was hammering painfully as he crouched at the display case and fumbled with the key ring. Too dark—he couldn't make out the lock. As the keys clinked against the glass case, he cast an anxious look down the corridor. Sheer nerves. He'd had no problem using Esther's keys to open the front door and to turn off the alarm, and there was no security guard. He straightened up, laying his free hand against the glass case, and told himself to slow down, take his time—no one could possibly know he was here. He had to carefully choose the article he'd come to steal.

The flashlight he'd put down on the floor illuminated the Holocaust artifacts around him in a ghostly light. The walls and pillars were covered with photographs—family snapshots of lost loved ones in the hundreds; photos of crematoriums and burial pits; a photo of a barrel full of teeth extracted from the gassed victims for their gold fillings. In the middle of the room were samplings of the millions of personal items confiscated from camp arrivals, to be shipped off and sold: a small hill of shoes, a bin of buttons, a crate of eyeglasses. In the glass case before him was a collection of hair. Some of it lay in mounds, some in braids of varying shades and lengths. The typed card beside the braids read, "The Nazis exploited their victims for economic benefits beyond slave labor. Here is some of the hair from women murdered at Auschwitz. Seven tons of hair were found at liberation, packed in parcels of twenty-five kilos, ready to be sold, at fifty pfennigs a kilo, to German firms who used it for suit linings."

From the walls the shadowy Holocaust faces looked down on him, faces so familiar from the many times he'd passed through this room. *Familiar as family.* One of these braids could even have belonged to a sister of Esther's . . . or to Heinrich Knelmann's wife.

His sweaty palm moving off the glass made a squeak. He froze. *Too jumpy.* But at least it had broken the spell.

He unlocked the case and made his selection.

An overgrown sumac nearly obscured the metal back door of the Tre Stelle. He knocked, his knuckles rapping the spray-painted black swastika. There was a reek of nearby garbage. Underfoot was broken glass. He could hear a dog barking inside.

The door opened. A teenager built like a linebacker, all in black, stood scowling. His small eyes flicked over Knelman.

"Mr. Nardi?"

"Fuck off." The teen started to close the door.

Knelman stiff-armed the door. "Please tell Mr. Nardi I have brought something that will interest him." He held up a cardboard stationery box. "An item of memorabilia. Very valuable. He will be most disappointed if you turn me away."

As the teenager led him down a dim hall, the dog's barking became louder. Knelman could see the barroom at the far end, lit by blue TV light, where several young men at the bar were watching a wrestling match. His guide opened a door on which "Office" had been written in black felt marker. Walking in, Knelman stiffened as a barking black Alsatian lunged for him. Then he saw the chain that restrained the dog. A young redheaded man in black jeans sat with his bare feet up on a pool table, reading a tabloid newspaper under a bare bulb. "Shut up, Heidi," he told the dog. He wore a German World War II leather bomber jacket. Knelman recognized the cut. Luftwaffe issue.

"Mr. Nardi?"

The redhead turned. "Who wants to know?"

Knelman came to the pool table, holding up the box to display the embossed lettering on the lid: "Isaac Rosenthal Center." Interest sparked in Nardi's freckled face as Knelman set the box on the table and lifted the lid. Inside was a thick braid of chestnut-colored hair about fourteen inches long, plus the typed card of explanation. "As a connoisseur," he said, handing over the card, "you know this object's great worth."

While Nardi read the card, Knelman observed the shrine-like bookshelf where Nazi items were displayed. Panzer divisional badges. Knives, stilettos, bayonets. A Sam Browne belt with Gestapo insignia. A Luger pistol, the model not unlike Knelman's own, hidden at home these twenty-eight years.

Swinging his feet to the floor, Nardi reached into the cardboard box. He fingered the braid like a lover, but when he looked up, the gleam in his eyes was like a hunter's over his kill. "How much you want?"

"Not money—I am not a trader. I want you to bring me Nick Morgan."

No sign of recognition. "Who's he?"

"The thirteen-year-old runaway who recently joined you and your friends in, shall we say, a little rough business."

Nardi's lips curved in a cold smile. "What's the little shit done now?"

"That does not concern you. But something else should. The police are looking for him, and if they find him, he will undoubtedly betray you. I have come to suggest that we work together. A mutual solution to our problems."

Nardi sat back. "Haven't a clue where he is."

"I know someone who, I believe, will lead you to him. His mother. She is staying in the East Village with a man named Yuill. Follow her. Once she finds the boy, I want you to capture them both."

"What's in it for me?"

"Access to the Rosenthal Center's Memorial Museum, after hours. I'm sure you are aware how valuable their collection is. I can get you inside. What you take away is up to you."

The green eyes flashed with interest. "Word among collectors is that Yid place has a safe, and in that safe is a book. Bound in human skin. Know if it's true?"

Knelman felt sick. "It is."

"I'd get access to that too?"

"Yes." He put the lid back on the cardboard box. "In the meantime, please accept this as my gift. Do we have an agreement?"

CHAPTER 17

"HEY, ALANA, YOU ever make a movie with Raquel Welch? Now there's a good-looking broad. Think she might have a little gypsy blood in her?"

"Couldn't tell you, Vesh, I've never met her."

Alana sat in the back of a cherry-red '69 Camaro, her half-brothers Vesh and Nicu on either side of her, her cousins Walter and Danny in the front. It was ten-thirty A.M., and they were inching along with the traffic on Second Avenue, on their way to Gus's on East Sixth Street. Because of the threat from Knelman, Rajko had ordained that she couldn't go out without a bodyguard, but she felt more like a prisoner. Not that the guys here were a problem; it had actually been nice how the whole family had welcomed her back to the fold. Nice at first. Now it was bugging her, being treated as one of the sheep. She hated the waiting and hiding. She'd almost prefer to take her chances alone against Knelman's gunman.

"I sure would like to," Vesh said, combing his Elvis pompadour. "Meet Raquel, I mean."

"Dream on," Walter said at the wheel.

Alana's thoughts strayed to Gus. He'd left a message on her service saying that he'd picked up her knapsack from Luba's Café. "Looks like wallet and car keys inside," he'd said, "but you can check for yourself if everything else is there." Alana was eager to get the keys so she could pick up her impounded Fiat. That's what she and the guys had come for. She knew that as soon as they delivered her car back to her father's enclave, it would become family property, but she was clinging to what the Fiat symbolized: a chance to take off with Nick. She needed to believe that was still possible.

"See his shiner, Alana?" Danny said with a giggle from the front seat as he nodded at Vesh. A pudgy sixteen-year-old, Danny had never known Alana in the old days, so he was somewhat shy with her, but he took his joshing cue from her brothers. "Ask him how he got it."

Walter chuckled. "Yeah, I heard him last night going on to Simza about Raquel this and Raquel that, and how they oughta name the kid Raquel if it's a girl. Simza, she hauled off and socked him."

Vesh shrugged. "Pregnant women get jumpy." He winked at Alana. "Guess I had it coming."

She couldn't help returning his smile. Vesh was her favorite brother. His eighteen-year-old wife, Simza, was expecting any day, and her mother and sisters had already arrived from Chicago to help. Alana had to admit that this was one good thing about communal gypsy life: when the baby came, Simza's mother and sisters would do all Simza's work in Rajko's household, including taking care of her two other kids, leaving her free to rest and suckle her baby for months. And even after they'd gone home to Chicago, Simza could still rely on Rajko's other *boris* to share the chores. If I'd gotten support like that, Alana thought, having a baby at fifteen might not have been so bad.

She caught herself. Her baby hadn't been like any other. Her *life* wasn't like any other, and neither was Nick's. They had a unique bond, and they faced a unique danger, and they had to stick together. Except, Nick had fallen in love with gypsy life, and he was so hot now to carve out a future with his clan, he didn't seem to care if that cut the bond with her. The change in him scared her; she didn't know what to do about him. He wasn't listening to her these days, only to Rajko. Rajko's golden boy.

She turned to Nicu. "Any word on Ruby?" Her half-brother Boldor's wife had been arrested yesterday; on what charge, Alana didn't know. No one in the family did, it seemed, except Rajko. She had an uneasy feeling that Nick was somehow involved.

"The *rom baro*'s got it under control," Nicu said. Scraping a toothpick under his fingernail, he seemed unconcerned. He accepted Rajko's leadership without question, just like all the others. Sheep, Alana thought. "Heard him talking to his lawyer this morning," he went on. "They'll get Ruby out today. Don't worry about it."

She *was* worried. What were her father and son up to?

"This the place?" Walter asked her, pulling over.

She looked out at Gus's crummy brick walk-up. Chipped stone steps, rusting fire escape. "Yup."

Vesh got out. Alana stayed. They'd earlier agreed that since Knelman had tracked down Gus's address, it wasn't safe for her to be seen here, so she'd called Gus to tell him Vesh would be picking up the knapsack. She'd come along just to claim ownership of her Fiat once they got to the car pound. "Say hello for me," she told Vesh through the open window. "Gus is a good friend."

He exchanged glances with the others, and she knew what they were thinking: We make money off the *gadje*; we don't make friends. "Back in a sec," he said.

"Saw a cop ticketing down the street. We'll drive around the block," Walter told him, and pulled out into the traffic.

The guys nattered on as they cruised along Avenue A. Nicu said he wanted to stop for lunch once they were done here, because Walter had forgotten to bring the food the women had made for them. That got them going on about where to eat. On and on. Alana almost rolled her eyes, knowing what the problem was: they wouldn't eat off restaurant plates, because all dishes used by the *gadje* were considered polluted. They'd have to find a place that had paper plates and plastic forks and foam cups. Idiotic.

"There's that Portuguese joint on Ninth," Nicu said.

Walter made a face. "Their sausage gives me gas."

"So order something else. Soup or something."

"Jesus, who knows what they put in their soup."

Alana tuned it out; she'd heard it all before. When she was a kid in the fifties, half the *kumpania* had gone on the road for months, carloads of them camping all the way to Mexico where they made good money trailering a mini movie theater around to the hands at remote ranches. A buck to see a grainy two-reeler; Westerns were the favorites. On those trips Yanka had constantly warned the kids about diseases they could catch from filthy *gadje* plates and cups.

I'm living the old life again, she thought uneasily. Stuck in the enclave, secluded with the women, locked in a gender status quo that hadn't changed in centuries. If she stayed, her father might even try to marry her off; in his world no woman stayed single unless she was so handicapped no man would have her. It gave her the creeps. The charm of the family's scams, too, had worn awfully thin. For one thing, the whole *kumpania* now worked the welfare system as a way of life. Gypsies had never bothered with marriage licenses, so the women claiming benefits listed their children all as fatherless. She'd felt revolted this morning over breakfast when her cousin Liza, the family's welfare queen, had proudly displayed her monthly checks from five states. Using aliases, she was on the welfare rolls in New York, Newark, Boston, Philadelphia, and Baltimore. All she did to maintain the scam was pay chicken-feed rent at rooming houses in each city to establish residency. Even with one of the guys constantly driving her around to collect the checks, they pulled in a good profit. But what bugged Alana most was the way the *kumpania* kids were kept out of school. They attended for a few years, because that was an official condition of their parents collecting welfare, but they got yanked out at ten or eleven, before *gadje* ideas could take hold. "Gypsy smarts" alone had value, and the kids were trained to gloat at giving the slip to well-meaning social workers. Alana was fed up with her family's ignorance and bigotry. She could hardly believe she'd defended gypsy life to David that night they'd met.

David, she thought with a pang. No message from him on her service for two days; she'd called several times from her father's to check. She felt such a hollowness, sure now that David was out of her life forever. She remembered his face at the London Grill when Knelman had confirmed the gene's existence—the realization sinking in for him that she was a freak of nature. He was probably relieved to see the last of her. Why else would he have stopped calling? She told herself she had to forget him, but the essence of him lingered in all her senses. His wonderful, good-natured laugh. The smell of his skin—that trace of male sweat under the scent of a freshly pressed shirt. The thrill of his hands on her, making her crazy. She loved him for all that, loved him with a passion she'd never felt for any other man. But even more she loved his goodness, his decency. It gave her a strange pain to realize that part of that very goodness was his steadfast loyalty to the man he believed was his father. The scribbled indictment she'd handed him couldn't stand up against a lifelong father-son bond. Losing David felt so hard.

But it sobered her as well. She didn't have a shred of hope now that he would take action against Knelman. She was on her own. It was just her and her son.

She desperately wanted to leave town with Nick, but how could she get him to go? He was dead serious about getting married. That really shook her. Scared her too. He was high on the idea of having pretty Mimi Toma, and blithe at the idea of fathering children. She hadn't told him Knelman's horrible theory. Why should she, when she didn't believe it? But an edgy voice inside whispered, *What if Knelman's right?*

"You're way too young," she'd told him when she'd finally got a word alone with him last night in the scrap-metal yard, desperate to talk some sense into him. "Marriage will tie you forever to this world. It'll warp you, Nick. It's already screwed up your judgment. Why can't you understand that we have to get away from Knelman? He's insane."

But he had it all figured out. "He can't touch us here. Anyway, the faster I can have kids, the safer we'll be—even *he'll* see he can't kill us *all*. Besides, it's going to put this family on top. I'm gonna have superkids. Nobody'll mess with them. And one day I'm going to be the *rom baro*." He'd smiled at her with a strange fire in his eyes. "It's like—what do they call it? My destiny."

It seemed surreal to Alana. Nick was on a roll. He was back at the enclave right now with Rajko, entertaining John

Toma in the marriage negotiations. They were planning the wedding for the day after tomorrow. She couldn't see any way to stop it.

"Hey, what's with Vesh?" Danny said.

They had pulled up at Gus's building again, and Alana saw Vesh hurrying to the curb. His face was pale as he opened the car door. "The guy's place was busted into. Jesus, somebody got him good!"

Alana jumped out and ran up the front steps. She found the inner lobby door broken, like it had been jimmied with a crowbar. She sprinted up the three flights. The apartment door was open. "Gus?" she called, coming in.

No answer. An Aretha tape was playing. "Do Right Woman."

Down the hall she heard a groan. Reaching the bedroom, she gasped. Gus was bound to a chair with duct tape, his head slumped to one side. Blood soaked his clothes. "Gus!"

He blinked at her through swollen eyes. Blood dripped from his nose. "Alana?" His voice was only grating breath.

"Jesus," Vesh whispered behind her. She said in a strangled voice, "Give me your jackknife." When he handed it over, she rushed to Gus and cut the tape. He fell into her arms. She saw that his bloodied shirt and pants had rips like punctures, as if he'd been knifed over and over. The puncture at his throat frothed with tiny red bubbles. She tried to haul him over to the bed, but his dead weight was too much, and she had to lower him to the floor. "Gus, I'm calling for an ambulance! Just hang on!"

On his back, he groped at her ankle. "Get out . . . they're after you . . ."

A gust of fury hit her. *Knelman.*

". . . didn't . . . tell . . . where you were . . ."

She snatched the bedside phone and dialed, her eyes

locked on Gus as she waited for someone to answer. Her heart twisted as she saw him pass out. Vesh cautiously walked over and stood looking down at him. When a woman came on the line, Alana's voice broke as she asked for an ambulance and gave the address.

"Hang up, Alana," Vesh said. "He's dead."

Aretha crooned, "If you want a do-o-o right, a-a-all day woman . . ."

Staring at the body, Alana couldn't take it in. Gus . . . gone?

". . . you gotta be a do-o-o right, a-a-all night man."

She hung up, and found she was shaking. Who had done this? Not the gunman's style. Gus had said "they." Had Knelman hired someone new?

Vesh was eyeing Gus's wounds with revulsion. "Looks like from fangs. Jesus . . . a dog?"

Alana looked in horror at the punctures—the ragged gash at his throat . . .

Her legs buckled. She staggered to catch hold of a chest of drawers, but it couldn't hold her up. As she thudded to her knees, the drawer knob gouged her shoulder, shooting pain down her arm. But the truth that stabbed her hurt far more. *Gus is dead because I ran away. Because I tried to hide.*

"Alana, you okay?" Vesh said, coming to her. He took her elbow. "Come on, we gotta get the hell out."

She stared up at him. Couldn't tear herself away. She wanted to yell, He's my friend!

But she saw that Vesh was scared and itching to run. She thought: Run—hide—it's all I've been doing. Beneath the agony of grief for Gus, she felt something harden inside her. No more hiding. She would strike back. There was only one way to make sure that Knelman could never hurt anyone again. Kill him. The vision of action galvanized her. Somehow, she would take this madman down.

"Come *on!*" Vesh was pulling her to her feet. With a choked good-bye to Gus, she left the bedroom, grabbed her knapsack on the hall floor by the door, and hurried down the stairs with her brother.

The Camaro was idling at the curb. As they went for it, a dog growled behind Alana. She whipped around. A German shepherd was straining at its leash, a woman in jogging sweats struggling to control it. The dog sniffed Alana's sandal, and she flinched at the cold wet muzzle.

"Prince, stop that!" the woman said, and wrenched the dog away.

As Vesh and Alana climbed into the car Nicu said, "What took you so long?"

"The guy's dead," Vesh said.

Danny looked frightened. Walter, at the wheel, said, "Christ, let's go. We don't want nobody seeing us here."

They drove past a boarded-up Avenue A storefront plastered with angry red graffiti, and in the lurid spray-painted swirls Alana again saw Gus's bloodied body. She was fighting not to cry. The savagery of what they'd done to him shook her. But so did her own hard fury. I'm becoming like my enemy, she thought in shock—planning a cold, premeditated murder. An awful question gripped her. Could she be wrong about Knelman? Not about his trying to kill her and Nick: the bullet that had scarred her was proof of that, and besides, later the gunman had come to the St. Moritz, and only Knelman had known she and Nick were there. She was sure, too, that he had to be behind this savage attack on Gus. But could she be wrong about him being Schiller? About him killing her mother and the other subjects? Was he truly the Nazi who'd masterminded the gene, or an innocent Jew who'd been forced to collaborate, just as he claimed, and whose sense of guilt had driven him out of his mind? Did she really know this man she intended to murder? Her evidence that he was Schiller was thin. Circumstantial, David would call it. She was relying on her inherited knowledge, and Nick's, but that knowledge was freakish. *What if it's all in my head?* She had to find a way to disentangle the lies from the truth. Because if Knelman really was telling the truth about himself, he might be more right than she'd allowed about the awful threat Nick embodied. She felt a fear that chilled her to her bones. But she had to face this straight on. She had to find out who this man really was.

There might be a way. An eyewitness. Her father said he'd seen a doctor shoot Lina right in front of him. Could Rajko confirm whether Knelman was Schiller or not?

"Walter," she said as he drove through a yellow light, "I need you to make another stop."

The lobby of the Rosenthal Center was quiet as she and Danny waited for the elevator. Alana had prepped him on the way, and he seemed eager. Maybe too eager. She wished she had Nick with her instead; he'd pull this off so slickly. She also hoped that Esther Knelman wasn't working here this morning; that could be dicey. She was relieved when the doors opened, and the elevator carried her and Danny up to the second-floor archive room.

"Back again?" The librarian offered a professional smile over the name plate on her counter. "Otzenhausen, wasn't it?"

Alana nodded. "Brought my nephew this time, Mrs. Rosen. I'm on a mission—educate the youngsters one by one. Poor kid was home from school anyway. Bad asthma." She added in a whisper behind her hand, "Between you and me, his mother keeps him home too much. Overprotective, you know the type."

The professional smile softened. "I'll get you the files. Have a seat."

Slipping so easily into the old con patter, Alana felt ashamed at her earlier holier-than-thou annoyance at her family. There would be no more holding her nose at their ways. To get to Knelman, she was going to need all the ancient instincts of her people.

She turned to the two long research tables. Both were close to the librarian's post. At one, a milk-faced young man wearing an embroidered yarmulke was reading a large volume, and an austere Asian woman was writing with a fountain pen in a loose-leaf binder. No one was at the other table. Alana counted four people browsing the open shelves across the room. She led Danny to the empty table, and they sat down. The librarian brought them the box of files, then went back behind her counter.

Alana flipped through the three-ring binder's plastic sheets that encased the black-and-white photos. She was looking for a group shot of officers that she'd glimpsed when she was here with Nick. She hadn't suspected Knelman at that point; they'd been searching only for information on Hilde Wentzler. Though she'd spotted the group picture then, it hadn't rung any bells.

Suddenly, his face was looking up at her from the photo. White lab coat open over his gray SS uniform. He stood with a handful of other medical personnel dressed the same among a group of maybe thirty camp officials. They were milling in the commandant's rose garden, apparently enjoying some kind of impromptu afternoon party. The caption, listing no names, said only: "Otzenhausen SS officers and senior medical staff. July, 1944. Commandant Reinhardt's garden." The man she was looking at seemed to be in his thirties, he was clean shaven, and his thick dark hair had a youthful sheen. Knelman, in his sixties now, had close-cropped white hair and a trim white beard. But the steely eyes and ramrod bearing in the photo sent a shiver of recognition through Alana. It was him all right, and he was no prisoner doctor. Almost certainly Viktor Schiller. Hot tears pricked as she thought of Gus. Only one question remained: Was this the same man who had murdered her mother? Rajko alone might be able to tell her that.

She turned to Danny and whispered, "You're on."

He coughed, gasped a breath, coughed again. It became a coughing fit. Pushing his chair back from the table, he fought for air.

"Breathe, honey," Alana cried, rubbing his back. "Breathe!" She felt everyone in the room watching. As Danny gasped and wheezed, she called to the librarian, "Mrs. Rosen, a glass of water, please!" then turned back to help Danny. He staggered to his feet, red-faced, and lurched a few steps from the table, sucking tortured breaths. Alana saw the librarian scurry into the washroom. Satisfied that all the others' eyes were locked on Danny, she tugged the photo from the binder with one clean jerk and slipped it under her shirt, flat against her stomach. She shuddered, its glossy surface cold on her skin. The librarian arrived with the water, and Danny grabbed it as if he were dying. He began to breathe more freely, but was still making gasping sounds as Alana put her arm around him, saying, "I'd better get him home," and guided him away from the staring faces, toward the elevator.

Downstairs they crossed the lobby with its plate-glass wall of windows onto West Eighty-second, and calmly walked out, and as they met the Camaro down the block and climbed in, Danny was grinning. He regaled the others with details of the prank, and they laughed. Alana hadn't told them what was at stake. She couldn't laugh along. Her mind was on the Nazi against her skin.

"He's in the big room with Toma," Yanka told her. She was stirring a pot of lamb stew, while a menthol Kool with a half-inch of ash dangled from her mouth. The kitchen was crowded with women running the lunch feast, Nadja and Liza and pregnant Simza busy at the counters, chopping onions, folding cabbage leaves around savory fillings, arranging platters of sliced meats and salads. Three little girls were giggling over walnuts they were shelling at a table. Watching Liza pick up a platter of potato pancakes, Alana said, "I'll take that up," and lifted the plate from her cousin's hands.

Yanka muttered, cigarette bobbing, "About time you made yourself useful."

Alana went upstairs to the "big room." When she was a kid, her father had entertained important guests here: out-of-state *rom baros* passing through town, or visiting *kris* judges. As she passed the seated men, they chatted on, oblivious to her presence. Bright woven hangings covered every wall, softening the room like an opulent tent, and a display of gold plates gleamed on a shelf. Half-eaten platters and bowls of food covered the table, along with whiskey glasses and beer cans. Cigarette smoke was thick in the air. Rajko sat at the head of the table in a shiny navy suit, red polka-dot shirt, and his green fedora. On his right sat two of his brothers and Yanka's three uncles. The Toma men sat opposite. At the other end, Nick sat beside Mimi, the bride-to-be. Pretty and shy, wearing a modest white blouse and pink full skirt, she kept her dark eyes lowered, darting a look every now and then at Nick, or her father, or Rajko. Nick, scrubbed and combed and got up in a too-big pin-striped suit like a pimp, looked very pleased with himself. He infuriated Alana, and so did this *diwano*; as a woman, she had no say.

She set down the platter in front of Rajko and bent to whisper in his ear, "I have to talk to you outside. Now."

He scowled. But she made sure he caught her determined look, and as she left the room, she heard him start to excuse himself. They met in the yard beside his Cadillac. Men were busy banging at car fenders and door panels, a gaggle of boys hanging around to help. Two preteen girls were dancing on the grass like a wedding couple. A fat old woman sat snoozing in the noon sun. No one paid Alana and Rajko much attention.

"Now, don't you butt in about this marriage," Rajko warned her. "It's a solid alliance. Toma's got good connections—he's respected at every *kris* in the country. This is gonna bring our family up in the world, and put Nicky in line as *rom baro*. So you better get used to the idea."

She bit her tongue. One battle at a time. "It's not about that. It's about Knelman."

He seemed startled. "You heard? Look, it's business, it had to be done. They'd taken Ruby in."

What the hell did Ruby have to do with Knelman? "What are you talking about?"

He looked at her hard, then a door seemed to close in his eyes. "Nothing. My mind's stuck on my lawyer getting her out, is all." Using his thumb, he rubbed a speck of dirt off the Cadillac's gleaming hood. "What's this about Knelman?"

She handed him the photo. "Look carefully. You see the man who killed Lina?"

His gaze zeroed in. He pointed, hatred sparking in his

eyes. "That's the Nazi bastard. He put a bullet in her heart. Would've put one in yours too, if I hadn't knocked him back and grabbed you."

Now she was sure. Pain flooded her at the memory of Gus. Those fang punctures, the froth of blood at his throat . . . his tortured eyes as he'd warned her with his last breath. "His hired killers just murdered my friend Gus. They were looking for me and Nick. Knelman's not going to stop." Again, she let the icy resolve harden inside her. "So I'm going to kill him. I'll need your help."

"Kill him?" Rajko's eyes narrowed, whether in disbelief or interest, Alana couldn't tell. "How?"

She flashed on Lina and thought, with a small shock, I've done it before. Winter, 1943. Austria's Burgenland. Her half-starved *kumpania* in their huddled wagons had been hiding in a beech woods near the Hungarian border. Rajko and his brothers had gone out that morning to forage for food, and she was anxious for them to get back. Already the governor's police had rounded up most of the province's gypsies, as well as the Jews. With the family crowded together in the wagon for warmth, Lina heard a man outside stomping toward them and hoped it was Rajko. He threw up the heavy canvas flap at the rear, letting in a gust of icy air. It was Milosh, her oldest brother, his face haggard.

"Papusza's dead," he said. Lina froze. Her seventeen-year-old sister. Papusza and her husband and what was left of his *kumpania* had been holed up in an abandoned barn. "Somebody tipped the police," Milosh said. "They bolted the barn doors and set it on fire. Papusza . . . all of them. Burned to death."

The family sat in silent horror. Lina was the first to speak. "Who betrayed them?"

"That sheep-fucker, Hoche. So I heard."

A tightfisted farmer. Lina knew him from the market square, where she and her mother used to make a few pfennigs sharpening knives, telling fortunes.

Vendettas weren't the gypsy way. Not practical. So the next day, market day, the *kumpania* prepared to move out in their wagons at nightfall, Rajko organizing the horses. But Lina had something to do first. She found Rajko's bone-handled knife and tucked it in her skirt, then pulled from her uncle's trunk a patchy cloak that would let her pass as a *gadje* peasant. She slipped out on her pony to the market square and waited for Hoche. When he came, she told him she had a milk cow she could sell him for a good price.

"Belonged to some Yids got rounded up," she said. "I stole her myself as they got carted off. Gotta be quick, *ja*?" Seeing his hooded smile, she felt she had him. "So I can let her go cheap. If you're interested, meet me at the bridge over the creek behind the beech woods."

He was so greedy, he came. And on that stone bridge filmed with ice Lina sliced his stringy throat. Left his body turning the creek red as she joined Rajko and her people, and their wagons pulled out of the woods. She'd done it for Papusza, and it had felt very good.

Alana pushed away the chilling memory. But she held onto her mother's dark wisdom: To murder with the least risk, make the victim disappear. "First, we get him off his own turf," she answered her father. "To a place where there are no witnesses."

"Kidnap him?"

"No, we get him to come to us. Not here. Some place he'll feel safe walking into. We lure him there."

"With what?"

"Me. I'm the bait."

Rajko frowned. "What if he sends his gunman?"

"I'll take out whoever shows up. But if I set the trap right, I'm betting he'll come himself. We'll send a phony traitor to tip him. Vesh could pull it off. When Knelman comes, I'll be waiting for him."

Rajkos eyes glinted in admiration. "You always were the smartest."

"So you'll help? All you have to do is give me Vesh. And—" She swallowed. The only killing she'd ever done had been movie make-believe. "And a gun."

He shook his head. "I've never kept a gun. And you're wrong, that's not all I have to do. It's my wife he murdered. My daughter and grandson he's trying to wipe out. This is my job, *shori.*" She heard passion in his voice; this seemed to mean as much to him as to her. "When the bastard comes for you, he won't get near you, because I'm the one who'll be waiting."

Something like love swelled in her throat, surprising her. She hadn't expected this offer from him, but she felt so grateful to have him on her side. "I can live with that."

He chucked her under the chin. "That's the whole idea."

She could have hugged him.

He said, "If he sends his hit man, we'll get rid of that problem, at least." He looked again at the photo, and Alana saw the lust for revenge rekindle in his eyes. "But I hope you're right and the Nazi comes himself. I'll rip out his heart with my bare hands."

"Bit extreme," she said, almost smiling. "You used to be pretty good with a knife, though. Lina always thought so."

A smile played on his lips. "You and Nick, you know it all, don't you?"

Nick, she thought, anxious again. She couldn't bear him knowing she was plotting murder. "Listen, don't tell him about this. Not about Gus, and not about what we're going to do. None of it, okay?"

He nodded. "Just you and me. This job's ours. And once it's done, no one has to know anything."

He made it sound simple. But could it be? She felt a shiver of dread, remembering Lina. Soon after she'd cut the farmer's throat, the governor's police had rounded up the last of the Burgenland gypsies, and she and Rajko and their *kumpania* were shipped in cattle cars to Otzenhausen. Most didn't make it out.

"Taxi? Sure thing, Dr. Knelman, let me get you one."

"Thank you, Bill."

As the doorman stepped to the curb and raised his arm to hail a cab, Knelman stood under the marquee and checked his watch, anxious to reach Detective Lipranski before he might leave for lunch. David's friend was his only lead now for finding Alana Marks. She was no longer staying at Yuill's apartment. "We got that much from the guy while he could still talk," Nardi had told him on the phone moments ago. "Nothing else, though." Knelman had shuddered, imagining what had befallen the stuntman at Nardi's hands, but he could not let such qualms sidetrack him. Then a thought had come to him: Could she and the boy have sought sanctuary with her gypsy family? It seemed so obvious, he wondered why it hadn't occurred to him before. Only, where was her family? That's when he'd thought of the detective. David had referred to Lipranski as a gypsy expert.

"Here you go, Doctor," Bill said, holding open the cab door.

As the taxi took him downtown, Knelman's aggrieved mind turned to David. They hadn't spoken since yesterday, when he'd confessed everything. *I had to make him see.* But

David hadn't understood. David despised him. The pain festered like shrapnel in Knelman's chest. The ties of family love had meant everything to him, binding his life, but now they had been blasted away from him, and he felt adrift, sinking. The misery was almost more than he could bear. He repeated to himself, like a prayer: *No time for grief. Find the carriers. Finish this.*

At the Ninth Precinct office he gave his name at the desk and asked to see Detective Richard Lipranski. He waited, impatient. An intoxicated woman in fake fur was being led away, shouting obscenities, when the frosted glass door opened and a wiry, sallow-faced man came to meet him.

"Rick Lipranski. You're Dr. Knelman?"

"Yes. Could I have a moment of your time, Detective?"

Concern flickered in Lipranski's eyes. "The DA okay?"

"Oh, quite. It is a professional matter that brings me. David once mentioned your expertise concerning gypsies."

Lipranski seemed mildly surprised. "You talk to him today?"

"No."

The detective seemed to shrug off his fleeting concern. "Come on in," he said as he opened the door.

They went through the busy office amid ringing phones and clacking typewriters. They reached a cluttered metal desk, where Lipranski, sitting down, picked up a half-eaten corned beef sandwich. Taking a bite of it, he gestured to the chair opposite. "Sit down, Doctor. Take a load off."

Knelman explained his dilemma, just as he had rehearsed. He had a gypsy patient who might be suicidal, and it was urgent that he reach her, but she had left him no contact number. She was, however, related to a man of some reputation in the gypsy community, a man named Marks. An

Austrian immigrant. Could Lipranski furnish information on Marks's whereabouts?

The detective chewed. "Funny, I never met a gypsy who'd admit to a mental health problem. Makes 'em seem almost human, huh?" He opened a drawer with hanging files. "Your man sounds like Rajko Marks." He lifted out a file and opened it on the desk. "Good luck getting through. His people will give you the runaround." Swallowing his mouthful, he offered a sour smile. "Or maybe that's just the house special for cops."

Minutes later Knelman left with what he'd come for. An address in Sunnyside, Queens. He would inform Nardi directly.

As he reached the curb, about to hail a taxi, he heard a voice behind him. "Doctor Knelman?"

He turned. A swarthy young man in a yellow flowered shirt and red bell-bottom slacks stood looking at him with a guarded smile. His slick black hair was shaped in the kind of pompadour Knelman associated with gigolos. "Yes?" he answered, uneasy.

"I hear you're looking for Alana Marks."

Knelman was amazed. And instantly wary. "Who are you?"

"Call me Stevo. I was at her old man's place in Sunnyside yesterday, big party. She's there. Heard her say a Dr. Knelman was looking for her, but she didn't want to be found. Didn't think much of it at the time, but when I woke up this morning, I thought, hey, maybe there is something in this for yours truly."

"How did you find me?"

The man gave a wolfish smile. "Followed your taxi. Took a little digging to find where you live, but my ma didn't raise no dummies. Look, you want this Alana. I don't know why—girlfriend, whatever—but I'm telling you you'll never get into Marks's place. It's like a fort. Me, though, I know how you can get to her."

People jostled past them on the sidewalk, and Knelman motioned the man to come with him out of the foot traffic. "How?"

"On account of the partying, Doc." He pulled a comb from his trouser pocket and smoothed back the sides of his hair. "Big celebrations. Marks's grandson Nick is marrying a Toma girl. Day after tomorrow, I hear."

"Marrying?" Knelman was stunned. "He's only thirteen!"

The man shrugged. "To us gypsies, if you can get it up, you're a man. The kid's ready, and Rajko's found him a prize wife."

This was the worst thing Knelman could imagine.

"Anyhow, here's the thing, Doc." The young man tucked away his comb. "This Alana you want is dead set against the marriage, and she's squawking about it to anybody who'll listen, really mouthing off. Far as her father's concerned, she's a royal pain in the ass. Told her right in front of people he's gonna move her into town tonight, leave her there till the wedding, some apartment where she'll be all alone. Smarten her up."

Alone? It was like a gift. As for her remaining there, he knew this woman: she would not flee without her son. "Where?"

"Don't know that yet." Again, the wolfish smile. "But, what with all the liquor and excitement over in Sunnyside, there's gonna be loose tongues. So here's what I'm offering. I go to the party and ask around, find out where he's sending her. Then I come back to you with the address, and you give me three hundred bucks. Fair?"

Knelman felt frantic. What to do first? The male carrier was the priority . . . a male now poised to impregnate a young bride. *But it's his mother who's out to stop me.* He asked, "Nick will remain at his grandfather's home for these celebrations?"

"Sure, he's the main attraction. So, Doc, what do you say?"

Which one, which one? With mother and son separated, Nardi could not get to both at once. Time was running out. David knew everything . . . and now hated him. *How long before he sends the police to arrest me?* He made a snap decision. Nardi must get the boy immediately. *That leaves Alana Marks to me.* He thought of the Luger hidden at home. Smuggled out of Otzenhausen in his pant leg, the gun had been with him as he'd struggled out of his war-wracked homeland into Switzerland, then across France to Le Havre on the coast. Weeks ago, he had so hoped to avoid spilling more blood by his own hand. It would surely lead him to prison this time. Yet, what did that matter now? His life was over. Only God's judgment mattered.

"Doc? We have a deal?"

The Alsatian growled at Knelman as he entered the Tre Stelle office. The dog strained at its leash to take down the intruder. Nardi looked up from the orange vinyl easy chair where he was shining his boots beside the pool table. The big teenager in black T-shirt and camouflage pants, the one they called Tank, continued shooting pool. The room smelled dankly of beer and dog.

"What have you got for me, Santa?" Nardi asked, dabbing on black shoe paste with a rag. As they'd parted last night, Knelman reluctant to give his name after bringing the braid, Nardi had seemed to relish devising this nickname:

the white-haired old man bearing gifts. "Not another blind alley like Yuill, I hope."

Knelman recoiled at Nardi's composure. The attack on Yuill had been mere hours ago. Yet wasn't such brutal calmness precisely why he'd hired this man? "No. I have learned that both the woman and the boy have taken refuge at her father's gypsy household in Sunnyside. I have the address. We must act immediately."

The big teen looked up from his pool cue in astonishment. "Did you say *gypsy*?"

Nardi seemed equally surprised. He snorted a skeptical laugh. "What, they got their wagons and ponies parked in Times Square?"

"More likely automobiles. They deal in used cars."

"Can you beat that? Gypsies." Nardi made a face as he polished his boot. "Not exactly niggers, but close enough. Stand downwind, I bet you can't tell 'em apart."

Knelman plowed on. "I've had word that the woman will be leaving soon, and I shall deal with her myself. Your focus is capturing the boy. This may be difficult. He'll be protected within his relatives' household compound, but somehow you must get to him today. He is to be married the day after tomorrow. That *must* not happen."

"Married?" The White Pride leader exchanged an incredulous look with his friend. "You gotta be kidding. The kid's barely out of diapers."

"It is gypsy custom to marry young," Knelman said. "He is old enough to procreate."

Nardi snorted. "Perverts."

Knelman felt himself losing patience. "Time is of the essence. Let us discuss how you can reach the boy."

"Shouldn't be a problem. We're his pals. Especially Tank here."

The big teen scowled over his pool cue, aiming at a ball. "Little runt seemed okay, yeah—till he ran out." His tone sounded to Knelman like a jilted lover.

"So," Nardi went on, "Tank goes to the joint in Sunnyside, asks to see Nick, the kid comes out to say hi to his buddy." He snapped his fingers. "We nab him."

Knelman saw that it might work. The relationship between these two and Nick could allow them to get close to him, the very access he lacked.

Nardi got up from his chair, eyes on his shiny boots. He took a few steps as though testing brand new footwear. "Sooner the better, Santa. I sure don't wanna wait for Christmas. You get me into that Yid museum, I'm gonna pick up some collector's items, position myself for a little trading. Got my heart set on that skin book."

Knelman suppressed a shiver.

"Trouble is, I been thinking," Nardi went on, his expression turning hard. "Say your plan to get me inside doesn't go so smooth, and you leave me holding the bag. Call me crazy, but the idea of doing hard time for busting in there doesn't thrill me. I'm gonna need some assurances here. Personal guarantees. Like, just what's in this for you?"

"Perhaps it is time you knew my name."

"I don't give a flying fuck what you call yourself, I'm talking about—"

"I am Dr. Viktor Schiller. I was a medical officer in Hitler's Schutzstaffel, the SS, under Reichsführer Heinrich Himmler. I performed medical experiments on prisoners at Otzenhausen concentration camp from 1943 to 1945, and for the last twenty-eight years I have been hiding under an assumed name. If my true identity were ever exposed, it is I who would be sent to prison, for the rest of my life. Does this assurance satisfy you?"

They both gaped at him. Nardi said, "You're shitting me."

"I have never been more serious."

"You . . . knew Hitler?"

"I was introduced to him once. At a luncheon in the Waffen SS officer's mess in Berlin in 1942. The führer looked, shall we say, preoccupied."

"Wow." The big teenager said in awe. "So, like . . . what do we call you? Colonel? General?"

"Doctor. That is what I am." He couldn't waste any more time. "Mr. Nardi, the gypsy woman and her son have found out about me, and that is why I must deal with them. It is also why you can trust me. Don't you see? I would hardly betray you now, since you are safeguarding my secret." Of course, it was no longer a secret. David knew, and soon all the world would. But if this assurance sufficed to recruit these thugs, it was all he wanted. Nothing else mattered.

"Okay," Nardi said, collecting himself. "That's cool. So, I guess we got ourselves a deal. Doctor. You get me inside the Jew joint, I'll pick up the kid."

"Pardon me, but the question now becomes, what assurance do I have about *you*, that you will carry out your part? Let us establish specifics. You want into the Rosenthal Center, and I have the keys. I want the boy removed, and your friendship should allow you to abduct him. So I suggest the following. I'll give you a copy of the key to the basement door, as well as one for the alarm. Inside, you will have a free hand. The most valuable artifacts, however—such as the book you desire—are kept in the director's office in a climate-controlled vault, for which I have the key as well. No copy for that. This evening, when the center is closed, we'll meet inside. Once I see that you have Nick Morgan with you, I'll hand over the vault key. At that point, we can each conclude our missions."

Nardi picked up a pool cue. He bent over the table and jabbed a ball, sending it cracking against another, which rolled into a corner pocket. He smiled up at Knelman. "Heil Hitler."

CHAPTER 18

"YOU SURE ABOUT this raid, Counselor?" Lipranski asked from the hall, a chocolate doughnut halfway to his mouth. "Maybe you oughta see a doctor first."

"No time." David was finishing getting dressed as he came out of his bedroom. Pulling on his shirt, he winced at the stab of pain.

"You don't look so hot."

"Never had the shit kicked out of me before." Yesterday, bleeding and hunched, he'd reached a pay phone and called Lip, who'd brought him home, cleaned him up, doped him with painkillers, then went home himself and left David to sleep. And sleep he did. Waking up groggy when Lip had buzzed twenty minutes ago, he'd been dismayed to see that it was almost noon. Then, at his bedside, Lip had stunned him. "Your father came to see me this morning."

"Dad?" David now hated that name, but he was stuck with it. "What about?"

"Looks like we're not the only ones interested in Rajko Marks. Your old man is too. Did you know he has a gypsy patient? Some dame that's related to the *rom baro.* Seems she's wacko, and she split, so your father wanted to know where Marks lives, try to reach her. Small world, huh? By the way, I didn't tell him about Marks's boys rolling you. He didn't seem to know, and I figured it was your business."

"Yeah, thanks. No sense worrying him." David felt dread in his gut. Dad was tracking down Alana to kill her. He must have deduced she'd gone to her father's place. David himself had known it since Nick had delivered that final kick to his ribs, with the warning to stay out of Rajko Marks's business. "She's with him?" he'd managed to ask, curled up in pain on the asphalt, and Nick had confirmed it. *"Where she belongs."*

David had gotten out of bed fast. "Lip, I want to raid Marks's place. Tonight."

"Now you're talking, Counselor."

They'd laid the groundwork while David shaved and got dressed. But now that the drug had worn off, his right side ached so much that every deep breath hurt, and his skull throbbed. His bruised face in the mirror looked like a boxer's, his split lip scabbed, his left cheekbone an ugly greenish yellow, and below it pinprick scabs where the asphalt had grated his cheek.

"Need another of these little beauties?" Lip offered as they reached the living room. He dug into his pocket and brought out a half dozen shiny red capsules.

"Jesus, no," David said, tucking in his shirt. "Those things would knock out a horse."

"Work pretty good, don't they?" He indicated the table where he'd set the cardboard tray of doughnuts and takeout coffee he'd arrived with. "Better eat something, at least. Gonna be a hard day's night."

David shook his head; it hurt to even think of eating.

He'd have to stick to aspirin, though. In a few hours they'd be on their way to Marks's enclave, and he needed to stay on his feet and thinking fast until the raid was over and he'd gotten Alana safely away. The pain was small beer compared to his fear for her. He had to keep one step ahead of Dad.

Grabbing his windbreaker off the couch, he pulled it on, holding his breath at the stab in his side. Damn rib had to be cracked. "Let's go."

"More backup would be regulation," Lip said as they got into his unmarked Dodge at the curb. "You ask me, the eight officers we're planning is plenty, more's just overkill, snafus almost guaranteed. But I know you're a by-the-book guy, so if that's what you want, I'll get the ball rolling."

David had to level with him. "Lip, we're not going to get approval for this raid. Rintoul would deny it if I asked. He's authorized surveillance only." There hadn't been enough evidence even to bust the woman they'd arrested at Howard Jaffe's home, let alone the *rom baro* himself; Marks's lawyer had already got the woman released. Rintoul might reconsider if he knew the gypsies had beaten up one of his ADAs, but David had asked Lip to keep it quiet, saying the red tape might hold them up, maybe for days. "When this is over, my boss will likely want my head," he went on, "but I'll take the heat. I'll tell him you acted on my instructions. The longer we put this off, the bolder Marks gets. We couldn't detain the woman, and her release could be deadly. I want Marks—to save Howard Jaffe's life. We have to move in this evening."

At the wheel, the detective scratched his cheek. "Gypsy bastard's gotta be stopped. You'll get no lip from me."

The lame joke made David smile. Which hurt his cut mouth. The lie he'd just told hurt too. He wasn't organizing this raid to bring in Rajko Marks. Only to get Alana out. Far away from Dad.

In the yard, dusk was gathering. The campfire had been lit, and the party was in full swing. Nick, feeling no pain, sat at the foot of the table beside Mimi, a bottle of Bud in his left hand, his right arm thrown along her chair back. He loved being close enough to smell her.

"Think your mother's ever going to like me, Nicky?" she asked above the party noise: laughter, guitars, people dancing, squealing kids. Her eyebrows tugged in an anxious frown as she poked her spoon into her melting strawberry ice cream. "She's awful quiet."

"She'll love you. Don't worry about it."

Mimi turned as a guest, an old man, handed her an envelope. She thanked him with a bright smile and added his gift to the basket of other envelopes—all containing cash—then chattered on to the man. Watching her, Nick couldn't believe how pretty she was. Sparkling eyes, the whitest teeth, hair like black silk. Her giggle made him high. The thought of being in bed with her made him hard. At school no girls had ever come near him, like they knew he was a freak. But to Mimi he was a prize, Rajko's favorite, in line to be *rom baro.* That made her father happy, so it made her happy too. She accepts it all, Nick thought with a shiver of amazement. Accepts *me.* He was hungry for more. He wanted her to know how special he was. He might not be big and strong, but he was powerful, and he longed to share that with her.

"Mimi, there's something about me I want you to know."

She turned to him. "Yeah?" The old man drifted away.

"It's a big secret. You can't tell anybody. Not even your *taté.*"

That seemed to throw her. "You saying you haven't told anybody?"

"You're the only one I want to know."

She blushed. "Nicky, you're sweet."

He drank it in. *She's mine.*

"Mind if I dance with my daughter?"

Nick looked up. John Toma stood grinning and perspiring in his powder-blue suit.

Nick answered in his most formal Romany, "Be my guest, sir."

As Mimi got up she whispered to Nick, her eyes alight, "But I wanna hear the secret."

He squeezed her hand. "Later."

Alana was inside, cramming her few things into her knapsack, waiting to be driven to the place where she hoped to lure Knelman. The apartment was in midtown Manhattan, her father had said, and she wasn't sure how long she'd have to stay there. Maybe overnight, maybe longer. Much as she hated Knelman, she was so horribly nervous she felt on the edge of nausea. She'd never set up anyone to be murdered.

Rajko joined her. They stood beside the family's mattresses, stacked high in a corner across from the kitchen, where relatives and guests were moving in and out, talking, joking, eating, arguing. Leaning against the wall with his can of Coors, Rajko frowned at her. "God, you're stubborn. If you'd wait, I'll take you myself. Vesh is just leaving, and he's gotta get to Seventy-third and Park and meet Knelman and get paid. Plenty of time. Stick around for the toasts, at least."

She shook her head. They'd already been through this. Nick's looming wedding appalled her, and she wanted no part of the celebrations. She still hoped there might be some way she could prevent the marriage, but in the meantime her priority had to be Knelman. She wouldn't sit here twiddling her thumbs as if all was well. She said, "Walter's set to take me." Her father earlier had given his consent to that. "I'd rather drive myself, you know," she added. "Not get Walter involved."

"No, I don't want you going out unprotected." He drained his beer, then crushed the can in his hand. "So go. Soon's I finish the toasts, I'll be along."

She groaned inside. The endless toasts.

Nodding at her bulging knapsack, Rajko said, "You won't need all that stuff. Be all over tonight. Then you come back."

"Can't be sure he'll come tonight."

"Vesh will spin some story. He'll get him there tonight."

She looked at him in alarm. "Vesh has to be careful—does he know that? Does he know how obsessed Knelman is?"

Rajko tossed the beer can on the floor by the mattresses. A *bori* always picked up after him. "Vesh knows what he's doing." Smiling, he chucked Alana under the chin. "So do I. You leave all this to me, *shori*. Tonight, that Nazi takes his last breath."

How could he be so calm? It was strangely reassuring, tough. His instincts for survival had kept him alive through far worse. She'd lived the war in her head, through Lina, but for him the lessons were in his blood.

"Something I wanted to ask you," he said. Hesitating, he looked almost sheepish. "See, you know all about her. What she thought, and such. I just wondered—" He cleared his throat, uncomfortable. "Did she love me?"

It rocked her—the flood of memories. Lina's love-hungry

lows, longing for him before they were married. Her orgasmic highs, those first nights in the wagon with him. Alana had to look away, blood heating her face. She said quietly, "She loved you."

He grinned.

Walter joined them, bouncing car keys in his hand. "Ready?"

"Ready." Picking up the knapsack, she felt the familiar thick ball of yarn crammed at the bottom. It struck her how different her life had been a mere two weeks ago, how she used to sit on a film set, knitting to kill time during the long lighting setups and actors' rehearsals until it was time to do her stunt. Prepping the gag, joshing with the crew, knowing she was great at her job . . . now, all of that seemed like another life. So innocent. For here she was, plotting the worst of crimes. Murder. Could she go though with it? It couldn't even bring back Gus.

"Walter," she said, "give me a sec. Just . . . wait here a minute."

She pushed out through the crowd in the yard. Nick sat at the end of the long table packed with guests. She followed his gaze to Mimi, who was dancing on the grass with Toma. Chords from two high-spirited guitars melded in harmony, and someone whooped with laughter. Alana made her way to Nick and sat down in Mimi's chair.

"Nick, look at me." She kept her voice quiet and calm. He didn't know what she and Rajko were planning. Everything in her world depended on his answer. "I'm asking you one last time. It's not too late. We can take a car and drive out of here right now, just you and me. Get the hell away from Knelman."

As he looked at her, she saw the fevered glow in his eyes that so often had made her uneasy. He said, "Meeting you was the best thing that ever happened to me, because it got me here." As he looked around at the party guests, Alana saw his hunger for this life, for acceptance. "We're going to look after you, me and Mimi. That's what family's for. She likes you, you know. You should try to be nice to her. Try to . . . accept." He gazed again at the girl as she danced. "Like she does."

Alana sensed something new in him, and suddenly she felt the grip of a discovery. A boy's love for a pretty girl was nothing special, but *this* boy's was, and it sent a thrill through her. It was evidence that Knelman was wrong! Until this moment she hadn't faced how terribly afraid she'd been of his theory—a "switched-off conscience." Born psychopaths. But right before her eyes was *proof* that he was wrong. *Nick has the capacity to love, so he must also have the capacity to be good.* It struck her how he'd risked himself for her—and not just once. After the gunman's attack on the bridge he'd risked coming to pick her up when he could easily have taken off. Later, he'd risked the cops seeing him when he followed her to the café and phoned to warn her of David's trap. And then, when she'd arrived here and come up against her father's wrath, Nick had defended her like a lion. Like Lina. Tears stung her eyes. How could she have missed such signs of love?

A memory flashed. A gold nugget. That indistinct mental image, which she hadn't been able to make out that first time at the Rosenthal Center, suddenly glittered hard and clear. *A gold filling.*

Now, finally, she felt she could see the big picture. Otzenhausen, and before. No wonder Knelman had been blinded by his so-called data—he didn't have the knowledge she had! Lina's knowledge. Lina had got to know those two other experimental subjects personally, as Knelman never had, and the brutal truth was that Hilde and Sophie were habitual criminals who'd honed tough survival skills long before the war. And so was Lina. Hard-nosed, opportunistic, amoral. All three were selected by Mueller, the medical block kapo, because they'd *bribed* him to select them, gambling that it would keep them alive. Lina had paid him with oral sex whenever he wanted, Hilde and Sophie with some gold they'd hoarded when they were sent to extract gold-filled teeth from gassed Jews. Gold nuggets.

It told Alana something essential—that the traits surviving in their offspring were more or less natural. The amoral streak in Hilde's son and Lina's grandson was no mutation, as Knelman feared; it wasn't a predestined behavior. No, Jacob and Nick had *learned* amorality from these hardened women—a response enabled by the passed-on knowledge gene. I fended off that tendency, she realized. So can Nick. He has free will, the chance to choose. He's been screwed up by Lina's ferocity, and from knowing my demons, too. And from living with all of that in ignorance. It hasn't given him wisdom, just a will as hard as steel. As hard as Lina. But he can change. He *has* changed. Love changes us all.

It was love that welled up in her now. She had wanted to give her son a better life, to guide him past his own demons. Well, this was it: *this* was the life he wanted. It wasn't for her; she could never stay. But the acceptance and communion Nick longed for were here. *These are the people he wants to be with. They will make him human.*

It fired an answer in her heart. Nick would not leave, and Knelman would not give up until they both were dead. Her only course was to go through with what she and her father had planned.

"Want to dance?" Nick asked her.

Smiling through tears, she hugged him, about to go. "Got something to do first."

"Says he knows you," Yanka told Nick as she opened the door to the tarot room. She'd brought him in from the party in the yard, and they were heading for the one-way window that, on the other side, in the *ofisa's* front parlor, was a mirror. Nick knew that watching a customer from here was how she picked up tips on them before telling their fortune. It was past business hours now, but the door to the street was open for arriving guests. "That right, Nicky?" she asked as they reached the window. "You know this *gadje* goon?"

It was Tank. The big idiot stood there in his grimy jean jacket and camouflage pants and army boots, picking his nose right beside the mirror, not knowing they were watching him. It made Nick very nervous. He didn't want Rajko knowing he'd ever been mixed up with a Bensonhurst gang, the lowest of the *gadje* low. Acting as cool as he could, he told Yanka, "I'll get rid of him."

She scowled; he hadn't answered her question. But Nick didn't volunteer any more. "Make it snappy," she said. "Guests are coming through here, and he's giving them the creeps."

As Nick walked into the front parlor, Tank turned to him. "Holy shit, man, it *is* you. Saw you on the street yesterday. Couldn't believe my fucking eyes."

Nick remembered that after bolting from Jaffe's place yesterday, he'd walked home from the subway. But why the hell was Tank in Sunnyside, and for two days in a row? "What're you doing here, Tank?"

"What're *you* doing here? Not hanging with these scummy wetbacks, are you?"

Stifling his anger, Nick made his face blank. "Nah, just came to see about a girl."

Tank grinned. "Hear their bitches bend over for man or dog. Even for a little prick like you, huh?" Laughing, he punched Nick's arm hard enough to hurt.

Nick thought how satisfying it would be to have his uncles and cousins beat the crap out of this fat-ass like they'd done to the DA. "So, you didn't say. How come you're out this way?"

"Waiting on a body shop. Nardi's Trans Am got dinged. Found a good joint down the block yesterday and left 'er there."

"Bruno's?"

"That's the place. Like I said, saw you on the street, thought I'd come say hi. Where you been this last week, anyway?"

"Here and there."

Tank seemed uninterested. His small eyes narrowed slyly. "I got a little time before I pick up the car. Got a little weed, too. Wanna do some? Looks like we're alone in this dump." Digging in his jacket pocket, he pulled out a joint.

"Not here. People could come in."

"Okay, the alley. Come on, man, this place gives me hives."

Nick wanted to get back to the yard, but he couldn't risk pissing off Tank. He'd once seen this guy smash his elbow through a convenience-store window just because the Asian behind the counter took too long getting him change for his gum. "Sure, let's go," he said. Hopefully, after a few tokes the fool would lose interest and get lost.

They reached the alley. Partway down it, blocking it,

Nick saw an idling black Trans Am. Nardi at the wheel. "I thought you said—"

The truth hit him like a fist. *A setup.* He spotted a fire escape above some piled crates and turned to run for it. Tank's arm caught his throat. "Too late, jerkoff. Nardi wants your ass."

CHAPTER 19

THE GYPSY YARD was in an uproar. The police raid had interrupted a party, the place was packed, and David was surrounded by angry men yelling at him and women screaming in fright, some old ones keening as though he'd come to slaughter them. Even kids were crying like in some old melodrama. All for show, he reminded himself as he pushed through the crowd, looking for Alana. An officer caught up to him, a rookie named Fantino. Above the noise David could barely hear what he was saying.

"Mr. Knelman . . . a call . . ."

"What?"

"In the cruiser . . . Detective Lipranski."

David looked around. Jumping out of Lip's unmarked car when they'd pulled up with the cruisers, he'd come through the house with the cops, assuming Lip was right behind him. He headed back out to take the call, passing through the big room festooned like a tent, where officers were trying to question individuals. The gypsies' strategy was to respond as a group; several talked at once, and almost every answer was followed by curses or tears or a sudden change of mind—or all three.

"Where's the *rom baro*?" Lieutenant Phelps asked a man in a powder-blue suit.

"Who?"

"Rajko Marks. Aka Roman Mitchell."

"Never heard of him. Get the hell out."

A woman with tears running down her cheeks grabbed Phelps by the arm and cried, "Don't hurt my husband, he's all I got!"

Reaching the squad car by the curb, David leaned in for the radio transmitter. "Lipranski? Where are you?"

"Going back to town, it looks like. I'm on Marks's tail, and he's turning onto the Queensboro Bridge. At least, I figure it's him. As you went in, I saw his Caddy tooling down the block, so I took off after him. I don't think he has a clue what's going down at his place as we speak. I'll keep you posted. Tell Phelps to bring in the small fry."

"Will do."

"And, Counselor? See if you can ID the pricks who beat you up."

No time for that, David thought as he went back inside. Nor for Rajko Marks. He'd come only to get Alana to safety. He relayed Lip's message to Phelps, then shouldered his way out to the yard again, wincing at the pain in his ribs when anyone jostled him. He headed for a middle-aged woman standing at a table spread with food. She was calmly piling dishes as though to clear them away.

"Ma'am, could I ask you a few questions?"

She turned hard eyes on him. Setting down the dish in her hand, she pulled a pack of menthol Kools out of the top of her dress. "Like what?"

"What's your name?"

"What's yours?"

"David Knelman, Manhattan assistant district attorney. Are you Yanka Marks?"

She stuck a cigarette in her mouth. "My mother calls me Mary."

"Look, I don't want to hurt you. I'm just looking for Alana. Is she here?"

She picked up matches from the table and lit the cigarette. "Don't know anybody by that name. You got the wrong place, mister." She blew out the match. "You busted up a real nice party for nothing."

This one wouldn't crack. Leaving her, he approached two men raising their voices above the din. "Walter, you call the lawyer?" the younger one asked.

"He's on his way."

Seeing David, they fell silent.

"Walter," David said, reaching the older one. "Tell me just one thing, then I'll let you alone."

"Yeah? What's that?"

"I need to find Alana Marks. She's in trouble. Not with the law—someone's after her to hurt her. Can you help me?"

He thought he saw concern spark in the dark eyes, but as the two men exchanged a glance, the spark died. "Don't know her. But, hey, ask around if you want."

The damn gypsy code. He left them. As his eyes raked the crowd for Alana, he thought of Lip's comment: *"The pricks who beat you up."* Nick had been their leader. But not only was there no sign of Alana, there was no sign of Nick either. It gave David a bad feeling. Dad was after them both.

Alana looked out the window onto night-dark Irving Place. Nice address. A few doors away was Gramercy Park, an immaculate little Eden of foliage surrounded by its cast-iron fence. A sprinkler there was wafting droplets, causing the glossy-leafed trees and pink rose bushes to gleam under the park lamplight. Looked like a scene from a fairy tale.

And me the ogre's captive, she thought. Waiting. She had all the lights on in the living room so that if Knelman was out there by the park, watching, he'd know someone was home. It made her skin crawl, but the whole idea was to lure him. Slipping in wouldn't be hard, she figured, not for a nicely dressed gent. Just wait until some tenant was leaving and take advantage of the open door. She didn't doubt that he would get to her.

But when? She looked at her watch. Almost two hours since Walter had brought her here, then gone home, but her father still hadn't arrived. Stupid endless toasts. Sentimental "brothers forever" baloney.

Turning from the window she paced the living room. The apartment felt so alien. Spacious, but an old lady's place, sour-stuffy smelling. China knickknacks, African violets, overstuffed chintz chairs with doilies, ornate antique furniture. How had Rajko got access? she wondered. This was no gypsy relation's hideout; it was a wealthy *gadje* woman's home. She stopped at the polished dining table where some mail was scattered, and picked up an envelope. Addressed to an Iris Larson. Had Rajko somehow got his hands on this place? She had an uneasy feeling it might be connected to Ruby being held overnight by the police, and had something to do with Nick.

A noise outside made her turn. A faint, mewling cry. She went to the window. A cat streaked away from the park fence, leaving another one mewling on top of the railing. A taxi beetled down Irving Place. On the far sidewalk an old couple in English-looking raincoats were walking twin poodles in plaid doggy coats. Alana watched the dogs frisk along, and when the couple reached the park's iron gate, the man unlocked it and they went inside. She'd heard that this was the city's only private park; only residents who lived directly around it got keys. Perks of wealth. As she looked back, she saw the gold Cadillac slowly turning onto Gramercy Park East. Her skin prickled. She'd missed seeing her father arrive, though he'd driven right under her nose. If she'd missed that, could she have missed more? Knelman coming into the building?

She went to the kitchen. Opening drawers, she rummaged past cutlery and paring knives. She wanted a weapon.

A scrabbling sound at the door. Walking through the living room with a boning knife, she forced herself to imagine plunging the blade into his chest. Lina could do it. She'd cut that farmer's throat. Rammed deadly phenol injections into kids' hearts. *Fifth rib.* Her mouth dry, Alana opened the door.

Rajko looked up from inserting a key. He seemed surprised at the knife in her hand. He chuckled. "Doing some cooking?"

Nick shut his eyes and turned his head as Tank kicked in the museum display case, shattering glass.

Nardi shone his flashlight inside. "Get the silver stuff," he ordered. "Leave the other crap."

Tank climbed into the ceiling-high case and began stuffing silver loot into a gym bag as Nardi pointed with his gun to things he wanted. Heidi growled at Nick, her fangs bared inside the wire muzzle. Nick was trying to think straight, but fear churned inside him. Nardi had warned that if he made a run for it, he'd shoot. Pins and needles shot up and down his arms, bound tightly behind his back with duct tape. His lips were gummy with saliva under the tape plastered across his mouth. His nose was dry from breathing too hard. He was afraid he was going to piss himself.

In the car, before Tank had taped his mouth, he'd burst out to Nardi, "Why me? What did I ever do to you?"

"Nothing to me, runt, but you sure pissed off a certain old guy. And he's the kind of Nazi you don't mess with. The real thing."

The truth had flooded him like poison gas. *Knelman.*

Now, he forced himself to look around the museum room for some way out, or for something he might use. It was dark except for the glow from Nardi's flashlight. High glass cases lined the walls, and a sign read, "Tradition and Community." Nardi had turned off the alarm system with a key as soon as they'd dragged him inside, so Nick knew that no help would be coming from the cop shop. He looked at Tank grabbing a candelabra with branches, then a dish thing hanging on chains, then a platter. Cards beside them read, "Silver menorah," "Engraved silver Hannukah lamp," "Seder plate." He looked across the dim room, where formal black lettering had been carved into two gray granite walls. On one: "*Remember. Never forget.* Deuteronomy." On the other: "*There is hope for your future.* Deuteronomy."

He started to shiver. He didn't believe there was *any* hope. He thought of the people he'd never see again. Mimi. Alana. Rajko. Danny and Vesh and the guys. He'd never wanted so much to live.

Tank dragged him to the next room. A sign read, "Persecution and Holocaust." Nardi threw his arms wide in glee. "Mother lode. Go, Tank."

Tank kicked in a glass front and bundled up a huge red Nazi flag with a black swastika, then grabbed a silver Nazi eagle, then a book. The card by the book said, "Himmler's copy of 'Mein Kampf' with penciled margin notes." He grabbed handfuls of ghetto money in paper and coins, a Hitler Youth armband, an SS belt buckle. When he reached a headless dummy wearing a prisoner's ratty uniform with faded stripes of gray and blue, he stripped the dummy.

Nardi's flashlight beam played over a wall of photos: people being herded onto boxcars, skeletal prisoners, crematorium ovens, burial pits littered with corpses. The beam flashed over a row of pillars plastered with faces of the dead. Nardi snorted. "They were told they were gonna be resettled. Stupid Yids didn't even figure out it was the end." Leaning back against a pillar of faces, he casually aimed the gun at Nick. "How dumb can you get?"

Nick's legs went weak. He tried not to show his fear, but he couldn't help shutting his eyes. He knew he was going to die.

Nardi said, "Not yet, runt. We got an appointment with the doctor."

"Just like the old days, eh, *shori*?"

Alana turned from the widow. "What?"

Rajko smiled at her from the chintz armchair, his legs stretched out, his green fedora tilted against the doily behind his head. "A team again, you and me. Partners. Remember those slip-and-fall insurance jobs? You were a sight to behold."

She glanced at his rough, bone-handled knife, which he'd set on the dainty round telephone table beside him. Partners in murder, she thought with a shiver. Only, was Knelman ever going to come? They'd been speaking in hushed voices, and in the silence the antique filigreed clock ticked on. She could faintly hear someone upstairs playing an opera recording, some soprano. She felt how out of place she and her father were here. She was so on edge, so tense with the waiting, she had to talk, if only in whispers. "Who does this apartment belong to, anyway? And what did you mean this morning when we were talking about Knelman? You said, 'It's business, it had to be done'—something about Ruby being taken in by the police. What did that have to do with Knelman?"

He cocked his head at her with a shrewd look. "The other Knelman."

She was taken aback. "David?"

His lip curled. "Kind of familiar with him, aren't you? That's over, Alana. You're one of us again. From now on, you stick with your own kind."

"*What* had to be done?"

"That Jew DA's after my hide. Nicky and the boys took him down."

Her stomach plunged. "You don't mean—"

"Nah, they just roughed him up a bit, he'll live. Make him think twice about butting into my business, though. He was getting too damn close." He nodded at his bone-handled knife. "After tonight, *shori,* you'll be blooded, so you might as well know everything. This place? Belonged to an old *gadja,* sick old dame, kicked the bucket. She's the third. They were all sick, all on their last leg. We helped them along, magic salt in their food, a little every day. This one here got to be best friends with Stefan and Ruby, and believe me, those two earned what we pulled in. Hell, they even nursed her. By the time she croaked, she'd signed the place over to them. Nicky's working another mark, real prime, fingered the old guy himself, name of Jaffe. That Nicky, he's a sight to behold."

Alana couldn't speak. Nick . . . beating up David . . . poisoning Howard Jaffe. It terrified her. Sickened her. Was he Knelman's genetic monster after all?

David. *Was* he all right? Dear God, she had to know. Call him. She went to the little phone table and lifted the receiver.

A thud down the hall. She stiffened. Her eyes met Rajko's—this was it. Putting down the phone, she whispered, "The bedroom."

He got up swiftly and silently, putting his finger to his mouth for her to be quiet. He picked up his knife and started for the hall.

She stopped him, her hand on his arm. She flicked her finger in a gesture that said, "Me and you," and nodded toward the hall, indicating they go together; better odds. She had left the kitchen knife across the room, but her open knapsack was on the sofa right beside her. She pulled out a knitting needle. *Fifth rib.*

Her pulse drubbed in her ears as she and her father slipped down the hall. Two bedrooms on one side, a den on the other. The master bedroom door was shut. It had been open before. She glanced at Rajko. Understanding, he nodded.

Heart in her mouth, Alana opened the door.

No one in the room. Slowly going in, she noticed that the gauzy curtain was stuck under the windowsill. Outside, she could make out the black railing of the fire escape. She thought: He's inside.

The den.

She spun around. Knelman stood in the doorway, a gun in his hand.

"Forgive me, Miss Marks." He aimed at her.

Rajko lunged from the hall and kicked the back of his knee. As Knelman sprawled forward, Alana snatched the gun and turned it on him. Knelman caught himself before he fell, and twisted around in surprise.

Rajko was there, knife ready. "Remember me, Herr Doktor? I've never forgotten you. A Luger like that's what you used to shoot Lina. Almost used it to kill my baby girl, too."

"In saving her you did more harm than you can know. She has bred a killer species."

Alana's heart pumped rage, remembering Gus's savaged body. "This is for Gus Yuill." Her finger curled on the trigger. But she couldn't shoot him in the back. "Turn around."

"No, *shori,* that's not the way." Looking at Knelman, Rajko's eyes narrowed, calculating. "Doctor, we got ourselves a problem here. Much as I'd like to rip out your stinking heart, there's the law to think of. Too many people know that my daughter knows you. You turn up dead, it could be bad for her. Bad for my people. So we're going to work out some arrangement. Live and let live, you know? Like, you agree to move to San Francisco and never come near her or her son again, and I'll agree not to blind *your* son. Friendly arrangement like that. I'm open to suggestions. See, we just need you to disappear." He took the gun from Alana. "My car's outside. Let's go."

As they walked down the hall, Knelman in front, Rajko winked at Alana and mimed firing into Knelman's back. She understood. He'd been blowing smoke to keep Knelman hoping and passive, because a desperate man could be a dangerous man. They would keep to their plan: drive him to Brooklyn, find a deserted spot by the waterfront, leave his body. No ties back to them.

Stupid, stupid, monumentally stupid.

Knelman cursed himself as he sat immobile in the Cadillac's back seat, Marks beside him with the Luger while his daughter drove. Of course, it had all been too pat! The "traitor's" street-corner information, the scenario that she would be alone. He'd been blinded by his need to have it all over with tonight, both carriers dispatched. But now, because of his blunder, both would be at liberty. Marks had saved his daughter again, and Nardi, cheated of his reward, would set the boy free. It terrified Knelman.

She was going south on the Bowery. Would she take the Manhattan Bridge to Brooklyn? Around them were neon signs, honking cars, night people busy on the sidewalk, but he sat in silence with the gypsies who had duped him. A silence whose significance was dawning on him now. There would be no discussion about a truce. That had been a bone they'd tossed him to get him into the car. They were going to kill him. They were just taking him as far as possible before he struggled, but any struggle would end in his death. He did not doubt that even a move to the door would bring a bullet. The gypsy's vengeance was quiet but deadly.

The realization had an unexpected effect on him, like a mild anesthetic. Numbing. He did not fear death. His life had been over since he'd seen the hatred in David's eyes. Death would be a release. He welcomed it.

But not yet.

He focused his thoughts. He must not die until his mission was complete, but it lay in two parts, both stalled—the woman here, the boy at the center. What if he could join the halves? Bring this one to the center. Dispatch them both, perhaps with Nardi's help.

"Miss Marks," he said. He saw her eyes snap to his in the rearview. "Your father is keen to have his revenge, but you must not allow it. Not if you want to save Nick. He is a captive at this very moment, betrayed by his own friends. Listen to me, or Nick will die."

Rajko snorted. "Bad opening for a negotiation. Let's talk about your new life in 'Frisco instead."

"Drop this charade. I know that you intend to kill me."

Marks's voice hardened. "Well, seems one thing you don't know is that Nicky's safe and sound at my place. So why don't you shut up and enjoy your last ride."

Knelman's eyes hadn't left the woman. Her gaze on him burned into the mirror as she said, "What friends?"

"White Pride."

Her eyes widened with alarm. "My God," she whispered.

Knelman felt a jolt of hope. He knew this woman. She would risk anything to save her son.

Marks said, "It's a bluff, Alana. He's lying to save his skin."

"It's no lie. I hired these neo-Nazis. Miss Marks, earlier you mentioned your friend Yuill, so perhaps you are aware of Nardi's methods. Believe me, I alone can stop him."

She hit the brakes to avoid a man who'd dashed across the street. A horn behind them blared. She drove on slowly. "Go on."

"Nick walked into a trap. They have taken him away to kill him. I know where."

She and her father shared a glance. "Pull over at a phone," Marks said. "Call home."

Knelman sat in silence with Marks at the curbside, the engine running, while they waited for his daughter to finish in the phone booth. When she returned and slipped behind the wheel again, she looked shaken. "There was a police raid. Under control, Liza says. But Nick . . . even before the cops came, nobody'd seen him for hours."

Marks threatened Knelman with the gun. "Where is he?"

"If you shoot me, you will never know. I can take you there."

"If we go," Marks warned his daughter, "we'll be walking into the same trap."

"If we don't, they'll kill Nick."

"Hell of a choice, *shori*."

"No choice." She fixed Knelman in the mirror again. "Where to?"

If he told them that, they would no longer need him. "Nardi will stand down only if I give him the order face to face."

"Then you better not give my father any reason to blow your brains out." She demanded again, "Where to?"

"The Isaac Rosenthal Center."

"Counselor? Boy, am I glad I caught you. This has turned weird."

Outside the gypsy enclave, David stood beside the open passenger door of the squad car and spoke into the radio. "Weird? How?" Fantino, the only remaining cop here, sat at the wheel filling out a report. Phelps and the other officers had gone, taking Yanka Marks and a couple of other characters in for questioning. David felt a frustration close to fear. He hadn't been able to prod anything from these people about where Alana might be.

"Weird as in, I follow Marks's Caddy midtown, and he stops on Gramercy Park East, goes into Mrs. Larson's brownstone. I give it about twenty minutes, and I'm about to go check it out, when who comes out but your father. And get this—he's with Marks. Plus a woman. They all get into the Caddy and take off. Could've knocked me with a feather. I mean, what kind of a house call is this?"

David's grip on the radio tightened. "Describe the woman."

"Between twenty-five and thirty, short dark hair. Jeans, leotard kind of top. A looker. She's driving."

Alana. With Dad. And her father. What was going on? "You're still on their tail?"

"Yeah, and it gets weirder. They were southbound on the Bowery, then all of a sudden she pulls this slick U-turn. We're uptown now. She's just turned onto Eighty-second, and I . . . hey, hold on, she's pulling over."

"Where on Eighty-second?" David was climbing in beside the rookie.

"Between Fifth and Madison."

The Rosenthal Center? Why?

"Counselor, I don't know how to put this. Is there something about your old man I oughta know?"

David clamped down his dread. "Afraid so, Lip. Plenty." He reached to activate the siren. "Stay there. Call for backup. Fantino and I are on our way."

CHAPTER 20

NICK WAS SCARED to death. Nardi's flashlight beam in his face half blinded him, but above the sound of Tank's boots crunching broken glass as he gathered loot, Nick was sure he heard a man's voice down the hall: ". . . likely in the display area farther along here."

Knelman's voice. Nick stiffened in terror. Knelman was coming to kill him. Only, who was he talking to? Straining every nerve to listen, he heard another man answer in a growl: "Shut up, or I'll fix your jaw."

Rajko? Nick couldn't believe it! Then a woman's voice: "No, don't hurt him, he has to stop Nardi."

Alana! He almost fainted with relief. Alana and Rajko had come to save him!

But he saw that Nardi had heard the voices too. Nardi switched off his flashlight and whispered fiercely, "Tank, shut up, listen. The doc's not alone."

They stood still in the darkness, all eyes strained toward the dim corridor. Even the dog had gone still. Nick heard footsteps coming. He saw Nardi's shadowy arm rise with the gun, aiming at the hall. Nick was bursting to yell a warning to Alana and Rajko, but he couldn't budge his gag of tape.

The three silhouettes appeared, moving forward in the shadows. Hope shot through Nick. Rajko's outstretched arm was unmistakable—he had a gun on Knelman!

Nardi whispered to Tank, "Get him out of sight."

Tank dragged Nick behind the display case and shoved him up against the wall. With the case jutting out beside him, blocking his view, Nick couldn't see anything but Tank's fat face up against his. But he heard the footsteps coming. His heart was hammering. Alana and Rajko didn't know Nardi was waiting for them in the dark. If only he could warn them!

The flashlight burst on.

A gunshot!

Tank leaned out to see, loosening his hold. Nick ducked beneath Tank's arm and head-butted Nardi, knocking the flashlight from his hand. It hit the floor, and the light went out. Tank's arm whipped around Nick's throat, and he dragged him back and pinned him to the wall.

The blast of light in her face had blinded Alana. Then a gunshot! Who'd fired? Where from? She couldn't see anything past the light! But what happened right beside her flashed like a nightmare snapshot: Rajko hit and staggering back, his gun falling to the floor, skidding toward Knelman. Rajko collapsing, bleeding . . . *Taté!*

The light went out.

Alana was about to lunge for the gun in the dark. Knelman was closer. She heard him snatch it up.

Rajko gasped, "Alana, run!"

Panic hit her. How could she leave him wounded? But if

she stayed, Knelman would shoot her . . . no way she could help her father then. Or find Nick. *Have to find Nick.*

She could just make out the corridor ahead because of a faint red glow. Blindly, she ran toward it.

David and Fantino pulled up in the squad car in front of the Rosenthal Center. David jumped out, telling him, "Wait for the backup Lipranski called in." He ran ahead to Lip sitting in the Dodge and called to him through the open window, "Lip, I'm going inside," then started for the entrance.

Lip got out and caught up to him. "What's going on in there?"

"The woman is Marks's daughter. My father means to kill her. Can't explain now. Got to get to her."

At the entrance a security night-screen of steel bars made a barrier that shielded the door and adjoining plate-glass walls of the lobby. David gripped the screen and tried to rattle it. It didn't budge.

Lip was already going down the steps to the street-front basement door. But David knew this place. Hearing Lip kick at the locked door, he yelled down, "It's steel. Forget it."

As Lip came back up, David said, "We have to rip this screen away."

They both turned to the squad car. It had a reinforced front bumper. Lip said, "Towing chain in the trunk."

"Let's do it."

Running, Alana reached the end of the corridor as it opened into the next room. It would have been pitch dark if not for the faint red glow, which she now saw came from an emergency exit light. She slowed down as she approached three looming structures, and her breath snagged in her throat at the scene. She'd been in this big high-ceilinged room before, that first day she'd come to the center. It was the museum's highlight, the camp tableau room, the final stop on the tour. This was the end.

To her right, a boxcar on steel tracks. Dead ahead, a wooden watchtower. To her left, a cross-section of a prisoner barracks with tiers of bunks. Fronting the barracks, barbed wire bristled in zigzag lines ten feet high, fencing the invisible inmates. She stopped cold before the boxcar. She was in Otzenhausen . . . *freezing night, blowing snow. Searchlights from the watchtowers blinding us as they herd us off. Guards with machine guns. Leashed dogs barking. Doctors making selections.* Rechts! Links! *Right! Left!* . . .

Footsteps pounded behind her. She twisted around. Knelman. She couldn't see him yet, but she heard him coming. She spun back to the boxcar. No where else to go. If she was fast, she might make it before he saw her. She dove beneath the boxcar, scrambled across the tracks, and sprang to her feet on the other side. Pacing the back of the car, she blindly felt for the ladder. A splinter dug into her palm, then she felt an iron rung and grabbed it. She climbed to the top and lowered herself facedown on the metal walkway along the roof ridge. The metal under her cheek was cold. Her heart was banging as she lay still, trying to stifle the sound of her breathing.

In the faint red glow she saw Knelman arrive, gun in hand. He slowed down, looking for her, clearly unaware she was on the boxcar roof. He stopped.

But footsteps still sounded. Alana lengthened her gaze in the dim light and saw four figures come in behind Knelman. Two men. A dog. And Nick!

Her heart seized. Nick's hands were bound behind him, his mouth taped . . .

* * *

Nick's shoulder sockets screamed in pain as Nardi dragged him toward Knelman's back. He was wildly sucking air through his nose, light-headed with fear.

"What about the woman?" Tank said behind them. "Where'd she get to?"

"Who gives a shit? If she had a gun, she'd have used it by now."

Suddenly, the scene they'd walked into hit Nick like an electrode to his brain. Boxcar. Watchtower. Barbed wire. He was in Otzenhausen . . . the unloading ramp. The snow, the barking dogs, the terror. It unleashed a shudder he couldn't control. *Got to get out. Do anything it takes . . . escape.*

"Okay, Doc," Nardi said, "here's the kid. And that guy I shot's out of commission. So let's get this show on the road."

In the faint red glow Nick saw Knelman turn, face like a zombie. Their eyes locked. Knelman lifted the gun. Nick's legs turned to water.

"Hey, not so fast!" Nardi shoved Nick behind Tank's bulk. "The kid keeps breathing until I get into that vault. That's the deal. I get the stuff I want, *then* you get his carcass."

Knelman lowered the gun. "Yes. Come. The director's office is this way."

"Hold on a sec." Nardi bent and pulled the wire muzzle off the dog. "Insurance, runt. I don't recommend you mess with Heidi."

They started for the hall, Tank dragging Nick. Knelman led the way. Nardi was at Tank's other side. The dog's claws clicked over the floor as it followed. Nick's terror became sheer panic.

* * *

Alana squelched her own panic and grabbed at hope. She saw she had a chance to save Nick. One chance.

The way Nick's little group was heading, they would pass by the boxcar's end in seconds. Nardi and the big guy were side by side, Knelman just feet ahead, all three targets bunched together. Perfect.

In a crouch she moved quickly and silently to the opposite end of the boxcar roof. When she reached the edge, she turned, visualizing the whole thing, like a stunt. She would race the length of the car, achieve velocity, and launch herself onto them. In other words, run like hell, jump, and knock them down like bowling pins. But this wasn't movie make-believe. She'd have no soft air bag to land on. No box rig to break her fall.

She would die. She knew that. If the fall didn't break her neck, Knelman would shoot her, or Nardi would. But if she could surprise and confuse them enough, it might give Nick the chance to break loose and run. A head start was all he needed. In this near-darkness, with his smarts and Lina's survival instinct, he just might make it out. Was he the genetic monster Knelman claimed? She still didn't have that answer. She knew only that she'd abandoned him once, when he was born, and she wouldn't do it again. She had nothing to give him but this one last chance.

She pushed off. And ran.

"Move my heap, Counselor, we're ready to haul!"

David ran back to the Dodge. Lip had attached one end of the towing chain to the screen of bars. The other end was around the squad car bumper, and Fantino, at the wheel, was ready to reverse. Lip's Dodge was in the way.

David jumped in it and backed up, giving Fantino room to maneuver.

Down the block sirens wailed, coming this way. Our backup, David thought. He just prayed he wasn't too late.

Alana sprinted along the roof. The metal walkway spurred her feet. She picked up speed, pounded over the last stretch, reached the far edge . . . and hurled herself on the air. Every muscle strained to carry her all the way to her target.

"Run, Nick!"

She crashed down on the big guy, sending him sprawling against Nardi. Nardi staggered, tripped, and fell. The dog yelped and spurted forward. Knelman whipped around as Alana hit the floor on her shoulder. Pain stunned her. She flopped onto her back in agony. Her shoulder was broken.

"Nick . . . run," she managed.

Through her blur of pain she saw Nick dash off. Saw Knelman stumble with the confused dog underfoot, in his way. But he still held his gun.

As David reversed the Dodge, its headlight beams shone through the expanse of windows and across the lobby to a glass door on the far side. He knew that door was the emergency exit from the camp tableau room. He could see between the wooden legs that supported the watchtower, and glimpsed someone moving. Dad . . . with a gun. And Alana.

He rolled down the window, set the roof light flashing and the siren wailing, and yelled to Fantino, "Go! Go!"

Fantino backed the squad car. The chain wrenched the screen free. It clattered to the sidewalk, exposing the door and the plate-glass windows.

David threw the Dodge into gear and drove forward across the screen, tires thumping over the bars. He gunned the gas and smashed through the lobby window.

* * *

Staggering to her feet, Alana was blinded by the sudden headlights. Disoriented by the scream of sirens. So were the others—Knelman looking stunned as the barking dog ran in circles around him, Nardi looking terrified.

"Cops! Tank, get the fuck up! Come on, there's gotta be another exit!" The two of them took off down the corridor. The dog scrabbled after them.

Nick was running for the tower, clumsy, unbalanced by his bound arms. He felt dazed by the lights and sirens, but dizzy with hope. Cops! Safety! He could see them through the glass emergency door . . . see their flashing lights. In seconds he'd be around the tower and at the door. *Once through it, I'm home free!*

Alana couldn't believe it—police! Hope shot energy through her. Awkwardly, she ran, following Nick, her shoulder on fire, her mind fogged with pain.

A gunshot! She gasped . . . Knelman had fired . . . but missed her! She ran on behind Nick toward the flashing lights and wailing sirens. She glanced over her shoulder. Knelman was aiming at her again.

Something snatched her sleeve, whipping her to a stop. She was caught on the barbed wire! A top strand bit her neck, and lower barbs cut through the fabric into her arm and back and through her jeans into her thigh. She wrenched and thrashed, but the needle teeth just hooked her clothes tighter and cut deeper into her flesh. She couldn't loosen herself. Her other arm was free, but the broken shoulder made it useless. She hung on the wire, desperate, panicked, her heart raging as she watched Knelman take aim. She turned her eyes to Nick and willed him: *Please, Nick, make it to the door.*

The door . . . a man running through the lobby toward it . . . David!

Knelman tried to steady his trembling arm as he aimed at her. Tried to block out the awful blaze of lights and the din of sirens. *Aim carefully. Miss again, and the carriers will escape. Can't let them leave the camp.*

Too far away. He started to walk toward them.

Behind the tower the door burst open. He blinked. A man was running in, a black silhouette against the stark lights.

"Schiller! Stop!"

His heart seized. David.

But his legs kept taking him forward.

Alana watched Nick in horror. He was running *back* to her. No, this was the last thing she wanted! She yelled, "Nick, don't! Run! *Go!*"

He reached her. Mouth taped, arms bound, he looked frantic—there was nothing he could do for her. He glanced at Knelman, who was coming on, grim as death, and then looked back at Alana. He'd always been so cocksure, but all she saw in his eyes now was abject confusion. A misery to match her own. She knew Knelman would kill them both. "Please, Nick," she begged him, "go!"

Instead, he stepped right in front of her. Face to face with her, he presented his back to Knelman—a human shield. To protect her. The stab of joy in Alana's heart was torture. This was her answer, finally. A monster didn't feel the misery of love.

She longed to push him away, but couldn't even lift her damaged free arm. And the barbed wire held her fast.

The gunshot slammed Nick's body against hers. Breath burst from his nose. His eyes went big in shock. She saw his struggle to stay on his feet, to keep protecting her, and she thrashed in the wire, her heart breaking. Another shot slammed him against her again. He forced himself to keep standing, his anguished eyes on hers. A third shot. He slumped against her, then slid down her front to the floor.

A wail ripped from Alana's throat. "No-o-o!"

"Schiller!" David charged in, the gunshots ringing in his ears. He saw Nick slide to the floor, hit. Alana wasn't—yet. Blinded to everything but the murderer with the gun, he lunged the last yards and tackled him, knocking him down. They sprawled together on the floor. David scrambled to his knees and straddled Schiller and clamped his forearm across Schiller's throat, pinning him down. With his other hand he chopped Schiller's gun arm, the blow springing the Luger from his grip. David channeled all his fury into pressing the life from that throat. "Damn you, Schiller!"

He was aware of cops rushing to Alana and Nick. Alana seemed all right. But Nick? Breathing hard, fighting to control his rage, David told himself to let up on the throat he was choking. Told himself the man was now disarmed. Arrest him. It's over.

Still straddling Schiller, David lifted his arms. The murderer would live.

Viktor Schiller wanted to scream. Failure. Despair. And the hatred he saw in his son's eyes burned with a white-hot passion like God's own fury. Perhaps it was. In this place of suffering, beneath the watchtower, this was surely God's verdict. A sentence to hell.

But to live would be a torture he could not bear.

He snatched his son's hand and gripped it tight. "Kill me."

David flinched. He jerked his head, No.

"Yes! I know you, David. You are compassionate, like your father was. I saved him as long as I could. I saved you too, and loved you as my own. Please, save me now from a living hell. I beg you . . . do me this one last kindness. Kill me."

Tears glinted in David's eyes. Schiller's vision, too, clouded with tears. He felt his son's forearm come down gently across his windpipe. And then David pressed. Harder . . . harder . . .

Vision darkened. Breath stilled. His soul reached out for oblivion. In the final seconds he clung with his mind to a prayer. *Forgive me, Father, for I have sinned . . .*

Officers were working to free her from the wire, and she could only wait in agony to get to Nick, who lay at her feet. In the commotion around her she was dimly aware that David had taken down the madman . . . that Nardi and his partner, handcuffed, were being led by officers out to the cruisers . . . that another officer, crouched over Nick, was calling on his radio for paramedics. But she saw nothing but Nick's pale face, his startled look . . . blood pooling on the floor beneath him.

The moment they freed her from the wire, she dropped to his side on her knees. She cradled his head in her good arm. Gently, she pulled the tape off his mouth. His body felt so slight. Thirteen years old. Just a boy.

His blood felt warm on her arm. His cheek felt cold. Trembling, he looked up at her with eyes as clear as a child's.

"We'll get you to a hospital," she said, stroking his hair. "You'll be fine." But she felt the life draining from him with his blood. She'd never known such harrowing grief.

"You didn't . . . abandon me," he said. "I always had you . . . here . . . inside."

Then a sheen like steel came into his eyes. Lina's eyes. The faintest smile twitched his mouth. Lina's smile. His voice was only a whisper. "Go for it, Alana. Life. Don't let the bastard win."

CHAPTER 21

December, 1986

THE SKY WAS a cloudless blue, the sun as bright as a smile, but Hannah had her mouth open to catch falling snowflakes. "Snowing!" she squealed. It was because Riley, nine, and much taller than his sister, was trotting behind her and grabbing handfuls of the stuff from the snowbank and sprinkling it over her. Alana, behind them both, liked the way it drifted, sparkling, onto her daughter's head, like fairy dust. She knew that Hannah, being five, was keen on fairies. And Riley was keen on making unexpected things happen.

"He's fooling her," David said, not quite approving.

"He's being innovative," Alana said, slipping her arm through David's. Their boots squeaked over Central Park's snow as they turned off Seventy-ninth onto a path among bare trees.

He shot her a sidelong glance. "Like back there, entertaining the folks?"

She groaned. "My children, the ignoramuses." They'd just come from a Saturday afternoon at the Museum of Natural History, where Riley, in the Hall of Mammals and Their

Extinct Relatives, had loped around like a chimpanzee, making ape noises, and Hannah, in the Hall of Reptiles and Amphibians, had loudly sung out verses of "Froggie Went a-Courting." Alana had shooed them past the less-than-charmed patrons. "I should have studied more science when I was pregnant."

"No way. Bad enough you were memorizing the entire works of Shakespeare."

She had to smile. It had taken David two years after they were married to convince her she was ready to have kids, and then, through that first pregnancy, she'd crammed in as many courses at NYU as she could manage, wanting to learn as much as possible to pass along to their baby. She'd actually found it exhilarating; she'd always liked learning things. No time for such a luxury these days. She was directing films now, in the middle of cutting her second low-budget feature, a Cape Cod sailing thriller that had wrapped in October, and what with juggling her crazy work schedule with David's as a U.S. district attorney, plus the kids', she sometimes felt like a general organizing an invasion.

Hannah veered off the path and plopped on her back in a patch of virgin snow. Fanning her snowsuited arms and legs to make an angel, she crooned, "Good night, sweet prince, and flights of angels sing thee to thy rest."

David shot Alana an amused glance. "See? Top-heavy with Hamlet."

Alana looked at Riley, who was stomping like a dinosaur around Hannah, trampling snow and growling. "The brainy stuff didn't exactly take with Riley, though, did it?"

"Kids never turn out the way parents expect. Even ours."

She watched them with a small rush of wonder. Riley was as smart as a young wizard, but nothing intellectual interested him; everything physical did. Like I was with stunts, she thought. Hannah was like David: bright and kind, a bookworm in the making. Both of them had all her knowledge, and both of them *knew* they did. Before the kids were born, Alana and David had been in total agreement about leveling with them.

"So, you see, you're special," she'd explained. "So special, we have to keep it a secret. Nobody except our family knows, and that's the way it's got to stay."

David had gone further. "And because this is an exceptional gift, you have to use it well."

"How?" Hannah had asked.

"By thinking about other people, not just yourself. By trying to be a leader, and helping others. Gifts are made to be used, so use yours to do good. Okay?"

"Okay."

Alana loved the straight-ahead way he talked to them. But then, she loved the way he was like that with everybody. Even during the trial twelve years ago. It had to have been such hell for him, charged with murder for killing the man he'd once revered as his father. Alana herself had gone through that period in a fog of grief over Nick. The police who'd been at the center that night testified that Schiller had shot Nick in cold blood, and that David had stopped him from killing Alana next, and she, too, had testified that he'd saved her life. But David had told the court that it was really Nick who'd saved her, by making himself a shield. A hero, he'd called Nick—and she'd never loved David more than at that moment. The judge acquitted him. But, of course, things hadn't ended there. The bombshell about the respected Dr. Knelman being a former Nazi had exploded in the media, blasting their lives for months. Esther had been hard hit. Through it all, Alana had been amazed at how focused David had stayed. It had helped her get through it, and stick with their decision not to utter a word about the gene. They'd agreed that if that ever became known, the public scrutiny would be unbearably oppressive, and would never end. It had to remain their secret.

Luckily, Rajko, when he'd recovered from his wound, hadn't spoken of it either. It had never been his way to volunteer information to authorities, and Alana had been very thankful for that. He'd checked himself out of the hospital early, but the bullet they'd removed from his lung had badly weakened him. For good. She hoped his condition at least was keeping him at home and out of trouble now, though she didn't know; she hadn't seen him in years. When she was pregnant with Riley she'd gone to visit the enclave in Sunnyside, but because of her marriage to David she was no longer welcome. Her father's stony silence, plus the cold shoulder from the rest of her family, had made her feel almost leprous. She'd never gone back.

My family: that's David and the kids now, she thought with a glow. And Esther, of course. Esther had married Howard Jaffe and enjoyed four happy years with him before his heart gave out, leaving her a widow. Alana and David had immediately asked her to live with them. The kids adored Aunt Es, and so did Alana. Family, she thought with a pang, remembering how much Nick had craved these bonds, this sense of belonging. She still missed him—the son she'd known for only nineteen days. Just long enough to learn that, far from being a monster, he had the heart of a hero.

She hugged David's arm. She was thankful for what she had.

"Isn't that Ralph Evans?" he asked, looking at a man in a fur-collared coat coming along the path, his breath steaming.

"Who?"

"Appellate Court Judge. Let's go say hello."

"They'll be yakking for hours," Riley said to his sister. "Come on, I'll race you to that shed."

"You'll win."

"Give you a head start."

"How much?"

"Five Empire State Buildings. Go."

She took off.

Riley counted, "One Empire State Building, two Empire State Buildings," all the way to five, then sprinted after her. In a moment he zipped past her, laughing. No contest! Hitting a patch of path as smooth as ice, he skidded cleanly, stretching it out, savoring the slick, fast feel.

He heard her voice behind him chirp, "Rajko."

He turned. Hannah stood looking up at a man in a bulky black overcoat, his back to Riley. Seeing the green fedora, Riley felt his heart kind of jump. He'd never met Rajko, but he sure knew that hat. He loped back to Hannah, and Rajko turned to him.

Riley was surprised by the face. It wasn't like what he'd seen in Mom's memories. Thin, gray around the eyes, and the skin on his cheeks looked as pale as Aunt Es's raw strudel pastry. Riley checked over his shoulder for his parents. The brick shed was in the way. He couldn't see them.

"So you're Riley. Know who I am?"

"Sure. Rajko Marks. My grandfather."

"Got that right. You know lots, I bet, huh?" He coughed. Riley saw that the black overcoat was too big for Rajko. Like the ski jacket he'd gotten for his birthday, and Mom said she'd made a mistake with the size, so they'd changed it. Only, this looked like Rajko *himself* was the mistake. Like he'd shrunk inside the coat.

Even coughing, Rajko hadn't taken his eyes off Riley. But he didn't have that sappy smile most grown-ups had when they looked at you. This was like a look deep inside Riley, to see who he was really was. It kind of scared him, but excited him too.

"Know what a *rom baro* is?"

"I do," Hannah piped up. "Big man. Like a chief."

Rajko smiled at her. Holy cow, Riley thought, even his teeth are gray.

The old man's dark eyes flicked back to him. "Here's the deal, kid. I'm sick. Only got a few years left. My people are gonna need a strong *rom baro*. I been wondering, think you got what it takes?"

A shiver ran up Riley's back. He snapped, "I'm not Nick."

Rajko blinked, like he was surprised but impressed. "See, now that's good. Standing up for yourself. Real good." He coughed again. "You come see me sometime. We'll talk. Know the place?"

"Sure. Sunnyside. Van Dam Street."

"Think you can get there on your own?"

Riley was insulted. " 'Course I can. I take the subway to my dad's office." He didn't mention that Aunt Es went with him. She was a bit dozy and forgot stuff. He was always the leader.

Rajko was looking over to where Mom and Dad were, behind the shed. Riley turned to look too. Were they coming?

Nope. By the time he turned back, Rajko was walking away, already hard to see among the trees. Riley felt a sort of tug inside. He almost wanted to go after him. Sunnyside.

Hannah said, “I’m cold.”

He looked at her. “Wanna go home?”

She nodded. Riley tucked away the thought of Sunnyside. Later.

As they started down the path toward their parents, he said to his sister, “Better not tell Mom and Dad about Rajko.”

She nodded again. “It would just make her sad.”